STARS FALLEN SERIES

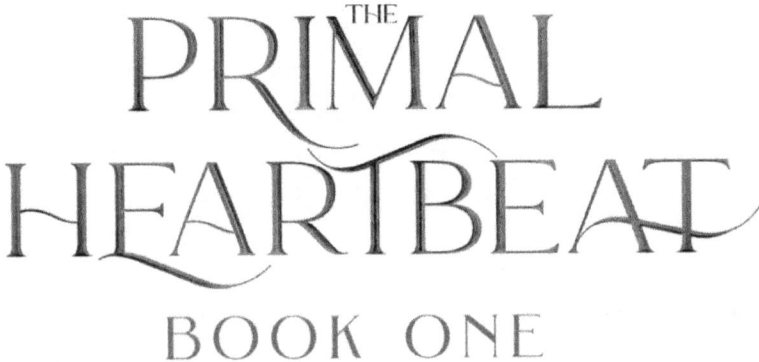

THE PRIMAL HEARTBEAT

BOOK ONE

NADINE ABRAHAMS

The Written Word Publishing
Australia
Contact: keltoidrui@hotmail.com
https://nadineabrahams.wixsite.com/author

ISBN: 978-0-6457722-7-2 (paperback)
        978-0-6457722-6-5 (ebook)

Cover design by Mibliart: https://miblart.com

This book is dedicated to all those who have been through painful experiences. Your wounds may be internal, but they are your battle scars. Remember, you are warriors.

Disclaimer

This book is a work of fiction. Certain historical words or places with some similarities to our own world may be used to immerse you fully, in this fantasy world. All characters are imaginary, while teeming with humanity and struggles that the reader can relate to, they are not based on any persons living or dead.

Trigger Warning

This book contains references to sexual assault, gore, incest and larger age gaps. Reader discretion is advised. The recommended age for the reader is New Adult with recommended minimum reader age of 16+.

The Primal Heartbeat, book one, was first published in 2004. Originally meant to be a trilogy for my *Stars Fallen* series, it took me many years to be inspired to write the sequel.

The books are centred around the characters' enduring love, despite going through terrible ordeals. These novels helped me through my own experiences. They are dedicated to all those who can still love and find beauty in the world despite the sad things other humans cause them to endure. It is also a story of redemption, and never losing hope that your dreams will be fulfilled in the end.

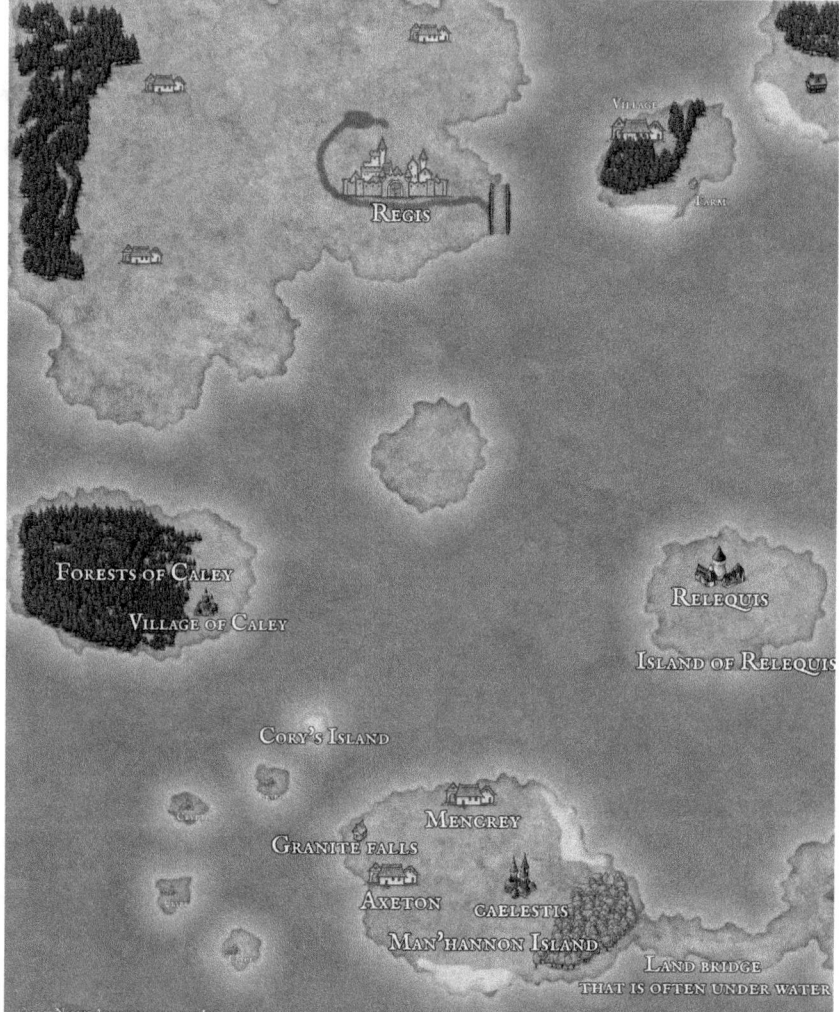

VILLAGE

REGIS

FARM

FORESTS OF CALEY

RELEQUIS

VILLAGE OF CALEY

ISLAND OF RELEQUIS

CORY'S ISLAND

MENCREY

GRANITE FALLS

AXETON   CAELESTIS

MAN'HANNON ISLAND

LAND BRIDGE
THAT IS OFTEN UNDER WATER

© 2023 Nagini Abrahams made with Inkarnate

PART ONE: THE PROPHECY

CHAPTER ONE

On a cold winter's night in 1700 CE, an adolescent boy stirs the embers of the hearth. His grandfather sits in an old wicker cane chair. The man is ancient. He rubs his scabbed and wrinkled hands, trying to keep the certainty of death from his failing body. He is to tell the lad his heritage. *Someone must carry on the knowledge, or all that I know will be lost forever.*

A horse and carriage clatter by, a sign of the changing times. A smithy puts hammer to cooling steel as the sounding work-bell releases coal miners from their workings on the Earth Mother's inner self, her primal heartbeat.

'We begin this tale in 306 CE, a time when magic is at its peak, romance made its greatest stories and where anyone could become a hero. We are in a time where mankind has been corrupted and disease and murder reign free.

'I hope to lighten your heart with the tale of a very special lass: Stars Fallen.'

Fear, cold sweat, twigs snap underfoot. *Danger, flee, must save unborn child.*

'There she is,' shouted Ankanlee.

The three hunters released their taut bowstrings in choreographed action. Twang, fft, fft. One arrow missed, two hit the target. One pierced the mother doe's heart, the other through that female's world striking her love, her child.

'Praise the spirits of creation as mother of all deer gives her body to be nourishment for the Crykenuak, the children of the stars,' said Mejanuak.

'Now, the three bold hunters of the best people will eat of mother doe's heart, drink of her strengthening blood,' said Telutanka.

Like most men of their tribe, the three hunters were nearly bald except for a long ponytail at the back of their heads. Dressed in loincloth and sandals, all three had brown eyes. They were on the hunt for a great feast for the jovial spring celebration. And the doe was the symbol of springtime life.

'Our women and children will eat of intestine and blood meats. They will rejoice in our prowess,' said Ankanlee.

'Let it be so,' said Mejanuak.

Ankanlee placed the animal on the ground and slit her underbelly—throat to urethra. They drank her warm blood as it steamed in the morning air. After they had gorged themselves greedily, they unravelled the intestines and set them aside, withdrew the heart, liver and fetus. Then, with their fleshing knives, they skinned the doe. Lugging everything over their shoulders, they headed back to the camp covered in the lifeblood of the once wild and free animal.

A female child, not worthy of a name, scabbed marrowbone and unfit meat from the smouldering ashes of the once glorious springtime celebration. They had spit roasted mother deer. Everyone had partaken except this child and her mother, who her tribe had named Taboo Breaker. *If I was a boy, Mama would have been murdered and Auntie would have raised me.* She lived in a male-orientated world. Gathering the precious morsels of food, the child snuck back to her mother, who was asleep.

The nameless girl sat down outside her hut and sucked the tangy white marrow from the bones she'd scavenged. Piercing a hole in an eyeball, the child drank the tangy but sour liquid inside. She looked at the rest of her meagre meal and wondered if she could eat a little more. There were two more marrow filled bones, another eyeball and a kidney. *Yuck kidneys, Mama can have that.* As the child ate, her eyes followed the other little girls and boys playing.

There were fifteen other children in the tribe. The eight boys were wrestling each other for the prize of a new bow and seven little girls looked on in admiration, occasionally squealing when a pair rolled their way.

Can I sneak off before Mama wakes? Today was washing day, and the girl hated helping her mother display their few meagre cloth items while all the other girls pointed and laughed. The girl grimaced. *They always laugh.* The girl rose and scratched at the large sores on her legs from her past beatings, two of them a new gift that morning. The girl had walked in on her mother being harassed by Ankanlee, as his wife was too heavily pregnant. He had struck her as he shooed her out.

After he had finished with her mother, for extra humiliation, he left her mother twelve yams, making her seem worthless. The nameless girl spat harshly on the ground at the memory and rose. Her eyes darted to their tent and she scowled. 'I will help you, Mama, especially after what you have been through today,' she whispered.

CHAPTER TWO

In sleep, Taboo Breaker lost herself in the world of her past, dreaming fond memories of passionate embraces, loving words and unforgivable crimes, as she let her story flow.

The sun rose above the village. A beautiful summer morning like any other. Women rose and built fires for the morning meal. Children swam in the gleaming waters of the village lake. It looked like any other village with its conical huts covered in the skin of wild animals and structured with their bones. However, who was to know the events that would unfold that day.

Melowy, or Singing Bird as she was often known, awoke to these familiar sounds and thought of the men who were out hunting. They were hunting for the feast that would occur tomorrow in honour of Telutanka, or Sun Warrior, who was to wed Melowy. Only a virgin female could wed, and even then, could not choose who to. Other women became objects of pleasure for the tribe's men when their women were pregnant.

Melowy secretly wept at night, dreaming of a love that might be. Dreaming of a man she could love and be loved by in return. Melowy thought about the man she was being given to. Even in her innocence, she knew that Telutanka did not love her, only lusted after her. Melowy knew she was appealing with her slender figure, dark green eyes and honey blonde hair that ended at her feet, her baby-soft skin, supple young breasts and a voice like the birds she was named after.

Melowy was frightened of what Telutanka was to do to her. She knew children did not come of kissing, but of something more. Melowy had become a woman two moons ago. She was the pride of her father, who also had three gangly adolescent sons and two homely barren daughters. Melowy sighed and rose to do her chores.

The father of the stars, the tribal god Sorendee, who was one with Earth Mother, took pity on this young beauty. While his perfect sons slept, he sent his youngest and most beloved son, Gepatok, on a comet to fulfil Melowy's dream. But the green-eyed monster, jealousy, that no star knows, hides in mankind's hearts and allows innocent eighteen-year-old girls to be named taboo breaker when they fall in love.

Melowy looked up from hauling in her fishing net to the sounds of drums beating. The women around her started chatting excitedly; children ran laughing towards the noise. The villagers headed to the central fire. The hunters had returned boasting of their skills and lugging bear and deer carcasses. Trebrelan, or Star Scryer the mystic, had arrived with his clowns, who gave out gifts, cartwheeled and juggled. His circus included dancing women and strange animals that nickered and pulled their burdens and his wolf-like dogs. He brought stories of dangerous adventures and funny jokes. He had two new foundling apprentices that stood next to him, cold eyes staring straight ahead, taking everything in.

Melowy ran towards the jovial celebrations but stumbled and fell at the feet of one of the foundling mages. Looking up, she gasped.

⁓

Gepatok knew his purpose. He had woken on earth with his father's encouragement. The five-thousand-year-old being looked no older than eighteen.

He remembered the words his father had told him. 'Fall in love, my son. Bring forth a child worthy of the stars.'

Fall in love with mankind? Impossible, Father. Gepatok hated the ways of men with their dominating masculinity, destructive wars and yet … their women were gentle, yearning for the sun in their directed lives and bringing forth life from within that secret woman's world.

Thump. Brought forth from his thoughts, Gepatok looked down. His heart paused and started at a double pace. Gepatok's words stuck in his throat. The warmth of a man's longing spread throughout his body and beads of sweat formed on his skin. He blushed and offered Melowy his hand. 'Are you okay Melowy?' Gepatok stuttered.

Melowy's eyes widened in shock. 'Who are you?'

'I am Little Star, or Gepatok. Our souls just mated, and our hearts linked. You are to be mine and I will be yours. The stars have spoken, and our names were among them,' said Gepatok.

The crowd turned and laughed at Gepatok.

'Ahh, we have a poet among us. You can announce your work at mine and Melowy's wedding which will take place tonight in honour of Trebrelan, instead of on the morn,' announced Telutanka, angered and displeased at Gepatok's display.

Melowy was led away by her mother, Kenra, or Little Woman, to ready her for the ritual.

Gepatok, hurt and confused, stalked off into the woods for solitude and advice from his father.

'Mother, I do not want to marry Telutanka.' Melowy wept.

'Hush, my child. I did not want to marry your father, Teja, but I do love him now. I loved the chief when I was but a wee one like you. It is not a woman's world me love. We must endure and draw what happiness we can from what we are forced to do. Now dress, my child,' said Kenra.

Kenra left the hut. Despairing, Melowy dressed.

—∿∿—

As the moon arose in the distant sky, no stars were present to give their blessing to the forthcoming ceremony. The flames of the feast fire consumed the raw meats hungrily. Smoke billowed high into the air as a chilling wind began to blow. A figure lost in thought stood motionless near the tent that Melowy shared with her family as the wind toyed with his long hair. Thirteen-year-old Trebrelan thought about the bride-to-be. *A teenager is being forced to marry one she does not love; one I do not trust.*

Unlike these tribal people, he was of a different race, one that lived in the forests. One that mankind called elves. *I must help her escape.* He withdrew a scroll from the pocket of his robes and began to recite the words.

'*Calmatis Stormus Surgerious.*'

The wind began to howl and loosed the ribbon from his hair. Trebrelan began to chase it, snatching at the air as the wind carried it away. As grey storm clouds began to form, tears welled in the boy's eyes. *That was Father's last gift to my mother and now it's gone.*

—∿∿—

Melowy stood ready, waiting for the return of her mother. Her mother did not come. She heard footsteps. The skin flap door was pulled back suddenly and Gepatok stood silhouetted against a sky that was beginning to rage. A storm that would sweep the tracks of the young couple away as they started running towards the forest.

Gepatok and Melowy took shelter in a cave they had found after running for half the night. They had thrown off their pursuers in the storm.

Gepatok had packed enough food to last two days, and brought kindling, tinder, flint, and wood. He had also brought water and a huge bearskin blanket. This was packed into a bag made of deerskin. He lit a fire and rationed the food into six meals. That night, the couple ate of a hastily prepared stew with slivers of dried meat and chunks of turnip, onion and potato. After their meal, they talked of their likes, hates and misgivings. The sky outside stayed dark, raging with thunder and torrential rain. Tiring, the young couple lay wrapped in each other's arms and covered by the bearskin blanket. Their eyes met and something clicked.

'I'm in love with you Melowy.'

'I love you too.'

Gepatok drew Melowy close and removed their clothing and he took her mouth with his own. Their shadows danced in the light of the dying fire in response to their passion.

The storm subsided in two days. Melowy and Gepatok travelled on for four weeks like hunted animals, the truth of the chase reflected in their haunted eyes.

Melowy touched her abdomen and smiled sadly at Gepatok. 'My menses haven't returned.'

Gepatok kissed her, he drew back and grinned. 'You will have our baby in nine moons.' His eyebrows furrowed in concern. 'We need to tread where other's rarely venture to keep you and our child safe.'

He grabbed Melowy's hand and they left the known tracks, hoping to throw their pursuers off. They heard a shout and Telutanka came into view. The couple began to run.

Twang. Too late. An arrow pierced Melowy's stomach.

'You bastard,' shouted Gepatok and threw himself at Telutanka.

One of the village's tracking dogs cornered Melowy as she slumped to the ground. Gepatok hammered Telutanka into unconsciousness with the back of the dagger he had managed to capture.

'Gepatok, help,' whispered Melowy. She had begun to miscarry.

'Melowy, oh Melowy. Listen, I know you love me, but I must leave you. I must go. I will live on in our child because I'm giving up my soul to become one with her,' said Gepatok.

'No, I need you, don't,' Melowy said urgently.

'If I don't, you will both die too,' said Gepatok.

Gepatok slit his throat, the warm blood seeped down his arm as he knelt next to Melowy. The arrow wound in Melowy's stomach closed, she screamed and sat up.

'No, my love … no.' She placed her hand on his cheek as he collapsed to the ground. His hand clasped hers and the warm blood dried on their arms, bonding them for eternity.

'I was honoured to love you Melowy. I will find you in the palace of the gods if you find a way to give yourself for the greater good.' He closed his eyes and his hand slipped to the ground.

Melowy sobbed and kissed him repeatably. Her elven father, Teja, approached her and dragged her away from the body as the sun's rays sparkled over Gepatok. The body erupted in specs of dancing light that enveloped Melowy.

'Her lover was a child of the stars. We cannot execute her for fear of the Gods' wrath. Melowy, you are hereby banished to the outskirts of the village to fend for yourself. Be grateful you are allowed to live. You are now named Taboo Breaker and your child will not have a name. Strip her of her belongings.'

Melowy struggled and scowled at her father as she was stripped by Ankanlee. Teja turned and picked up her belongings and strode towards the path. 'Bring her, Ankanlee. She is soiled.'

Melowy whimpered as Ankanlee ripped her clothing and ran his hands over her body. She turned and kicked him and he grabbed her arm and yanked her towards him. 'After the brat is born you are free game as long as I trade for your services. How else will you feed your spawn?'

Melowy was thrust away from him and the frigid air hit her body, she shivered and followed the others towards the village.

Chapter Three

Taboo Breaker awoke to see Trebrelan standing over her.

'I have your daughter and will take care of her.'

'You're taking my child?' asked Melowy.

'Yes, because I know what you intend to do to yourself. Is there no way that I can prevent you?'

'No, if I give myself to be sacrificed, I can leave to be with the stars.'

'Come with me, my friend,' said Trebrelan gently.

'No, they come for me now, look after her, my dear friend.' Melowy wept.

The villagers came for her. Trebrelan stood in the doorway refusing to allow them to enter.

Teja mumbled something and a gust of air caused Lan to stagger.

'That should have thrown you,' mumbled Teja.

Lan grinned. 'I am a mystic. I can stay on my feet when others cannot.'

'Step aside elfling.' Teja took a step towards Trebrelan.

'I will forgive the insult.' Trebrelan stepped towards Teja. 'She has a child. How can you think of letting her kill herself?'

Teja stared at Ankanlee who darted behind Trebrelan and dragged Melowy outside.

'Leave, elfling, and take her child to that school of yours. Hanton's prophecy has come to pass.'

'I cannot be responsible for a child. Especially a divine one.'

He backed towards Melowy. 'Melowy, how can you abandon your child? My mother can offer you and your daughter refuge.'

The village men lowered their spears at Trebrelan and he eased away.

'Go, Trebrelan. I am over this life.' Melowy was dragged towards the centre of the village and tied to a post. Trebrelan sprinted towards the forest where he had left the sleeping child. He picked her up. She blinked and yawned as he left the village.

'Mama, Mama,' screamed the child. The village erupted in flames.

Oh, my gods, what a powerful and dangerous child. He cast a sleeping spell on the girl.

Trebrelan headed through the forest and into a rich and fertile valley. The girl slung over his shoulder began to grizzle and awaken.

Geez, two hours and she's already thrown the effects of the spell. Most people cannot for at least four, thought the mystic.

'Hello, young one. I'm here for you,' he whispered to her.

'No, I want my mama,' cried the child.

'She has passed into the summer lands, dear child,' Trebrelan said, trying to soothe her.

'But she be alive a short time ago,' said the child.

'The summer lands is not a place of eternal rest. It is but a place of viewing your life before so that ye may go on to another life,' said Trebrelan.

'Ha? What da that mean?' asked the child.

'It is something like heaven except you have the opportunity to return,' said Trebrelan.

'Oh, so when ya get dead you go and sit in the sky and wait till the Goddess says go on downed,' said the girl child.

Trebrelan placed the child on her feet. 'Yes, something like that. Now come inside and we can commence the evening meal,' said Trebrelan.

The mystic led her into a small brick cottage. The smell of cooking stew wavered on the air. A large iron pot bubbled over a blackened hearth. The house was lit by candles and smelled of wildflowers in the summer. An elderly lady sat in a rocking chair by the fire. She had long silver hair that cascaded to her feet, a face ravaged from years of bracing the elements and blind white eyes.

'Ahh … Ahh … Witch, wun or da the witch will get ya,' stuttered the scared girl.

'Settle, child, it's just my mother. And yes, she was a witch in her day. She travelled, giving help to those who needed it. But she be a good one,' said Trebrelan.

'Son, is that you?' asked the old lady.

'Yes, Mother,' said the mystic.

'I smell a young child.' She sniffed the air. 'Feed her to me,' said the old woman.

'Nooooo!' screamed the girl and she started bawling.

The old woman began to laugh. 'It's okay, young one. I'd do no such thing.' With that, the elderly woman removed the glamoire spell upon herself and resumed her proper profile as a woman around fifty with long, plaited, silver hair, caring and loving brown eyes and a smile that was hard to beat. But the corner of her mouth suggested cunning and a love of pranks.

'I am Regona of the earth, Lan's mother. I will tend to you,' comforted the old lady.

The child stopped bawling.

'You should not have scared her so, considering her mother has just passed away.' Trebrelan glared.

'What? You told me you were just going to get her, not kill her ma,' gasped the old woman.

'I did no such thing,' said Trebrelan.

'Who did? By the way, I was going on the fact that an ill-treated child would want cheering-up.' The old woman hushed him.

'Fine, fine, Ma. Leave it at that,' stated Trebrelan.

Regona looked down at the child and spoke calmly.

'I'm sorry if I scared you so. I hope that you will forgive me. I wish you to be like a granddaughter. I will love ya like the daughters I lost to the Shadow Masters. You need a name.'

Regona looked at her son.

'She has one, one that is stated in the prophecies. Stars Fallen, Telewanake. On the night she was pushed into this world stars zoomed overhead and crashed upon this earth. She is the daughter of Gepatok, a child of the stars,' Trebrelan said enthusiastically.

'This is she?' whispered Regona, exchanging looks with her son. Telewanake looked at the two adults.

'What's a profisee?' questioned the girl.

'You will understand child, one day. Now come, Telewanake, time to eat. We do not eat of the animals here as the great mother provides enough for all her creatures,' said Regona.

'Who is Tellawonky?' asked the confused girl.

'You, child, that is your name,' said Trebrelan.

'I have a name? … Did my mummy give it to me?' asked Telewanake.

'No, the gods ordained it,' said Regona.

The three sat and ate the vegetable stew.

'Dis is nice even dow there is no flesh from the Goddess,' murmured Telewanake.

'Why eat of another living creature when the mother has given us the green of the land, the fruit of the tree, her breath that rustles our hair and her tears which quench our thirst?' asked Regona.

'But animals are part of Mother Earth. If we want to be a part of her, they must be a part of us,' said Telewanake.

'Precious child, we are all born from the earth, how can we not be a part of each other?' Regona smiled.

'I never thought of it like dat afore,' whispered Telewanake.

'Do not worry your pretty face lassie.' Regona laughed. 'It will all make sense one day.'

'I not pretty, I a bad girl, not supposed to have a name cause Mama was bad and my Dadda a demon,' the child whispered.

'No, Ake, you are but a wee lassie with your parents gone. You were treated poorly by your tribe and have come to live among us. We will look after thee. Now it is time to get ye off to bed.' Regona smiled.

CHAPTER FOUR

As the god Mercury lit the lantern on a new day, the north wind caressed a great oak tree's leaves and water shimmered on a lake in a forbidden valley. An old man put flint to stone and prepared his morning meal of tubers and summer berries. His grandchildren splashed in the lake, absorbed in their youthful innocence. This would seem like a normal scene if it weren't for the tears streaming down the elderly man's wizened face as he listened for the screams bound to come. He whiffed the air for the taint of blood and body excretions where the slaves were being beaten into submission, for this valley was a slave hold. The man's blind eyes could not see, but his heart remembered the anguish of his own enslavement.

Three thousand kilometres away a child woke crying from the vision she had seen.

'Ake, Ake are ye alright youngin?' asked Regona, hugging Ake.

'There be a man and he sees no light but scents life on the winds. He pains for what I now know, to be free. But he will not taste it but go into der heavens at moonrise. I don't wanna him to go away, help him old Ma,' stuttered an anguished Ake.

'Hush, child, it is but a nightmare.' Regona tutted.

'No, it's not, it's real,' cried Ake.

'I'll consult the runes, sweet, and then we will see but now we must break our fast. Today you have been with us two months and the grief for your mother seems to have lightened somewhat. Lan will take ye yonder in der village for some learning,' said Regona.

'But old Ma, the man, the man,' said Ake.

'I will read the runes, but off to breaky and your learning or you'll be late,' Regona firmly stated. And she ushered the girl out of the room.

Ake sat down at the table pondering on what she had just seen. The girl looked down at her half-eaten breakfast of thick porridge with milk and honey. Lan was looking at some ancient scrolls and sipping a mug of tea, he looked over to her and told her to eat up. She finished her breakfast and rose.

'What's wrong Ake?' asked Lan.

Ake explained the vision to Lan.

Lan's face creased with worry. 'It is probably best you don't worry about it, Ake, I will look into it for you.'

Lan stood and handed her honey cakes for her midday snack and Regona kissed Ake on the cheek and watched Lan and Ake leave.

—⁓—

'Children, after me. Eriu, land of bog and hill where Sidhe do dwell,' said Ms Bozz.

Schooling took place inside a stone building. The children of the Axeton village school chanted in time as they sat on logs surrounding a central fire pit.

Just then the door opened and a small girl with blonde tresses to her shoulders and grey-blue eyes entered. She had lips as red as blood and cheekbones that finished where her eyes began. Ake moved with an unearthly grace more likely found in an older maiden. Oozing an aura that revealed her energetic tribal heritage, Telewanake approached Ms Bozz.

'Ahh, mam, I'm here to get some learning,' said the child. The recipient ignored the child.

'Mam, mam, I'm here to get some learning. Old Ma sent me, I'm not too late 'cause it's just after breakfast,' said Telewanake, pulling on the skirts of the teacher.

Slap! The sound rebounded off the stone contours of the schoolhouse. The chanting children watched in awe as the teacher hit the young girl across the hand with some kindling.

Telewanake, stunned and with tears coursing down her angelic face, stumbled and fell against the stone wall.

'Why, mam, what did I do?' asked the innocent child as her hand began to turn red.

The teacher sniffed and slowly lowered her eyes to the child shivering and curled up in the fetal position against the cold stone.

Ms Bozz opened her mouth and, deliberately choosing her words, she uttered, 'Children should be seen and not heard. They should always obey adults and never speak out of turn. Little girls should curtsey and wait and always step in line when a man says. You, child, have broken two of these rules.'

Ms Bozz pointed to a log and Telewanake rose, and half walked, half stumbled to the seat as her sobs faded.

'Time to buy your midday meal. Be sure to return when I ring the bell,' said Ms Bozz uncaringly.

The children filed out in two orderly lines, eyes to the front. Telewanake, still shaken, ran and vomited in a nearby bush. A young boy, about twelve, wandered up to Ake and offered her a scrap of material ripped from his shirt to blow her nose.

'Don't worry, shez just a prig with an apple stuck up her hiney.' He gave her a kind smile. 'She's only filling in though, lovely Miss Karin died of the pox, but me mam will be teaching next month. I'm Little Fella. I get me name when I turn thirteen. I'll be a man. You don't get names till they know you will live past all the normal childhood diseases. Do you have any idea what you may get?

See I'm gonna get a good name because I'm in the training.' He pointed to the set of throwing knives belted at his hip.

'I don't have folks, but I have a mystic and an old Ma and I got a name,' said Ake smiling up at him.

'Ah come on, you got no name, you not be past eight summers. And you got no mystic.' Little Fella laughed.

'I do so, his name is Trebrelan. And I'm Telewanake.'

'Telwonkee,' pronounced the boy.

'No, Tel-a-wa-narkey,' spelled Ake.

'Do you have something shorter?' asked the little boy.

'Yeah, Ar-key.' Ake sounded out her name.

Ding-ding-allying sounded the handheld brass bell. Ms Bozz yelled for school to restart. All the children re-entered the building.

CHAPTER FIVE

School finished, and the children returned to their homes before darkness fell. Ake waited anxiously for Lan. Ten minutes passed, fifteen, twenty. It slowly started to grow dark. A wolf howled in the surrounding forest. A hooded man headed towards the school. His countenance was that of an angry man, his anger beyond redemption. The man lifted his huge black eyes towards the child. They had lost their normal lustre. Dark clouds gathered and a light drizzle began. The man pulled back his hood and ran his fingers through his long, scruffy black hair. And then he uttered a cry filled with malice. 'Shadow Scout, show your true self for ye shall never appease my anger until your whole race is decreed dead.'

Ake stepped up to him. 'Are we playing a new kind of game Lan?'

'No, Ake, Ms Bozz is a spy for the Shadow Masters who take a flesh tithe of children from the villages to satisfy their hunger needs. She is what is called a Shadow Scout. She wants you but I will kill her first. Now, Ake, you must go on home to Old Ma. Do not dawdle as night approaches and with it unmentionable darkness that wipes away souls as if they did not exist,' explained Lan.

Ake, trembling with fear but determined to help Lan, stated she would not leave his side.

This is one courageous child; how can I not undermine her but make her leave? Then an idea sparked in his sharp mind. 'Who is to look after Old Ma if we both stay here?' asked Lan.

'Oh, how come I did not think of this by Dee. She is needing my looking after,' Ake stated proudly.

Ake half ran and half stumbled home with her love for her family seeping into her soul.

Lan headed to the door of the schoolhouse and entered quietly and carefully as not to upset the shadows that concealed him. A sudden movement out of the corner of his eye captured his attention and his gaze followed and settled on a figure in the middle of the room.

'Ah, elfling, you have come to meet your untimely end,' snarled the apparition.

It was more commonly known as Ms Bozz, even though her disguise was not needed now. Her red eyes were small, and her face was that of death aged beyond recognition. Just a few layers of skin stretched over ancient bones. Her hair, now straggling ends, were once luscious and had known the grip of countless lovers' hands as they experienced the pleasures of love. Her teeth were cracked and black.

'These ancient and withered hands that had caressed so many endeared ones and took the life of many fair and innocent maidens. Oh, the memories of youth that no one can deny me. When the men found their loves dead, in their grief I comforted them with my own body. Drianna has similar plans for you, elfling.'

In the few moments Ms Bozz was reminiscing, Lan had managed to cover the distance between himself and the spectre.

'Ahh, Bozzwanna of the once great city of Gloriu Reigisn is now but a downcast, murdering hag.' Lan laughed.

'Manling of a mystic not past twenty-two summers, child of Regona who's many whoring daughters provided for my blood lust,' Bozzwanna growled.

'Bitch, you had Liken, Kora and Goriard raped, and you call them whores? You killed the innocent babes of theirs. Then, when they were barren, you had them tortured to death. You are the cow that ruined the lives of many!' yelled Lan.

'*Ad-jurac minsing artruro Lan dos elflin minsing arturo nigima-tre hun sen hun sen*,' Bozzwanna cried, casting her spell in the language of darkness.

Fear flooded his mind then Lan collapsed from an agonising scream inside his head. A fiery burning began in his legs and travelled to his lungs, causing him to gasp. It was agonising to breathe. Bozzwanna's evil laugh echoed off the building and hail began to fall. Lan's last cry as he drifted into darkness was an earth-binding spell.

'My heart is pure, my mind is canny. Bind me to this plane,' he whispered.

Bozzwanna cackled and left the building only to come face to face with Regona.

'Ahh, ancient whore mother, have you come for what now belongs to me?' cackled Bozzwanna.

'Mother of all, father of air, to my side. Destroy a child of Drianna. Lay your blessings on my child and bind him to this plane. So, mote it be,' Regona yelled.

Before Regona could finish Bozzwanna teleported herself and Lan to her crypt.

Lan awoke groaning, bringing a hand to his head. He sat up, noticing the expensive rug beneath him in a strange, richly fur-nished room. He shivered in the cold as he had been stripped of his clothes and weapons. He still felt groggy following Bozzwanna's attack, and it took some time for him to regain enough strength to stand. A guard stood at the door, listening as Bozzwanna gave him instructions. Bozzwanna turned and approached Lan, cast-ing a binding spell over him. Lan couldn't move, he tried to strug-gle, but in vain. A strange feeling crept into his mind and spread throughout his body. Fear surged through him and sweat beaded down his body. His thoughts began to cloud, and he began to lose his sense of self as he tried to fight the confusion spell.

Bozzwanna laughed as she saw Lan's eyes glaze over. She cast another spell on Lan and his muscles relaxed, and he knew he could move again. He flexed his hands and tried to make a run for the door. A pained cry filled the room. Lan stopped and turned. A woman sat on a red feather bed, freshly bathed and dressed in red silks. The woman wept; a sword held to her throat. Lan stared at the ground in despair. His shoulders slumped. He uttered a guttural cry. 'Don't hurt her! Please don't do this,' he begged.

'Enough! You will perform at Drianna's bidding,' said Bozzwanna. She whispered into his ear, casting a lust and fertility spell on him. Lan smelt the sickly scent of incense burning in the holders by the door and saw the flicker of a dozen candles. Up surged an animalistic urge he had never experienced before. He looked up, his eyes drawn to the woman on the sensuous bed. She looked no older than twenty-three. His mind said he should know her, but the ever-increasing oppressive fog would not clear. The girl spoke but her words were incoherent. Bozzwanna's spell ripped away his senses and reduced him to the status of animal. A man's need overtook him, and he slunk on all fours across the bed.

The girl was beautiful but cowering in the corner. He grabbed her, forced her down and his cloudy mind caused him to ignore her screams as he put his full weight on her. When dawn came, and the spell was broken, he realised what he had done.

Lan turned to his sister cowering up against the wall.

'Oh, Goriard, what have I done?' he cried. Tears slid down his cheeks. He reached for her but she whimpered and moved back.

Lan hung his head in shock and shame. He pushed down the urge to vomit as a bout of nausea threatened to overwhelm him. *I can never be forgiven for this.* He looked at his sister. 'Goriard, I did not know what happened, words cannot abate what I did, but I will get us home to Mother.'

'Mama, my mama,' the woman whimpered. Hesitantly she reached for her brother. They embraced, weeping together.

———

Meanwhile, Bozzwanna gazed into the room through her crystal ball. She laughed and turned to her goddess who was visiting in the form of an ample and sensuous woman.

'You have done well, Bozzwanna, you shall be rewarded with the looks of your youth for eternity. The child born of this coupling will be my tool against Regona, the messenger of Dee. Now, we must get rid of this mystic and make the girl bear her child so that you may raise him to do my bidding,' ordered Drianna.

———

Lan cracked open the door and peaked outside. He realised they were alone and might be able to escape. He closed the door and looked around for anything that could be used as a weapon. His search was futile.

Lan reached for Goriard's hand but she pushed him away.

'Goriard, I am so sorry. But we must get away from here,' whispered Lan.

Lan reached for her hand and this time she accepted. Lan pulled her from the room.

They entered a small hallway and turned left. A guard spotted them. Lan threw *Mystic Fire* at him and the man clutched at his face. They ran past him and through an opening to outside. Lan ran and Goriard stumbled behind him. She began to weep. Lan held strong for the fight he was sure would come.

Lan looked about. The crypt was built from human bones. The ground was but sharp stones and shells, which cut their bare feet. The sky was dark and cloudy, the wind lashed against their shivering bodies as ghosts of the innocent cried out for revenge. To their right, as far as the eye could see, was water. The island smelled of freshly spilled blood.

The mountains on their left suggested mountain goats could supply meat, cheese and milk, as Lan could see slave shepherds on the hill. Wheat grew for bread and there was a large orchard growing apples, potatoes, beans and grapes for wine. If only there was no evil on this island, then the orchard and shepherds would seem welcoming, but winter was about, and with it snow was bound to come. To survive, Goriard and he would need necessities, so he picked her up and headed towards the mountain slopes.

They had been travelling for an hour when a sudden downpour occurred. Lan saw a cluster of trees nearby and made a run for it. As he entered the trees, he saw it was a forest and nearby was a miners' cottage. The door lay unhinged on the ground. Lan went in. He was welcomed by dusty furniture, cobwebs and startled mice.

There was a bed nearby, so he laid his sleeping sister down upon it. He looked around. There was a woodpile but nothing to light a fire with. An old hearth stood nearby.

'What am I thinking? I am a mystic,' said Lan.

Lan lay the wood in the hearth and conjured a flame. Within an hour, a roaring fire was blazing, and the cottage seemed more homelike. Lan explored the cottage and, to his surprise, managed to find a trunk with boots that were just a little too big, socks, a man's tunic, women's shoes, scarf and dress, a pair of men's trousers and a darning and sewing kit. He dressed himself in the men's outfit and his sister in the women's, minus the shoes and pulled the bed coverings up to her chin. Then he lay on the floor and fell asleep.

———

Bozzwanna screamed with rage, her crystal ball could only gaze into her crypt. Drianna promised her, if the pair were not found within a year and a day, death himself would find her. Bozzwanna, anguished, began her search for the escapees.

———

Morning, the sound of cawing echoed on the air. A large black crow announced his delight about a freshly caught mouse in his talons for breakfast. Lan stirred awake at the eerie cry. Hunger pains gripped him, he ran his tongue across his parched lips. *I must find water and food, even if it's flesh of Dee.* He shook his sister gently awake.

'Goriard, I must find us nourishment. I'll try not to linger,' explained Lan.

Goriard nodded and closed her eyes as the waves of exhaustion overtook her again. Lan took his leave.

———

Back at the cottage where Lan grew up his mother and the apprentice, Ake, wept.

'My only child remaining, oh Lan come home safe.'

'Old Ma, we can find him if we find the horrid Bozz. I miss him, please use your power to get him back,' said the little one.

'Child, there is one person who might help us, but he may be dead. My children's father. The Arch Druid Dun Norix. He was my partner before he felt the blood of his forefathers calling him to the sacred school of the druids. We must leave soon, but first it is time to mourn. It is the month when my daughters were taken from me fifteen years ago.' Regona sighed.

Regona and Ake spent the next two days wearing black and picking sweet grass and burning it to purify their bodies in the smoke. They lay wildflower wreaths at the spot where the girls were taken and sang songs of sadness and said prayers in Regona's darlings' honour. She grieved like a mother who had just lost them, and her heart seemed as if it would be pulled asunder. Tears were wept endlessly, and they did not rest or eat for forty-eight hours. The elven fifteen-year grieving period was finally up and now it was time for Regona's grief to become a tool for revenge.

———

A man in green robes opened the front gate to the little cottage. He had black eyes, a long white beard and flowing white hair.

Regona felt her heart flutter and looked up from where she and Ake were feasting and breaking their fast. It was as if an older Lan stared back at them from those eyes, for this was the Arch Druid, Dun Norix.

'Hello Regona,' he said.

Regona nodded.

'Who is this wee one that sits beside you with adoring eyes?' asked the druid.

'My grandchild!' Regona glared at him.

'That must make her my granddaughter then too, doesn't it?' asked the druid kindly.

'No, it does not,' said Regona.

'Then you must have had another babe when I left. I can't blame you though,' said the druid sadly.

'No, you up and left me with three little lassies under seven summers, and you call yourself a man.' Regona spat on the ground.

Ake, a little taken aback with this side of Regona she'd never seen, tried to comfort the old lady by putting her small arms around her foster grandmother.

'I can't undo what I did, but the calling was strong in me. I thought you and the girls would be fine. But this is not the time to discuss this. You called me for some purpose,' said the druid compassionately.

'I did, my only child remaining, my son Lan was taken by Bozzwanna, my twin sister and I need to know if he be dead or alive. If alive, he needs to come home,' said Regona.

Oh, Dun Norix, the love, the soul connection we shared. He is the child of your seed left to me the night you left and didn't tell us except for the note two moons later. If I told you, it would hurt you so because every man desires a son to take after him and you have missed him growing up.

'Regona, may I know his father please? To put me at ease that you chose someone better than me,' said Dun Norix.

Regona chose her words to sting. 'Your old enemy, Triston.'

'Regona, he wanted you since we were together, he always wanted what I had. He is cruel and violent. How could you sleep with him after knowing this?' asked the druid, visibly shaking.

'He was here, you were not,' said Regona.

'We should discuss this later. We must find your son,' said the druid, his face a mask of emotional pain.

'Child, gather me sweet grass, water, and flat stones near the river. Regona, I'll need birds' feathers, a messenger pigeon and a large piece of amethyst. While you gather these, I must regain my strength because I have come a fair way,' said the druid, sitting down on the veranda where they had been talking.

The girl and the woman left. Dun Norix looked around. He

had missed the green pastures of the cottage and the woodlands nearby. The river flowing peacefully over the rocks of granite falls. And he and his family watching the sunsets whilst drinking cordial on warm summery evenings as the great spirit's breath blew the dresses and hair of his girls. They had been happy. The laughter and their faces he missed most of all. A gentle cough woke him from his thoughts.

'Here is the equipment you need,' said both Ake and Regona.

'Leave me now, till the moon rises,' said the druid.

Regona and Ake left and went inside.

The fire was blazing and wildflowers of red and yellow stood in a vase on a table near the hearth.

'Old Ma, why did you fib?' asked Ake.

'Ake, child, he hurt me, so I hurt him back. Don't tell him. I will in time but it's too soon. It would hurt him more if he knew about Lan, especially if he has passed from this world,' Regona said, putting a finger to her own lips to silence the child.

'That is true.' Ake nodded and they clung to each other.

The druid took the sweet grass and burnt it in a fire he had lit of feathers and grass on top of the rocks. He cleansed the amethyst in the smoke. Taking the amethyst, he said a chant three times over it, 'Dee, find the man-child Lan for me. Keep him safe, keep him strong. Bring him home to his mother and child. So, mote it be.'

The druid took a piece of ribbon from his pocket and bound the amethyst with it. Uncaging the bird, he whispered his message to the animal in the language of air and sent it on its way. He rose as the moon showed herself, and entered the cottage.

CHAPTER SIX

Two months passed by and the three people living in the cottage near Granite Falls had fallen into a routine. It's amazing how the body and mind still go about daily routine whilst soul and heart are partners in grief. Ake went to school and enjoyed it because Little Fella's mother was teaching. Ake helped Regona with the chores of gathering, gardening, washing and cooking. The druid Dun Norix was a guest and was using Lan's room while he was away. He insisted on helping with chores and told many amazing tales by the hearth after the evening meal. *If only Lan was here,* thought Ake, *then everything would be perfect.*

'Miss Ake, please stop daydreaming and concentrate.' Mrs Ginger laughed.

'Oh, sorry mam,' mumbled Ake.

'Okay children, for homework ask your parents if they know any stories that are special to them that we can share. Ake, are you coming tonight?' asked the teacher.

'Yes, I wouldn't miss it mam,' said Ake.

It was Little Fella's birthday. He was to be named at sundown, the time he was born thirteen years ago.

'Okay children, home time,' said Mrs Ginger. The children left the building.

—///—

Lan and Goriard had managed to survive. They had been running and hiding from the horned guards, Bozzwanna's army. They had used the rest of their firewood and stripped bark from the weaver's tree, weaving the wood together to make a raft. Lan knew the magic to make it watertight. *Now, if only we had a map.* He had made three waterskins from the hides of animals, dried their meat, and gathered fruit so that they would have supplies. His sister barely ever responded when he spoke to her, almost as if she lived in her own little world. He knew if he didn't get her home to Mother that she would be lost to them forever. Lan thought of Ake and his mother and hoped they were safe. A pigeon suddenly alighted on his shoulder and spoke in an old man's voice. 'Lan, I will guide you home. I'm Dun Norix, friend of Regona. You must trust me.'

Lan gave a whoop of joy and pushed the raft out to sea.

Bozzwanna's angry screams echoed in the distance as she came upon the place Lan and Goriard spent last night, a cave near the edge of the island.

———

The sun set. A plainly robed boy, now thirteen, walked towards the descending sun and raised his arms to Sorendee. 'Father of stars, Dee, mother of earth, give blessings to me. Karma, point me right so I never meet your wrath. Great Spirit, whisper to me this night the name I will be given for this lifetime.'

The child sat down upon the hill covered in wildflowers. This hill was the naming hillock on the outskirts of the village. To walk further one would find his death in the sea yonder because two feet from where the boy sat was a thirty metre drop to the sea. The child shivered from the cold as a sea breeze suddenly whipped up. A sign was supposed to come from above and he must interpret it.

—⁓—

The old man telling Ake's story saw it was getting late and stopped, to the lad's protests. He sent the lad to his supper and bed. He told him he would continue in the morn, as he didn't want the lad to wither away from the lack of necessities. The lad tried to disagree, but his father entered the room, scowled at the old man he disliked with a vengeance, and agreed for once the old man made a decent decision.

The old man hobbled to his room with pride, ignoring the younger man. Over the next week the story would unfold, and the boy would know his heritage. *Good then, he will know what to do next, for I'm stuck and he must help me,* the man thought. The man lay down upon his bed, closed his eyes and fell asleep. Morning woke the man. The boy entered his room and pestered him to continue. He did. 'Ah yes, Little Fella's naming, well …'

—⁓—

Above, an owl was circling. It hooted and dived as Little Fella looked on in awe. Still descending, it was swift and powerful. It grabbed a field mouse for its meal and flew to a dead tree atop the hillock to devour it. The boy smiled and continued down the hill to the elders' house so that they could draw blood and he would say his name aloud for the first time and tell them how it had come about.

He entered the hut erected in the naming tradition's honour. It was made of mahogany and was more like a cabin. It was rectangular in shape and had shutterless windows. Inside, the floor was dirt. There were four long logs on the ground for seats and a central fire, four other boys waited there because they too were thirteen tonight. All had been through their naming ordeal earlier.

'Lucas Ginger's son step forward and state your name,' ordered Linton, the head elder.

'Heta Falcon, as swift as night descends. I am of the owl tribe. He is my spirit guide as he swiftly kills the prey in the night.' Heta Falcon puffed his chest out proudly.

'So, Falcon, know your name but be careful, for people you give your name to may be enemies and could control you by such. Names hold much power so don't be too quick to state it,' advised Linton.

'Behold, son of the ginger grower, you must become a man,' said Cristoff.

Cristoff took hold of the bone dagger and sliced Falcon four centimetres diagonally on each cheekbone. Blood welled up and Falcon bit his lip to stop himself crying out. Adrenaline set in and he wiped the sweat from his brow. He started shaking as the chilly night air whipped his long brown hair wildly and cooled his burning skin. He moved to the shutterless windows, allowing the other boys to step into the elder's circle. There was the blacksmith's son, Grudran, Rilikin the herbalist's boy and Furrier the baker's boy. Falcon turned his hazel eyes to the night sky and waited for further instruction.

———✦———

A great bonfire in the central square roasted wild boar on the spit. Stout was brought, chilled from the lake, and bread, cakes and ginger ale sat on long tables. The fire dancers, jugglers, jesters and all slaves waited to entertain the village when the new men came forth. Ake watched in awe as thirteen young women in gold chain underwear and halter-tops were led by town men who held ropes connected to torques of silver at their necks. These women were slave dancers owned by the village and would dance as entertainment for the villagers. Another table held gifts for the young men.

Ake waited for her best friend in admiration and quiet happiness. A storyteller stood up and bowed, the loud merrymakers began to settle and whisper in hushed tones, a stark contrast to their earlier exploits. A lone drummer began to tap out a steady ancient beat as the storyteller began to tell the story of creation.

'Sorendee is the Great Spirit, the breath of every creature, and the air on which departed souls whisper their memories. He is formless and empty, yet he fills the gaps in everything that is motion and energy. Sorendee's soulmate, Dee, is the goddess of the earth, the core is her forgiving heart. Magma, hot and strong courses through her veins like blood throughout the veins and arteries in a single human heartbeat. She is manifested in the trees and the plants that nourishes all mortals——'

The storyteller was interrupted as the new men were led from the cabin to the table. Heta Falcon was surprised Regona had let Ake come as she didn't believe in the villagers' ways. Heta Falcon turned to Ake.

'What's your name?' The little girl giggled.

He took the little girl out of hearing of the villagers by walking hand in hand with her behind the main buildings.

'It is Heta Falcon, but you can call me Het for short,' said Het.

'I like that, owl boy, hoot hoot.' She laughed and ran off.

He caught her and tickled her. They both fell backwards giggling in the fields of sweet grass. Then lay on their backs looking up at the dark, star-free sky.

'Maybe we should go back to the feast cause I'm hungry and I have to be home after it,' said Ake.

'Yeah, let's go,' said Het.

Het and Ake watched the jugglers, dancers, the fire-eaters, and jesters. They clapped when Mrs Ginger sang with her angelic voice. They ate of cakes, fruit and breads. Ake had ginger ale and Het had stout. Het thought it was strange that Ake would not eat any boar, but he ate her given share. When the feast was finished, Het walked Ake home. There was a big commotion inside, candles were lit on the veranda. Het said his goodbyes and went home. Ake went inside.

Dun Norix was warming last night's soup in a cauldron over the fire. Lan and some lady sat in chairs shivering with blankets wrapped around them and a tearful Regona was laughing with relief. Ake ran up to Lan and put her arms around him.

'Oh, my Lan, my mystic,' she cried and rubbed a tear from her face. 'Who is this other lady, Lan?'

Regona answered, 'This is my Goriard, my youngest girl. Oh, she's still alive but seems lost. But Mother will fix that, oh yes, she will.'

'Where was I? We made a raft and your pigeon guided us home. Thanks to the Great Spirit and Dee, a mist surrounded the island and stopped Bozzwanna. It took us four days and we nearly ran out of supplies. But then we came insight of land, and it took us two days' trek overland to get here. I managed to catch game to sustain us,' said Lan.

Regona let Ake hear about Lan's quest but then put her to bed. Ake couldn't sleep. An hour later, unknown to the adults, she listened from the shadow of her bedroom door. The fire was down to glowing embers and a wind whipped up outside. A storm was on its way and everyone in the kitchen sat talking and drinking hot soup from earthenware mugs. Goriard's body functioned for her, but her mind was elsewhere.

'Lan, it is disrespectful to allow your young one to call you by your name,' said Dun Norix.

Lan rung his hands and looked away before composing himself. Then he looked up happily and laughed.

'She's not my daughter, she's my apprentice, Dun Norix. I found her about four months ago. Ake's part of a prophecy.'

Lan dropped his gaze to stare at his feet. *Mother can never know what I did. I will never forgive myself. I must appear happy for her and Ake's sake.*

The druid turned to Regona. 'Regona, I thought she was your grandchild.'

Regona looked up and replied, 'In the heart she is, Dane, in the heart.'

'Oh, right. Hey, you remembered my old name.' He sighed.

'Hey, how long have you known each other?' asked Lan.

'We were close friends over twenty years ago,' answered Dane.

'How close?' Lan laughed.

'Oh, I'm tired, perhaps we should rest,' said Regona.

'Lan, do you care for this child?' asked Dane.

'I have been charged with the responsibility to see she gets educated. Once she is settled with her teachers, my job is done.' Lan shrugged.

'That seems a little harsh to me,' said Dane.

'All part of the job,' said Lan.

'Where are we all going to fit?' asked Dane.

'I'll put Goriard in with me and Lan you could share with Dun Norix,' said Regona.

'That would work,' said Lan.

'Okay, that's settled,' said Dane.

They each went to bed. Lan fell asleep as soon as his head hit the pillow. Unknown to him, Ake roomed in with the women. Ake cried until dawn when, wretched and miserable, she finally closed her eyes.

CHAPTER SEVEN

Sunlight filtered in through an open window and birds sang in the distance. Everyone sat at the breakfast table. Goriard began to show improvement, muttering thank you when Regona handed her food. Everyone smiled except Ake whose eyes were swollen from crying. No one noticed, but something strange was happening between Regona and Dane. Dun Norix had told them that Dane was the name he was born to but his druid name is Dun Norix. He laughed and told them to go ahead and eat. Regona gave Dane a secret smile, noticed by Ake. Then, when Lan and Goriard were eating and they didn't think anyone was looking, Dane and Regona clasped each other's hand.

'Ake, you best be off to school. When you finally get your reading good and your numbers, Lan's gonna teach you special magic. Did you know he is the principal of a mystic school?' asked Regona.

'No, I didn't old Ma.'

'He will have to return to that school soon. I have already started packing, my dear. You will get to go to school there, Ake. Isn't that exciting?' Regona smiled at Ake.

'Yes, old Ma,' said Ake without enthusiasm.

Ake wandered from the house with her little backpack. Lan looked at the child as she left, wondering if something was amiss but then shrugged, happy to be home.

School ended, and Ake returned home to the smell of cookies.

Strange, old Ma normally lets me help her cut out the shapes. Ake raced inside to see Lan, Regona and the druid laughing happily. Goriard's eyes were aware, and she spoke, 'Ah, ginger cookies Ma, we all used to bake these together before my father left and then after with Lan.' They all agreed. Ake entered the building, gave them a put-on grin, grabbed a cookie and headed to her room to do her homework. This seemed to happen to Ake every time she came home over the next month. Everyone else was doing something special without her. Ake felt hurt and angry and when Het asked her what was wrong, Ake confided in him.

'I think it's just for a little while,' Het said tenderly.

Ake told him what Lan said on the night he came home, about him not caring for her.

'I'll tell you what, come and stay with me and my family for the summer holidays when they start in a month.' Het paused and spoke gently. 'Ake, I won't be going back to school after the holidays, sweetheart.'

Ake's eyes brimmed with tears.

'Oh, don't be like that. We will still be friends. So, what do you say, want to come?' Het grinned at her.

'Yeah, I'd like that,' said the little girl.

Regona agreed to Ake spending the time with Het, as she believed children should have friends. The night Ake went to Het's, Lan came in and asked where Ake was.

'Oh, that's right,' Lan said and went out the door.

Ake spent the next six weeks having a wonderful time with her friend. They swam in the river, played knuckles with sheep bones, had running races and enjoyed a many great tales around the fireplace after scrumptious meals. Ake enjoyed it so much she cried when she left. Mrs Ginger hugged her, said what a quaint little girl Ake was and what a good choice for her boy. Mrs Ginger gave her some ginger snaps and ginger ale to take home to old

Ma. Ake didn't understand but Het smiled at her and winked, and she skipped home in the bright summery sun.

When Ake arrived home, she knew something was amiss. Lan was pacing back and forth scowling on the front veranda. Ake walked past him into the house to give old Ma the gifts. Old Ma was crying in the druid's arms and Goriard sat on the couch looking lost again.

'Old Ma, Mrs Ginger gave you these,' said Ake.

'Ake, hi dear, you best go to bed,' said Regona and dismissed the child.

'Old Ma, it's lunchtime, I can't go to bed.' Ake laughed.

'Well, go play,' demanded Lan, entering the cottage.

'But Lan,' Ake whined.

'Don't Lan me, go outside,' he said and shooed the child outdoors.

Ake, with tears in her eyes, knelt on the veranda, looking in at the people she loved most of all. Her young heart knew the feeling of rejection once more. Ake decided it was time to make her own way in the world. The girl would bide her time and decided Het and her would run away together. She listened to the conversation going on inside the cottage.

'Son, she's your full sister, Lan, the child will be Bozzwanna's tool if is to live,' said Dane.

'When did you ever care? You left your family for a career and if we were to raise it, what harm is there in an innocent child? By the way when did you find out?' asked Lan.

'Son, your mother told me.' The druid shrugged.

'Don't call me son. You have no right too. I'll at least be there for my child,' said Lan.

'But son, it's being carried by your sister.' Dane gasped.

'I will not kill my child.'

Lan stormed outside and saw Ake crying. 'What's your problem, kiddo?'

'Nothing I can't handle, unlike you,' Ake grumbled.

'Don't speak to me like that again girl, I'm your mentor,' said Lan.

'I was never yours until you stole me. You don't own me,' spat the girl.

'I didn't want to take you. But after what I've don——' said Lan.

Ake interrupted him. 'You, you did nothing, it was Het and old Ma that did everything, not you. I hate you. You use people and you're like the Shadow Masters and their flesh tithe.'

'I'm nothing like them!' Lan stared at her shocked.

'You want to use me for your own gain just like them, but it seems more right because you don't destroy many lives. You've destroyed mine but what does it matter that you don't care for me,' cried Ake.

She stormed off angry, her tears dried. *I am going to stay. I will learn all I can from Lan.* Now Ake had a purpose to stay.

—⁓—

Lan rushed inside with tears in his eyes. 'Give Goriard the herbs. If that is what she wants. I still think it's dangerous this far along.'

Regona brewed the simple tea and offered it to her daughter. 'Like I explained a month ago when you drink this, you will miscarry the baby. If you don't it could be born poorly, having siblings for parents.'

Goriard shrieked and threw the cup. 'We have already discussed this. I don't want to lose another child.'

Lan sat on a chair, head in his hands.

Regona tried to hand her daughter the cup again.

'Mother, leave it be.' Goriard wept.

Lan stomped out of the room, tears sliding down his face.

Drianna looked in upon this heart-wrenching scene and laughed with glee.

Chapter Eight

As the months wore on and the year ended, Ake could read and write fluently. Her little family seemed as if it was drifting further away from her. Regona, Lan and Dane were arguing about the child-to-be to the point of exhaustion and had no time for her. It seemed as if it didn't matter if she came and went. The first few months of her coming had been the highlight of her life. If it wasn't for Het and the other Gingers, it seemed pointless hanging around this village.

The child had put her heart into this term and spending time with her friend. Ake was a quick learner, and she soon came to be head of her class. Mrs Ginger came to realise this was one very special girl.

To reward the girl, the woman set about putting on a birthday celebration because Ake had told her, her birthday was within two days. With the little silver she had saved, Mrs Ginger bought Ake new shoes, a robe and girls leggings as the winter was nearing. She also knitted her a rag doll and prepared biscuits, sandwiches, a cake and some ginger beer. Mrs Ginger baked enough for the little school of twenty-five and the Gingers.

Someone must take an interest in Ake. It seems as if her foster parent doesn't want her anymore. Her few clothes are ragged, her hair scruffy and her socks need darning. The child is being fed but what of her emotional needs? thought Mrs Ginger, a mother herself. *I think it would be best if Ake came to stay with me for good.*

Two days later, Ake entered the schoolhouse to a birthday celebration in her honour. A local miner's three daughters hugged her and wished her a happy birthday. Het was there and his two older brothers, Danu and Mikeal, who all winked at her and clapped her on the back. Mr Ginger smiled and nodded his agreement and Mrs Ginger hugged and kissed her. They consumed the food happily and sang the birthday song. All the other children joined in. Then came the gifts. Ake could not stop the tears falling from happiness and when Mrs Ginger said it would be an honour if Ake came to live with her family, she was too happy to disagree and nodded her answer.

Meanwhile in the cottage of Regona, a baby was brought into the world. A little boy, both Lan's and Goriard's son. There was sadness as well as joy. During the pregnancy Goriard retreated into her tortured memories of earlier births. Goriard passed from this world giving birth to the new baby. To the three that watched the birthing, they knew Goriard had been lost to them for a long time, but it seemed as though she had been reborn in her son. It was Goriard's eyes that looked back at them from that young face. Regona would embalm Goriard on the morn then cremate her on a berth of mahogany and wildflowers.

Ake skipped home hand in hand with Mrs Ginger and Het and was shown to the room she was to share with Het. It had two beds in it and wooden floorboards. It was quite small but had shuttered windows and stone walls. There was a little hearth with a warm fire glowing and a black kitten on her designated bed with a ribbon around her neck. The little kitten mewed softly and jumped off the floral sheep wool coverlet and rubbed herself affectionately around Ake's legs. Ake noticed she had white tufts on her ears and paws.

'Mrs Ginger, Mrs Ginger, there's a kitty on my bed, she must have snuck in here,' cried Ake wondrously.

'Child,' said Mrs Ginger, entering the room, 'I put her there, she's yours. Mrs Gibbs's female had a litter six weeks ago and I thought you might like one.'

'Oh, Mrs Ginger, I'll call her Socksy,' cried Ake, clinging to Mrs Ginger's waist.

'You can't keep calling me Mrs Ginger. Why don't you call me Ma and I'll call you daughter.' The woman smiled down at Ake.

'Oh, I'd like that, Ma.' Ake laughed.

'Welcome to my humble abode Ake, daughter,' said Mrs Ginger.

—∿∿∿—

The happiness continued long into the night for Ake. She had brothers and a Ma and Pa now, life was looking up. Ake kept thinking about Old Ma. But Old Ma probably wasn't thinking about her, and with that, the girl fell asleep.

During the night the three oldest inhabitants of Regona's cottage were discussing what to name the child.

'Well, Father, it's normally your job to name the grandchildren,' said Lan.

'Well, I was thinking, your mother told me your full name was Trebrelan, Star Scryer, and I know Goriard's translates to Sweet Flower. Humph. I know, let's take scryer and sweet from both your names so it becomes Sweet Scryer. That makes it Orilan in the elven tongue,' said Dane.

'Orilan, I like that,' said both Lan and Regona.

'By the way, when do you leave for your mysticism school with Ake and Orilan?' asked Regona.

'In the morn. It's a four-day journey on foot to the end of this island where the school stands. I know you packed Ake some special things over a month ago, so she's been having to wear her worst clothing. I'm going to have to hire a wet nurse for Orilan.

She can help me with Ake too. I'm afraid I was a little harsh on her not long ago,' Lan said awkwardly, looking away.

'What did you do?' asked the older two.

Lan told them.

'Oh dear. So, that's why she's been distant! And with all the surprise planning I've done for her birthday and working with Goriard and packing for the trip, I haven't taken much notice of her lately,' said Regona.

'Yeah, she was supposed to be home a while ago,' said Dane.

'Well, I'll go look for her. I bet she's with that friend of hers,' said Lan and left.

'Oh, dear Regona. My druid senses tell me something's amiss. Maybe I should go help Lan,' said Dane.

'Maybe you should. I'm going to spend the time with Orilan and get a wet nurse for him,' said Regona.

'Okay, see you soon Regona. I leave too in the morn, Regona, but remember what we talked about, it's going to happen.' Dane winked at her.

Regona laughed at his straightforwardness.

'Oh, Dane, I remember and yes, I forgave you a long time ago. I too understand the calling and it has been a long time, and we're not too old,' whispered Regona.

Orilan stirred restlessly in her arms and Dane kissed Regona gently on the mouth and left.

Meanwhile, Bozzwanna drew ever closer, her time nearly up. She felt the hold of her power growing weaker. She must act soon. *Ah, when my wretched nephew is on the way to his school, Caelestis. Ha, it means celestial. No way is he divine.* She laughed evilly and flew off in her owl form, away from the cottage window.

—◊◊◊—

Lan and Dane knocked on the door of the Gingers' house. Mrs Ginger answered the door.

'Ahh Kathy, how are you tonight? You haven't seen Ake, have you?' asked Lan politely.

'Yes, she has decided to live with people who care about her,' said Kathy.

'What are you talking about? We see to her needs and my mother treats her like a granddaughter.' Lan glared at her.

'Well, Ake doesn't see it that way. She hasn't had any attention or decent clothing and you didn't even remember her birthday.' Kathy shrugged.

'What? We've been planning that for months and when she didn't come home tonight, Regona was worried,' said Lan.

'What about you, Lan? Do you care for her? She adores you; she's always talking about her mystic.' She gestured at him.

'She's my apprentice and I don't have to answer to you,' said Lan.

'No, but you have a duty of care to Ake. She's head of her class, beautiful and honest. Don't you feel she has a say in her life?' asked Kathy.

'What would you know, villager, following in barbaric rituals? Your men don't even give women a choice,' said Lan smirking at Kathy.

'Wrong, Lan. I married a villager but I'm a cleric of Dee, of the old way. In the tradition of tribal way, I have a say and any woman in this household does too. My home is a sanctuary for girls and women. As you should well know. Your own mother is one too,' said Kathy.

Dane spoke up. 'People, let's ask Ake, as she does not belong to any of us. Ake is an orphan and Lan you should learn to remember she's not your property.'

'Father.' Lan turned and glared at him.

'Lan, quiet, here she and Het come,' said Dane.

A sleepy-eyed Ake, holding Socksy and sucking her thumb, wandered up to Kathy and asked what was going on.

'Old Ma and this druid want you to go home. They did not mean to ignore you Ake,' said Kathy gently.

'Old Ma wants me! Sorry Mrs Ginger but I have to go home,' said Ake.

'I understand sweetheart,' said Kathy.

Dane offered to pay back the money Kathy spent on Ake's presents when she went and got them. Offended, Kathy replied, 'It's a labour of love.' Apologising, Dane allowed Ake to say good-bye to Het and the rest of the Ginger family. Het and Ake cried in each other's arms and the Gingers all had tears in their eyes when Ake left. Dane took Ake by the hand warmly.

Lan suddenly felt jealous and was surprised. *Why is it he favours others over me?*

'Ake, you can take your pet on your journey and guess what, I'll be coming along and will stay at Caelestis with you as long as I am able. And child, call me Grandpapa,' said Dane.

Ake happily answered back, 'Oh Grandpapa, I'd like that. I'll have someone that loves me and can teach me on the way.'

'I'll gladly teach you a few things,' said Dane.

The druid picked Ake up and headed towards the cottage while waving to Het and his family.

Lan, proud and undermined, seethed and wandered closely behind. Upon returning home, Ake received another party. There was a young woman there with her own baby slung in a carrier over her shoulders. To Ake, he didn't seem older than Orilan, the new baby in the household. Orilan, with his deep blue eyes and tiny features, fascinated her. When he smiled at her and Regona said it was just wind, Ake laughed.

Ake received another doll and supplies for her trip from Regona. A clear quartz from Dane and from Lan nothing. He had made her something but was too annoyed to give it to her yet. Dane, understanding jealousy, shook his head sadly at his son.

Unknown to the rest of the household, Dane could speak many languages. Everyone looked on in amazement as Dane found out the name of the girl who was nursing Orilan. He told the others.

'Her name is Sidon or Sun Dew, daughter of a chief. Her son is named Torrid,' he said.

Dane whispered to Ake his forte was speaking languages. Ake asked him if he would teach her a few words so she could talk to Sidon. Dane smiled and nodded. Then it was time to rest. Sidon shared with Ake. Lan went to his own bedroom, closed the door and lay down on his bed in annoyance. The two babes were put together in an old cot brought up from the cellar. As the babies drifted asleep, Regona sat talking with Dane of their continuing love until they were sure everyone was asleep. The couple took each other's hands and went for a romantic walk outside.

'Oh, my love, I have not forgotten what it was like the first time, my sweet,' said Dane.

'Oh, Dane, neither have I, my darling, my heart,' whispered Regona.

'Regona, I have come one last time. I will travel with Lan and teach him what I can. Either of you may not see me again. I return to Eriu for good. I have about two decades left to me, and I must train a replacement,' said Dane softly.

'Oh, Dane, my darling, then we must make this memorable for both of us.'

'Yes, well, I was going to give this to you a few months ago but I'll do it now.'

Dane pulled out a single gold band that had engraved on it: No parting of our souls. Even when the sun last sets.

'Oh, Dane, I have nothing to give you except my love,' said Regona, tears in her eyes.

'And the knowledge of my son and grandson. I need nothing else to sustain me on those lonely nights but the knowledge that you love me,' said Dane.

Dane slipped the ring on Regona's left index finger. It fitted perfectly.

'The night is young. Just like we can pretend we are too, my Dane,' enticed Regona.

The couple embraced each other tenderly and consummated their love physically.

Morning saw the band of six set out on the road early. Regona kissed Ake, Orilan and Lan tenderly. Regona paused when she came to Dane. Weeping, she embraced him passionately.

'Sssh, old bird. Remember me in your dreams,' said Dane.

'I will my love, my Dane. Tell Sidon good luck,' said the woman sadly.

'I will,' said Dane, wiping tears from his eyes.

CHAPTER NINE

The band of six left Regona standing on the porch waving and weeping. Then the old woman turned and entered the house to prepare the burning ritual for Goriard, alone.

By midday, Lan appeared cheery and more himself. *As soon as I get to Caelestis I can let this mask down. God, I hate myself. I caused Goriard's death.*

Orilan started crying and Lan handed him to Sidon, who took the child to her breast. Ake watched fascinated as Orilan's face became a mask of complete bliss. After Orilan finished, Sidon's own son cried, and she fed him too.

Ake, Lan and the druid stopped to consume the midday meal. Sidon watched, then took supplies from her own backpack Regona had given her. Sidon had resisted at first as she had not owned anything in five years. She had calmed herself after the druid Dane had talked to her and soothed her and she had accepted the gifts.

Ake kept trying to speak to Sidon in her own language, but with little luck. The poor kid kept getting muddled. Sidon laughed at her attempts.

They were on the road again shortly after, until dusk. Lan took Ake aside.

'Hey kiddo, I got something for you. I should have given it to you yesterday, but I was being a fool.' Lan grinned at the child.

'Yeah, I agree with you. I don't know if I want to forgive you,' said Ake cheekily.

'Ahh, come on.'

'Umm, no.' Ake grinned up at him.

'Why, you cheeky runt.' Lan laughed. He grabbed Ake and held her upside down.

'Put me down Lan.' Ake laughed nervously.

'Nope.' He grinned at her.

'Lan, please.' The child whimpered.

'Why, you scared?'

'Yes.'

Lan put the child down. 'I am sorry.'

'You mean man, you,' screamed the little girl. She knuckled away her tears and stormed off.

Dane walked into view.

'What was that about, Lan?' asked a puzzled Dane.

'I don't know,' said Lan.

He was just as puzzled. Lan told Dane what had occurred.

'Hmm, I reckon this is linked to a trauma of some kind. I'm going to go find out. Lan, next time, mind your manners,' chided Dane.

'But I did,' said Lan.

'Not enough.' Dane shrugged.

'What do you expect from me, Father? I'm not as great as the druid Dun Norix, am I? You come here and try to take over and boss me around. Well, I don't have to listen to you,' Lan yelled and stormed away, as hurt as Ake. He pouted and headed towards a rocky outcrop nearby and sat there scowling at his father.

'Jealous elfling,' cried Dane to his son's retreating back.

Lan turned to see his laughing father heading back to camp where Sidon was gathering firewood. Lan started writing an apology note to Ake on the hand painted writing set he had made for her. He looked at his craftsmanship and sighed. *Why does it always seem as though I'm the cause of trouble? Well, I've had enough of this interference. Dane can teach her. I want nothing to do with her.* Lan erased the note he was writing and headed down to camp. He stormed up to Dane, Ake and Sidon and threw down the writing set at Ake's feet.

'There you go, missy. There's the gift I made for you,' Lan said.

Ake looked at it. The pages were white, rare because most paper at this time was yellow or brown. She saw swans in flight over a lake and her old village painted there.

'If you make a mistake on it, it erases by magic.' Lan shrugged.

Impressed, Dane tried to apologise for his mistake.

'Hush, druid, you teach her. I want nothing to do with any of you.' Lan growled.

'What about Orilan?' asked Dane.

'If you think you can do a better job, druid, you raise him,' said Lan.

Lan stormed off to set up his own camp. Dane sighed sadly and resumed his conversation with Ake.

'So, girly, how did they punish you?' asked Dane.

Lan with his elven hearing heard the conversation without trying to.

'Well, me and my mama were starving. Because no woman is allowed to carry a man's weapon. And when Lan wasn't bringing us food, we needed something to live on,' said Ake.

'Wow, was Lan trying to look after you and your mam?'

'Yeah, they were good friends.'

'Do you know if Lan was just trying to get to know your mam, so he could take you to the mystics?' asked Dane.

Lan growled to himself. 'Druid, you just became my enemy. Melowy was my friend. Just because Ake was hers doesn't make the mother any less my friend.'

'Continue, girl,' said Dane.

'Lan would never do that. Before he took me, he said something to my mama,' said Ake proudly.

'What was it child?' asked Dane.

'He said something like, come with me, friend, is there no way I can stop you?' said Ake.

'Now I understand. Ake, what happened to you to make you have a fear of being upside down?' asked the druid.

'Umm, I saw them hang up a dead animal and I didn't like it,' Ake's voice wavered.

'Oh okay. Let's have this meal and rest,' said Dane.

Why did Ake lie? Is it that she is unsure of the druid's purposes, as I am? Lan knew Ake so well he could hear the lying tone in her voice.

Lan rolled his eyes when he heard Dane give Ake an explanation on the maturity of elves.

'I am sorry Lan is so immature towards you and everyone else. You see Ake, Lan is only a teenager. Elves stop growing physically at eighteen, but their minds develop slowly as they can live everywhere from fifteen hundred to two thousand years. Elves reach adulthood at one hundred. At twenty-two, Lan is a long way away from that. He will likely have the maturity of a teenager when you are an adult.'

Lan heard Ake giggle and reply, 'That explains a lot. Then why is he in charge of a magic school?'

'That was pure circumstance. He inherited it as a boy. I will try to guide him from now on,' said Dane.

Lan had heard enough. *I am sick of everyone undermining me and deeming me immature. Especially him. How dare he!* Lan sighed and rolled himself up in his bedroll and fell asleep.

—⁓—

Bozzwanna and her horned guards were hot on the group's trail and were camped a little way off. Her guards and their hellhounds were little more than animals, brought about by a strong appreciation for pleasures of the flesh and bloodlust. The latter was the most important attribute and easiest to supply. Bozzwanna looked over her little encampment. There were thirty guardsmen and seventeen hellhounds. The hellhounds were as big as small ponies, and as black as the darkest night. They had the face of a jackal and layers of teeth like a shark and just as sharp. Their eyes were as red as blood and their mouths frothed from the rabies they carried. They were as skinny as a whippet and always hungry but were never satisfied or put on flesh. Their paws were as big as a lion's and their talons as sharp as an eagle. But strange enough, when they moved, their paws padded soundlessly, and they could cross any terrain. Their voices were the sounds of bones continuously creaking and only sounded when they were chasing down prey. Their stench was of bodies long since decayed and they had no shadows.

Bozzwanna turned and saw two of her horned guards fighting over raw bits of entrails from the body of a dead raven. Their horns were part of their human bone helmets, two upright humeri. The guards wore nothing apart from these helmets and a loincloth made of human skin. They carried weapons of wood hardened in fire with a long glass blade on the end that would shatter into fragments when they wounded someone. These creatures were blind. Their supernatural senses were hearing and an unearthly sense of smell.

They could smell life hundreds of metres from where they stood. Maggots and tics crawled in the sockets of their eyes and nasal cavity. Their only teeth were two extremely sharp canines. Their fingernails were yellow and dried with blood. The creatures' skin was grey and drawn tightly against their bones. One slash of the claws had the effect of the bite of a Komodo dragon, lingering death. Their breath rasped in their diseased lungs and had the sickly sweet and metallic smell of blood.

Bozzwanna laughed and turned into the owl that Het had seen and flew to where Ake lay with Orilan in her arms. The little girl sighed in her sleep.

—⁓—

Lan, camped on the rocky outcrop a little way from the other campers, awoke in a night sweat and raised the alarm as the sound of creaking bones filled the night air.

'Ake, Father, wake. For Dee's sake, wake up,' Lan screamed.

Ake, witnessing Bozwanna's army in a vision, was the first to hear his screams.

'Lan, help us,' screamed the little girl as she tried to wake the sleeping druid and Sidon.

Bozzwanna laughed aloud and resumed her normal profile. Lan saw this happening and jumped from where he was camped onto the back of the filth that stood before Ake.

'Off me, boy scum,' screamed Bozzwanna.

Distracted, Bozzwanna could not maintain the concentration needed to hold a prolonged sleeping spell. The druid and Sidon woke, and the two babies opened their eyes, screwed up their little faces and wailed.

Ake, in her heart, knew she must do something. Ake helped the old druid and Sidon up. The horned guards came upon the little encampment. Ake's sharp mind flared, and the girl grabbed the two infants and, with unnatural speed, ran towards the nearby granite falls.

'Get her,' said Bozzwanna.

Lan twisted her head back sharply, snapping her neck. Bozzwanna's last thought was the sight of Ake's courageous deed. The lifeless body was thrown into the oncoming horde of hellhounds and horned guards. The once seductress would become carrion for vultures and other scavengers who would fight over her entrails, again becoming part of Dee.

Lan the mystic, an unarmed combat master, readied himself for a fight. Dane's countenance grew serious, and Sidon grabbed her pitiful eating implements for weapons, but her brave heart was ready. The threesome fought hard. Meanwhile, darkness chased Ake. Drianna, the goddess of eternal fear, hunted her.

Lan went flying into the onslaught. A roundhouse kick embedded itself in a horned guard's skull. A twist of the ankle and his neck snapped. Druid's fire was sent forth with the wrath of Dun Norix. Sidon slashed off the hands of a guard trying to drag her down. Black blood spurted forth, covering her face. She choked on the blood and went down. Lan and the druid turned to look but the girl was lost among the horde. The druid sent his green, smokeless fire forwards once more and took down three of the hellhounds trying to overpower him.

Lan somersaulted backwards and put the heel of his boot into the side of a guard he landed on. A sound of creaking bones came from behind him, and a claw pinned his left arm down. The talon went through his bone. Blood streamed forth and he heard ligament and muscle tearing. He screamed as his bone was crushed under the hound's weight. He sent forth mystic flame in a wide orange arc and burnt the hound to ashes. Screaming in agony, he drew the talon from his arm. He saw his father fall. Dane's green robes were shredded. Dane cried out and Lan believed he saw blood weeping from the gaps in the fabric.

'Father!' screamed the young man.

He heard the sound of creaking bones again and rolled to the side just in time as another hellhound landed where he previously stood.

Meanwhile, Ake was stumbling under the weight of two wailing infants. Ake sensed someone following and saw a bramble bush nearby. She pushed her way inside, ignoring the blood that welled up on her tiring body as the thorns tore and caught on her fair skin.

The babies were still wailing. She lay them down on the mossy floor and hummed to them. Ake stilled her fluttering heart. Orilan stopped and turned his big, blue, unearthly eyes towards her. He looked deep into her soul and wrapped his little fingers around her thumb. The other child began to wail again. Drianna stopped and listened.

'Come out wherever you are,' laughed Drianna hideously.

The Dark Goddess then cast a spell in the language of darkness and blew the bramble bush into the air, exploding it. Ake stood and faced her. The child began to glow with an unearthly light and Dee began to speak through her.

'Drianna, sister, jealousy has brought this evilness upon you. I am in the earth and not on this physical plane, so I cannot stop what you are about to do. But your downfall will come at the hands of this child's own son,' came the angelic voice of Dee.

Drianna laughed. 'Not if she dies this night.'

'I will protect one tonight as it is in my capability. Take the child that has come about by your means. Know this, that what I have said will come to pass,' said Dee.

Ake screamed as the voice faded and she was held to the earth. Drianna laughed. She picked up Orilan and cradled the sleeping child in her arms. She teleported the broken and battered body of Regona to the spot.

'Old Ma! Orilan!' Ake yelled.

Drianna started to chant some horrid verse. She slit open the still warm body of the dead Regona and dipped her fingers in the blood and put it to Orilan's lips. The child opened his eyes and wailed. Drianna laughed and disappeared with the child. Ake's screams echoed into the night.

An infant wailed. Ake turned and gripped the child to her heart.

Lan grimaced in pain and turned to the sound. They'd won the fight as Dun Norix's group of druids turned up in time. He looked at the body of poor Sidon. The druids had knitted the wound of his arm closed and strapped it to his side. Dane sustained nothing more than cuts and bruises. When the druids turned their backs, Lan arose painfully and headed towards Ake.

Dane, resting, turned to his son's fleeing shadow and cried out, 'Dee's blessing Lan. They are taking me against my consent as the druids protect what they believe they own. I'm sorry, my son, for all I have done and missed. I am proud to be your father.'

Lan turned and yelled out as the druids disappeared with his father among them. 'Thank you, Father, I love you.'

Dane's soul smiled. Lan wiped a tear from his eye and headed towards the screams.

Ake sat near the body of Regona, her face covered in the old woman's blood. Ake kissed the face repeatedly. Her tears washed and purified the body. Ake rocked back and forth. The child held Sidon's son in her lap. Her eyes showed the pain that dripped like an open wound into her soul, staining it with a permanent memory.

Ake turned to the sound of gasping breath and crunching footsteps. Her aura cried out, *let there be no more pain.* She saw Lan. He had his hood up to cover up his tear-stained face and blood-shot eyes. He looked over the scene. A child covered in the blood of the grandmother of her heart. He began to cry too. An infant cry answered, but not with the voice of his little son, Orilan.

Ake cowered down on the ground awaiting her punishment. The child believed she had failed the mystic, and that he would send her away to again know the rejection she had felt a thousand times. Lan stopped and his heart finally broke in two. He fell to his knees and screamed.

'Dee, why must it be this way? First my sisters, then my mother and son, and now Melowy's child. Do you always damage and torment those you eventually wish success?' Lan wept.

Ake walked towards him after placing the infant in a bed of nearby moss.

'I have failed you and Orilan.' The child cowered.

'No, Ake you have not. You did a great deed. It is humanity who has to know suffering. I thought by not showing you I cared it would make you stronger, but it has failed to do that so far. I vow to protect you.'

With his one good arm he pulled the child towards him. Keeping the child at his side, he said a chant over Regona and picked some nearby herbs. Placing them atop his mother, he then picked up the infant with his one good arm and handed him to Ake. Lan then conjured *Mystic Fire* and incinerated the body of his beloved mother. Turning, he headed back with Ake to the battlefield and did the same to Sidon's body. Lan headed up towards the rocky outcrop and turned to survey the carnage. Shivering, he lay down. Ake stood there lost and alone.

'Ake, lay down upon this blanket.'

The child didn't seem to recognise him. Angry, he grabbed Ake and placed her and the infant on a blanket and tucked it around and under them. The exhausted baby drizzled feebly and then closed his weary eyes.

'Ake, take heed of me.'

The child raised her frightened eyes towards the mystic. 'Lan, when are you going to make me go away because of what I've done?'

'What? Ake don't be a fool. I wouldn't do that. You did what was right.' Lan shrugged.

'No, you must make me go. I made everyone dead.' Ake whimpered.

'Hush,' said Lan softly.

Lan then cast a sleeping spell on her. Feeling exhausted himself, he went to sleep nearby. The god, Sorendee whispered to Dee. Dee hearing her husband's plea, teleported the three on the rocky outcrop to a field full of sweet grass outside Caelestis.

CHAPTER TEN

A baby's cry of hunger woke Ake and Lan from their vivid nightmares. Lan wiped his tearful eyes and shivered. Ake listened to the morning chorus and felt sunlight warm her cheeks.

Lan felt a change in the atmosphere and looked up. There stood the gleaming whitewashed stone walls of the mystic tower, Caelestis. He remembered how he was schooled there and the principal who had no children made his promising advanced student heir to it when he passed on. He wondered how he got here but then shrugged.

Lan then cast aside the wood and rope his healing arm was strapped too. He picked up the infant and grimaced against the remaining pain. Ake walked up to him and took his hand, and they headed inside Caelestis together.

Several days passed and to Ake it seemed as if she was in a dream. Ake learnt to deal with her fear of rejection and the grief that had so horribly ripped a tear in her soul. Ake had not seen much of Lan except over the dinner table at mealtimes as he had to see what had happened at the school while he was away. Ake realised the splendour that Lan was used to and how rich he was. Lan had her given her own room until she was to start her training in the mystic arts and so that she could have her own time to come to terms with her grief. On the notepad Lan had given her, she began to keep a diary of her thoughts, and events that had happened. Slowly the pain disappeared.

For the first two weeks Ake stayed in her room, mainly crying and barely eating. When Ake wasn't crying or sleeping, the child was writing. But soon her cat's curiosity drew her out of hiding and into exploring the fortress. Her little cat had managed to survive the battle by hiding amongst a clump of rhododendron. And they explored the place together.

Lan managed to find a mother who was a wife of one of his servants and was nursing, she took Torrid in. On the following day Ake was taken into the tutelage of a lower mystic to teach her the basics, and a combat master would teach her basic unarmed combat over the next year.

The year passed, and Ake fell into a basic routine. Ake loved to learn and caught on quickly. Her occasional highlights were the rare Saturday mornings Lan invited her and the senior students to a staff party. He would play the harp and several other teachers would sing or play the lute. He talked at length with the older students before he briefly asked her how her training was going. Then he ignored her for the rest of the meeting and discussed any issues within the school with his staff.

Often Ake left early, without anyone noticing her departure. Her birthday came and went, and Lan surprised her with a collection of texts on elven lore. He told her he had forgotten to get her the textbooks when she had started.

After her birthday, Lan seemed to retreat into his research and running Caelestis. Ake only saw him around the school on occasion or when she rushed into his office for some rebellious misdemeanour with a teacher chasing her. He would laugh and innocently tell the teacher to deal with it, unaware why the child played up.

Torrid grew quickly, Ake was fond of him and would babysit him when Mrs Callum, his foster mother, went to market on Thursdays. Then came Ake's exams where she had to conjure a flame in the palm of her hand and put it out with her mind. Ake had to know the herbal cures for warts, boils and acne. As part of the final exams, Ake had to perform two martial arts displays in front of her unarmed combat master. The summer solstice approached and with it, Het. He spent the next fortnight at Caelestis.

Ake and Het spent many hours searching the numerous secret passages Ake had found. One time, they got lost and Lan had to come and find them. All too soon it was time for Het to leave. Ake cried and begged him to stay. But he could not because he was in training, he was learning to become a warrior, proficient at many arms. He said he would return the same time every year. In time, the lonely Ake turned to Het for solace, and he became a brother to her.

CHAPTER ELEVEN

Five years passed, and Ake grew into a tall and clumsy teenager, who was always falling over or getting into mischief. She was always sent to Lan, who tried not to laugh when he had to punish her. One time, Ake conjured up rats in the kitchen. When the non-magical old lady chef saw them, the woman went screaming in a flood of tears into Lan's office. At the time, Lan was marking mid-term papers. He looked up and groaned. *What am I going to do with her?* He knew it was Ake again.

Ake was ushered into the room grinning ear to ear. Lan, trying not to laugh, scolded her and sentenced her to plenty of fresh air outside the fortress walls gathering herbs for her so-called scary herbology teacher.

'But Lan,' Ake tried to charm. But Lan dismissed her back to her chores.

One day, when Ake had just turned fifteen and Het had come to stay, Ake woke up with gut-wrenching stomach pains. Standing up, she was tired and ached all over. Ake noticed what she hadn't noticed a few months ago, breasts were beginning to form. Ake was becoming a young woman. Ake was angry and annoyed about it. Ake went to relieve herself and noticed some bleeding. Little did she know she had begun her moon cycle. Ake dressed, using a towel to sop up the mess. She ran screaming into Lan's office.

'Calm down,' said a flabbergasted Lan.

'I will not,' said the young woman.

'Why not?' asked Lan.

'I'm dying.'

'You don't look like it to me.'

'Yes, I am.'

'Okay, tell me when you have one minute to live and I'll record your last wishes,' Lan said and turned back to his budgeting.

'But I'm bleeding and I'm tired and feel dizzy,' said Ake. Lan looked up at her mortified. 'Oh, um, you should go see nurse.'

'But she's always busy and I might die before I get there.'

'Well, go see Het. You're growing up. He might explain it to you.'

'But he's a man,' said Ake.

'And I'm not?' asked Lan.

'No, you're an elf.'

'I thought I was a man. But thank you for that startling piece of evidence.'

Ake laughed. 'You know what I mean Lan.'

'Yes, I think I do.' Lan blushed. 'It is not my place to explain it to you. I am your principal. Go to the library and look under this reference.' Lan handed her a piece of paper ripped from his pad.

'But first go to the nurse and she will teach you to take care of yourself.' He dismissed her.

Happy to know she wasn't dying, Ake headed to the healers' quarters. After seeing to her physical needs, Ake went to the library to deal with her information necessities.

The library walls were made of white stone as was the high ceiling. Shelves lined the walls from ceiling to floor. A rail ran along the top which had a ladder on wheels connected so one could climb to get to a certain book or scroll. The floor was dark, polished mahogany.

Ten long tables and chairs of oak sat in the centre. The scrolls and books looked like they hadn't been read in years as they were yellowed with age, dusty and made Ake sneeze when she picked one up. After her look around, Ake sat down at one of the long tables with a few of the books under Lan's given reference number, as well as several on elves, and began to read.

—◦◦◦—

Lan stood alone in his room ready to part on a mission he had been planning for the last six years to retrieve his son Orilan from the underworld. His trusted adviser was to be in charge while he was away. There was a gentle knocking at the door.

'Come in Falcon,' said Lan.

Het entered.

'You wanted to see me, master mystic?' said Het.

'Yes, remember what we talked about last summer?' asked Lan.

'Yeah, the thing about you going to find your little boy. My answer is yes, I'd do anything for Ake.' Het shrugged.

'I know you would, son. But this journey could take months or years and Ake won't understand why I didn't tell her. And in her curiosity, she'd want to come. I need you to protect her, as I know you are a master at arms. Six years training, phew. You'll be paid of course. Two silver a week plus room and board. I would also like you to teach her to ride and learn to track and know the land. You would know it as well as I, being a farmer's boy,' said Lan.

'It's okay to be nervous, dark uncle. I'll take good care of her. You know I love her, don't you?' asked Het.

'It's obvious. I'll tell you now, her son is supposed to bring about Drianna's downfall. So, be careful what you let yourself in for Falcon. I think you will suit each other,' said Lan.

'It's okay, sir, we'll be fine. You better leave now. I saddled your horse for you, boss,' said Het.

'Don't call me that, I'm no one's boss. My father taught me that. Falcon, there's a possibility I won't come home, if you know what I mean?'

'Be positive, you've got your school to come home to.'

'Well, yes. Goodbye friend. Tell Ake goodbye.'

'I will,' said Het.

They both left the room. Lan turned the key in the lock and they went separate ways down the hall. Horses' hooves thundered out the gates and the rider, with his long black hair waving in the wind, didn't look back. Meanwhile, a young woman cried in Het's arms when he told her Lan was gone.

CHAPTER TWELVE

A sixteen-year-old lass and a twenty-two-year-old lad sat in the library on a bright sunny Saturday morning. They were setting about planning the biggest prank of the era. Het had become the biggest part in Ake's life since Lan left the year before. Ake was now the most popular girl in the school among the cool kids. A year had seen amazing changes in the once gangly and clumsy adolescent. Her blonde tresses ended at her slender waist. She was graceful and could out-ride and out-run any man on campus. Ake had become an amazing tracker. Her studies and unarmed combat were failing as she spent most of her time in the forest tracking and riding with Het.

Ake stood at five foot six inches with a dainty build. Her skin was pale and without blemish. Het was the eye of many a girl, but his eyes always followed Ake when she wasn't looking. He wore his curly brown hair shoulder length. His biceps rippled with muscles, as did his calves and thighs from the unrelenting weapons practice and riding with Ake. Ake had become strong, proud and rebellious. None of her teachers could control the pair. Het was strong, unyielding except for the wants and needs of Ake, his smile was mischievous and harsh.

Ake had a keen sense of someone watching but it went as quickly as it came. She shrugged the feeling off and she and Het continued their whispering long into the afternoon.

—⁓—

Lan entered the crypt of Drianna on a strange, dead, volcanic island. The sands that he traversed after landing his canoe here were white, the pathway to the crypt was paved with obsidian. This was the fourth crypt he'd searched. The other three were on similar islands, the buildings were built from the bones of slaves. He wondered if he would have to fight his way out again. *What injuries may I sustain this time?* Lan looked down at his left ankle, still bruised and scarred from his last fight against followers of Drianna, her clerics.

They dressed in the colours of lust. Hideous blood red capes and scarlet robes, wielding axes. He had barely escaped with his life. He had looked in on Ake today with the use of a scrying spell. She was in the library with Falcon, probably planning some huge prank.

Oh, Ake, why must you be this way? You are a brave and cunning thing. Why do you not use this to put into your studies? I wish you were here to brighten my days with your antics. Lan pulled out his mystic long knives.

Orilan, are you worth all this, my little son? My heart tells me you are. But my head tells me it may be too late to drag you from Drianna's clutches. A sound behind him dragged him from his thoughts. A little elven boy was playing in a rock pool, poking a starfish with a stick. Goriard's eyes stared at Lan.

'Hey mister, why are you crying? Didn't you get enough warm blood from the slaves with your breakfast?' asked Orilan.

'I could never get a taste for human blood.' Lan shrugged.

Orilan laughed. 'Drianna says that one day I'll get to taste the blood of my father and it will make me strong so that I will destroy the followers of Dee.'

The boy grinned showing sharp, snow-white teeth. Drianna

had filed each of his teeth to a point. His huge supernatural eyes and angelic face could draw you to him. Every morning he awoke to find a slave grey from loss of blood in his bed. His taste for blood had gotten stronger and, instead of mere mouthfuls of blood, he drained all the blood from the neck of slaves. His hug could end your life.

'I like blood. I hug my slaves and draw out their life force. Drianna still lets me feed from her sometimes. Her blood makes me grow quicker. These teeth are a gift from Drianna. Shaped with her own file.' The child laughed hideously.

'I'd best be getting on home, Orilan,' said Lan.

Lan started towards the beach with tears in his eyes. *I will suffer my Orilan to live, for I will not put my hands to work in the death of a child.*

'Hey mister, how did you know my name?' Orilan asked, coming up beside him. He slipped his little hand into Lan's. Lan released the boy's hand, realising the mistake he'd made. Hurt, tears formed in the little boy's eyes. He started screaming at the top of his lungs.

'Hush child. I'll tell you my name,' said Lan.

Intrigued, the little boy suddenly stopped.

'What is it?' asked the boy angelically.

'Umm, it's clam man,' said Lan.

'You lie to me,' whispered Orilan.

'Okay, it's sugar carrier,' hurried Lan.

'These must be jobs you do,' said Orilan.

'Yes.' Lan laughed anxiously.

They reached the little canoe.

'I can't let you leave, Lan. Drianna has told me all about you.' Orilan grinned.

'Well, I'll be going now Orilan. Ta ta,' said Lan.

Lan made a grab for the boy and missed as his mystic senses

kicked in. The sound of pounding feet on stone caught his ears. Orilan suddenly latched onto his hand.

'Ahh, you little horror!' yelled Lan and shoved the kid in the mouth.

The boy let go, taking half the index finger on his right hand.

'You … You,' gasped Lan.

Lan leapt into his canoe and invoked Man'hannon, the Galli god of the sea to whip the waves into a current that would carry him home. The last thing he saw was a little boy grinning gleefully as a horde of followers of the dark goddess Drianna lifted him into the air. The child munched on the finger, enjoying the sensation of tissue, gristle and warm blood sliding down his throat.

CHAPTER THIRTEEN

Two young adults crept towards the supply room hand in hand. Het and Ake were hoping to pull off their planned prank. It was dawn and Het laughed as Ake's stomach grumbled. The hallway was void of students and teachers. Early morning sunlight filtered in through the stained-glass windows that adorned the white-stoned hallway, depicting scenes of elven history. Ake stared at one window of two elves, their backs turned to her, standing on a hillock, the sun shining down on them as if they were special. The words Din and Dage were written in elvish beneath the window. Ake turned back to the supply room door and tested the handle, it was locked.

'Damn, we didn't plan for this, did we Het?' asked the girl quietly.

'Het to the rescue, drum roll please. I did, I nicked the caretakers keys.' Het grinned.

'My hero.' Ake laughed sarcastically.

'Well, that's gratitude for you,' said Het as he playfully cuffed the girl around the head.

They unlocked the door and returned the keys to the caretaker's quarters.

A woman screamed and ran to a wizened balding man late in age and very short in stature.

'Vice principal, someone has died in the well and their blood contaminates our water supply,' screamed the woman.

'Oh, dearest me, what must be done?' whispered the frightened little man.

'First you must see,' said the woman.

They headed to the well. The vice principal saw the water was red and not one, but two bodies floating within. One male, the other female and around Het's and Ake's age. The team of maids and cooks were gossiping nearby in audible whispers. Ake and Het had not been seen since dinner the night before.

'Maybe it's Falcon and that poor orphan lassie without a father or mother to care for her,' they whispered.

'I heard that the principal left to find her missing brother, but he died,' they continued.

'Maybe the wee lassie could not bear the loss of a father-like figure gone so threw herself in,' they gossiped.

'And her beloved threw himself in after her because he could not bear to be parted from his love,' said the four maids.

In truth, the water was a potion brewed by Ake. Of course, any potions that could be tricks should be learnt in Ake's eyes. The figures were dolls made with wax and wood, and spells cast upon them. The spells were created by Ake so could not be detected.

―⁓―

Ake and Het had broken into Lan's dusty office intending to hide for a few hours. Hushing their giggles, they looked around. The room was full of dust as it hadn't seen a cleaner's touch in over a year. A huge oak desk and chair took up the centre of the room. The wood was ancient and stained. It was dark and looked impressive in the small room. A set of draws near the door on the right held files on each of Lan's students and staff.

Ake and Het crawled behind the desk and stifled sneezes as dust shifted with their movement. Het lifted his eyes to the whitewashed stone walls and saw four candle brackets at each corner: north, south, east and west. A shuttered window was central on the south wall adjacent to the door, no windows held glass, as glass was a rarity. Ake saw a water jug and clay bowl on Lan's desk. To her, it looked as if all the elements had been accounted for. Hardly any light entered the dark and dusty room.

Ake looked under the desk and, to her surprise the floor, seemed wrong. She tapped with the palm of her hands on the wooden floorboards and found it felt hollow. The dust shifted again, and Ake coughed. Het, starting to catch on, felt around too. His hands came into contact with a brass ring. He pulled on it and a dusty trapdoor opened.

There was enough room between the top of the massive desk and the floor for one person to crawl into it at a time. Ake could hear dripping. One drip, silence, two drips, silence, went the cycle. Ake put her hand into the trapdoor. Feeling around her hand touched cold damp stone.

'Wow,' whispered the two young adults in unison.

'I wonder what's down there?' asked Ake.

'You're not going to find out young lassie,' warned Het, taking charge. 'I think this is Lan's secret and we should not be interfering.'

'But Het, he keeps secrets about my purpose away from me,' charmed Ake.

'Oh no you don't, girl. That's not going to work on me.' Het laughed but did not heed her protestations.

Het wanted to make sure they were not caught. He decided they needed to wait a little while before returning to their daily routines. The pair spent the time playing rhyming games and telling lude limericks. Two hours later Het deemed enough time had passed. They left Lan's office and headed to the mess hall for lunch and to hear what had occurred since their prank.

The pair were seen and reported to the vice principal. One of the students going to the privy saw them and snitched. The quiet vice principal, with the aid of the cook's input, suspended Ake for two terms.

'As Lan's charity case, Ake is allowed to stay,' stated the cook. 'A poor little orphan who should be disciplined and loved more, as her own mentor left her in the lurch.' Het dragged a raging, kicking and biting Ake from the presence of the vice principal.

The cook and vice principal smiled, satisfied. If Lan was absent more than two years, they intended to take over the school and hand the reins to the Shadow Masters. This pair of Shadow Masters in their true form were ten times more unnerving than Bozzwanna. They laughed, closed the office door, and continued setting up their plans.

—◊—

Lan huddled under a crude shelter, a long black cloak stretched over driftwood pushed into the ground and a watertight spell cast over it. Blood dripped through yellow linen that had been wound around Lan's amputated finger. The linen, once white, was the flax woven handkerchief from his mother and embroidered with three silver stars. His salty tears had cleansed the wound.

The island showed no mercy as winter set in. Lan was too weak to kick the dead trees nearby into slivers and light them with mystic flames brought about in the palms of his hands. His boat had capsized and with it everything he had carried. He had lost his boots and had managed to be washed ashore with his torn and damp robes and long cloak. The drizzling rain had not stopped since he left that terrible island a day and a night ago.

Lan sat up cold and miserable and knew that if he didn't stop the bleeding, infection would set in. Using all his effort to stop himself losing consciousness, Lan unwrapped the linen and looked at his finger, bitten off at the knuckle. He shivered, remembering the leering face as he turned and saw his son, no, a demon boy consuming his flesh. He shivered at the thought. Casting a small but fiercely hot flame in the air he placed the amputated part in it and cauterised the wound. Grimacing and screaming, Lan fell into unconsciousness from the pain.

—∿—

Lan's body convulsed as poison seeped into his blood stream. His eyes rolled back into his head.

Ake woke from the vision of Lan in danger. Ake remembered the power and pain of Drianna and her death worshippers, the Shadow Scouts. Throwing off the feeling of impending evil, Ake got out of her bed in the dormitory she shared with twelve other girls who had come to dislike her intensely because of her masculine ways and popularity with the boys. They always tried to trip her up, throw food at her in the mess hall, spit curses at her and hide her clothes. Ake quickly dressed and snuck out of the dorm on her way to Lan's office.

Halfway there, a hand covered her mouth and dragged her into the shadows as a teacher walked by. The captor then pushed her against the wall with his body. Gasping, Ake tried to push the assailant off her. A pathetic attempt at *Mystic Fire* went shooting past the man's ear. The supposed teacher, a Shadow Scout turned as he sensed the energy of magic.

Ake's assailant's hearing kicked in and he put his full weight on top of her and whispered in her ear. 'Shut up, there's a dark one heading this way.'

Ake, hearing Het's voice, stopped moving and tried to settle her pounding heart.

The Shadow Scout sniffed the air, and he turned his blind eyes towards the sound. Listening intently, he ran his impatient tongue across his dry and cracked grey lips. He turned his pointed, once elven, ears to the sound and shuffled his dead feet towards the energy source. He appeared to float as his human-skin-robes reached the floor and covered his feet as he drifted across the stone surface.

This was a prodigy Shadow Scout, blinded so that he cannot see his masters' faces as he sits in their presence.

'Magic,' hissed the creature as his serpent-like tongue darted out of his quivering, toothless mouth, his skinny arms stretched forth.

Unlike the lower Shadow Scouts, this one consumed the magic of its victims and along with it, their souls. The purer the better. But any would do, as he would turn on his own kind if they were not more powerful than himself.

Het and Ake ran for the nearest secret passage they knew. As they disappeared, the Shadow Scout came upon where they were before. Angered, it raised the alarm and its superiors, the vice principal and cook, were soon running towards the eerie cries. It was as if a coyote and a raven's cry became one and now sounded into the darkness of night.

Ake and Het found a new passage that led into Lan's office,

'Het, how did you know I would try to come and explore what was beneath the little trapdoor?' asked an exasperated Ake.

'Your cat curiosity. That creature is like the Bozzwanna thing you told me about. Remember the first time we met, and I said I was in the training?' asked Het.

'Yes,' said Ake.

'Well, the training is understanding and trying to put an end to these creatures. Druids run the committee. The headman is Dun Norix himself. Ake, there is something you should know. I am his replacement if he should die. You know those few hours I'm away on Saturdays, it's because he has teleported here to teach me. I'm involved in the guiding of your life. But the problem here is Lan. He is less in charge of this than he thinks he is, for he has a significant role to play unknown to him,' said Het.

'No, Het, no. It can't be true. I thought you were my friend,' Ake cried, pounding on his chest.

He crushed her to him. 'I'm sorry, Ake. I will always be your friend. I feel bad about all this, I was not supposed to become more than an encourager. For my deeds, we will search Lan's quarters together. Maybe we can find a way to rid at least Caelestis of evil,' he soothed.

'No, I will not trust you,' yelled Ake.

Just then, flashes of candlelight could be seen underneath the crack of the door.

'Quick, head on down,' said Het.

Too frightened to disagree, Ake opened the trapdoor and rushed down. Het followed and, trained in druid art, cast a spell that created an orb of blue light. The orb followed them down the stairwell.

CHAPTER FOURTEEN

Lan awoke in the night, his head throbbing, his body shivering with the cold. His elven senses picked up the sound of talons clicking on the ground. His nose ran and his breath rattled in his lungs. Snow had fallen while he was unconscious and covered his little canopy made of robes in a thin, icy layer. Lan lay there, he had lost the will to live and awaited death quietly and fearfully. An aging griffin came into view.

A griffin is a beast made by the trickster god, Bel to scare children and old ladies on cold, dark winter nights. For these beasts had a sense of fun, though they only ate horses. Many a farmer had lost one or more to these magnificent beasts. They had the hindquarters of a lion, and the wings, head and talons of an eagle. Its back legs were a lion's and so was its tail. It was about the size of a stock horse and had the quirky antics of a young child. It was intelligent and could speak. It was not immortal but lived between two hundred and two hundred and fifty years.

'What do we have here?' asked the beast.

'Master, take my life for I am not afraid to die, but end it quickly,' cried Lan. He knew nothing of this beast, having never encountered one.

'Now why would I eat an elfling?' The griffin laughed.

'For you are a demon wishing the satisfaction of human flesh,' Lan mumbled weakly.

'I am Cory. I won't take offence at that, for I see you are nothing but a death-like wraith in need of a good meal yourself,' said the griffin.

'If not demon, what?' whispered Lan, his strength failing.

'I am a griffin made to entertain the god Bel with my mischievous tricks. I have strength of eagle and nobility of lion. And I was about to eat a donkey before you caused a ruckus. Now, what is a young elfling doing on this dangerous island?' asked Cory.

But Lan had again drifted into unconsciousness.

'Am I that boring?' asked an annoyed Cory.

Seeing the young elf's predicament, he carried Lan back to the sanctuary of his cave. Lan woke up to a yawn-like humming.

'Ouch, my head,' Lan groaned.

'Now, don't you tease my singing, elfling. You lay yourself back down on that hay. When I was young all the maiden griffins used to tell me I was the best singer in all of Eriu.'

'No, my head. It feels as though a dragon used it as part of his collection of knuckle bones.' Lan winced.

'That bad ha? You see that dead horse over there I think he's worse off than you are, maybe we should ask him? Hey horse, how you feeling this morning? Your head not screwed on the right way?' Cory laughed.

'Yeah, but he isn't feeling any of that,' said Lan.

'I can arrange that for you.' Cory growled.

Lan's face drained of all colour. 'I thought you didn't eat humans.'

Cracking up in laughter and rolling around the floor, Cory spluttered, 'Oh, it hurts to talk, you kill me kid. People, yuck, the worms can have you when you go.'

Lan lay back down, sighing with relief.

CHAPTER FIFTEEN

The dripping that Het and Ake heard when they first opened the trapdoor continued. Above their heads the Shadow Masters and their scout began to tear Lan's office apart. But the trapdoor had a glyph engraved in it to protect it being opened by those of evil intent.

Ake heard a voice in her head, *'It says, he who passes through must only seek enlightenment.'*

'What the hell is that?' said Ake.

'It is me, hoot hoot,' replied the voice.

'What, is that you Het? What the hell are you doing in my head?' asked Ake angrily.

'I thought this way we could talk without those things hearing us as their ears run deep into the earth,' explained Het.

'I can't do it back,' whispered Ake.

'That's the great part, if you get too annoying like you usually do, I can sit there and hear your thoughts, but you can't talk back,' Het projected.

'I can still think unpleasant thoughts.' Ake grinned.

'Hey Ake, that's disgusting,' said Het.

'I thought you'd like it. That's probably why you're in my head.'

'Whatever, stop thinking of the toilet. Can we please proceed?'

'What, more crude thoughts?' Ake laughed quietly.

'No, you fruit, we are trying to kill those things above,' said Het.

'Yep, bring on the pie, I'm a fruit,' said Ake.

'*Stop being sarcastic.*' Het suddenly stopped talking in Ake's head, leaving her with a slight headache from the intrusion she wasn't yet used to. They came to the end of the stone steps and the orb of light illuminated a large underground cavern.

'Oh,' said Ake.

'Holy hell,' cried Het.

Ake looked at Het as if he'd gone mad. 'You idiot, how is hell holy?'

'It's got lots of holes in it made by all the dead bodies pushing their way towards the centre.' Het laughed.

'Now I know you're utterly and completely mad.'

'Yep, that's Het.' Het winked at her.

Ake groaned. 'You're incorrigible.'

'Wow, the girl that hates to study knows big words,' he said, putting a hand to his face in mock shock.

They both started looking around. It appeared the underground cave was Lan's secret living quarters. The cavern roof was uneven, as the aeons of water that once flowed here had shaped it. The roof glowed. It seemed as if a thousand different coloured fairies were moulded into it. On closer inspection, as the orb guided by Het rose, countless crystals and precious metals were embedded in the ochre rock.

'There are bits of gold, silver, hematite, tiger's eye, jasper and the many varieties of agate, citrine, amethyst, rose quartz, ruby and crystal,' said Ake, surprisingly adept at geology.

The floor was green limestone, and the other walls were white quartz. In the centre was an underground spring and it bubbled and frothed. Ake could see the steam rising from it. Het pointed to a nearby wall and the orb floated over to the indicated wall. Het had noticed strange incantations and drawings upon them and went to examine them.

Ake, meanwhile, started going through papers on a nearby

desk and looking through the drawers. She found nothing of interest except a few ideas and thoughts scribbled on paper. Ake walked past Lan's double four-poster bed and started looking in his wardrobe at the interesting array of cloaks and robes. That's when she noticed a black leather-bound book at the bottom of it.

'Hey Ake, come look at this, it's really odd,' called Het.

Ake placed the book in the folds of her yellow robes and headed over to where Het stood. The faerie orb glistened purple and then the colours of red, then yellow.

'What's wrong with that orb?' she asked.

Het looked over at it and replied, 'It's a faerie-natured orb, it changes to represent the mood of the caster.'

'Okay, so what's odd, apart from me?'

'Aren't you over that already. Be serious for once Ake, this may concern you,' Het said.

'Ppplll.' Ake gave Het raspberries.

'Shut your face and listen up,' said Het harshly.

'Okay, what?' asked Ake testily.

'I'll tell you what each of these symbols means. For starters, the glyphs state these were the last words said to the people of the earth by Dee and Sorendee,' said Het.

'Isn't Sorendee the god of the cosmos and Dee the mother of the earth?' asked Ake.

'Have you forgotten the time with your mother and what she taught you?' questioned Het.

'My mother taught me nothing as she was always pining for my father who died before I was born. I barely remember what she was like. Then she got herself killed and left me behind,' said Ake sadly.

'I'm sorry to bring it up Ake.'

'Ahh, nothing I can do about it now. Just continue.' She shrugged.

'Okay. This symbol of a bird and a star walking through starlight is supposed to represent coupling. Then here's a baby with a star smiling at her. So, the bird and the star had a baby, and the stars smile at the child. Then this arrow pointing to this woman represents her growing up. Interesting, this is the symbol for a handmaiden of Dee. Wow, this is a new piece of information,' said Het.

'What?' Ake asked, looking over in interest.

'Well, this symbol represents a handmaiden of Dee and next to it the symbol of mother then the symbol for child. A handmaiden of Dee has a child, and the star woman marries him. See the handfasting symbol here?' said Het.

'Yeah.' Ake shrugged.

'They have two children. Ah, interesting,' mumbled Het.

'What?' asked Ake.

'See how they are close together they are possibly twins. Wow, here's a shadow man, evil but the symbol for brother is quite obvious. Then it shows the symbol for either pain or death,' said Het.

'Right, I wonder what person drew these?' asked Ake.

'Well, it's tribal. Hang on, there are two more symbols. One that means Drianna, the goddess of darkness and this one means battle or enlightenment,' said Het. 'Ake?'

'Yeah,' said Ake.

'This is about you.'

'Het be serious.' Ake laughed.

'I am.'

'How do you know?'

'This is the prophecy that Lan said you were a part of.'

'It can't be,' stuttered Ake.

'It is Ake and I'm surprised about the husband bit. I didn't know it would be someone so special. I knew who it was but didn't know he had the title of the son of a handmaiden of Dee,' said Het.

'Who is he and what's a handmaiden of Dee?' asked Ake. Her heart pounded in her chest.

'When Dee comes to earth on Beltane week to see her son Bel, a handmaiden is sought to serve her while she stays for the week's festivities. The handmaiden is chosen for her kindness and courage. To do this Dee turns into an old and very eerie crone and from a group of many young girls the one to step forward and offer her services is chosen to wait on the crone. Many girls are encouraged. The girls aren't told it is Dee, just some rich merchant's old mother and that many great rewards will be showered upon them. Only the elders know who she is and when seven days pass, Dee changes in front of the gathered elders and handmaiden and her parents. The parents are given gold and the girl gains the honoured title and the gratitude of Dee for her lifetime. These girls have the freedom of men and any daughters that they have will too and so forth for five generations,' said Het proudly.

'That explains the handmaiden part but whom am I supposed to wed?' asked Ake nervously.

'I cannot tell you that Ake, for all will reveal itself in time,' said Het.

'I thought you were my friend Het.'

'I am but if you hear it, it's possible Drianna might too and try and stop the coupling,' explained Het.

Ake shivered at the memory of Drianna and nodded her understanding but was still disappointed. Het noticed this.

'Hey, are you going to help me rid this place of evil? Your diversions might prove useful.' Het grinned at her.

Ake perked up at the thought and they set about their planning.

CHAPTER SIXTEEN

Lan lay back down in the hay and rested for another four hours.

By then his head had stopped throbbing. Cory brought him some ice-cold water in a glass. 'How did you get this?'

Cory smiled proudly. 'I collect human possessions. I have in total thirty objects. Would you, my guest, be willing to see the amazing collection?'

'Of course, after what you did, taking me into your pleasant home,' said Lan.

Looking around, Lan noticed the cave was about the same size as his underground one back home. A collection of bones from Cory's meals lay in one corner. A small, half frozen spring was near these. The hay Lan was resting on was Cory's bed he realised, and he was touched. *Cory must have spent the night on the cold floor.* He noticed the shelf of human possessions in the corner. Cory strutted over to it proudly. Lan rose to follow him but had to sit back down, for dizziness threatened to overwhelm him.

'No, you don't! I'll bring each of them one at a time so they can have their limelight,' said the griffin proudly.

Cory brought a fork over.

'This is a nose hair plucker. Humans are always grooming themselves. I study them,' Cory announced.

'Ah that's a fork and people eat with it.'

'Oh okay,' said Cory. He was a little disappointed that his new friend wasn't overwhelmed with the amazing implement.

Trying to impress Lan, the next object Cory brought over was a feather quill and ink pot.

'This is a pot of amazing magical stuff, and this sharpened feather is what they use to put it into themselves,' said the griffin.

'That is an ink pot and quill. We write with it. I'll show you,' said Lan. He took the two objects and wrote the alphabet on the floor.

The mystic looked up and saw that Cory was sad and disappointed.

Lan realising he had stolen his host's livelihood, said, 'Well, it could be. What else do you have?'

Cory looked happy again and went off and got a spoon.

'This is a tongue shaper,' said Cory.

Lan smiled and clapped politely as Cory showed him the objects in the collection and explained their interesting new uses.

———

In the heated walls of Drianna's crypt young Orilan was undertaking his new naming ritual. The now seven-year-old was to finally rid the dishonouring name given to him by the evil druid Dane. Orilan was always told Drianna's ways were the good ways and any other was evil and unsanctioned. The child thought himself a man and stood proudly as Drianna named him.

'Now, child, you will be renamed. You shall be Vampyr, Beautiful Death. Named for that which you so readily enjoy. Come, you must bathe ritually in the waters of this island.' The goddess cackled.

Orilan, now Vampyr, was taken, and handmaiden slaves cleansed him with belladonna and sage. They plunged him into the cold saltwater and rigorously towelled him dry as he stood on the rocky shore.

'Now, you must awaken the vengeance against my banishment in you. You must find a griffin. End his life and consume his soul. He will become your totem. Dress and take up your knife and your ten horned guards and bring me back the hide of a griffin called Cory who is your father's friend. Then you shall forever be my favourite human, worth more to me than the slaves I so readily collect. Now leave, Vampyr, but I gift you with invisibility so that you may not be noticed. Your journey will take several days. Be wary of the charms and evilness that calls you to Eriu and your father's side,' said Drianna.

With those words, Vampyr mounted his saddled hellhound, who he thought beautiful and pure, and gathered his guards. Then he made his way forth to kill the griffin his Drianna said was evil.

CHAPTER SEVENTEEN

'Okay, here's the deal. The Shadow Masters are now searching above for us. You will conjure an illusion of us running down the hall so I can get to them with my short sword. Pity I don't have my other weapons with me,' said Het.

'How many weapons can you use?'

'Six, but I normally carry three,' said Het proudly.

'Wow, I can't even use one.' Ake shrugged.

'What, how about your unarmed combat?' asked Het.

'Missed too many classes,' said Ake.

'*Mystic Fire?*'

'Same,' said Ake.

'Oh dear, if we get out of this I'm going to teach you at least one weapon.'

'That would be good.' Ake nodded.

'Ake … I've got to tell you something. My parents thought I would marry you.'

Het waited for her obvious reaction.

'Really, that's hilarious.' Ake laughed.

'Well, I love you.' Het blushed.

'What. Het, no, we are friends. Are you my intended?'

'No. I'm sorry. Any regrets Ake before we do this thing?'

'One. I've never kissed a boy.' Ake looked at him meaningfully.

'How about that first kiss from a man? Especially one that loves ya,' asked Het.

'Okay, but only this once.'

'What if you want another?' Het charmed.

'Het!' Ake glared at him.

'Okay, okay,' said Het.

Het closed the gap between them. He took his enormous hands and lifted her chin. Looking into her eyes, he asked, 'Ready?'

'Yes,' said Ake.

'Close your eyes. I heard it makes it nicer,' said Het.

Ake closed her eyes. Het opened her mouth with his and touched her tongue lightly with his own. He kissed her gently, then harder. He caressed her face then drew away. Ake stood there, eyes closed and ran her tongue across her lips savouring the touch. She opened her eyes.

'How was it?' asked Het.

'I had no idea that kissing felt like that,' said Ake.

'It feels nice if it's wanted and the two people love each other. Do you love me Ake?' asked Het.

'I do-nnoott know,' stuttered Ake. 'You awoke strange feelings in me. I don't know how to explain them.'

'You don't have to. Savour them. They aren't wrong. They only become wrong when you kiss someone who isn't right for you,' said Het.

'So, that's what these feelings are.'

'You gave me something I'll remember forever. Your kiss and friendship.'

'Het. Thank you for being here with me all this time since Lan has been away.'

'That's okay. I'm envious of the boy. But then again, you are a handful.' Het grinned at her.

'Het. What do you mean by that?' She punched him playfully.

'Okay, okay. You're killing me,' cried Het in mock horror. 'Let's get those things.'

'Yeah,' said Ake.

Ake cast the spell and the creatures uttered their eerie cries. Like a pack of slavering wolves, they ran after the apparitions in the hallway. Het lifted the trapdoor and locked Ake in by pushing the desk on top of the trapdoor.

'Het, what are you doing?' asked Ake's muffled voice.

'Doing the duty Lan gave me and looking after the girl I love.'

The master of arms then gave forth his battle cry. 'As swift as night descends.'

The Shadow Masters and their scout turned and came at Het. Het knew without the entire druid magic he hadn't finished learning, he stood no chance. But he would try and not let Caelestis fall. The Shadow Scout came at him first, its blind eyes staring and serpent tongue darting out of its toothless mouth.

The evil spectre hissed. 'Pure boy full of magic, mine to consume.'

'Not for the likes of you who takes the life of innocents as they lie in their beds,' said Het.

'Sssssss. You shall die at my hands,' the creature hissed.

'I don't think so.' Het grinned at the creature.

The Shadow Scout, angered, cast *Poison Arrow*. Two magical arrows formed and shot from a magic bow. The arrows would paralyse whomever they hit. Het sidestepped both easily as he was very agile. Het somersaulted into the air and landed behind the creature. His short sword came down in a blur. The head of the Shadow Scout went flying and hit the far wall, as it slid down, its acidic blood smeared and burnt a hole in the stone wall.

The cook threw off her disguise and took the form of the dreaded Shadow Master. Dark blood poured out endlessly from its eyeless sockets. There was a pig snout and raven's beak where its nose and mouth should be. Its ears were daggers tipped with poison. The creature's arms were mere stumps. It had no legs, but a serpent-like body. The monster's tail had three prongs like that of a trident and this was its main weapon. It came at Het swinging wildly.

This creature was blind but could use the eyes of its victims to see. It wielded a deadly mind attack known as *Wails of the Banshee*. Screams echoed off the sconces of their victim's skull, eventually their head would not be able to withstand it and explode. This weapon was very rarely used as these creatures were charged with the blood of dragons giving them great strength, therefore making almost all their victims easy prey. The only way to kill these creatures was with a specialised druid magic.

The spell was known as *Starlight*. It took a lot of effort to cast, and one could get lost in the casting. This was the most beautiful and deadliest spell for any druid to use. The Shadow Masters were absolute darkness but the druids were warriors of Dee, and pure in her sight.

When cast, a huge bright light with many colours swirling in its depth surrounded the druid. This was the gate to Sorendee's palace. It beckoned to the druid and whispered of all the wonders the druid loved. Only druids of the highest rank could control it. There had been many a time when a minor druid had come into contact with a Shadow Master and tried to control the spell and failed. When successful, the light destroyed all darkness in an explosion of colours.

Het drew in a deep breath. The creature came at him with its trident-like tail. It sniffed the air and howled. Het turned sharply as the creature's weapon went zipping past his head. Ducking he tried to push his weapon into the belly of the beast. The creature sensed his intention and it headbutted him using the daggers on its ears. It hit home and Het's arm was sliced open. A burning sensation started, as if his blood was alive and consuming his flesh. His arm was now useless, he changed the short sword to the other hand.

Het rolled out of the way as the tail came crashing down. Stone bricks went flying from the impact. Ake screamed as she heard Het's cries of agony. Ake started pounding on the trapdoor, drawing the attention of the other Shadow Master. The once vice principal took his true form and its tail splintered Lan's desk apart.

'Ake, shut up, it's atop the door, it cannot find you if you make no sound,' said Het in Ake's mind.

Ake stopped screaming. The assailant screeched in anger and looked through the eyes of Het who had just mind-spoken to Ake. Het, knowing that it could use his sight against him, closed his eyes so that he could save Ake. Het tried to fight blind. But the creature's poisonous daggers went through his other arm making it useless too. He opened his eyes for a split second and kicked the creature in the head and rolled out of the way.

Ake, scared for her friend, cast an illusion of Het running to help her. The once vice principal growled and went towards it, giving Ake enough time to open the hatch. She jumped out and made a run down the hallway with the creature following. Then the sound of running feet heading their way was heard. Ten mystics came onto the scene. The teachers' beams of *Mystic Fire* hammered into the Shadow Master chasing Ake. It howled in pain and turned on them. They held it at bay, but for how long? Het, nearly useless with pain, cried out. Ake went running and rolled under the slashing tail of the vice principal Shadow Master. The love she felt for her friend flared up and a strange sensation overtook her.

Voices called to her, and many colours began to surround her. She felt so happy. Suddenly a doorway appeared before her, and Ake saw her mother and some handsome young man beside her.

'Mother,' she called. But they didn't beckon her towards them.

'But mother,' said Ake, tears in her eyes.

'Daughter,' said the man. 'I died to save you. Use the gift of life to save your friend. If you come here, you stay forever.'

'Father,' whispered Ake.

'Save Het. Don't let him die trying to save you,' said her mother.

'Don't leave me. Mother, Father,' Ake cried.

Ake noticed the feelings were fading as if they weren't real, and realising the danger of this spell, sent it sweeping towards the Shadow Masters. They screeched in agony as they were torn asunder. The light faded and Ake collapsed into unconsciousness.

Ake woke from her dreams of her mother and father in the infirmary bed, warm and refreshed. Across from her was Het, wounds dressed and looking worse for wear. A warm hand was placed on her forehead, and she looked into the eyes of an aged Lan.

'Dun Norix, ww-hat are you doing here?' stuttered Ake.

'You called on the ancient magic and were able to control it. We were worried for your safety and Het's. You truly are she, the earthbound goddess. At first, I thought Lan had it wrong. But it is true. Most can never wield *Starlight*. But you have done so at an early age,' said the druid.

He kissed Ake on the forehead, and she drifted back into sleep. The druid turned to Het. 'Now, you lad, had a fine first fight. You too must rest.'

The druid kissed Het on the forehead too and Het drifted off. Dun Norix disappeared on the spot. *I must find Lan.*

CHAPTER EIGHTEEN

The griffin's powerful wings beat soundlessly as he glided through the dark midnight sky. He flexed his powerful talons, and his eagle sight spotted its prey. His lion's tail whipped back and forth excitedly as his body filled with adrenaline. The stallion below sensed danger and the herd whinnied and thundered off in a cloud of dust. The griffin eyed his prey once more. A young mare full of life and not with young. He dared not take the stallion, as the herd could not be without the powerful beast. He dived; quickly and kindly he ended his victim's life then carried the kill home.

'I will not eat of horse, Cory,' said Lan.

He had been with Cory four days and knew he must leave soon. Cory had returned from his hunt. Again, he offered to share his meal with him.

'You can't survive on a few mere berries and leafy plants elf. You need meat in your life.' The griffin grinned.

'Cory, I don't mean to sound rude. But I'm not an elf.'

'Yep, you are. It's obvious you're trying to trick me,' said Cory.

'You must see something I don't see.' Lan shrugged.

'Sure do,' exclaimed Cory.

'Okay point them out.' Lan laughed.

'Let's see, the pointed ears, high cheekbones, huge eyes, melodic voice and slanted eyebrows. You also smell like magic. Probably Eriu descent. You seem like one of those folk that come from the mountains. What do they call them? Ahh, now I remember, the Sidhe or faerie folk,' said the griffin.

'Do you know where these people are?' asked Lan.

'That I do, and I can take you to them, it's only a little way off,' said Cory.

'Okay, do this, for I need supplies to make my way back to Caelestis,' said Lan.

'You'll leave me lonely,' muttered the griffin.

'Come with me Cory.'

'And have everyone try and kill me for sport, I do not think so. But it has been nice having company, I will not forget you, Lan,' said the griffin.

'I will not forget you either Cory. How will I ride you, for I have no boots?' asked Lan.

'My collection has the things you need. I found most of it in a backpack on a dead guy,' said Cory.

'But you love that collection.'

'You're my friend and it will be like passing it on to family,' said Cory.

'Oh, Cory, that's very nice of you.' Lan looked away, touched by the gesture.

'Don't think on it. Let's pack the stuff and get thee to Eriu before deep winter sets in. I intend to hibernate then,' said Cory.

———

Orilan dismounted his hellhound. Grinning ear to ear, he allowed his horned guards to kill for themselves, flesh to sustain them. With the aid of his water scrying bowl, he watched his father talking and rubbing shoulders with the griffin. The child remembered the taste of his father's blood, the power that ran through him. He wished to savour more, to feel his father's heart pounding against his own as he drew the life force from him, and the power that would be his. He licked his lips excitedly. He watched the griffin. *Ahh a lovely prize for Drianna, the mother of my heart.* He ushered his guards forward.

'Take the mystic but do not kill him,' said Orilan.

Orilan whispered some magic words and turned invisible, ready to kill the griffin.

CHAPTER NINETEEN

Ake woke and felt for the little black book she had hid in her robes. She licked her lips and opened the book. Mould had caused the pages to stick, but Ake managed to tease the pages apart. Ake looked over at Het who was fast asleep and dreaming by the look of the way he was moving about. Ake turned her attention back to the book and began to read.

This is the history of the tribe, Crykenuak, the children of the stars, believe in. I, Hanton, principal of Caelestis, have studied the local tribe, first out of interest then out of necessity. The Shadow Masters are watching, waiting for the child Telewanake but I must find her soon. Before they do.

Most of the paragraphs were barely legible. Halfway down, an entry caught her eye. It appeared to be written in a rush, the words were hard to make out.

Lan, they have come for me, … glean the knowledge from my head. Find her … only thirteen, but you … only hope. The corrupt sit among the druids … highest ranks … stolen … druids' gift of glamoire … do not know.

Ake looked closer at the page. *Is that a bloodstain? Ah, what happened here?* Ake turned the page. Scrawled at the bottom it read:

They are here ... I go ... their blades ... poisoned ... Lan I ... only father ... you have known. Forgive me, my son, but if I stay, I ... not ... same ... turn ... against the truth. ... trusted Tok ... holds you back ... going after me. My heart weeps ... my mind will change, ... this log ... my love for you dear child.

Ake turned back to the beginning of the book. With painstaking care, she separated a few more pages. With tears in her eyes, she read on:

Feb 1

Dear Log,

My name is ... I am a master mystic and principal of ..., the school of mysticism. We are located on the island of ... The druids have not yet penetrated the mists that protect this ... Yet someday they will. And the corrupt among them will steal the ancient ... of a religion older than them. The old way, the way of Dee and ... Then they will turn the ancient white walls of ... to the ways of the one god.

It is not up to the gods to pay ... way to the other world with their blood. Man ... freewill, what he chooses ... do with it is his desire. But destiny will flee if ... evil mind and fate will draw near to create mischief. I ... hope that the white-walled school does not fall to the new ways, for the old knowledge will be forever lost in time. And with it, mankind will turn his soul to the comforts of his own hands and murder the gods with his heart.

March 6

Dear Log,

This is my ... entry many days after the last. For I have ...to mingle with the natives. I cannot yet speak their ... The women beautiful ... treated as nothing more than workers. The men strut … believing they own the world. I bring gifts of clothing … sample the sweetmeats and sugar biscuits I bring. I … one word, *ginkou*, thank you.

June 6
Dear Log,

Sorry to leave the gentle caresses of ink from … pages for so long. It has been … since ink has touched your skin. But I have … news I have … the language of the natives. Strangely … it is of an ancient tongue. A … of Elvish, my ancestors' tongue. Rarely spoken except by the Sidhe of Eriu. Could it … the Daione Sidhe were banished to …s and their ways forsaken, or … be that the elves mingled their blood with the natives? I must … out more.

June 18
Dear Log,

Only … since the last entry. Lan, my heir, son of my heart, …with me on one of my regular visits to the … These … call themselves the Children of the Stars or the Crykenuak (Kray-N-Yik). Only four people every decade can learn to read and write their language. Only… blood of two families, three males and one female (surprisingly about the girl) they believe …be this way because the blood of these families is closest to the blood of gods. And … families must never marry outside these two pure families.

There was a large clatter as someone dropped something metal on to the stone floor.

'Ake, time for your sustenance and a rest,' stated the fatherly physician Tok, picking up a metal bowl.

Ake put down the book and looked out the window. By the sky it looked late.

'What will happen now Tok, since the vice principal and cook have been seen for who they really were?' asked Ake.

'Young Tom has been promoted to head chef and Dun Norix has left a druid in charge and gone in search of the headmaster,' said Tok.

'Oh good,' said Ake.

'You best be resting mistress.' Tok bowed.

'Why do you call me mistress?' Ake looked at him confused.

'You killed them Shadow Masters and Lan said that … Oops, I be not allowed to say,' said Tok.

'What Tok? You can tell me,' said Ake.

'No, I can't mistress,' said Tok.

'Fine. No need to get anxious.' Ake shrugged.

'Now, mistress, you be resting. You are not to leave here except for bathroom interludes. Dun Norix said ye must stay in the infirmary a week,' said Tok.

'All that time?' asked Ake.

'Yes,' said Tok.

'Oh, hell cat,' exclaimed Ake.

'Hush, mistress, don't you go talking like that now you be a lady. Oops, I said too much again. Please forgive me Dee.' Tok bowed.

Ake looked at the elderly man with long white hair and green eyes. His robes hung loosely over his waning physique.

'You best see to others now,' said Ake.

'Yes, mistress,' said Tok.

Tok turned and headed over to touch Het on the forehead, checking his temperature. Ake placed the black book under her pillow for later and consumed her meal.

Then she closed her eyes and fell soundly asleep.

At dawn, Ake woke and continued to read.

Jan 23

Dear Log,

The men have … to respect me … honour my magic. They believe … one of the sons of Sorendee and have … a name to suit the honour. They believe me to be Bel, the … of mischief and lovemaking, Sorendee and Dee's oldest. His domain is fire, a… I once lit one of their wood stacks on fire to try and explain myself as a mystic, they believe this … more. So strange, Bel is Galli and not to … an elvish god. Soon I will have the answers t… Soon friend, soon.

March 6

Dear Log,

Lan has also … the native tongue. I know Lan to be … pedigree Sidhe. Soon I wish to take him to see the last … few in their township, Relequis or remaining. How do I know this? His … Regona, a Galli, came from Eriu. And she has … in me his parentage. Her father was a fighter from Relequis but alas the new … conquered his soul. Lan's father is a druid whose name I dare not utter for fear of Lan reading this and being taken by the druids.

I know this … selfish but my love for the boy is powerful. The druid is … elf and his magic and insight powerful. If Lan were to … his name, he'd surely come. I … be just paranoid but the wind from the north seems to be … more feverish and at night the delicate feel of past voices drift in open windows … wrap their addictive touch around sleeping minds.

April 5

Dear Log,

The history … Crykenuak is so close to elven history that if varied but a little it would be the same. Two days after learning

... interesting piece of news, Lan ... playing the game ... throw a spear through the centre of a hoop as it rolls down ... hill. This was ... done with two native boys when ... a sudden, the two natives fell down in pain covering their ears and their eyes were rolling back in their heads. Lan turned to see a black-robed man pointing at the two boys. He ... over to help ... friends, but their heads exploded. Lan stumbled backwards and looked towards the stranger. His countenance seemed familiar but then he disappeared. Lan lay on the ground curled up in the fetal position weeping. That's ... I found him at nightfall. He ... missed the evening meal, so I came to look for him. He sobbed ... story out, I knew this to be the work of a Shadow Master. Today I banned anyone leaving the fortress walls. Demons are gathering strength and darkness seems to be deepening.

May 1

Dear Log,

The mists ... surround the Isle of Man'hannon have disappeared. I watch over the battlements of Caelestis and see darkness gathering on the rocky shores. Am ... lose everything? There may ... hope that the natives told me the night ... told their story of creation. Sorendee carved two spears, one which he handed to the Sidhe, ... other to the druids. The male spear of Mbel Daione (*Mystic Fire*) is in the hands of the druids. Its handle ... carved from ash, the tree of the mystic. The blade ... carved ruby ... if wielded by the blood of Bel sends forth unlimited *Mystic Fire*.

Then t... is the obsidian blade, carved oak spear, Empon Searto. The seemingly dull, useless spear that looks as ... needs a good polish. Its brother ... is bright and its blade glows as if it is on fire. I believe I will try ... find the Mbel Daione gifted to the Daione Sidhe, for the Empon Searto can only be wielded by the blood of Daione Sidhe crossed ... blood of a god, ... example this Telewanake. No one knows much … the Empon Searto. It is recognised as a feminine blade. I … translated the name, but … still does not say what it is used for: "Wielding Water". Maybe it does the same with water as her brother does with fire. Maybe she controls the weather. I must go see the druids, enter … foreign land to get my answers. Tomorrow, I head to Eriu for two months. … leave Lan here to keep an eye on things.

July 1
Dear Log,

I fear this will be … my last entries. Lan … finished … training early and top of the school. Thirteen this day, … is more powerful … I could have imagined.
To Lan … book must go, for while heading to … boat that would take me to Eriu, I … pierced by a thrown dagger … unearthly poison on … blade and I am feeling … seductive power of evil tainting my blood. The masked stranger, whose face I … not see, laughed hideously before fading away. I managed to get back … Caelestis. But I think … evil stranger may be able … get in. Lan will leave … his mother's cottage in the morn for … holidays … I know the shadowy ones will soon come for me.

Ake turned to the last page, which she had read thrice. This was the third time she had read the log over the week between sponging the unconscious Het, who had still not woken, and her trips to the privy. After getting over the shocking coincidence between her and the girl in the prophecy, Ake had found it fascinating. Her only other highlights were her meals and casual conversations with Tok. Tomorrow she was allowed up but only to be kept under strict supervision according to Dane's instructions. Being the father of the current Headmaster, Dane was in charge until Lan returned. Ake was to put all her effort back into her study or Dane would discipline her further. After a week of complete boredom, Ake was only too happy to agree.

CHAPTER TWENTY

Lan shivered in his feverish sleep. The nightmare continued as he relived the events that led to the sickness now ravaging his body.

Lan had stood ready to mount the griffin when Cory cried out in pain. An evil laugh penetrated the air and Cory swiped around him with his menacing claws. Lan turned at the familiar scent of death and sound of grating bones. A hellhound had leapt onto his chest and started tearing at his clothes. Lan sent the demon flying against a nearby wall with *Mystic Fire*. Cory bellowed. Lan turned to help his friend, but three horned guards came into sight.

'Ahh, lovely to see such a devilish creature in pain.' Orilan laughed horridly.

'Who, or what, are you?' asked Cory.

'I am beautiful death,' said Orilan.

Cory lunged towards the direction of the voice but tripped on an invisible leg. Lan threw himself out of the way just in time as a glass-bladed weapon thrown by a horned guard went whizzing past his ear.

'Phew.' Lan panted.

A sound of grating bones behind him warned him of another hellhound's whereabouts. He turned sharply and his bad ankle went down. Lan sent his *Mystic Fire* flaring out just in time. Dark reinforcements appeared. Lan kept trying to defend himself, but it was not enough. A beast screamed and crashed to the ground. Lan turned to see Cory's slumped body.

'No!' Lan screamed.

An unearthly laugh shattered the air. Lan dodged another blade. His mystic senses kicked in and he felt harsh breathing on the back of his neck and kicked up sharply.

'Grrr, Father, no need to hurt your beloved son,' hissed Orilan.

The blow shattered the spell, and the boy became visible again.

'You are no child of mine,' said Lan.

Another sound of grating bones warned Lan and he rolled out of the way.

'Enough, my friends. This one's mine. But you may hold him for me,' said Orilan.

'You won't catch me.' Lan rose to his feet.

Lan sent his last use of *Mystic Fire* arching outwards hammering into Orilan's mount and two horned guards trying to get at him.

'Ahh, Lan. Nooo, you killed my sweet!' screamed the boy with tears streaming from his eyes.

Maybe there is still a chance for you, as you feel emotional pain. Four more horned guards came at Lan. He had no more *Mystic Fire* as it could only be cast four times a day. He slid his long knives from the sheaths at his wrist and into his hands. *If I can just get outside, then I can manipulate the weather.* He tried casting sleep on Orilan but as he was almost a full blood elf, it had no effect on the child. Orilan sucked his thumb and sat down upon the ground. *Could this just be another try at trickery?* thought Lan.

The mystic turned sharply to the left as deadened hands groped for him. He sliced off the hands and black blood spurted up into his face. He choked and spat out the foulness. He felt himself grabbed and held. Four pairs of these hands pushed him down against the cold floor of the cave, they were surprisingly strong for their corpse-like appearance. Lan thrashed against their pressure.

'Orilan, don't do this to me. I have only ever loved you since I first held you in my arms. And I have been looking for you ever since you were taken from me so cruelly all those years ago,' cried Lan.

Orilan looked up, his young eyes full of hurt. 'But Father, dear Drianna is the goddess of all things good, and you are a demon out to trick me.'

'Son, that is not true. Look into your heart. My sisters before me were taken and hurt by your goddess. Then Drianna did terrible things to them. Then to your own half brothers and sisters. She then tried to kill my apprentice, Ake. You were born from the terrible things I was forced to do,' Lan shouted.

'You lie. That is not how it was. Drianna saved these women, and you came to take them back again as your slaves,' said Orilan.

'You have been lied to son.'

'I am not your son as you have already uttered.' The boy hideously gnashed his teeth and came towards Lan.

'No, don't Orilan,' screamed Lan, thrashing against his captors.

'Afraid of death from your own body?' asked Orilan.

'Is this it Orilan? Kill your only parent left. The one that loves you and knows the truth.' Lan looked at the child pleadingly.

Orilan's countenance changed back to that of an angelic young boy.

'Father, do your really love me?' Orilan asked.

An unseen hand signal from Orilan to his guards saw them reopen the wounds on Lan's ankle. They slashed him on the face, from the right cheekbone down to the corner of his mouth in ragged diagonal lines with their long, sharp nails. Tears welled up in Lan's eyes and his body went rigid with shock. He started fitting and his eyes rolled back in his head from the foul touch of the disease-carrying guards.

Orilan laughed happily. 'Oh dear. Baby wants to play with Dadda.'

He closed the distance between them. Orilan knelt by his father and dipped his fingers in the blood seeping from the wounds on Lan's face. He shivered as he put the blood to his lips. 'So pure in magic. More,' said Orilan. He bit into his father's pulsing neck with his sharp teeth. Lan's body went stiff at the intrusion. A few memories were gleaned from the taste of his blood, as it did with all his victims. At first Orilan was very delicate. But then he clung to his father, his little arms wrapped around him. The guards released their hold on Lan. Orilan gorged as the silky feel of magic entered his veins.

The magic came gushing fast, too overwhelming and pure for his dark intent. He tried to draw away, but the pulse of Lan's heart beat in unison with his. He felt bonded with his dying father. At this point, the last of his victim's memories and emotions flowed through him and into his mind. The memories forever safe. Lan's heart began to slow and Orilan realised he didn't want this man dead. He wrenched himself away. Orilan tried to stand but he was too bloated and collapsed.

'Get me a new mount. Men, carry the corpse of the devil animal,' he mumbled.

'What about the elf, master?' asked a guard.

'Leave him to die. Now fall out,' said Orilan.

He and his party left the cave on their way back to Drianna's crypt.

Lan had lain between unconsciousness and reality for two days. Slowly dying. The shadow of death came ever closer. His breaths became shallower as the hours increased. A saviour came in the form of a true Sidhe, the druid Dun Norix. He teleported himself and his son back to the druid school in Eriu.

This was where Lan now lay, between cool clean linen. His wounds had been cleansed and bound. Then they had bathed the toils of the road from his weary body. When he woke up screaming, they managed to get him to sip a warm, nourishing, thin soup. Five druids chanted a sentence of healing five times over Lan, every sunup and sundown. It was eerily beautiful to hear the elven words sliding off melodic tongues in unison,

'*Lan vyasht Dee shtys syl Dee clerc Sidhe.*'

Dun Norix stayed near his son almost all the time, bathing his forehead with cold compresses. Two weeks from the day he had been brought here, Lan slept a peaceful sleep and morning found him awake and asking to use the privy. Dun Norix had fallen asleep in a chair across from him. The lower druids wheeled in a hollowed out wooden chair with an iron pan in it.

'I will not use this,' said Lan weakly.

'*Cyb Sidhe non ska,*' they said.

'What?' asked Lan.

Dun Norix, hearing the commotion, opened his eyes and translated.

'He says you are not allowed up elfling.'

'Who says?' Lan, turned towards his father's voice.

'I do, son. I'll tell you what, I'll tell them to leave and so will I. Then ye can use it yourself,' said Dane.

'That seems a little better. Hey, I'm no elfling,' said Lan.

Dane laughed. 'Ahh son, you are! Don't be mad. Fine, believe what you will. How old do you think I am?'

'No more than seventy,' said Lan.

'Try fifteen hundred years.' Dane shrugged.

'Whoa. But Ma ...' said Lan.

'Your mother was two hundred and fifty when she was killed. She lied about her age, as women do. Half elf, you know,' said Dane.

'I didn't. Now I got to go,' said Lan.

'Of course. Move.' Dane waved away the lower druids and followed them out of the room.

After relieving himself, Lan washed his hands in the bedstand basin. Dane returned with a lower druid who wheeled the commode away.

'Lan, all new elven recruits cannot speak Galli and we here speak Elven within these walls so that no outsider may know our business. I will teach you a few basics, if you are willing to learn,' said the druid.

'No, I do not wish to speak it, for I am not an elf,' said Lan.

'Fine, your body will recover in a month, and we'll give you supplies and send you on your way,' said Dane.

'Father, don't you want me to stay?' asked Lan.

'No. Only truth is spoken in these walls. If you believe the facts of creation is just faerie talk, then forsake your mystics to doom, for I will not suffer my druids the same fate,' Dane said angrily and left the room.

Lan sat on the edge of the bed brooding. *I do not need to know that I will outlive the many people I will come to love. And if I learn elven ways then my father may bond me to the druids' fate, and I do not want their ways. Hanton didn't trust their ways. Mysticism is older than druidry, yet they are kin. I just want to go home, but in my absence has my father turned Ake his way? I will learn their speech by listening and hear what they have to say.*

Lan closed his eyes and began to astral travel. He soared above the school of druids, past Relequis, to the island of Man'hannon. He wanted to see what was happening to Falcon and Ake.

CHAPTER TWENTY-ONE

Ake was choosing her classes for the upcoming year. But instead of eight she was only allowed to pick six because Dane wished to develop her magic further in one of the time slots. Het was slowly recovering, and he wanted to use another slot to train her in weaponry and thievery. The last week Ake had spent catching up on her lost studies and was barely awake. She had barely passed. If Ake hadn't aced geology and healing then she would have failed. In unarmed combat she had forgotten so many moves and her balance had fallen sharply that she had ended up on the floor.

In spell casting Ake had failed at casting full *Mystic Fire*. Water seemed to be her element. She had managed to spin the water in the glass bowl so quickly she had knocked it off the table. Earth, nope, Ake managed to kill the plant she was trying to grow quicker. And air, well, let's just say the book she was trying to float in the air was warped beyond repair. Ake managed to get a C average in language and mathematics and a D in cultural studies.

At Caelestis, most students usually started at six years of age, she had at eight. Schooling went for thirteen years so most students left at nineteen. The first three years were dedicated to simple reading, writing and arithmetic. Ake had been worried she would be much older than the others. But Lan, believing in her, had put her in with the other eight-year-olds. At eighteen this was going to be her last year where she would choose all her subjects, and she had to master them all.

Ake headed to the registration desk where ten mystic teachers sat. In Lan's place was Dun Norix. She saw twenty six-year-olds lined up with their parents. Some were crying, others were biting nails. Some looked as though they were ready to bounce off the wall.

On front of each of the desks were posters stating the subjects that corresponded with the appropriate year level and the teacher that took them. While lined up behind twenty other eighteen-year-olds Ake read the year ten poster to herself.

Year Ten – Principal Trebrelan/"Grand Master Mystic"
Choose eight of the following in which you wish to master:
Healing
Geology
Elementary
Aromatherapy
Meditation
Cultural Awareness
Unarmed Combat
Weaponry
Tracking
Horse Husbandry
Mathematics
Galli

'Next,' called Dane.

Ake looked up and noticed that she was three people away. The line shuffled forwards again. Ake looked at her options. Healing suited her. Geology she was good at. Ake was furthering her magic with Dane and one slot was filled with Het so that left four. Elementary, yes, Ake could take that in water. Maths and Galli, she would also study tracking. To all the year tens' delight, each student got their own room. As they would need all the privacy they could get for the hard year ahead.

'Next,' called the druid.

Again, the line shuffled forward, another person stepped in behind Ake. That's when Ake realised something. If all the students pick different subjects how could one teacher be there for all of them.

'Next,' called Dane.

'Hello Dane … I mean Dun Norix.'

'Hi Ake,' said Dane.

'What have you selected?' he asked.

Ake told him and he wrote it down.

'Dun Norix, I'm confused, if all the students pick different subjects how could one teacher be there for all of them?' she asked.

'Simple Ake. The students pick and the classes with the biggest numbers go ahead. You should know Caelestis doesn't allow registration of more than twenty-five students a year for all grade levels. And if each student goes on to the next year, then the only new students are the six-year-olds that come at the start of each year,' said Dane.

'Oh yeah, I forgot about that.' Ake blushed.

Dane laughed. 'Don't worry about it.'

Ake smiled at Dane then headed back to her dorm. That's when she sensed someone watching her and looked around. Nothing out of the ordinary, so she continued on her way. Lan returned to his body after seeing Ake shiver from his presence. A minor druid brought in his meal, and he consumed it ravenously.

CHAPTER TWENTY-TWO

Ake woke to the summer solstice and the first day of the holidays. The sun streamed in through the open shutters and the other girls were still asleep. She yawned, got up and dressed. Ake was now considered a senior and was allowed to visit the village during holidays, a two hour walk from Caelestis. The village was named after the tribe that once populated half this island. Mencrey, the people of Man'hannon. You could feel the excitement in every room of Caelestis. A big feast was held every year to celebrate the solstice and included games and dancing.

Ake went down to a tasty breakfast. Het was down there, grumpy and playing with his food. He gave Ake a half smile when Ake sarcastically tried to comfort him. Tok had told him that he wasn't allowed down to Mencrey. Ake whistled happily back to the dorm and grabbed three pieces of silver. Then she enjoyed a leisurely walk along a path that had felt the feet of many happy shoppers heading to and from Mencrey.

Ake bent down and picked several flowers and lifted them to her nose and inhaled the exquisite scent. She sighed as she looked out over the vast field of red and yellow wildflowers. Sweet grass whipped in the wind, tall as no one had touched it with a scythe in many a year.

She entered a small village that consisted of a well, a small cobbled market square and four long houses that served as shops. There was the smithy on the south, the baker on the north point, a general supplies store on the west and the Braying Burro inn at the east point. There was a field behind all this, in the opposite direction from which Ake had entered. Pitched on this field were large A-frame tents with various travellers selling their wares.

Ake headed to the tents, there were eight in all. A purple tent had two middle-aged, similar-looking women selling an assortment of natural products and crystals. A brown tent, that looked familiarly tribal, was selling feathery and leathery goods. A blood red rounded tent had a couple of foreign people smiling and tempting buyers with interesting foreign foods and art. Ake walked among the stalls. In a green tent a big jolly man was selling smoked meats and marzipan.

A man cried out from a yellow tent, 'Roll up, roll up, test your skill with the hoop game. All you have to do is get three iron hoops around these blocks of wood and you can win a prize.'

A raven black tent had eerie music coming from it and Ake's nose wrinkled as she smelt sulphur. The outer flap was closed over but to Ake it seemed as if eyes were watching her every move from within. A bright blue tent had jesters and jugglers performing their countless hilarious acts. Ake watched this for about an hour then decided she liked the look of some of those crystals the women were selling. Ake moved towards the purple tent, her eyes sweeping across the colourful wares of vibrant gemstones and simple woven bracelets.

A middle-aged woman approached Ake. She was a vision, clad in her striking dress of violet satin and mauve lace. Her dress billowed out in rippling folds that ended at her sandalled feet. She had long black hair that ended at her waist and her eyes were the colour of a summer-lit sky. Her cheekbones were high and proud, yet her face was delicate and yielding. Baby pink stained her lips, and her body was supple yet thin.

'Hello there, miss, canna I help ye?' she asked.

'Ah yeah, those crystals are stunning and have a good shape to them,' said Ake.

'Yes, they do. Any special one that suits you?' asked the merchant.

'They are all nice. But I'm supposed to feel attracted to a cosmos stone, so says Dun Norix.' Ake smiled at the woman.

'Ah yes, the star stone,' said the merchant.

'What? I haven't learnt about that one yet,' said Ake.

'Ah, it is very precious. It has a gold base and tiny slivers of silver crystal weaving its way to the heart of the stone,' said the merchant.

Ake grinned. 'Do you have any?'

'Why yes, we do. We have a few.' The woman gave her a kind smile.

'Where do you get them from?' asked Ake.

'From the core of deep dark caves,' answered the merchant.

'Yik, I wouldn't want to go in there, there may be Shadow Masters in there.' Ake's eyes widened in fear.

The lady gave a little laugh. 'Why don't you run your hand over these, drawing in their heartfelt energies yet never letting your fingers touch their hardened surfaces. Crystals be personal, each one needed by their user.'

'Wow, I was just taught that they came from the earth and were made up of this and that. And they are good for making your spells stronger.' Ake shrugged.

'They also have a grounding and comforting effect,' said the merchant.

'When Lan gets back, I'm gonna tell him to teach his trainees a little better.' Ake pouted.

The lady laughed.

'By the way, pretty lady, what name feels blessed to be owned by you?' Ake gave the woman a toothy grin.

'Why you are precious. I am called Tirian,' said the middle-aged woman.

'Does that mean something special, as it should?' asked Ake.

'Yes, it does, it means calm like water,' Tirian said.

'Lucky, I get a star that doesn't know where it's going and ends up here.' Ake smiled.

'Here, why don't you take this star stone, as a stone given as a gift is more precious.' Tirian handed Ake the crystal.

'If ever any of your friends or relatives are in times of need contact Telewanake and I will come. For with a name given I have given you a gift of friendship,' said Ake.

'Beautiful name meaning Stars Fallen,' said Tirian.

'How did you know that?' Ake stared at her, mouth wide with shock.

'Very few moments pass in which a seer doesn't see most things,' said Tirian.

'Lan thinks I'm some kind of super freak, and that I must stop some evil goddess.' Ake shivered.

'Freak is much too strong. But I'm sure you'll do well. Well, I say, Clara would really enjoy you,' said Tirian.

'Is that your sister?' asked Ake.

'No, Clara is my niece,' said Tirian.

'How old is she, if it's not to rude to ask?' asked Ake.

'She's seventy-four now,' said Tirian.

'Wow, I'm only young. Het is older than me but he's a grumble bum lately and wants to slash everything,' said Ake.

Ake noticed the two merchants were half-elves and asked if this Clara was one too.

'I believe our father had the blood of a few ancients in him. That's why we age slower and live a little longer than most humans. My other sister, Clara's mother does too. And by the way, I'm sure you care deeply about your sweetheart.'

'No, Het isn't my chosen. By the way, Tirian would you be able to check in on Lan's whereabouts?'

'What's Lan like?'

'He's a mystic who was full of himself from what I remember. He was kind when he needed to be, but immensely proud. Hey, what is your sister's name?'

'She be Charian.'

'Yeah. I like both of you even though I haven't said anything to her.'

'Well, that's sweet.'

Ake looked at Charian who wore her long, black hair up. Charian turned to Ake and spoke for the first time. 'I sense trouble with this one who is close to you.'

'What, Lan? I'm not close to him.'

'I feel as though he is suffering great pain,' whispered Charian eerily.

'What! Is he dead?' Ake dug her nails into her palms, causing them to bleed.

'He is in spirit,' said Charian.

'Has his spirit left his body?' asked Ake.

'At times it does to watch over you. But no, this isn't what is meant. He is losing himself. He is not sure who or where to be. Heed the words of the wise who speaks through my lips,' said Charian.

'I'll tell Dun Norix,' said Ake stoically.

'He might want to be quick,' said Charian.

As though he had heard Charian's words, Dane teleported beside the stall.

'Ah Ake, here ye are. Oh, hi ladies.' Dane bowed to them as if they were queens.

'I have foreseen that your child is in danger,' Charian began loudly and ended in a barely audible whisper.

'Wow,' said Ake.

'Sorry to disappoint three lovely young ladies. But I have got him at the druidic school in Eriu,' said Dane.

'He suffers greatly inside; I know you believe the physique is all that needs healing. What about spiritual and emotional health?' asked Charian.

'And his head, don't forget that he doesn't teach things properly. Maybe that needs fixing too,' said Ake.

'Ah, our ways are ancient and true, but it is nice to hear of alternate ways. Lan's tough,' said Dane.

'I guess a father would know, being there all his life,' said Charian.

'Hmm, Ake, it's best if we go. There's danger present. Nice chatting with ye,' said Dane.

'Wait, Dane,' Ake said.

Ake ran up and hugged both the women. Some innate sense told her she'd never hear their sweet voices or look upon their faces again.

'Goodbye,' said Ake.

'Fare thee well precious,' said the women.

They hugged Ake again before she left with Dane.

'Hey Dane, I want to see what's in the black tent before we go,' said Ake.

Dane drew in a breath and smiled at Ake. To her it seemed as if he was holding something back. Something snapped in her. She felt a ball of rage and hurt that had been held in since her years as a young child, build. Her face screwed up into a scowl and Ake stopped walking. Dane turned and ushered Ake on.

'Nope. You'll not boss me around anymore or decide my future,' Ake said.

'But it's already written. Now come on, we cannot dawdle. The odour of evil is wafting on the air,' said Dane.

Ake turned back, searching for the warm and inspiring faces of the women but they were gone, their stall had disappeared. Ake blinked in shock.

Ake was finally beginning to show the traits of the strong and defiant woman written in the prophecies. Had those women known that she had needed them? They were now a rich and delightful memory in her heart.

'Hurry along child. It is time to leave,' said Dane.

'I can handle any danger aimed at me,' said Ake.

'You cannot, you're just a wee lass,' said Dane.

'The Shadow Masters didn't seem to think that way when they were destroyed!' Ake glared defiantly at him, her hands on her hips.

'Don't throw a childish tantrum girl. Now move it or I shall have to cast a sleeping spell on you,' Dane said.

'Go ahead,' said Ake.

'Bloody insolent child. You'll do as you're asked,' said Dane.

A crowd had begun to gather. Some of the youths cheered Ake on. The adults nodded sadly at her, believing the druid was in the right. There was a strange humming and Ake smelt sweet flowery scents in the air. A sweet, endearing, feminine voice whispered in her ear.

'Do not be afraid. We know who you are, we have been watching for you since before you were born. Your curiosity drew your eyes to where we wait as you walked among the stalls. You may know of us from legend. We are the elven priestesses of Ea. Come to us now for the druid wants you to be owned by their kind. They say your destiny is written. Can a page not be torn from a book? We know the way of your magic. Learn to wield it and not be owned by mankind.' The melodic voice drifted away on a draft of cool air.

That lapse had been but a mere minute, but it had felt like an eternity within Dee's heavenly embrace. Ake turned to Dane who had gone pink in the face from embarrassment due to Ake's defiance. It seemed as if the voice and scent had been for her alone. No one else seemed any the wiser.

Ake turned and walked off leaving a stunned Dane. She headed back towards the rows of stalls and walked right up to the black tent. The flap opened just as she neared it and a maiden not much older than herself, beckoned her in.

Ake noticed the lady was naturally pale but slightly tanned from hours in the sun. No blemishes anointed her skin. Her hair was chestnut brown and worn to her hips in a spiralling plait. Her eyes were the most outstanding features on her face, wide and luminescent violet. Her eyebrows were deeply slanted, and her nose was button-like. Her lips were a light pink and full. The dress she wore was but a mere slip, long in length yet almost totally transparent and swirling with the colours of the rainbow. She was no more than five foot. Her cheekbones were high, and her face was thin but not gaunt. The woman was a full elf.

'Hello Telewanake, daughter of Gepatok, who was sired by Sorendee. I salute you child of the future. I am Elder Flower, daughter of the high king of the elves, Serenade. I am a priestess of Ea,' said the elf.

'Hello Elder Flower. Yes, my name is Telewanake but I do not believe me to be the girl worthy of the title stated,' said Ake.

'Oh, but you are, for your chosen himself wrote me and I came,' said Elder Flower.

'My chosen? You know of him?' asked Ake.

'We know him to be the one but he himself does not see the truth.'

'Who is he?' Ake asked.

'Enter my tent.' Elder Flower beckoned.

'How do I know you can be trusted?'

'Trust can only be believed within your heart. Does your heart whisper of mistrust?' asked Elder Flower.

'No, it does not.'

'I would rather you feel more comfortable about what I have to say. So, if it pleases you, shall we walk among the fields? That way Ea can protect us from harm,' said the elf.

'Yes, let's. But first who is Ea?'

'Ea is Dee, mother earth and many other names. But foremost she is everything on which we stand,' said Elder Flower.

'Elder Flower,' said Ake.

'Call me Flo.' Flo smiled.

'Call me Ake.' Ake grinned.

The maidens walked among the flowers and Ake couldn't get over the alluring beauty of Flo.

Flo turned and whispered, 'Enchantress is what I be, not many men and very few women can resist my charm. I am here for six months to try and help you on your way. No pay I ask for, I was sent by your chosen and the high priestesses you have just met.'

'Ha … explain to me some more about your purpose,' said Ake.

'Okay, I am a priestess of Ea and have just finished my training a year past. Girls are sent to the academy from as early as five and as late as ten. There we train them to be clerics of Ea. A cleric of Ea has a lot of knowledge of healing spells, potions and charms. They also make great singers and poets. They can talk to animals and heal them. The academy is very select about who they take. Noble men send their daughters there for an education as not many other places believe women should be educated.

'When the priestess comes of a marriageable age, men clamour for her hand for her uses on the battlefield. Some people live far away from towns and physicians are costly. There are two other things that men like about them. They are supposed to be trained in the ways of loving. All females that reside in a household with a cleric of Dee gain equal status to a man under the law. His wife gets a pension of five gold sovereigns annually; normally meant for her, but he usually takes it.

'Once a year the women come back to us for the summer solstice to tell us how they are going. They are also required to help in the big annual healing. This is where we help the poor locals and cast fertility spells over the seedlings and animals in hope of a good harvest the following year,' said Flo.

'Wow, that is a lot to take in. How long has your academy been around?'

'Forty-one thousand years.'

'Wow, that's old.'

'Not really, only six elven lifetimes. Your Caelestis is older.'

'How old?' asked Ake.

'Forty-five thousand years this year. Built by the great Din and Dage, the elven explorers in the time of the alliance.'

'The what?' asked Ake.

'You haven't been taught the history of Din and Dage?'

Ake blushed bright red. 'I've heard of them, but I missed a lot of cultural awareness classes.'

'Oh dear, I think I must request a year to teach ye before we allow you use of Empon Seato,' said Flo.

'You have that spear? I thought it was lost from mankind.'

'Yes, mankind but not elvenkind, let alone womankind for it can only be wielded by a woman.'

'Yet Mbel Dai——'

'Can be wielded by both, I know,' interrupted Flo.

'This is very overwhelming. Can I think on it?' asked Ake.

'Yes, don't leave it too long. Return at dawn tomorrow with your answer.'

'Okay. By the way, who is my chosen?' asked Ake.

'Lan.'

Ake stared at her confused. 'Lan sent you?'

'Yes, he wrote to the academy about a year ago requesting we look in on you. He thought it would be good to show you a strong female presence,' said Flo.

'How kind of him,' Ake mumbled. 'Wait, Lan? That's kind of ridiculous don't you think? He's an old man.'

'Lan is an elf. I am older. He is a mere youth in elven culture. In terms of ageing Het would be much older than you in maturity than Lan is. Lan is now the equivalent of a twenty-one-year-old human, and will be for a long time.'

'Explains a bit.'

Flo embraced Ake and turned and left. Ake returned to Caelestis alone to find Dane had left.

CHAPTER TWENTY-THREE

'They are coming after you. They are going to hurt you and when they're finished with you they are going to hurt her until she's not herself anymore!'

Lan sat with his eyes screwed up and his hands pressed against his ears. The voice was back but this time it seemed more real, like the person was standing over him and hissing their cruel intent in his ear. The druid that had been tending him these last few weeks entered the large and spacious room.

To Lan, it had become a terrifying jail and he barely got out of bed except to use the lavatory. He peeped out from under the covers, more animal-like than man. The druid looked outside the door and down the corridor, seeing no one he closed the door. Turning back to Lan, he grinned harshly. He had brought in a tray and placed it on the bedside table. He picked up the pitcher of water and turned his back towards Lan. From within his robe the man took out a tiny clear vial with some clear liquid in it. He poured the contents into the pitcher and with the power of his mind stirred the fluid.

Lan covered his face as the man placed the pitcher back on the bedside table. The man turned and strode from the room. Lan looked around the whitewashed rectangular room and sighed. He was even afraid to eat and was growing weaker by the day. He had scared himself yesterday by looking at his own reflection in the mirror on the side dresser.

His throat was parched and the water that the druid brought him always tasted clear and fresh and he craved after it so much. He sat up and his hand shook as he poured himself a glass.

You're being drugged, came his unclogged thoughts. His thoughts soon began to cloud, nothing mattered but to drink the water.

'Ake, what did she ever do for you?' something asked in his mind.

She tried to save my child and always had an antic to cheer me up.

'That doesn't matter. The water.'

She was always honest with me, calling me out for my immaturity. A true friend.

'She's one of them, a Shadow Master.'

No, she isn't.

'She is going to get you!'

No, she's just a girl.

'An evil one in disguise. Like your auntie who tricked you, just like Bozzwanna. She will hurt you!'

'Please, no,' Lan said.

Lan had begun to lose control of his sanity.

Unbeknown to the rest of the druids, the druid that was tending to Lan was a Shadow Scout. It was slowly poisoning Lan's mind using the venom from a basilisk. He had begun to poison Lan from the morning after he had arrived. The poison was addictive in small amounts and brought the victim's innermost fears to the surface as if they were reality. All that was needed was one more dose.

Chapter Twenty-Four

'Ake, not like that. Magic flows in the user's veins as does his or her blood. Be water and the magic will flow,' said Flo.

Ake had taken Flo up on her offer to teach her. Het sat nearby trying not to laugh. Dane had returned a week ago from Eriu and had totally ignored Ake. Ake had decided Dane had Lan and she was going to train for six months with Flo and then go rescue him from the druid's clutches.

'Ake, concentrate,' said Flo.

'Sorry, Flo,' said Ake.

Ake was trying to cast a simple levitation charm on a feather.

'Okay, I'll go through it again. Close your eyes and gather your most happy thought. Then focus on the emotion behind it. Hold that energy. Now think of the feather and push the emotion into it,' said Flo.

Ake tried and Het burst out laughing.

'Don't you have a training session?' Ake opened her eyes and stared at him.

'Yep, but you should have seen the expression on your face. You looked all squished up like a prune.' Het doubled over in laughter.

He rose to his feet but almost tripped over a rise in the ground. He chuckled and threw both Flo and Ake a kiss.

'Get outta here you mutton head.' Ake laughed and pointed towards Caelestis.

Flo's cheeks were slightly flushed. Ake looked at her as if she was mad and shrugged. Het left and Flo and Ake returned to their learning.

CHAPTER TWENTY-FIVE

The Shadow Scout parading as a druid brought in Lan's evening meal. Lan cowered under his covers. He made a silent scream. Something within told him he was about to die.

Meanwhile, in the mess hall at Caelestis, Ake's heart felt like it was pounding through her chest, and she began to sweat. Ake heard a silent scream. She knew it was Lan and that he was in serious trouble. *Maybe Lan might be able to hear me.* She could only try.

To the rest of the students in the mess hall it looked as if she'd fallen asleep. Some girls jeered and called her an attention seeker while the oldest lads made lewd suggestions about her sleeping next to them. Ake ignored them and delved deep into her subconscious as Flo had been teaching her and tried to seek Lan's energies.

The Shadow Scout drew closer, and this time did not try to hide what he was doing. Lan felt the memory of that addictive touch on his taste buds. The urge came to reach out his hand for the vial. It will end the misery. No more worrying about Ake, Orilan or Falcon. Painless, empty and free. He felt his hands reach out.

Ake was suddenly filled with terror. It surrounded her very senses, overwhelming her ability to concentrate but she held on. Her tastebuds craved something, and Ake had an overpowering urge to fill her mouth with it. Ake felt her hands reach for a vial but knew she had to hold back.

Ake opened her eyes and turned to the mirror beside the bed. She was inside Lan's body and could feel the strength of the magic in his veins. Ake turned to the Shadow Scout and saw him for his true form with the blind, white eyes and the serpent-like tongue. She shivered and Lan's body responded.

What was she doing in here? Ake whimpered from terror and Lan's voice uttered the cry instead of hers.

'Intruder, fight her from within you,' cried the entity.

What the hell was that awful voice inside his head? thought Ake. It had the awful intensity of nails scraping across a blackboard. *Is this what Lan has come to?* Ake asked herself.

The Shadow Scout came closer to Lan, trying to force the vial between his lips. She screamed hoarsely, fighting the urges.

Lan's true self tried to take it, no longer strong enough to fight the urge.

I must take it, must, came Lan's weak thoughts.

No Lan, don't!

Ake, is that you?

'Intruder. She's come to get you,' said the entity.

Yes, it's me, I'm here to help you. Hold strong.

No, it isn't.

It is Lan. Hold on, for I fear I will have to leave soon.

'She's gonna get you,' said the entity.

No, she's my friend!

Lan's mouth was being forced open. And he could already taste the smooth addictive taste.

No, Lan, fight it, don't leave me. Fight it! screamed Ake's inner thoughts.

Lan rolled away from the Shadow Scout. Dun Norix with four trusted druids came running into the room. They had finally realised why Lan had not been recovering. The Shadow Scout screamed harshly before exploding in a burst of *Druid Fire*. The rays spurting from the druids' hands were as black as their anger. Ake, relieved, returned to her body and Lan collapsed into a dreamless and pure sleep.

Ake felt a gentle touch on her shoulder. She opened her exhausted eyes and looked up into hazel ones. Het looked at her tired face.

'I'm sorry to bother you Ake, but Sidon's son Torrid was accused of stealing apples while in the village. The kid tried to pick them up after knocking them over. He tried to run from the guard, and they mistook him for a slave and shot him. He may not make it. Please come to the infirmary they need your help,' said Het.

Ake rose and followed Het to the infirmary.

CHAPTER TWENTY-SIX

Lan woke in the evening. He opened his eyes slowly and groaned from the headache. He was bathed in sweat and shaking from the early withdrawal symptoms of addiction. He thought he had spoken to Ake. He sat up and paused, surveying the room. His father spoke gently from a chair adjacent to him.

'I'm sorry, Lan, I should have realised that my own son was suffering. And that one would try to glean her whereabouts from your mind,' said Dane. He looked down and muttered under his breath. 'And destroy the mate.'

Lan turned his large dark eyes to his father and began to cry from all the stress and hurt he had suffered since being absent from Caelestis. Dane rushed to his son and embraced him for a long time.

Lan stopped crying and gently loosened the hug. 'Is it true that my destiny is to live a lifetime as an elf?'

'I'm sorry, it is true, my son, that elves only live one mortal life-time. When an unborn elf is in its mother's womb, power from Dee herself creates a new soul to be his or a half-elf chooses the one last path. Pure, strong and worthy are you. A new soul,' said Dane.

'Father, is the dance of the stone circles true?'

'Yes, you will dance within them in death, awaiting your soul-mate's return.'

'Then I will never love for I do not want to see them pass from my loving embrace and never see them again,' said Lan.

'But son they return once a thousand yea——'

'But Father,' interrupted Lan weakly, 'one day out of so many to wait to embrace them and if they are human they may not heed the call.'

'I loved and I am proud of the experience. The one that is ordained for you will forever heed your call,' said Dane.

'I have made a pact never to love.'

'If it is true love, you will break every pact and promise to make them yours,' said Dane.

'You didn't,' said Lan.

'No, but I wish I had. But I could not turn from this path, for I was not strong enough. But you will be for the harsh journey ahead,' said Dane.

'Father, I will not change my mind.'

'Don't be too sure, for I know you have already fallen.'

'Who?' asked Lan.

Dane shook his head, refusing to answer. He helped his son rise and led him from the room.

CHAPTER TWENTY-SEVEN

Ake and Het entered the infirmary, which held twenty-five wooden-framed beds. The floor was whitewashed stone as was the ceiling. It was rectangular in shape and had two huge doors. One led into the hall, the other led to the healing supplies room.

Ake counted eleven patients, all suffering from mild illness such as heat cramps to more severe illnesses. Torrid looked awful. His little face was screwed up in pain. His small frame had a two-layered bandage wrapped around his middle. As soon as Flo saw Ake she leapt up from where she knelt by the bed in prayer and came towards her.

'Ake, you must delve within your mind and heal the child for there is no grand master healer within these walls,' said Flo.

'Me included. I cannot do this. Ask Tok,' said Ake.

Het stood there solemnly, looking from one girl to the other.

'You're more experienced than me Flo. Why can't you try?' asked Ake.

'I have prayed to Ea and laid my hands upon the boy's hurt. But to no avail. This task is for you,' said Flo.

'What about Tok?' asked Ake.

At the mention of his name, Tok returned from the supply room with four coloured vials. His apprentice, a little boy of eight, ran alongside, tiring under the weight of bandages and notes.

'Ah Ake, still terrorising the helpless.' Tok turned to Flo and bowed. 'Regal maiden of Ea and elfdom, I have brought all the herbal solutions you asked for. This purple vial contains lavender to clean the wound. This black one has bittersweet nightshade for sleep and reduction of pain. This green one contains St John's wort to help speed recovery, as does this red one containing comfrey.'

Tok placed the vials on the bedhead and ushered his apprentice forward. The apprentice handed his burdens to Tok.

'This is Lei,' said Tok.

Het, Flo and Ake looked on as Tok unwound the bandages on Torrid then cleansed the wounds with each of the solutions. The wound was serious. Tok had changed the layers of bandages every twenty-five minutes due to blood soaking through. Torrid grimaced and whimpered. Ake saw how Tok had tried to stitch the arrow wound across Torrid's stomach, but it had split open and Torrid was losing blood very quickly. Tok took his pulse.

'His pulse is barely felt, I fear we will lose him,' said Tok.

'Ake, I believe in you,' said Flo.

'As my oldest and dearest friend, and being who you are, I do too. If a priestess of Ea believes in you can, how can it hurt to try?' said Het.

Ake closed her eyes took a deep breath and placed her hands on Torrid's gaping wound. She steadied her nervous breaths and cleared her mind of all thoughts. Her heart leapt against her chest in quivering anticipation and the girl dragged in the eternal light of the goddess. The energy began to overwhelm her untrained senses and Flo sensed this. Flo closed her eyes and reached deep within herself offering up her balancing energies. Ake took a deep breath and bright green light streamed forth from her hands.

Het, Tok and the apprentice watched in fascination as the wound knit together. Ake fell but Het grabbed her and supported her exhausted body. Flo smiled and opened her eyes. Het put Ake on one of the beds. Once Ake was placed on the bed, he kissed her tenderly on the mouth.

Flo scowled at him as he wandered over to her.

'What is it, Flo?' asked Het.

'You should not kiss Ake like that Het. You know she is not in love with you, and she is intended for someone else,' said Flo.

Het grinned at Flo. 'I don't think that's your place to say. My background matches Ake's prophecy. I am in love with her and can protect her. The difference is, I am present, he is not. Who knows, with time Ake may change her mind. Do you not think that elf is a little immature? He is also prone to bouts of darkness, the opposite of our bubbly Ake.'

Flo sighed. 'This is where your romance ends with Ake, Het. You are not prone to bouts of darkness as indicated by the shadow man on those inscriptions you saw. Lan was born under a dark portent on a stormy and dark night. Flooding took the lives of many, a sacrifice for his entry into the world. Dane unaware, engaged in a dark ritual at the head druid's behest on the night of Lan's conception. That immature elf you refer to has powers greater than any normal mystic I have ever seen. His powers will continue to grow rapidly unless kept in check by a goddess of light.'

'How do you know of those inscriptions?' asked Het.

'The great Din and Dage created them when they built Caelestis. They marked that wall. All elves are aware of them and the prophecy,' said Flo.

Het sighed. 'You are right, I know this. It is hard to let her go.'

Flo reached out and touched his hand. 'It is the right thing to do Het.'

Het looked at Ake. He turned back to Flo and gave her a bitter smile, then left the infirmary.

Chapter Twenty-Eight

A month had passed and Lan recovered with the help of his father. Lan still felt the occasional urge to wrap his tongue around that tantalising drink. It often played on his mind when he suffered from the nightmares of his traumatic past. *Why is my father so insistent on merging the culture of druid and mystic?* Lan turned to stare at his father, distracted from his thoughts as Dane continued their conversation.

'Lan will ye accept the offer to unite the druid world with the way of the mystic?' asked Dane.

'Father, I do not know if this is the right path.'

'But then druid and mystic may fight side by side. Would that not be grand?' asked Dane.

'Yes, but how long would it take to get the stubborn to change?' asked Lan.

'Time, but when it comes to unity and learning should it not commence with cooperation rather than be paid for it by anger and blood upon Dee's skin?'

'Yes, Father but who's to say those that do not agree with it may choose to rebel with the sword?' asked Lan.

'Son, I have thought long and hard but the final decision ends with you.'

Lan sighed and offered up an option. 'I have an alternative. As a male child of royalty gets fostered out as a squire, why do we not let our acolytes train at the different schools for a period of time then return them to their teachers? A list of ideals to be taught to the students could be drawn up so there would be a form of unity without massive change.'

'Very wise answer, my child. Let's go at once and talk with the council.'

The two men stood and left the quarters.

CHAPTER TWENTY-NINE

Dawn rose to the east of Caelestis and Ake opened her eyes. *So, I've only slept the night. Thanks be to Dee.*

Tok turned as he sensed Ake awaken and ushered his apprentice forward with Ake's breakfast. Ake sat up quickly and thanked the boy. Ravenous, she started on the meal of fruits, bread, cheese and apple cider. Flo entered the room. She smiled importantly at Ake and the acolyte took his leave.

'Ake, your last year of schooling starts in but a few short hours so I will take my leave soon,' said Flo.

'Flo, I didn't want to approach Het or Dane with this. But I keep having strange nightmares. They seem more like visons than anything.'

Flo gave her a smile. 'Tell me of them.'

Ake gave her a quick explanation of the two visions she believed she had seen.

'Did they ever come to pass?'

'Not that I am aware of,' said Ake.

'Well then, they are most likely nightmares. Now, it is time for my departure,' said Flo.

'Must you go? You are like a sister to me,' said Ake.

'Yes, sister of my heart. But I go to do honour to Ea. I will return when the year is through, on midsummer's eve when you turn nineteen,' said Flo. They clung to one another crying, then Flo left. Two hours later Ake solemnly sat in class looking at the window.

———∿∿———

Lan woke up and wiped the sweat out of his eyes. Throwing off the wet night shirt, he tossed it on to the floor and clambered out of the bed. His gaze settled on a nearby mirror. His cheeks burned with embarrassment. He strode to the window and drew open the shutters, a slight breeze cooled his burning body and he tried to control the new urges coursing through his body.

I am disgusting. How can I be attracted to Ake like that? Why do thoughts of her in my bed haunt me since she rescued me? He watched the sunrise and he smiled. *I wonder if she is watching the sunrise too.*

'Stop this you fool.' Lan walked over to his desk and sat down and began to scribble a few words. Then he screwed up paper and tossed it away. *This ends now.*

'You are fooling yourself. She was destined for you,' something whispered on the wind. Lan shivered. *Must be the leftover effects from the poison.* Lan stood and stretched before exiting the room.

———∿∿———

Ake smiled as she hummed a song to herself. She was sitting outside Caelestis making flower chains in the late afternoon sunlight. Het paced nearby before he came over and crouched near her. Ake smiled up at him.

'Why are you so anxious?'

'It's a year until you graduate. I am worried for your future and mine.'

'I hadn't really thought about that.'

Het rolled his eyes. 'Typical.'

'What future?' Ake slipped a bracelet over his arm and he inhaled the floral scent.

'Unlike mystic males, the females are married off. You will need a husband who can protect you and your son so he can defeat Drianna.' Het lay down next to her and looked up at the cloudless blue sky.

Ake frowned. 'So, I am just a vessel for the saviour.'

Het turned and his eyes met hers. 'It doesn't have to be like that. You could marry for love.'

Ake sighed. 'The mystics won't allow that. I will be traded to some lower noble.'

'You could come back to my village and settle down with me.' Het grinned. 'Let's run away now.'

Ake laughed and Het's eyes flashed with annoyance.

'You were serious?' Ake reached for his hand and held it. 'I am sorry if I upset you.'

Het grabbed her arm and pulled her on to his chest. She struggled briefly before he rolled her on to the grass, her hair fanned out behind her. He ran his fingers through it. Ake's eyes widened in surprise. She pushed on his chiselled chest and glared at him.

'Lay off——'

Het grabbed her small chin in his huge hand and his mouth found hers. His tongue darted into her mouth as he deepened the kiss. He pushed his hips into hers with earnest. Ake closed her eyes, trying to match his passion as he increased the pressure on her mouth. Het's hands began to unlace the bodice on her gown and her eyes snapped open. Het pulled away from her, his eyes hazy with desire.

'Why did you have to go and change our friendship?'

'I am sorry.' Het laughed as Ake scowled at him and her eyes flashed golden for the briefest of moments. 'It has begun. I need to go talk to Dane.'

Het stood and sprinted towards another field as Ake stood and trailed after him. Ake touched her lips in remembrance of Het's passion and blushed. She approached Dane and Het in a heated discussion a few minutes later.

'You are my apprentice and their guardian. She is not destined for you.' Dane glared at Het.

Het stood with his arms crossed, his face darkened with anger. 'I am a better fit. I have all the elements of the husband in the prophecy. I am also madly in love with her. Please don't sell her to the highest bidder.'

Ake stood behind a tree and watched.

'She is a noble and a goddess and needs someone of equal standing who can control her budding powers. You are both reckless and impatient. You would destroy each other.'

'I disagree, druid,' growled Het.

'What does Ake want?' Dane sighed. 'Maybe we should ask her.' Dane walked towards Ake and she stepped out from behind the tree.

Ake's cheeks burned. She couldn't face the yearning in Het's eyes and the worry etched on Dane's face so she turned and sprinted towards Caelestis. She ran to her room and threw herself on to the bed.

What do I want? Or more importantly who do I want? I love Het dearly but when he kisses me there is no spark. He is like a brother to me. Ake grumbled and hid her face in her pillow. There was a knock at the door.

'Who is it?' Ake sat up.

'It is Sir Norris, mam.'

Strange. 'Ah, you can come in.' Ake stood and walked towards the door as it opened. A youth of eighteen years approached her and bowed. He looked peaky as his eyes met hers. 'Miss Ake, I would like to offer you my land in … I mean, hand in marriage. I am reliable and hardworking.'

Ake laughed at his unintentional joke and put her hand to her mouth as the youth blushed. 'Thanks for your kind offer but I cannot accept.'

The youth bowed again. 'There is still time to pick. Please keep me as an option.'

Ake gave an awkward curtesy. The youth smiled and rushed from the room as Dane knocked and entered.

'There you are.'

Ake scowled and turned away and grabbed a book, pretending to read.

'I know you are avoiding me as I am discussing your future with others.'

Ake turned a page and yawned.

'You are a lot like Lan, you know.' Ake's gaze caught his. 'Both still lacking maturity.'

Ake's heart beat faster and she felt her cheeks burn with embarrassment and lifted the book to cover her face. She calmed herself before tossing the book on the bed.

'Where is he? Is he safe. Did he find Orilan?' Ake asked a little too quickly.

'He is okay, but a sadness has settled within him. He misses his beloved dreadfully.'

Ake felt faint and she put her hand on the bed to steady herself. *No.* She turned and smiled sadly at Dane. *Why does Lan occupy my mind so often? How dare he love another.*

'Well, I hope he recovers as Caelestis has missed him. I hope him and his beloved are reunited.'

Dane winked. 'He will come for your graduation.'

Ake's heart beat quickly and she felt a wave of joy spread throughout her body. 'It is good the headmaster returns so he can see his students graduate.'

'Why are you so distant?' Dane stepped forward and squeezed her hand.

Ake sighed and cast her eyes to the floor. 'It matters little now.'

'Could it be you are in love with my son?'

The realisation hit Ake like a troll swinging a mallet into her chest. She blinked before sitting down on the bed. *I'm in love with Lan? No, it can never happen, it is taboo.*

'Lan is still without a wife.' Dane smiled and patted her shoulder.

'Mystics don't usually marry. And for headmasters it's forbidden.' Ake smiled sadly.

Dane smiled to himself. 'That elfling is a rule breaker.'

Dane turned and exited the room. Ake lay down on her bed staring up the ceiling. She closed her eyes and imagined Lan kissing her and laughed. 'You don't even know what he looks like now.' Exhausted by the strange events she closed her eyes and drifted off.

The year passed and a big change had begun in Ake. She gave herself over to her studies and rose within the highest ranks of her classes. She became a master at thievery and Dane returned to teach her as he'd said he would. Het taught her to wield a short sword. Ake noticed Het no longer flirted with her and her thoughts turned to Lan, yearning to hear any news of him.

Ake forever questioned Dane on Lan's whereabouts but Dane made an excuse of not knowing where he was. Dane knew that the Shadow Masters wanted to kill the seed of the future and if he entrusted this knowledge to a young woman who could not fully shield her thoughts they would be sure to find out.

Ake began to spend her evenings in the library researching all she could on elven culture. *I need to know all I can about their ways if I am going to marry him.* A sigh escaped her lips. Ake laughed at the ridiculousness of it and the librarian cleared her throat and Ake blushed and dropped her gaze back to the tome. She flipped the pages until something caught her eye. *Marriage ceremonies of elves.* She read on.

The wood elves of Caley do not enter into marriage ceremonies, instead they take periodic lovers and the children are raised by each clan. Most elves that dwell in the outer confines of Caley and Relequis marry for love and are generally as faithful as the average human relationship. This cannot be said of nobles of Relequis. While the mage elves marry for alliance, they rarely bare young and will take many lovers to try to bolster their population, almost as if the magic barrier encourages this hedonistic display ...

Ake shuddered. *Dane is from Relequis. Does that mean Lan will be tempted by others even if we marry?* She continued to read.

While many elves tend to be fickle in love there are exceptions to the rule. Elves and half-elves who take mystic or priestess vows appear to be free of overly intimate feelings including polyamorous ways.

Ake smiled. *Thats a relief.*

Most mystics do not marry but can, the headmaster must set an example and it is taboo for him to take a bride.

Ake slammed the tome shut in anger and stood. *I will read the rest later.* She picked up the book and checked it out and left the library.

Dane looked around his small quarters. There was a bed, wardrobe and small table. He had set the table for two. Simple wooden bowls and cups and spoons graced the table. He had acquired a bottle of fine red wine. A large steaming pot of Eriu stew sat in the middle of the table and he had placed hunks of soda bread in the bowls. *This is going to be a very odd discussion.*

There was a gentle rapping on his door. He had invited his son to dinner.

'Come in,' said Dane.

Lan came in and smiled at his father. Dane gestured for him to sit. Lan sat and opened the wine and poured two cups while Dane ladled out the stew. After a few moments Dane sighed and looked at his son. *The boy has become a little calmer this last year, hopefully he won't react poorly to what I have to say and strain our precarious relationship.*

'Great stew, Father.' Lan ladled more into his bowl.

'Lan, you aren't going to like what I have to say.'

Lan put the ladle down and looked at his father. 'So, this invitation is a pretence for another issue.'

Dane nodded and Lan looked hurt for a brief moment before composing himself.

'Lan, we need to discuss you and Ake.'

—∞—

Lan stared at him. *How can he know that I have considered that as a possibility?* When Ake had rescued him from the Shadow Scout their souls had bonded, each recognising the other for its mate. Lan was now plagued with the need to be with her and protect her. He hated himself for his lack of self-control and was tempted to make her his.

Lan blushed. 'What are you talking about?'

'Ake keeps asking after you whenever I visit Caelestis. She is a woman now and nearly nineteen. According to your mystic culture she will begin to court her future husband like the other girls have been doing so. Ake is ready to be married.'

Lan smirked at him and reached over and refilled his glass. He drained the contents of his cup. 'That boy Het, he would be fully grown now. Surely, he has made his intentions clear to Ake.' Lan's heart began to pound in his chest as he said those words. A feeling of despair washed over him. *If only I was a little younger and I hadn't been forced to rescue her. Maybe then it would be acceptable for me to court her.* Lan sighed. *What the hell am I thinking?*

'Het has decided their union is no longer in Ake's best interests.'

Lan glared at Dane. 'I don't believe Het would have suddenly decided that without someone else's input.'

Dane smiled and stood up. He walked over to Lan and put a hand on his son's shoulder. Lan looked up at him.

'Ake is destined for you, my son.'

Lan pushed his hand away and stood. The chair screeched in protest against the stone floor.

'Did you interfere in Ake and Het's relationship?' asked Lan.

Dane shook his head. 'No, she isn't in love with Het. Ake is in love with you.'

'That is a ridiculous notion. I am thirty-three, she is nineteen. Can you not see the problem I have with that?' asked Lan.

Lan realised that he had insinuated that he had thought of the possibility on more than one occasion and tried to cover his tracks. 'Not that I——'

Dane laughed. 'So, you are in love with her then. Every time I mention her your eyes light up. It was the same for me and your mother. Surely you realise I was much older than she was. We are elves, Lan. Human values don't really apply to us. Ake is a grown woman; I think you should marry her. You were born to protect her and no one else can love her like you can.'

'This conversation is over.' Lan walked past Dane and opened the door. 'Don't entertain the idea that I will ever marry Ake. She deserves someone better. I am tainted and will never forgive myself for what I did to Goriard.'

'Lan, you are worthy of a loving relationship. You were ensorcelled, how is that your fault?' asked Dane.

A wave of loathing filled Lan. If only that were true. *Could she possibly forgive me and really be in love with me? Silly woman, please don't do that to yourself.*

Lan turned and stared at Dane. 'Stop manipulating Ake's life. Let her finish school and move on so I can be free of her. I don't want the responsibility.' Feelings of anger welled up in Lan and he clenched his fists. 'I just want a peaceful life and I want to be alone.'

'You are lying to yourself, son.'

Lan scowled and slammed the door on the way out.

——◦∿◦——

The days grew warmer and longer and midsummer's eve loomed ever nearer.

Flo was returning from the temple of Ea where she had taken her last vows. Flo was now a priestess of the highest ranks. As a martyr, she had been sent forth with gifts of fine silks and a silver dagger to seek her chosen. She also brought a birthday gift to a friend.

Caelestis was decked out in all her finery for the celebrations of midsummer and the graduation of acolytes to masters. The chef was flabbergasted at all the preparations still yet to come. It was seven in the evening and everything had to be set by ten, just three hours' time. Everyone would be hungry for they had been fasting all day in honour of the gods and feast to come.

'Blasted kitchen hands. Good for nothing lay-abouts. The peacock still has to be dressed. The boar is spit-cooking. The stag already cooked is being decorated. There is still trifle and gelatine desserts to be made. Eclairs and fairy cakes need to be put in the wood oven. Oh, not to mention wines need chilling and the ingredients for the starters still haven't arrived,' yelled the flabbergasted chef from the kitchen.

Ake stared out of her bedroom window, her nose up against the windowpane, waiting for Flo. She laughed when she heard the chef bellow. Ake grew bored relatively quickly, so she started pulling faces at the servants setting up the marquees and decorating the tables and surrounding area. Her effort produced a lot of angry faces. She laughed and continued her ploy.

'You want to hope the wind doesn't change suddenly,' stated someone.

Ake jumped and whipped around in annoyance at being caught on the spot. She was about to state her anger at someone entering her room uninvited when her grey-blue eyes dilated in tear-drawing happiness as they stared into Lan's dark hypnotic ones.

'Well, don't I even get a hello?'

He'd barely finished his sentence when she rushed into his arms and he wrapped her in a tight embrace.

'You came, Lan, you came,' said Ake.

'Well, yeah, I have to make sure all my students are ready for graduation. Fire some kitchen hands. Make sure thirty more settings are set for the five druid masters and their acolytes. And now I have to go discuss the new training options with my fellow teachers. Okay, Ake, I've got to go,' he said hastily as he unclasped her arms from around his waist.

Lan left before Ake could say what was on her mind. *I missed you, Lan. Why did you leave me for so long? I feel as if you abandoned me. Now you've only come back for the school.*

There was a mass of commotion and happiness as word spread of Lan's return. Ake turned back to the window. And to her great joy Flo was walking towards the doors of Caelestis. Ake turned and headed towards her bedroom door. She grabbed for the handle, but it turned of its own accord. Het entered the room with Flo.

'No one knocks around here.' Ake laughed and embraced Flo and Het.

'Happy birthday,' cried the others in unison.

Ake laughed and she and her friends sat upon the rug and began chattering excitedly about the past year. After an hour, Het turned to Ake and from within his tunic he pulled out a cloth-wrapped gift. Ake went to unwrap it. Het's hand stopped her.

'Do not open this within these walls. Remember the incident with the Shadow Masters, we do not know who might be listening. And I reckon these druids that are coming might not be all good,' warned Het.

A haunted look came into Ake's eyes at the mention of the Shadow Masters. Flo noticed this, laughed and playfully slapped Het for upsetting Ake on her nineteenth birthday. Flo turned and grabbed the gift wrapped in purple cloth. It was easy to guess what this was. The cloth was tied gently around the shape of the spear.

'Ake, you are no longer a child. You are of the most desirable bloodlines. You are ordained by the gods as their salvation because in you is their continued existence made certain,' said Flo.

Ake laughed and was about to deny the possibility when she saw the worried expression on both her friends' faces. She listened as Flo explained the prophecy. It was familiar. She recalled it from Hanton's journal.

April 4

Dear Log,

Two nights ago, the natives told me their creation story. It is similar to ours with a few differences. They also mentioned a prophecy. At first, I believed it a faerie story, but then, so can the history of the elves be taken that way.

Drianna, unhappy, … her hate for the divine couple …t about causing terror and hate and turning humans away from the right path. But …not corrupt the Sidhe or the Second Ones, closest of humans to the creator, so balance … maintained. But the … humans had … many and made a new religion and were trying to turn other humans from the right way. They soon … to succeed, and their numbers battled the Sidhe … near death.

Balance, … Destiny, Sorendee's second son, was … pushed away. Drianna's only child, a girl called Fate had set her freewill … her cousin Destiny and helped her mother corrupt the face of Dee. Fate was a daughter fathered … demon, one of the corrupted pale humans.

The Sidhe trained their children harder, and they became mystics. They had recruited a few of the second beings and they schooled themselves and became the people of the Learned Oak, the druids. Again, balance reasserted itself. Sorendee had become tired and wanted to settle down to aeons of family-making with Dee. But …d not let his creativity… his wife's artworks be forgotten. So, he spoke the words of a prophecy to the Sidhe and a few druids and retired. Meanwhile, Drianna created demons, devils and evil in the heart and minds of men.

Tired and sad Sorendee spoke … words to three druids and the most intelligent of the Sidhe, the mystics.

'You have not strayed … my arms and … heart of my wife. A son of mine will take a half Sidhe from a star tribe and upon her conceive a babe. A girl child, Stars Fallen. My son will lose his life to be one with his daughter. The …will be ever living and… soul-mate a child of a handmaiden of Dee. Their son will be Drianna's downfall, yet … girl will be her saviour. The soulmate … guide her forever … as long as one memory remains, then time will go through her cycles again. Watch … wait and when the Masters of the dark are at their highest reign, stars will fall and so will she from within a woman's world.'

It had taken Flo the better part of an hour to tell the prophecy. She was pushing the hard truth on Ake, that she was the one spoken of.

'Ake, it is real,' urged Flo.

 Het had left the room to get ready for the feast.

'Flo, I was taken from a tribe that pushed me away,' said Ake.

Flo interrupted. 'Ake, you must believe, for time grows short and the darkness in the world deepens.'

'It's just a lot to take in, Flo. You're lucky you won't die lonely. If it is true, that I'm immortal, then my friends and the many people I'll learn to love will die while I exist. Immortality is not life, it is just an existence. I'll grow weary in time and then I'll just be a shell of memories. Not a person that once felt, loved, hurt and laughed. No Flo, it is not easy to come to terms with being cursed,' said Ake sadly.

'Think of all the wonders you'll get to see. You also won't be alone, you will have Lan,' said Flo.

'Lan will eventually die, and I very much doubt he will ever return my feelings. It's a very unlikely union. Can I be left alone with my thoughts for a while?' asked a melancholy Ake.

'Yes, but don't think on it too long, it will just hurt more,' said Flo. She kissed Ake on the forehead and placed her gift in her hands and left.

Ake rose solemnly and began to get ready. She had bought a

new dress for this occasion from the allowance Dane had given her. Ake took it out and held it against herself. It was white and stopped at her ankles. A seam of pearls ran the width of the waist, and the sleeves came down in fine silk to the elbows. The rest of the dress was in white cotton and five blue cardinals were embroidered across the bodice. Het had bought her a pair of knee-length white boots that laced up. She placed the gifts the others had given her under her bed.

Ake rang the bell at the side of her bed and her handmaiden entered. She asked the girl to bring her the hip bath and warm water. After the bath Ake took her towel and vigorously dried her long blonde hair that reached her bottom. As she brushed it, she wove in four red silk roses, two on each side near her ears. Then Ake put some lavender oil on her wrists and at the base of her throat. Ake sprayed the rest of herself with rose water then got dressed. By the time she was finished it was nearly ten.

Ake left her room and hurried outside where all the other acolytes were waiting to begin the graduation ceremony.

CHAPTER THIRTY

Everyone was seated waiting for the ceremony to begin. The youngest children were already in bed. Flo looked around at the torch-lit area. The outlying field of tall sweet grass had been prepared earlier by several mystics teaching the younger students how to control *Mystic Fire*. The ground still crunched underfoot as it mixed with ash and the remnants of grasses. Sixteen long tables were set up. The first years were bouncing around excitedly while their poor red-faced teacher tried to settle them. On a table adjacent them, the second-year teacher was in a similar situation. Across from them the third years were blatantly ignoring the first and second years. Each table could hold thirty people. Nine tables held excited students and their teachers.

Each of these tables was covered in silver tablecloths and held silver goblets and the appropriate cutlery and dinnerware. Three tables behind the students were decked out in white and a team of thirty waiters in black robes stood by, waiting to bring in the starters. Each of the white tablecloths were decorated with red lace and pearls on the seam and each of the three tables held an ice sculpture as a centrepiece.

One was of a unicorn pawing the ground nervously, but head held high, one was a phoenix with his wings spread wide, his face looking up to the heavens, and the other was a nymph and satyr with looks of mischief in their eyes, a toga hiding their naked-ness. Another table held scrolls, trophies and awards. A horde of acolyte druids took up another table that was decked out in green also holding the appropriate dinnerware.

The ten tables with druid and mystic students were in two rows of fives. North lay a table decked in gold and held twenty-five places; this was for the tenth years. East lay the tables ready to hold the feast. Another table sat next to the tenth years. The tablecloth was purple and held six places only, for this was the high table. Five druid masters were already seated. The other place was set for Lan. A horn sounded and announced the entry of the headmaster. Lan took his place.

The waiters brought in the starters. This consisted of homemade lemonade and cocktail dogs and scones for the first, second and third years. A watered-down sweet honey wine, stuffed olives and garlic bread was served to the fourth to seventh years. Everyone else had a light fruity wine and an assortment of breads, cheeses, fruits and continental meats.

When all the dishes had arrived at the proper tables, Lan invited the tenth years who had made their late entrance as the guests of honour to be seated so that they could commence. After the starters were finished, a harpist and a flautist began to serenade the gods and Flo rose and took her place among these two as the solo singer. Everyone stopped to listen as her angelic voice sang of lovers by a lake in midsummer and birds singing the morning chorus. When she finished everyone clapped and cheered. Het's eyes followed her from his place among the druid students as she made her way back to her own seat among the servants at a plainly decked round table.

Then came the main courses. These consisted of a boar with an apple in its mouth set in a gravy made from its own juices and surrounded by dumplings stuffed with potato and rosemary. This sat on the table of the unicorn.

The deer took up most of the phoenix table. It lay on a bed of lettuce, and he was stuffed with lemongrass, garlic, onions and a peppermint and cinnamon sauce sat in a terrene to be served with portions.

The peacock was stuffed with bacon and sat in a dark wine sauce, this was on the nymph and satyr table. On all three of the food tables were one of each of the following dishes: a capon laden in a white cream and spinach sauce and stuffed with sage and an assortment of crushed herbs, a large pot of baked potatoes smothered in bacon and onion gravy, boiled cabbage stuffed with fresh herbs and soaked in a cheesy white sauce lay in another pot, while a large pot held a collection of roasted vegetables in a delicate curry.

Sarsaparilla was served to those under tenth year while a velvety thirty-year-old red wine graced the other tables. The waiters went round to each of the tables taking orders.

Lan stood up and tapped his glass and everyone hushed and watched. 'I'd like to thank our three musicians for the wonderful entertainment. And *gratas ska sastn*.'

The druids toasted with Lan in the language of elves.

'For those that don't know elvish that was: thank the heavens for this meal,' translated Lan.

'Hear, hear,' everyone cried.

While they were consuming the meal, thirteen lasses danced the maypole, while thirteen lads chased them. This got a laugh from all the diners. After the main meal was cleared away it was nearing midnight and all the children under fifth year were escorted unhappily to their dorms. They would be served herbal teas laden with honey and petit fours with fresh cream before bed. The children complained, but most of them were rubbing their eyes and yawning.

The graduation ceremony was held very late at night to honour the phases of the moon. Everyone clapped as the ceremony began. Each student was asked forward in turn to the high table where they were handed their graduation scroll listing their majors, grades and recommendations. Each student received a medallion with their name and the school crest on it. They were in pure 18ct gold and an arch of *Mystic Fire* surrounding a black stallion rearing on his back legs was imprinted on each. Each of the graduates shook hands with each of the five arch druids and received a smile from Lan.

Awards were handed out based on the student's best subjects and behaviour. When Ake was called forward to receive her award for outstanding achievement in all fields of academics, Lan looked at her in astonishment. *What I wouldn't give to kiss her right now. I am so proud of her.* He composed himself and frowned, wondering if anyone had guessed his thoughts.

Lan was about to speak but several of the druids frowned at him, knowing what he would become to her one day. Instead, he looked past her as he handed her the award. He glanced down slightly and saw the innocent look of reproach in her eyes, but she kept her head high and walked off the stage.

As midnight arrived, so too the desserts with mugs of steaming coffee. There were two trifles and lemon and peach jellies served with fresh cream. An hour later, the graduates were applauded as they left the ceremony. Soon, the celebration area was empty apart from a few stragglers, and servants clearing away rubbish and preparing to do the wash-up.

Ake looked up from her dessert which most of her class had forgone. Lan was watching her with interest. She looked around and saw Flo and Het were absent. The servants were set on their duties. Lan rose and walked casually over to her.

'Happy birthday.' Lan smiled at her mischievously.

Ake smiled back, happy that he'd remembered.

'I've got something for you.' He placed a little silver box in front of her. 'I didn't have time to wrap it.'

Ake picked it up and looked at it. Lan sat down next her, watching her turn it around in her hands. It was about ten centimetres long, square and made of wood. While mostly painted silver, a golden star was engraved on it. Ake opened it and it played a beautiful unknown tune. She was amazed at it.

'I thought you'd like it. It's about the stars, like your name,' he mumbled.

Lan turned away and slowly began to sing in a slightly deeper voice than he used to. His voice still contained rich melodic undertones Ake noticed.

Destiny drew me away, wish I'd stayed.
Terrors lurked in the dark,
You alone had become my bright spark.
I remembered the stars above, are watched by all those we love.
Beautiful, like you.

Lan stopped suddenly. Ake cast her eyes down, embarrassed as Lan watched her intently, admiring the stunning way she was dressed. He had hated the feelings he had discovered for her these last few months and had tried to push them away with no success. He had never been in love with anyone before. *Why does it have to be her?*

———∿∿∿———

'It's all beautiful, Lan,' she whispered.

'Just like you,' murmured Lan. He leant in to kiss her. She felt his breath on her lips. His eyes blazed with desire before it was replaced with a dreadful sadness.

'What was I thinking? You are destined for someone else.'

He got up suddenly and stormed off. *Things can never be the same again.* Ake felt tears burning in her eyes. *I need to get away from here. From him.*

—◦◦◦—

Lan rushed past Het who was leaning against a tree near Caelestis's outer stone wall. Lan felt his cheeks burn as he realised Het must have seen what had just transpired. Het gave him a superior smile and strode towards him.

'Why if it isn't the Lord of Caelestis claiming his prophesised bride.'

Lan's jaw dropped in shock before he clenched it shut and ignored the comment.

'Backing off already?' Het stopped inches away and towered over him. His enormous size caused Lan to take a step back.

Lan began to turn away, trying not to let his pride better him but the quip escaped from his lips. 'Jealous?'

Het scoffed and Lan staggered as Het pushed him lightly, his enormous strength apparent in the slight movement.

'Dane said you had decided marrying Ake wasn't in her best interest.' Lan eyes darkened with annoyance and he squared up to Het. 'It is supposed to be my purpose to protect her.' Lan's gaze dropped to his feet, and he sighed. 'There is no need for jealousy. I will protect her as a friend but not as her husband. Mystics don't usually marry, and as the headmaster it is forbidden.'

'You know the traditions call for her to be married. She needs a husband who will protect her and their son so the child can defeat Drianna.' Het squeezed Lan's shoulder firmly. 'It would be improper for Ake to stay at Caelestis with you, unmarried. Considering how she is in love with you.'

Their gazes locked. 'Ake is not in love with me. She was embarrassed by my declaration.' Lan sighed. 'What if she doesn't want to marry and have a child? This prophecy is ridiculous. Do you really think our wild Ake will submit to a husband and the laws that bind them?'

Het glanced up at the sky, lost in thought. He dropped his gaze and saw Lan walking away.

'This conversation isn't finished.'

'I am tired, Falcon. You are dismissed from protecting her. You are free to live your life as I am home. As head of my household and head mystic I am responsible for Ake's safety. I will keep her safe and comfortable until she decides her future, even if this includes a lover.' Lan gritted his teeth, the thought of her in the arms of someone else nearly rent his soul in two.

'So cold even after you attempted to romance her. Is Flo the only elf that can show her emotions?'

Lan took a deep breath and turned and smiled, taking all his self-control not to confront the insolent man. 'I am a lord; I must retain my composure at all times. I can't let my feelings rage and be on display. As a fellow man you should know that is immature.'

Het laughed. 'I guess marriage for elves is more platonic. How can you protect her when you don't love her? You won't be driven enough to die for her. At least she knows I love her, even if she didn't reciprocate it in the way I wanted.'

Lan felt the jealousy weave its claws around his heart and squeeze. A rage swept through him and he rounded on Het. 'I am capable of protecting her. What have I done to warrant hate from you, of all people? I thought we had an amicable working relationship.'

Lan rolled out of the way as Het threw his trident at him. The air was suddenly static. The hair on Lan's arms prickled as lightning flashed brilliantly across the sky, the tension was palpable between them as the prophecy decided who was the destined mate.

Het rushed towards him and drew his sword Lan somersaulted over him and delivered a quick jab to Het's side. Het tried to grab him, but Lan ducked and rolled as Het pivoted and the sword crashed down where Lan had been.

'Stop this foolishness, Falcon. Are you possessed?'

'Ake calls me Het.'

Het grinned and summoned *Druid Fire*. Lan mumbled a counter spell and the flames that streaked towards him were snuffed out as he scrambled to his feet. Lan brushed off his clothes as if Het's direct assault was a mere annoyance. Het laughed and Lan grinned. Het threw a dagger at Lan and he caught it in his hand. A flick of his wrist and it sailed to close to Het's cheek as he barely dodged it. Het rushed him again and Lan withdrew his knives. Squealing metal assaulted the night air as Lan countered the blow with one knife and ducked under the sword. Het grabbed his collar and Lan rammed the hilt of his other weapon into Het's sternum with a staggering force, his jealousy permeating his body thinking Het could take his Ake. He shook himself and scowled at Het. 'She's mine,' he whispered. *Damn, now Het, of all people, knows.* Lan felt the heat burn his cheeks as he blushed.

'Finally, some emotion.' Het stepped forward, the sword hefted in both hands above his head.

Lan leapt backwards, his back slamming into the stone wall. His ears rang as Het's sword crashed into the stone, the blade inches from his skull. Lan's eyes widened and he glared at Het.

'If she doesn't want to marry you, that isn't my fault.'

Het's shoulders drooped and Lan placed his arm up in front of his face. As he slid down the wall, he delivered a harsh kick to Het's knee. Het stumbled back, pulling his sword with him. Lan winced as the blood oozed from the wound in his forearm, the cloth shredded.

'You've finally made a decision then.' Het sheathed his sword.

'You are a capable fighter at least.' Het sighed. 'Hopefully her feelings will be enough for the relationship to be meaningful for her.'

Lan watched as pain streaked across Het's face as he fumbled with something in his pocket. 'It is good you can protect her. I had to see it for myself as I return to my village in the morning.'

Het turned and walked away.

'Good luck, Falcon. Just so you are aware, I won't marry her.'

Het's hearty laughter carried on the wind. 'Ake won't let you get away.'

Het is ridiculous, Ake doesn't want me. Lan's heart skipped a beat. *Is it possible?* Lan sighed. *I will have to get Tok to heal this cut.* Lan entered Caelestis.

—‑ᴡᴡ‑—

It was the early hours of the morning when Ake arrived back to her room. The halls were crowded with shadows as only a few torches lit the way. After the incident with Lan, Ake had started thinking about her future. Normally someone would hire a male mystic as a court astrologer or there would be missions that required their skills.

Ake changed into a white cotton nightgown and took her hair down and brushed it. Most female mystics landed a thane or lord with large holdings and wealth as a husband. It wasn't necessarily a match of love but the female would be well supplied for, as the lord would be getting a learned and powerful protector for his lands.

As with most schools of the time, Caelestis was for the children of rich fathers. Boys were sent here for they could go far, while fathers just got rid of their female children in the hope that they would marry well and increase their father's own holdings. A lord marrying a mystic would often give a rich offering to the girl's father in thanks. This was another way of getting rid of their less beautiful girls.

What chance did Ake have in hoping to marry high? She was just a girl from one of the local tribes. Ake thought of her classmates and sighed. *Twenty handsome, strapping, young men rich beyond thought. Four beautiful rich girls and me, a girl who has no royal heritage but some prophets spouting shady information about her parentage. Maybe Lan as my legal guardian could arrange a lowly lord for me.*

Ake's full-grown cat, Socksy, mewed quietly and demanded a back rub. Ake tutted and picked up the black furred, blue-eyed cat and obliged. Socksy made a sound of pure contentment and closed her eyes. Ake smiled warmly at her friend and shifted the cat onto the end of her bed. Nineteen. Ake sighed happily. She got beneath the covers, blew out the candle and closed her eyes.

———

After Het had heard Flo sing, he couldn't stop thinking of her. The guilt flowed through him as his simmering need for Ake warred with his newfound feelings for Flo. He thought about Flo's pretty elvish face and long hair. His eyes swept his peaceful surroundings. He was perched upon a rock near the spring that led to Lan's underground spa. The heat rose in steady clouds of steam. The stars were shining brightly, and the moon was at her fullest. The long dry grass appeared as dark stalks of shadow, waving slightly in a sea-scented breeze. A movement out the corner of his eye caught his attention.

Het turned sharply to see Flo, barefoot and dressed in a white gown studded with diamonds. The moonlight caught the diamonds and it seemed as if Flo was caught alight in white fire. She wore a coronet of fine gold that arched down near her eyebrows.

The sleeves of the dress were so long that her hands were in hiding. Her elvish heritage was apparent in her movements. With each footfall she seemed to be walking on air.

Het's heart beat wildly and he fell in love with this maiden so deeply that he felt he would do anything for her. Flo reached him and there was no need for words. Het stood and pulled her clumsily into his arms. Flo laughed and kissed him.

CHAPTER THIRTY-ONE

Lan awoke in his jewelled cavern. He'd awoken in a night sweat from the terrors he'd been through on his journeys. He sat up and threw back the covers. He sat shaking for a few moments then rose and poured himself a glass of water from the bedside table. He sat sipping it then decided he'd get undressed and bathe in his hot springs. He lowered himself into the water. He sighed with complete bliss as the water caressed his skin. After swimming a few laps, Lan lay back against the edge, arms outstretched atop the ridge.

Lan was busy towelling himself dry when there was a knock on his trapdoor. *Who could that be? No one knows about this place but me.* He threw on his nightshirt and extinguished the candle burning on his desk with a single thought. The room was thrown into sudden darkness. Lan's elven sight allowed him vision and he moved out into the hallway towards the stairwell that would lead him to the surface.

The knocking came again. Lan flung the trapdoor back, knocking the person or thing on the other side unconscious. Lan dragged the body closer to him so he could see who it was. Anger flared at his overreaction as he took Ake in his arms. She was very light and could be carried in one arm. He closed the trapdoor and headed back down. Lan lay the lass on his bed and sponged her forehead.

Ake had come to talk to him about her future and return the

black book clasped in her young hands. It could have waited until morning, but she couldn't sleep. Lan sighed and shook Ake gently.

She murmured and opened her eyes quickly. Ake sat up groggily and stared around in the blackness. Lan sighed and remembered Ake only had a very thin strain of elvish blood within her and that her sight was nowhere near as powerful as his. With a thought, the candle on Lan's desk flared into life. Ake closed her eyes against the sudden brightness. Lan saw blood seeping from a slight gash on the right side of her head. He watched in amazement as the wound knitted back together within a matter of moments. He realised her ancient blood was waking up. Ake opened her eyes and watched Lan gently wipe the blood from her face.

CHAPTER THIRTY-TWO

Het and Flo lay sleeping, naked in each other's arms. An ancient magic began to take form within Flo. She sighed and nudged closer to Het. A sound of muffled voices carried itself on the wind. Flo opened her eyes quickly, dressed and alerted Het.

Het, fully dressed with Flo at his side, scanned the area. Sure enough, foul voices seemed to float on the air. He teleported himself and Flo back inside the confines of Caelestis.

—⚬—

Drianna, the goddess of tyranny and destruction, had hired enough bounty hunters, cut throats and slave sellers to create a small army. *Too bad for Caelestis,* thought Drianna. The druid masters and acolytes had already returned to Eriu. That left twenty-five graduate mystics, thirty servants, nine teacher mystics and one Grand Master. The rest were children.

'Ahh Tok, twice you have failed Caelestis for four sacks of gold. Once for the life of Hanton. Now for the life of the woman, Telewanake. You soulless, traitorous scum. Hanton entrusted Lan's life to you. And with it, all the knowledge of the child of prophecy. Thank you. But you will die tonight too. For one of those bags that you will receive contains your death. Ha Haaa.' Drianna laughed eerily as she watched through her mirror of sight.

Chapter Thirty-Three

Lan waited expectantly for Ake to speak, she didn't.

'Ake, how do you know about this place?'

'Umm, you know when you left for so many years …' said Ake.

'Go on.'

'Lan, what happened to your face and finger?'

Lan shuddered and was about to offer up the truth but instead his eyes turned cold and he growled, 'What about them?'

'Your injuries are so sad.'

'What would you know of sadness? I have no need of pity from a woman,' said Lan icily.

'I didn't mean to upset you.'

'Answer my question. How did you find this place? Were you up to mischief? Off course you were. Whenever trouble happens you always seem to be involved.'

'Lan, don't say that. That is unfair.' Ake could see he was suffering. 'I have dealt with my own pain, Lan. Would you like to talk about yours?'

Lan grabbed for her. She pushed his hands away.

'So, you know about pain. Tell me of a situation and I'll see if it outweighs any of mine,' he said.

'You chose to go,' cried Ake angrily.

'You think I chose for all this to happen, did you?' asked Lan.

Ake shook her head.

'Well, do you?' demanded Lan.

'No. Don't you dare put this on me.'

'What's your sad situation?' asked Lan. His eyes grew haunted.

Ake saw a chance to subdue his anger. 'Well, remember when you held me upside down when I was a child?' she asked.

'You still are a lass!' Lan interrupted and ran his hand through her long hair.

'Lan, I haven't been a child for years. Out in the real world I'm considered a woman, quite old to not be married yet. I'd come here to discuss my future and here I am, met with a rebuke,' said Ake wisely.

Lan laughed at her and pulled her towards him. 'You are the daughter of a prophecy; you can't just marry anyone. There's harm in loving you.'

Ake looked at him coldly. Hurt she pushed his hands away. 'I guess this could wait until morning as it seems you are not in a right state of mind,' said Ake.

'Wise words for a young——' Lan didn't get to finish.

Ake had managed to get to her feet and had already covered half the cavern at a run. Lan extinguished the candle again with a thought. Ake stopped suddenly unsure of where to go. Then the light suddenly flared again, and Ake covered her face with her hands.

'What would you know about me, Lan? Where have you been all these years?' Ake sobbed.

'How dare——' Lan started.

'No, how dare you say I wouldn't know pain. I do not know you anymore. So, you want to know? Well, Het and I took on two Shadow Masters and I did some kind of druid spell. I've graduated, shared my first kiss, and passed practically top of my class. The only good parts. Now for the bad,' yelled Ake.

'Ake, I'm sorry. I'm just exhausted from these constant nightmares,' said Lan.

'No, you wanted to know. Shut up and listen. My father's breath died in his chest before I even took my first. My mother and I were outsiders before I was even born. My mother was misused so many times by men from the village, then they humiliated her and would laugh as I cried,' she said.

'Ake.'

'Quiet,' Ake scowled at him. 'We were starved. I was beaten harshly whenever I stole food. This was before I was four and whenever you weren't there, for you and your circus menagerie managed to give them a sense of good will for a little while. Remember when you held me upside down when I was little, and I cried in fear? It happened when I was five years old. I'd hit a fourteen-year-old in the head with a rock because he was trying to beat me.'

'Ake. Please stop.' He had closed the gap and reached for her. The haunted look in his eyes had grown worse, like his soul had been tortured. She took a step back and Lan lowered his arms to his sides.

Tears streamed down her face as the full force of the memory hit her. 'They punished me by hanging me upside down, pelted rotten fruit and dung at me. And if that wasn't enough, I was left there until morning, then I was given eight lashes across the back in honour of the man's dignity. There, now you know.'

'Now my turn,' said Lan sarcastically.

'Go ahead.' Ake gave Lan an emphasised bow.

'When I was younger, I never knew my father, he ran away to pursue his own needs. My mother sent me to Caelestis where I found happiness. Then when I was thirteen, two of my friends' heads exploded. The only father, I'd known was killed by a Shadow Master. Then I was made to rape my sister under a spell, my friend the griffin was killed by my son, who bit off my finger and drained my blood. His creatures gave me the scars on my face and ankle and a disease. I then was found by my father. A Shadow Scout began to poison me slowly. Yay fun. Then you rescued me. And ...' Lan stopped and stared at her meaningfully.

'I am so sorry, Lan.' She slipped her hand into his, her eyes brimmed with tears. 'Go on.'

'When I found out a few months ago that you'd grown up, it was a shock. Then every time I looked in on you after that I started feeling strange towards you.' Lan stopped and looked away. 'Things that no thirty-three-year-old should feel towards a nineteen-year-old apprentice.'

'Dane told me all about elves when you slept on the rocky out-crop before Orilan was taken. I was never your apprentice. You were gone too long, and you often forgot I existed. You were never my mentor. That role fell to Het and Dane. I am a woman, Lan, and you know you aren't a man, you're an elf,' said Ake.

'Soon everyone will know I am an elf.' He winked at her. 'What did you expect from me Ake? I never wanted to bring you to my school. Hanton was originally supposed to find you and bring you here, but he was murdered, and it fell on my shoulders at thirteen. I had no idea what I was doing. Then your mother got herself killed. I brought you to my mother thinking she could help. I was going to leave you with her, but Hanton wanted you trained at Caelestis. So, once you were in the care of your teachers, I felt I had honoured Hanton and his obsession with the prophecy.'

'So, I was nothing to you?' asked Ake.

'I had made a vow to protect you and, of course I cared that you were safe, like any of the students. You often amused me with your antics, though. After you saved me from the Shadow Scout, I realised you were my equal and had somehow become my friend.' Lan smirked at her. 'You said you'd shared your first kiss. I won't ask with whom, for I'm bound to dislike the answer,' said Lan with a hint of jealousy.

Ake tried to let go of his hand but he tightened his grip.

'Lan, that's my business. When you find me someone suitable to wed, I'm bound to have to kiss him and more. That's what I wanted to talk to you about, since that's what happens to most of the girls here and they've got marriages arranged for them already. So, do you know of anybody?' asked Ake.

Lan had met all the other girls' beaus earlier, as he would do the handfasting tomorrow morning, as was the custom. The girls had been courted for the last thirteen weeks, as was the norm. Some arrangements were made on the day, as greedy fathers wanted more.

'I don't think that's a possibility,' said Lan.

'I know that Thane Norris's eighteen-year-old son was interested. But he's probably too good for me,' she said.

Lan glared at her. 'You're too good for him. Has he been courting you without my knowledge?'

'And why shouldn't he?'

'Was it he who kissed you? If it was, I'll deal with him,' said Lan.

'I can kiss who I like.'

'No, you can't. I won't let you. But you probably liked him kissing you.' Lan scowled.

'And so what if I did?' Ake blushed.

Lan crushed Ake to him. Ake's eyes widened and she opened her mouth to say something. Lan stopped her with his mouth against hers. He gently deepened the kiss. He held her to him for what seemed like an age but was a matter of moments. He looked down at her and his sadness had somewhat abated. Still holding her close, he asked smugly, 'My young Ake, you do realise that I am the head of our household? I make decisions for you until you marry and join your husband's family.'

'Do you know what the problem with that is?' asked Ake.

'What's that?'

'Under elven law you are a minor, as one hundred years is the age of adulthood because you live so long,' said Ake.

'We are under the law of mankind,' said Lan.

'But your father could come and claim you at any time.' Ake smirked at him. 'One hundred years is the equivalent of a twenty-five-year-old human. Dane explained to me how elves age.'

'Fair enough, Ake.'

'You know what else I've read? You only live one lifetime and one childhood and we humans have a chance to live many. An elven parent keeps their elfling under strict supervision in the first one hundred years, frightened the elfling will come to harm. When the elfling turns twenty their hormones and frolicking instinctual nature often get them into a lot of trouble.'

Lan stayed Ake with a hand, as she was getting off track.

'Ake, why did you learn all this?' asked Lan.

'Let me finish, then I'll tell you why.'

'Okay.'

'Humph. While elves cannot reproduce with other elves before forty, full blood elves may reproduce with a human when they reach twenty-one human years. Lots do so by seducing as many humans as possible to add to their lovers list. They are very immature for a long time.' Ake smiled at Lan meaningfully.

'Don't believe you. I'm quite mature,' said Lan.

'Elves can mature more quickly when raised by humans or overcoming adversity. But they still age slower compared to humans. Flo said you are approximately twenty-one and will be for a long time,' she said. Ake laughed when she saw Lan pout.

'So, basically, after all that interesting information all you've done is given me an excuse for that kiss I gave you by explaining to me that I am around your age. Very cunning Ake.' He grinned down at her.

Ake noticed the wet gown cling to his body and looked away.

Lan laughed. He proceeded to take it off. She looked away, blushing bright red.

'What are you doing?'

He pulled her to him; she couldn't look him in the eyes. He laughed and dropped his mouth to the hollow above her breasts and kissed her.

'Gods, you're beautiful,' he whispered into her ear.

Ake looked into his eyes and then looked away from the passion she saw there. Her face was hot with desire and embarrassment. He grinned and picked her up and carried her to the bed. She yielded to him.

'So, young elves add lovers to their list, do they? Will you become my lover?' Lan teased.

Ake looked up at him and whispered, 'Yes.'

His hand slipped under her gown and slowly caressed her inner thigh. Ake sighed. He lay on top of her, catching her mouth with his own. She began to respond to him as he kissed her, his mouth hungrily exploring hers. The need to make her his surged through him and he unlaced her gown and whistled through his teeth in appreciation as his eyes raked over her form. He drew back suddenly, a memory soiling this beautiful one. He sat on the edge of the bed dejectedly.

'Ake, I can't ruin you. After what I did to Goriard,' he said sadly.

Ake sat behind him, lay her head on his shoulder and wrapped her arms around him.

'You didn't do it; a spell forced your body to.'

Lan turned his haunted eyes, meeting her loving gaze.

Ake unlaced her arms and lay back down and reached for his hands, their fingers entwined.

Lan turned but he refused to look at her. She brought his hand to her mouth and kissed it. His eyes lifted and met hers and something primal passed between them.

'Let me heal you. Love me, Lan.'

His mouth crashed down on hers and the passion surged through them. Lan clasped her firmly to him, the pressure from his hips caused her legs to part.

Sounds of fighting interrupted the pair. They pulled apart from each other, breathing hard. Lan heard a scream outside and rushed to change into something more proper for a Grand Master mystic.

'Ake, you better go up, we can't be caught like this, master and acolyte. Hang on, you've graduated.' Lan paused to ponder on a thought for a moment. *I can get around elven and mystic laws with human ones.* He grinned at Ake cunningly, then sent her up the stairwell while he finished gearing up.

Chapter Thirty-Four

Ake ran out into the main hallway. Bodies of children lay lifeless and broken, blood pooled in dark wet spots on the cold, emotionless stone floor. Ake vomited then ran down the hallway to her room and grabbed the old spear that Flo had gifted her, and the small package Het had given her. She left the room and entered the dark hallway.

Unbeknown to Ake, the servants, first and second years had been slaughtered after Tok had opened the drawbridge of the white-walled fortress to the enemy. The teachers and the remaining students were tiring as they tried to defend themselves as best they could.

Het, the master at arms, fought side by side with a few stable boys and Torrid, while Flo sang the song of sleep at intervals when her throat wasn't dry. When her voice lapsed, Flo fired a composite longbow with a quiver full of poisoned arrows.

Lan came running up the hallway. He looked around him. He'd seen so much death. Now it seemed to him whatever he loved was destined to suffer or die. He dropped to his knees and wept at the bloodshed. The human and half elf children were a loss that wrenched at his heartstrings. But the soul-crushing infinite sadness was the deaths of the eleven elflings among them that would never be reborn. They had never met their soulmate so they would never have a partner bonding them to this world or at the dances of the stone circles. So, in time their soul would disappear as if it had never been.

'No, by the blasted gods. No,' screamed Lan.

Lan's screams were so distressing that anyone who heard them flinched.

Those who were fighting to save Caelestis had tears streaming down their faces. Ake turned and took one look at Lan. He rose and stalked straight past her. Rain began to pelt down. Forked lightning appeared in the air and wind from the west howled its anguish and rage. For wind from the west never had good intentions.

When the wind comes blowing in from the west, departed souls will never rest, thought Ake. She ran after Lan. Meanwhile outside, more children died and Master Bradly, the fifth-year teacher, went down with a crossbow bolt in the side of his head.

Tok masqueraded his evil by helping some injured on Caelestis's side. But Lei had overheard him speaking his evil agreement with Drianna over a basin of blood. Her face had appeared in the murky contents. Lei now raced through the hallways to try and find the headmaster.

The remnants of the people of Caelestis were forced to retreat back into the keep. Here, they might be able to hold the army off for a little while. But the walls of Caelestis were old. The people of Caelestis closed the wooden doors and slid the bars down and across. The people inside still had to fight one hundred cutthroats that were in the keep.

Dun Norix was in the druid school rallying what loyal followers were left to the old ways and not converted to the ways of the nailed man who had attained the godhead in one lifetime. Two druids sided with him. One was a druid called Fin Ra. The other Gan Rix. All three men teleported to ramparts above Caelestis where Torrid and Het were slashing at the hands of the enemy who climbed the walls attempting to get inside. The three stable boys lay among the uncounted dead.

Flo stood atop one of the chimneys firing arrows. Her shots were so accurate she had taken down sixty men out of sixty-five. She had the agility of a full blood elf. Flo saw someone get past Het and go for Torrid. Another arrow triumphed with a sixty-first shot.

Boulder-sized hail formed and hammered into the enemy army.

Lan appeared about fifteen feet to the left of Het.

'About time,' grumbled Het.

'Shut up, apprentice,' hissed Lan.

Het gave Lan an apologetic look and continued his failing game of hack and slash. Torrid yelped and flailed as a beefy man made it over the wall and used his axe to take the boy down. Het screamed as the boy died. An insatiable madness welled up in him. He jumped over the railing and pulled out his small axe. He cleaved a man's skull and landed his place on the ladder. He pushed the corpse off. The master at arms drew his trident and speared another.

Lan raised his hands and sent *Mystic Fire* hammering into two men about to jump Het. Four more times he had to do this before Het made the ground, his short sword in one hand, axe in the other.

Flo was beginning to tire. She felt the life in her womb leap. She cleared the distance from chimney to rampart easily. Het threw his axe into a man's skull, where it stuck. Het gained the man's scimitar, and he became a deadly blur in a complicated swordplay.

Dun Norix approached Lan. The remaining army of three hundred men pushed a ballista in sight of the keep doors.

'Where is the woman?' asked Dane.

'Safe inside, where no one will get her,' said Lan madly.

He saw Het go under and sent his last spell down to defend him. A triage of lightning bolts took the lives of fifteen men.

Het somersaulted backwards and landed on the back of another, driving the scimitar into his neck. Blood spurted into his face, and he lost his balance. A sword in the back ended his life.

Flo screamed in anger and sent her last remaining arrows into the back of the man who had slain Het. When she was done, he looked like a porcupine.

Lan slid his knives from the sheaths at his wrist and into his hands.

'We need her Lan. Call her with your mind,' said Dane.

There was a large boom and the doors to the keep crashed inwards.

'We need her. Remember the village, the flames,' said Dane.

'How do you know about that if you didn't know about me?' asked Lan hysterically.

'Where is she?' asked Dane.

'You're not my father. Demon,' screamed Lan.

The demon took its true form as a doppelganger. For the real Dun Norix was behind Lan where Het had stood.

Dane channelled all his energy into controlling a spear, Mbel Daione, as unlimited *Mystic Fire* barrelled into the doppelganger. Dane's friends cast druid spells over the army trying to rage past the last four mystics standing within the doorway of the keep.

Lan flew over the edge and landed on his feet, his mystic knives acting in response to his movements. His fighting talent became clear as he moved like a dancer on the battlefield.

Mbel Daione sang with a voice that surpassed human ears. Empon Seato, his sister spear, answered and the point of her glistened like a black diamond. Ake ran towards the doorway of the keep. She didn't know what she was going to do yet but was hoping she would when she got there.

Lei stopped her. 'Mistress, my master Tok. He's——'

'Slow down, Lei, is he hurt?' asked Ake.

'No, he let them in. That's what he did,' said Lei.

'How do you know this, boy?' asked Ake.

'I saw him talk to a beautiful head in … urgh,' spluttered the boy and he fell as the arrow from Tok's bow took his life.

Ake screamed and some innate power born from the very blackness of pain swept through her as the last of the Master mystics and the children were put to death at the hands of the last one hundred and fifty men of Drianna's army. A black flame flared around the tip of Empon Seato and her caster. Mbel Daione answered his sister's cry of pain by leaving the hand of Dane and flying towards Tok's skull, Tok was caught up in flames and was dust before he could cry out.

Ake burnt with the fever of suppressed pain and anger. A white flame engulfed the last one hundred men. But it did not kill them. They began to change forms into absolute horrors. There were ghouls, nightshades and vampyrs, giant spiders, diseased people and death. Ravens wrenched eyeballs from corpses. Ake collapsed as the spear drew on the last of her reserves. The entrapped men kept taking new forms.

Every evil thought, act and complete madness just kept on taking form in this once human scum. The change was horrendously painful. Skin peeled off hands as they were exchanged for talons. Pus oozed from leprous sores. Gout caused obnoxious smells and well-toned skin fell from bones as it was exchanged for feathers. Unearthly hell sounds rent the air as skin was flayed from bones leaving jelly-like lumps of quivering muscle. No one had known the use of the Empon Seato; to wield the water of life, blood.

Gentle hands lifted Ake from the blood-covered floor. The Isle of Man'hannon was no longer safe. Out of so many, so few remained.

Lan stood on the ramparts of his blood-splattered fortress. Rain made the blood on the ground run and a cold, chilling wind buffeted the hair and eyelids of the once life-filled corpses, mockingly mimicking life.

Life pushes us unwillingly from our mothers' wombs. We come, struggling, screaming and gasping for breath into a world corroded from centuries of stagnant emotion. There are fleeting moments of joy, youth all gone in a heartbeat as if death is constantly waiting, watching. Then as unwillingly as we came, we are taken, ripped from life as we were once ripped from our mother's womb.

Lan strode forth purposely into the keep strewn with the once living. He headed to the treasury and filled his pouch with a few jewels and limited gold. Then he went to his cavern and packed a few belongings, changed and washed the blood from his body. Lan took what he had packed and headed to the stable where he saddled his stallion. Then he returned to the keep to discern Ake's whereabouts.

Dane placed Ake's weary body down on her bed. Flo, Fin Ra and Gan Rix waited as Dane checked Ake over for injuries.

'Will you cope without Het, dear girl?' Dane asked Flo sadly.

'I will return to my father, king of the elves. He will have a grandson and heir. As you know, Lord druid, our race finds it hard to breed full elf children and age has caught up with my father. The son of the eldest daughter is next in line to the throne because a buck elf can't always get the doe elf with child, so it matters not if the father is human as long as the mother is daughter to the king,' Flo sobbed and continued. 'I found my soulmate so early in life and his child will be a king. I will show his son visions of his father and tell of the great battle he fought so bravely and died in.'

'Well-spoken dear. I wish you all the best. My friends and I must leave now,' said Dane.

'What about Ake?' asked Flo.

'Do not worry yourself, my child. Lan is on his way for her

now and he won't stop at anything to have her, for he has also found his soulmate so young,' said Dane. Then Dane and his friends disappeared.

Flo kissed Ake on the forehead and thought about Lan's oncoming insanity, and Ake who was being left in his care. *I know what, Ake can come with me to Relequis, back to my father's castle where I can tutor her, and I can have this babe.*

Flo heard Lan on the stairwell and decided she better move now, and fast. Lan entered the room and walked towards Flo.

'Hello. Where do you think you are taking my charge?' Lan asked.

'Your charge? How do you figure that?' asked Flo.

'Well, let's see, I became her legal guardian after her mother died,' said Lan in a voice racked with grief.

'Yeah, but now Ake is old enough to make her own decisions.'

'Well, Flo, have you asked her if she wants to go with you?' Lan scowled at Flo.

'No, but with the state you are in you could not defend her if danger sought her out,' said Flo.

'How do you know what I can or cannot do?' argued Lan.

'It's obvious that you are on the verge of madness!'

'I don't think so, daddy's little rich girl.' Lan glared at her meanly.

Flo shivered and took a step back.

'Calm yourself, elfling.' Flo began to charm. 'Relax and let Ea love you and be within and around you.'

For a while it managed to calm Lan but then the look of madness was back in his eyes, and he lunged for her.

'You will not have her,' Lan ranted. 'You want her for her power. I don't! I love her. I wouldn't hurt her.'

'Look at what you've become, boy. Goddess, show him,' said Flo.

Flo raised her arms and the goddess spoke through her in a voice as fresh as dew and as strong as stone.

'Lan, child of my heart, be at peace, my granddaughter will come to no harm within Flo's care. In fact, she must go, to learn of her heritage,' said Dee.

The madness in Lan's eyes subsided for only a millisecond. The goddess in Flo retaliated by casting a paralysis spell over Lan. He yelled out in anger when he could no longer move. Before leaving Flo, the goddess teleported Ake and Flo to the outskirts of Relequis. The spell on Lan failed quite quickly and he let out a hellish curse and began wandering around Caelestis, alone and afraid.

CHAPTER THIRTY-FIVE

Ake awoke to the soft caress of a lavender-scented breeze. She opened her eyes, in awe of her surroundings as she took in the sunlight streaming through an open window. Never had she seen such luxury. Ake lay in a queen-size four-poster bed with a red silk canopy that hung down into lace curtains. The floor was carpeted in crimson, lined with real gold.

Tapestries depicting scenes from elvish history lined the walls in magnificent colours, while a solid oak wardrobe sat next to a heavy mahogany door engraved with elvish words, 'Apolo dawn royl Sidhe.' Ake translated it: *the sun would always shine on the elven royal family*. Ake thought about what it meant but couldn't discern the hidden meaning. Ake threw back the coverlet, which was made of a thick wool dyed green and spun so fine that it almost felt like silk.

Ake got out of the bed; her stomach grumbled from lack of food. She stretched and winced as her body ached from overuse. Ake walked towards the wardrobe, as she passed by the window she gasped and took in the strange but compelling view. As far as Ake could see lavender, giant sunflowers, roses and daises were everywhere. Horses ran in paddocks fenced by a strange glowing substance. On closer inspection, they revealed themselves as pegasi and unicorns.

An outline of a village could be seen on the horizon and a forest spread out on either side of the building. The sky was a mass of every conceivable colour arching out in fanlike shapes from a bright orange sun. Ake wondered where she could possibly be. As Ake was looking outside, the door to her chambers suddenly opened and a male elf entered.

Ake turned bright red in the face as she tried to cover herself with her hands. The elf had a look of pure embarrassment on his face. He turned and exited the room. Ake rushed over to the wardrobe, flung open the door and hurriedly looked inside. Someone knocked on the door and spoke.

'Are you decent, mistress? I thought you still resting. May I come in?' he asked.

'Hang on just a moment.' Ake saw a variety of gorgeous dresses, but she chose a simple grey robe-like garment and threw it on.

'Yeah, you can enter.'

The young elf entered. His crimson face had dulled but his high cheekbones still had bright spots on them. The elf, Ake noticed was incredibly beautiful. There was no doubt that this lad was a full blood elf with aristocratic attributes. The lad waited patiently as Ake gave him the once over. His ears were sharply pointed, and Ake could see a resemblance to Flo in his face.

'You came to tell me something?' asked Ake.

'Oh yes, sorry mistress. The king wishes to see you in the great hall in an hour. I am to take you to the baths and see that you are presentable.'

'Is there any way I could get a glass of something cold to drink?' asked Ake.

'Sorry, mistress, how could I be so inconsiderate.'

'Don't call me mistress, my name is Ake.' Ake presented her hand to the lad in greeting.

The servant looked startled and angry.

'What did I do?' asked Ake.

'I shall surely be whipped for that,' said the servant.

'Why?'

The servant interrupted. 'Until I am assigned to you for physical duties, I am not to touch the skin of the fair one.'

'What? It's not like I'm of royal blood.' Ake stifled a giggle.

'You belong to the most royal of all families, the gods,' said the servant.

'You look fairly royal yourself.'

'I am the great lady Elder Flower's third brother. Just an exceedingly high-positioned servant,' he replied.

'But you're the king's son. Doesn't that count for anything? She's only a girl after all,' said Ake.

'That is blasphemous. But how are you to know? She was born of a lady and is the oldest female. The elven race is matriarchal. Our kings have always sired daughters first and their sons become the next king. The new king will marry his closest female cousin who will rule when the former first lady passes on or abdicates,' said the servant.

'But why is your father ruling?' asked Ake.

'Because the gracious queen, First Lady, his wife, died sixty years ago.'

'But they're related,' said Ake.

She began feeling a little grossed out by it.

'It's diluted because the daughter born to the king lays with a human or half elf outside of Relequis. When the male child marries his cousin, he won't be so closely related. Elves struggle to produce with other elves. So, the First Lady will often take other lovers, as does the king,' said the servant.

'How do you know the First Lady's child is always male?' asked Ake.

'Because it always has been.'

'Oh, so Flo is your half-sister, because your father took a lover and had her, but had you with the first lady, who is his cousin/

wife. The first lady is also related to Flo and you. But the first lady is your mother and cousin and Flo's cousin too. Flo is your sister and double cousin too,' said Ake.

'If you look at it from a human view, anyone not fully related, as in having same mother and father, are classed as cousins.'

'Then why did you just class Flo as your sister then?'

'To make it easier for you to make sense of. First Lady always greets me as a cousin.'

'That's why she once mentioned she had no brothers. Where I come from males rule the world. But why do females rule here?' asked Ake.

'Our women are wise, gentle, caring and motherly. They are more prone to the arts of magic, and they bring forth life as Dee once did herself. They have a profound sense of intuition and show their emotion so easily. The men are fighters, protectors. Women have always ruled us and there is never war among our own kind, if there is a problem it is talked over and sorted out. Your men are always fighting among themselves to gain power. We are not! But the First Lady takes advice from her high council, which are all males from the Learned Oak. So, there is balance,' said the servant.

'Wow, all that from one question.' Ake laughed at him.

'The pursuit of knowledge, and love, is the life path of elves. If someone knows the answer to a question, they will gladly answer anyone if they ask. For knowledge is power,' said the servant.

'Ah gee, lighten up already.' Ake grinned at him.

'My skin is the lightest it can get, mistress.'

'Silly, don't you know fun?'

'Yes, mistress, with the servants I take my leisure, not with one of the ever-living ones if I'm not asked to,' said the servant.

'Well, I'm asking you——' Ake stopped in mid-sentence as the lad began to relieve himself of his clothing. Ake blushed and stuttered, 'No, I didn't mean that. I meant fun, play, live a little.'

'I'm sorry, I mistook you, I will give myself a good whipping,' said the young man as he began to dress. 'But first we only have forty minutes to get you ready to see the king and the First Lady who are rejoicing at her being planted, for our line will go on,' said the servant.

'Wouldn't you and your brothers continue it on as well?' asked Ake.

'Yes, the first cousin will, and be given lots of land and security. Second cousin will be captain of the guards. The rest will be high servants and be given medium holdings on the most fertile land and marry when they come of age. The cousins become thanes to the First Lady and only her sustenance and supplies come from these farms. For they are loyal to the crown and will not try and destroy her,' said the servant.

'I thought you were peace loving people.'

'We are, mostly, but there are few confused among us. And if they are caught, they must give up all their daughters to be wives for our clan,' said the servant.

'I thought this was the whole kingdom.'

'No, kingdom of one clan. For example, we are the kingdom and clan of mage elves. Across from us in the forest province is the clan of the forest elves. We trade according to our specialties. We trade magic, they trade wood, forest fruits, certain meats and herbs and the elven healers are employed from them like mages are from us. Now, mistress, we must go.'

'I'm sure we must.' Ake sighed.

The lad let out a strange low whistle and an opening in the stone wall behind Ake appeared.

'By the way, do you have a name? I can't call you lad or you,' said Ake.

The lad smiled for the first time and his whole face lit up in magnificent beauty, like a sole candle in the dead of night. Ake held her breath. *God, he's beautiful.*

'My name is Mikaere, which means one of five sons for there will be two more cousins after me, as my father scryed ahead. I will not always be the youngest. But now we must hurry,' he said.

The two young ones went ahead through the opening where a blind lady waited by a steaming bath with a washcloth and towel. Ake looked around. The room was pure white, windowless and with only a stone bath set in the ground. It was filled with steaming water. The roof itself was square and about ten feet by ten feet. There was one shelf directly in front of them set into the wall. Upon it were six potions in coloured vials. Mikaere bowed to Ake and left. He whistled once more, and the door closed behind him. The old lady beckoned Ake forward as if she could see her. *But that is impossible,* Ake thought. *Her eyes are cloudy with cataracts.*

'Come, mistress, bathe and I will tend you,' called the old lady gently.

Ake stepped down some stone steps into the water, which was luxurious on her skin. The bath was about four feet deep when she was standing, which was okay, for when she sat, it rose to the perfect height for a bath. The old woman bathed Ake with the contents from the vials and washed her hair as well.

—⁓—

Meanwhile, the freak show caused by the Empon Seato was still playing when Lan had woken the next day. He sighed and cast *Dispel,* and the bodies of the once humans disappeared as if they'd never been. Lan cast the spell *Teleport Other* which allowed him to remove all the bodies of the scum that came and destroyed Caelestis to the bottom of a cliff. Lan was so weary, but he knew he had to finish before the madness took him. These would be the last spells he cast for a decade.

Lan cast *Quake*, which opened a huge pit in the gardens of Caelestis. He then teleported the bodies of all the students, servants and friends of Caelestis into the pit and closed it again. Lan then cast *Stone Form*, which erected a huge block of stone that lay flat on the pit. The next spell he cast was *Star Scry*, which told him the names of all the dead as he wrote on a parchment scroll. These spells took a lot of energy and time to cast.

Lan's last spell was *Engrave*, which engraved the crest of Caelestis on the stone and all the names of the dead.

CHAPTER THIRTY-SIX

Ake looked at herself in the mirror. *I can't face the crowds dressed in the way of my tribe.* Her blonde tresses flowed down her back. She wore gold anklets and bracelets engraved with various tribal signs. Her only article of clothing was a skirt of deer hide. Her long locks of hair at the front covered some of her cleavage, but the blind servant finished the outfit by clasping three heavy gold chains around her neck. Ake breathed a sigh of relief.

The chains were long and sufficiently heavy that they hung down over her chest. The woman brought a chain of gold links which she used to join the chains together and clasp around Ake's mid-back. Now it looked like Ake wore a crop top of pure gold. Then the lady brought deer skin moccasins, which Ake put on.

The old lady brought her a light mask made of gold, woven with various symbols. Ake put this on, wondering why. It started at the forehead and ended across her cheekbones. It was fine and very light. It had large eyeholes and fit snugly and didn't cause any disruption to her sight. It was delicately moulded around the nose and the lady closed the silver clasps at the back. Then, to Ake's amazement, the lady placed Empon Seato in her hands and placed Het's amulet around Ake's neck.

This had been her birthday present from Het. The amulet was made of stone and engraved on it were strange runes and a white leopard in full sprint.

A slow whistle opened the door which she had come through and Mikaere stood waiting. His face had that serious look again, but he held a glass of cold water which she drank thankfully. Placing it on her bedside table, they then proceeded to the main hall.

CHAPTER THIRTY-SEVEN

Lan whimpered in his sleep. It was dark outside, and the lost souls of the dead elves wandered the hallways of Caelestis, bellowing their pain and outrage. Lan woke, rested, but his eyes betrayed the madness that raged within. *Must gather food for winter,* said his animalistic thoughts. *Gather food.*

Lan, or what was left of Lan, stood and wandered through the halls, crying out to the ghosts to come and talk with him, forgive him.

The ghost of a young elf boy, who had been fatally speared, spoke, 'Forgive what, friend? You did the best you could.'

But it wasn't enough, cried Lan's soul. *I am not good enough. Hanton was wrong, Dane was wrong. I'm not strong enough for the years ahead. Not when the world's pressures keep forcing me to give up.*

'It's not up to us to free your soul, we will fade and be no more,' said the souls of the dead elven children.

There must be a way to let your souls exist, the gods cannot be so cruel. His heart cried.

A strange humming sound came from behind Lan and where before there was no one, now stood Bel.

'Hi Lan, how you doing?' Bel spoke to him as if he was an old friend.

'What the ... who are you?' asked the confused Lan.

'I'm Bel and I'm here gathering unattached elven souls.' Bel laughed, his red eyes sparkling.

Lan looked at Bel strangely. He was red-skinned, red-haired and it was as if he were a living flame. Bel was well muscled and naked. He was amazingly charismatic, despite his strange appearance and Lan blushed, finding himself attracted to the god, despite the fact he had never been attracted to his own sex before.

'Hey boy, you're allowed to be attracted to me, I'm that good.' Bel winked at Lan.

'Elvish souls; do not make them vanish,' said Lan.

'Who said anything about making anyone vanish?' Bel grinned at Lan.

'But elvish souls can only be held to the physical plane if——' said Lan.

Bel interrupted. 'If they've loved someone. Whooo, the physical plane. Hey youngling, it's not all it's cracked up to be. And I know you humans and elves think you know everything. The truth is, when the earth no longer exists you'll come home to, wait for it, to mummy and daddy. I crack myself up sometimes.'

'So, the elves won't vanish?' asked Lan.

'As if they never existed? What do you take us for? We are not the baddies who don't care about what they create. You elves stay in the stone circles helping humans and making love while the unattached ones go to the open plains in the sky to hunt and be free while they wait for the rest of you lot,' said Bel.

Bel grinned and pulled out a soul collecting stick and spoke to the spirits. 'Come on you lot, before Drianna tries to entrap you for her evil purposes.' The spirits gathered around him.

'Bye elfling,' said Bel.

The humming occurred again as Bel disappeared.

Lan, in shock, went back to his cavern to think. When he got there, he wrote down what he had seen and thought, and the madness left him for an hour.

CHAPTER THIRTY-EIGHT

Ake approached the throne and trumpets sounded as the seneschal announced her. 'To the court and the crown I announce Telewanake, granddaughter of Sorendee and Dee, child of Gepatok and Melowy, daughter of the tribe Crykenuak.'

The trumpets stopped their sounding and Ake was ushered forth by the man on the throne assumed to be the king. He wore a simple coronet of silver and he sat on the smaller of two thrones made of oak and covered in green velvet. His charisma had mellowed a bit in his old age but the son, Mikaere, had the look of him. His father's hair was thinning and grey. But he was muscular and dressed in the robes of a mage. They were well made, blue in colour and richly adorned. The seneschal continued in Elvish after the trumpets sounded again, 'Announcing First Lady Elder Flower, only daughter of King Serenade and First Lady Kenshay! Heir to the crown of the Mage Elves.'

Flo entered, dressed the way she had when she had gone to Het on the night of the graduation ceremony, except she wore a mask like Ake's that caught the sunlight from one of the six windows. Flo walked past Ake without even looking at her. Ake quickly surveyed the room, it wasn't huge, about the size of the main hall in Caelestis. There were six trumpeters behind her, dressed in gold leggings and tunics, while from their trumpets hung a small banner depicting a white leopard in full sprint and the same strange runic symbols as on Ake's amulet. The only carpet was red velvet and led from the thrones to the two heavy mahogany doors where two guards in chain mail, armed with pikes and sword at hip, blocked the entrance.

Flo was seated and the seneschal stood next to the king's throne. Four banners, depicting an oak tree crossed with the Mbel Daione on black, hung at the start and finish of the windows on either side. Then the king spoke, and Ake turned her concentration back on him.

'Child, why do you just stand there idly?' asked the king.

Ake thought she should do something and bowed. The king acknowledged it and beckoned her forward.

'Come here child, sit by me on the step,' said the king.

Ake proceeded forward and did so, noticing the king's eyes were kind.

'Sir, why am I here and where is my mystic?' asked Ake.

The king's eyes sparkled, and he laughed.

'And by the gods, why am I masked?' Ake looked at him in annoyance.

The king guffawed.

'Seneschal and guards, take your leave and wait outside so my daughter, niece and I may talk.' Old King Serenade grinned.

'Niece, how?' asked Ake.

'Shh young one and listen. My mother had me fathered by your mother's father. Making your mother my half-sister,' said Serenade.

'How? My grandfather would be dead unless he——'

The old king interrupted. 'Teja was an elf from here sent to renew the blood in that tribe from generations past. He went there to gain a wife and ended up a shaman, forsaking his elven heritage,' said Serenade.

'Who was the father of your cousin whom you married?' asked Ake.

'You politely asked a question so I must answer? Dun Norix, my chief of the elven druid council,' said Serenade.

'Well, I see blood is kept in the family, isn't it.' Ake dug her nails into her palms.

'The blood is diluted enough so that no birth defects can occur. Many royal families do it so loyalty remains to the throne through blood,' said Serenade.

'Is that Dun Norix also known as Dane who is father to other children? So, he wasn't loyal to Old Ma,' said Ake.

'Elven lore states he must lay with a First Lady if she chooses,' said the King.

'That's barbaric,' said Ake.

'No more than your human kings and queens. And besides, this was before he met his half human wife,' said Serenade.

Ake started crying, her respect for Dane dwindling.

'Calm yourself child. He is only male after all and isn't it natural for men and women to lay together? He was not taken at the time. I assure you, as soon as he met his wife, he lay with no other women. Do not judge someone who is only guilty of living and the weaknesses that come with it,' said the King.

'But he is a druid,' said Ake.

'He wasn't a druid then, just a carefree youth, and elves love to lay with humans and elves just as much as you humans do. Besides, from all of this comes the fact that the blood that runs in your veins is from loyal men and women who loved dearly and paid for it, sadly. Don't judge whom people should love when you have not experienced it firsthand.' Serenade gently brushed away Ake's tears. 'Besides, at least you have some living relatives. In your human terms, Elder Flower here is your half first cousin and——'

Ake interrupted. 'Lan is my second cousin or something. It's just too complicated. And Orilan is my third cousin or such, and loyal to that bitch Drianna. And if I have family on my side, I might be able to defeat her by using family heirlooms because of that blood.'

'Very good. I don't think we can defeat her, but we might be able to change her ways with force. To ease your worries, I will explain. Lan's link to you is via marriage only. Lan is related to Flo as her mother was his half-sister. You are related to Flo as I am your mother's half-brother. The shaman, your grandfather, and his wife were not related to Lan in any way. While you both may be directly blood related to Flo, as I am your uncle and Flo is his niece, I am not a blood relative of his, I would be his brother-in-law by marriage only in human terms. Orilan is not your cousin, but he would be Flo's first cousin. The druids and elves wanted to build a network powerful and loyal enough to both you and Lan. Now, let's eat, you must be famished,' he said.

'I am. But two more questions,' said Ake.

'Oh dear.' Serenade feigned mock horror.

'How old are you, Flo and Dane? And how long has Dane been a druid?' asked Ake.

'Wow, three questions in one. I am five hundred human years, my wife's father is fifteen hundred years and Elder Flower is a baby at sixty-three years,' said the king.

'Father.' Flo gave Serenade a disapproving glance.

'Ah, you can never please your offspring.' Serenade pouted.

Both the women laughed.

'Another thing, Telewanake, people live in small communities miles apart. So, a lot of close relatives occur. And Dane has been a druid since he was four hundred years old. But enough. Seneschal,' said Serenade.

'Please wait. Lan will need me, when can I go home?' asked Ake.

'I have forbidden it. The monsters will look for you as you have come of age. You are not strong enough yet. With Lan suffering they will think the threat has ceased,' said Serenade.

'You can't keep me here. I need to be with the man I love. I can't allow him to be Drianna's target just so I can be safe.' Ake's eyes filled with tears.

'We are mage elves. You will not be able to cross the barrier without our help,' said the king.

'So, both Lan and I are prisoners to this damn prophecy again. He is alone and suffering. Do you think that's fair on him?' asked Ake.

'We are tasked to keep you safe,' said the king.

The seneschal arrived and Ake was escorted to dinner.

Chapter Thirty-Nine

Ake spent the next ten years training in unarmed combat, sword play and magery with Flo and Serenade. On several occasions Ake had attempted to cross the barrier and sustained burns, much to her chagrin. Over time Flo and Ake became inseparable, and Flo was the sister Ake never had.

When she was first told about Het, Ake screamed and ran to her room and stayed there for three days without food, crying and remembering the boy that had been a brother to her. Over the years the pain eased. Flo's babies were born, identical twin boys, and celebrated as a miracle.

Meanwhile, Lan's unnatural madness overtook him. He lived like an animal, barely bathing, sleeping or eating but the pain lessened and in a few years Dane came to his son, and they bonded and Dane nursed him back to health.

A shadow, a recognisable darkness, was growing in the west. Soon terrible famine and drought ran rampant. Disease and starvation killed elf and human alike. Orilan grew strong and deadly. Shadow Masters laughed gleefully as their time came steadily nearer.

CHAPTER FORTY

Drianna looked at her spawn of dark beliefs and laughed gleefully at the result. 'You are great, my child. You are beautiful. Vampyr, are you ready to take what's rightfully yours.'

Orilan laughed with her.

'She will not even recognise me when I take her and give her child to you. Then my evil father will pay for what he has done,' Orilan said.

Drianna looked at the man in front of her, his hair was now a sandy blond and his eyes a stunning dark brown. He stood about five foot nine and already muscles were showing.

The elvish in him can alter his eyes and hair over time. With mere humans, it seems their eyes, skin and, almost always, their hair do not change with time. Plus, he has consumed a part of his father's flesh and lifeblood. Soon the lad will almost look like him and be able to fool the woman. Drianna laughed aloud in glee. Her plan was so perfect. The woman was so in love with the elfling Lan that she would jump into Vampyr's arms without thought, only thinking that it could be none other than her love.

'Vampyr. We must allow your hair to grow, and you can no longer ride your beloved hellhound, for you must learn to ride a horse,' said Drianna.

'Do I have to, great one?' asked Orilan.

'Yes, you must be like him in almost every way!' Drianna growled at him impatiently.

'Yes, great one. I am sorry for my impudence.' Orilan bowed.

'You once did well, bringing me the head of the griffin,' said Drianna.

'Yes, great one. Your compliments honour me, but I don't deserve them,' said Orilan.

'Yes, I know I am great.' Drianna picked up a jewelled mirror and grinned at her reflection.

'Now, Vampyr, time for you to know a woman,' said Drianna.

'I have,' said Orilan.

'Silence! I remember that woman you seduced then drained two weeks ago. You need to be gentle and seductive with Sorendee's grandchild, otherwise she'll know something's terribly wrong,' said Drianna.

'What about the scars on his face and ankle, and the missing appendage?' asked Orilan.

'An hour glamoire potion should do. Remember, after the deed is done, we want her to know you're not Trebrelan.' Drianna spat Lan's name.

'So, afterwards she'll never go near him due to her shame of running to anyone that looks like him. That way my downfall will never occur. Now, this is my daughter, mistress of seduction. Vampyr, I give you, Fate.'

Orilan's eyes widened in shock. The lass looked no older than twenty. Black hair cascaded down her slim, tanned body. Her eyes were dark brown and her teeth glinted bright white and perfect in the candlelight.

Orilan stammered, 'I thought she was older, like ten thousand years or something.'

'She is but her body will never change,' said Drianna.

Orilan watched as the lass came and took hold of his hand. Ori's body was overcome with desire. The woman merely laughed and when she spoke her voice was as light as air.

'Like all men. But I will not harm you as I do other men I seduce, just teach you the secrets of the bedroom.'

Fate led him out of the throne room. Vampyr surrendered to her.

PART TWO: SHADOW OF EVIL

Chapter Forty-One

The waves crashed against the sharp grey rocks. The body of a nine-year-old half elf lay on a small raft of oak lashed together with vines. Under the child lay dry hay, lightly covered in oil awaiting a flaming arrow released from taut bow. His mother's tears fell on the little one's angelic face as she kissed him and placed a wreath of white flowers around his small skull. A large group of elves were gathered, their unearthly wails assaulted the night air. Three guards had to hold the mother back as the little raft was pushed out to sea.

The mother wailed and tore at her hair. Falling to her knees she remembered his cherub-like stature. His sea green eyes and chestnut hair, the first time she held her little son and his fingers gripped hers as he screamed and drew his first breath. The pain she went through to hold him in her arms and now the pain of his loss. The mother remembered his first word and steps and the little tear-shaped birthmark on his arm the same as his father's.

'Falcon! No, don't take my son. Don't send him from my loving arms,' the young woman screamed.

Flo felt the hot, bitter tears roll down her cheeks and wiped them away. It was hard to maintain royal decorum when her heart was broken. Flo thought about Falcon's twin brother, Hau, and the surprise he had been, born fifteen minutes later.

He looked identical to his brother, minus the birthmark. She named him Hau, or spiritual essence, because surely there was one between the two. He lay dying of the same disease that had killed her eldest, crying for his mother and his brother.

The Astazian plague had finally reached Relequis. Astazian Merzeto the high mystic of Caelestis three thousand years before, had discovered it. The disease was magical in origin, an abstract of all pure magic. It slowly soured everything on the inside except the bones. The outside of the victim remained as if nothing had happened. But it was only diagnosable by a mage and not curable by non-magical healing. The scroll specifying the cure had been accidentally buried with Astazian. Their only hope was Lan, for he would know where Astazian was buried and could magically uncover the scroll. They had sent for him. Lan was due tomorrow, maybe Hau would live.

Unbeknown to Elder Flower, Drianna had set this upon them and now Orilan was ready. Lan would arrive but so would Orilan.

Twang! The archer's arrow caught the little raft alight. Ake's eyes swam with tears.

Ake sobbed and went to Flo. They held each other in silence as the little raft disappeared over the horizon, with their five body-guards standing a short distance away, long after Serenade and the other elves returned to the castle.

Chapter Forty-Two

Lan lifted the message from the pigeon's beak and quickly read it through. *Poor Falcon and the many others who have passed on.* He went to his cavern below and blew dust from a scroll and checked to see if it was the right one.

Lan saddled his stallion and teleported himself and the animal to the outskirts of Relequis. No mere human or elf could teleport within Relequis, for its walls were protected against the like. An hour's hard riding to reach it, hopefully in time.

———

'Perfect. You are divine. You look almost exactly like him. One last thing, take this scroll which will cure that infernal child of Elder Flower's so it seems you are him. Read it and look relieved. Check the boy's forehead and hug that elven girl and give the king best wishes. Before you leave, drink this potion.' Drianna handed him a small coal black vial. 'In it contains a crushed fertility draught and glamoire potion. Go now, you will be there two hours before him.'

Orilan heard Drianna's laugh as he was teleported into Relequis, for the spell wards were no match against a goddess weaving magic. Orilan swallowed the contents of the vial in one gulp and threw it away. His flesh began to contort as the appropriate scars appeared. He wiggled his right index finger, amused that half appeared missing.

—ᴠᴠᴠ—

A knock sounded on the door leading into the nursery. Flo sat holding little Hau when a man entered.

Is that really Lan? Maybe it's just that time has changed all of us, but something doesn't seem right about him. Ah well, as long as Hau can be cured. Orilan proceeded to do all the things he had been told to. *It is Lan,* thought Flo. *It couldn't be anyone else.* Tears of happiness streamed down her face as little Hau sat up and cried for his mother.

'I must go find Telewanake now Elder Flower,' said Orilan.

That doesn't seem right. He would call Ake, Ake.

'Hang on you,' said Flo.

Whomp! Orilan hit Flo across the side of the head with the hilt of his dagger. Little Hau screamed but Orilan gagged the child and tied his little hands together. The little boy's chest heaved with exhaustion, but he could still breathe.

Orilan thought about how tasty the both of them looked but fought back the urge to sink his teeth into their necks. He left the room, informing the guards that Elder Flower wanted time alone with her now healthy son. He asked if they knew where his lover Telewanake might be. Assuming this was the famous mystic Trebrelan the guards said she was seeking solitude at the edge of the castle grounds. He followed their directions towards the castle grounds.

CHAPTER FORTY-THREE

Ake wandered through the gardens at the edge of the castle grounds, hoping Lan would arrive soon and hoping Hau, her beloved cousin, would be alright. *Poor little Falcon,* she thought. *I loved him as dearly.* A shadow appeared at the corner of her eye, and she turned sharply and slipped over. Ake looked up at the figure standing over her.

Drianna screamed in Orilan's mind. *'Call her Ake like he does. Otherwise, she'll know you are not he.'*

'Are you okay Ake?' Orilan offered Ake a hand up.

'Lan is …' She stared at him.

'Hau is fine. God, I haven't seen you in many years and I could eat you right up,' said Orilan.

'Lan, are you okay?' Ake's eyes challenged him.

Orilan looked at the woman. She was tall for a female of elven decent, five foot six. He was five foot nine, a little taller than his five foot eight father. But she probably wouldn't be able to tell. Ake was slim but full in the right areas. She was dressed in ageing yellow robes and her hair was braided down her back. He knew he better answer.

'Yes, now I'm finally with you. I want to kiss you,' said Orilan.

Before Ake could pull back, he was doing so. Ake tried to resist, but Orilan was too strong and rough. Much rougher and muscular than Lan had ever been. *That's not Lan.* Her mind and heart screamed. *Get away.* The fake Lan looked down at her and she noticed his eyes weren't as dark as the real Lan's, they only held wickedness where Lan's had been full of kindness.

Suddenly the scars disappeared, and the missing appendage reappeared. Ake tried to thrust him away and scream, but it died in her mouth as the fake Lan's teeth sank into her throat.

—◦∿∿◦—

'*Ahhh!*' Drianna screamed, her voice echoing in Orilan's mind. '*How could she break through that?*'

With a little effort, Orilan blocked his thoughts from Drianna. *Maybe that is what humans and elves call love, a bond strong enough to break through the spell of a goddess?* Orilan was confused. *It doesn't feel evil. Just like when I am in pure pleasure drinking the blood of others, their heart beating in time with mine until they die, their faces peaceful. Don't think, don't feel, they are the evil ones.* Orilan wasn't so sure anymore.

He drained just enough blood so the girl was weak and not able to scream or struggle. Should he continue this, or shouldn't he? Orilan looked at the woman slumped in his arms and noticed the moonlight catch her hair. Her big blue eyes had closed, and the colour drained from her face. Her complexion was now ghost-like in the moonlight. He flicked through a few memories he had gleaned from that little taste of her and against his own will his heart took it upon itself to fall in love with her.

'Ah,' he said.

He must do what he was sent to do, or Drianna would seek him out as a traitor and kill him. But would she even know? For the first time in his life, he wanted to rebel against Drianna. But even now Drianna was breaking the barriers of his shield. He manipulated Ake's mind into thinking she had been with the man she loved before discovering the facade. Using a little bit of his own abilities, he tricked his mind into believing he had been with her.

At this moment, Drianna broke down his shield and encountered the joint thoughts and laughed with glee. The jolt to Orilan's mind made him believe the act had occurred and he could no longer unjumble the truth. Drianna teleported him home.

CHAPTER FORTY-FOUR

Lan arrived too late. As he entered the castle drawbridge the guards lowered their pikes at him, uncertainty clouding their eyes, for they were sure they had let Lan in before. Panting, Flo approached them at a sprint, her mask absent and blood trickling down the side of her head. The guards averted their eyes. King Serenade followed at her heels.

'Let him in. Lan, Orilan was here and he … he attacked Ake. Mikaere found her thirty minutes ago after he came in from bringing in the unicorns,' said Flo.

'Are Ake and Hau de …' Lan couldn't continue he was so numb inside.

'Hau was cured then tied up and I was knocked out. Ake isn't dead but her neck was bleeding and near the jugular are two puncture marks a thumbnail apart. And, well … she says was taken advantage of,' said Flo.

'Take me to her, please!' His body shook and his fists clenched the reigns tighter.

The guards moved aside, and Flo, Serenade and Lan hurried away.

―◈―

Ake lay whimpering and curled in a ball on her bed. A guard was at her door and a kindly old elven lady was fussing over her, trying to get her to talk about her ordeal and tempting her with sweet foods.

Serenade took his leave when they arrived at Ake's quarters and so did Flo who had already cried with Ake and tried to console her.

Flo knew that only time could heal the poor woman. Ake had been through so much. *Dear little mage.* All those years at Caelestis and her training here had proven her to be a mage. Ake had received the qualification two weeks ago and was ready to return to her mystic but now Orilan had attacked her.

Flo walked away as the anger fought for control of her. *What if Ake is carrying an innocent child? Would the mystic reject Ake? Or does he genuinely love Ake as I do Het? Oh, Het, if only you were here. You'd know what to say and do. But this will truly test the elfling's character.*

Lan stood at Ake's door, watching Serenade and Flo leave. He was still numb inside but anger at Drianna and his hate for his offspring began to build.

Bloody castle. Bloody elves. Even in my madness I could have protected Ake better. He pounded his fist into his open palm. *At least she would have been with me day and night. What if Ake is pregnant? Would I be able to accept the child, my grandchild?* He paced, clenching his fists. *Of course, I'd have to, it would be Ake's. I might even be able to bring myself to love it. If only I had encouraged my mother further to get Goriard to take the right herbs Orilan would never had been born and Ake wouldn't have been harmed.* He paused in front of the door. *No, I can't think like that.* He'd been taught to revere life. *What harm is there in a newborn child that will not be stolen by the evil ones? For I'll make sure of it.*

He turned to face the door; his mind made up. *As soon as Ake's well, I'm handfasting her to me and then taking her home.*

He sighed and tried to stop the tears from falling. But he couldn't. Angrily, he swiped them away. *You fool, be strong.* He pushed open the door and threw back his hood.

Ake turned at the sound of the door. Her heart skipped a beat. For this was the real Lan.

The elven lady bowed to Lan and kissed Ake on the forehead. 'Poor young thing, little quarter elf. Don't they suffer! Not knowing which legacy to follow, but their hearts win in the end,' she muttered as she left, brushing away a few tears of her own.

'Ake ...' The rest of the words died on his lips as he remembered Goriard and his own violation. He walked over and just stood watching her, waiting for her consent for him to be there for her.

'Lan,' she whispered.

That's all he needed. He bent and swept her up in his arms. He sat on the bed with her in his lap, her head resting against his shoulder. Ake's fingers brushed the scars on his cheek and his tears flowed freely. She wiped them away.

'Lan, say everything will be okay. Please tell me so.'

'It will be dearest, it will be.'

'I finally get to hold my mystic the way I wanted to. Lan, Het once told me something.'

'What sweetheart?' asked Lan.

'My intended would be a child of a handmaiden of Dee. Lan, that is you?'

'My mother was a handmaiden of Dee ... Ah, the book of Hanton's.'

'I read that,' said Ake.

'How?' asked Lan.

'Remember the Shadow Masters?' Ake grinned through her tears.

'Oh yes, and you ended up down there and managed to get the diary.'

'Lan, you know about Tok, don't you?' asked Ake.

'Yeah, he turned traitor,' hissed Lan.

'Lan, you know Orilan … attacked me and …' Ake wept.

Lan caressed her cheek, brushing at the tears. 'Yes, Ake I know.'

'Will you still want me?'

'Of course. I love you. What made you think I wouldn't?'

Ake clung to him, relief flooding her face.

'I'd been with someone else.'

'Don't fret. How is that your fault?'

'I tried to fight him.' Her tears continued to fall, and she clung to Lan.

'I know you would have. Oh god, my little darling.'

They were silent for what seemed like hours but was only twenty minutes, just savouring the comfort of one another. That night they slept in the shelter of each other's arms.

CHAPTER FORTY-FIVE

Two weeks later, Ake and Lan walked hand in hand in the forest of Relequis. They were catching up on what they had missed. It was a wintry morning and the leaves of trees and plants glistened with early morning dew. Weak sunlight filtered through the gaping canopy and clouds promised rain that evening.

'One thing I still don't get, your mother, how was she half elf if the blood of your tribe hasn't mixed with elves in centuries?' asked Lan.

Ake briefly told him what King Serenade had told her.

'I knew how Flo was my niece or, as elves say, cousin. Dane told me a year ago when he nursed me back to health,' said Lan.

'Nursed you back to health?' Ake looked at him in concern.

Lan quickly told Ake of the state he'd been in. One night he'd even considered doing himself in. Ake shuddered at the thought.

Lan looked at her gently and said seriously, 'Ake, I'm not leaving you alone ever again. I can't.'

'I don't want you to. Lan, what if I'm to have a babe? I don't want a child to anyone but you,' sobbed Ake, tears welling up in her eyes.

Lan tried to embrace her, but she turned away from him.

'How long have you felt this way Ake?' Lan asked.

'Ever since I read the diary, shared my first kiss and came to terms that it was you I wanted to marry,' she said sadly.

Lan let out a drawn-out breath.

'That long hey. But you were a mere youth,' said Lan.

'So were you elfling.'

'I know that now, but thanks for reminding me. Ake, I'll tell you what's going to happen. I'm going to marry you when the time is right. And you do not have to have a child if you don't want to,' he said.

'Lan, I love you.' She turned and stared at him, her eyes full of love.

'I know you do. Ake, come here, let me hold you. All right?'

Ake turned and moved closer to him, and he wrapped his arms around her.

'You know what?' asked Ake seriously.

'What?'

'We've never been with anyone of our own accord. Only forced to take someone else or have been taken,' said Ake.

Lan looked tenderly down at her, tears welled up in his eyes and he nodded his agreement.

CHAPTER FORTY-SIX

The day after Ake's attack Drianna ushered in Orilan.

'Did you do the deed?' asked Drianna.

Orilan remembered the sweet young thing he believed he had lain with.

'Certainly did,' he said.

'Good, now come here and lay with me, dark one,' said Drianna.

Orilan thought of Drianna's hissing voice and voluptuous body. To him, Ake had been the essence of femininity, with the musical quality in Ake's voice, the slightly pointed ears and delicate cheekbones.

That's when he saw Drianna for what she truly was, an old thought, a dying story waiting for forgiveness and clinging, bored and desperate, to the weak race of man for her crown. Before his eyes a new world opened. He saw the crypt and the creatures within for what they truly were. For Drianna had cast a disguise spell on everything so that it would look pure and perfect to Orilan.

Orilan looked at the now dispelled guards. Before the guards had looked like crusaders dressed gallantly in shining new leather, swords at the ready. Their kind, but sharp eyes regarding him and the goddess. Now the poor man saw them for what they truly were, and he gasped and stood frozen in shock. Drianna didn't seem to notice; she was preening again. Then an unfamiliar sound of creaking bones was behind him, and he turned to meet whatever it was. His once unearthly beautiful pegasus mount was so hideous he backed away. He would normally pet and tend his mount. Drianna looked up in annoyance.

'What are you doing? Don't play with Bemmin now, come here and tend my needs!' She glared at him.

Orilan looked up at Drianna and was disgusted with what he saw. For underneath the glamoire Drianna was nothing but an old crone hoping against hope that she would be eternally young. Her grey hair was tied in a plait down her back with layers of white warring for control. Her face had countless wrinkles and her mouth held a few blackened stubs.

Gods, he wondered, *what would that Fate girl look like now? And she, Drianna, wants me? Disgusting. I won't, not after Ake.*

'Vampyr, come here and satisfy me,' said Drianna.

'No,' said Orilan.

Drianna looked at him in astonishment and then anger. 'What did you say to me twerp?'

'Which part don't you understand? The N or the O? Do I have to repeat it again?' asked Orilan.

'What did that whore do to you?' hissed Drianna. 'I bet she took you over, not the other way around.'

Orilan, angered, lunged at and tried to strike Drianna. Strangely, that comment had hurt his feelings and he gasped, surprised at his new emotions.

Drianna laughed gleefully, amused at Orilan's failing attempt to come within one foot of her. Orilan's eyes widened in shock as he was flung against the wall when Drianna simply lifted her hand and spoke a few unusual words. Ori slid down the wall, raising a hand to the back of his head. He was winded and his breathing laboured.

Orilan opened his eyes and looked at his hand covered in blood. He drew himself to his feet and had to steady himself against the wall as a wave of dizziness threatened to make him lose his upright position. Drianna's hideous hyena laugh rang in his ears.

'You dare try and take me on you mere half-breed boy? Pathetic. After all I've done for you, you dare rebel against me?'

The dizziness subsided and Orilan faced Drianna bravely.

'I think what you have done to me is far worse. Taking me away from love and warping me into a kind of demon. A vampyr.'

Drianna laughed again, stood up and glided towards him.

'I may be old but I'm more powerful than a little obnoxious elven hybrid.'

Before Orilan could react, she had her old, gnarled hands around his neck and had lifted him in the air above her head with her unnatural strength. He began to choke on his own saliva.

'Do you beg mercy and forgiveness, scum?' she asked.

'Never,' he choked out.

'What?' hissed Drianna.

Orilan was starting to lose consciousness from lack of air, but he fought to gain control. He grabbed her hands with his and was able to release the pressure for a few moments.

'Well?' Drianna screeched.

'Never,' said Orilan.

'Ahhh!' Drianna screamed and threw Orilan across the room in a rage. Orilan lost consciousness before he hit the floor.

CHAPTER FORTY-SEVEN

Orilan awoke and opened his bloodshot eyes. He looked around at his gloomy cell. It was four feet by five feet in length and width. A wooden pallet with mouldy straw was to his left, held to the grimy walls by jutting chains. Outside the iron bars in front of him was a horned guard. Thankfully, its face could not be seen in the light from the sole burning torch.

Nine months in here with just the blood of rats to live off had seen Orilan shrink in size and constitution. His lungs wheezed every time he breathed, and he smelt like something so foul even he was appalled at himself. His clothing had rotted through long ago and he awoke from a fever every morning, sweat pouring off his naked body. Orilan rose and stumbled over to the pallet. The lack of hygiene wasn't a concern at the moment. Orilan dropped onto it and closed his eyes.

The sound of rusty bolts sliding back grated at Orilan's pounding head. His eyes flickered open to see Fate looking down at him. Age had not consumed her. Fate still looked as good as she had before Orilan had seen through Drianna's powerful glamoire.

'What do you want?' Orilan managed to force out.

'To help you.'

'Why should I trust you?' hissed Orilan.

'You have nobody else, and I want to see my mother defeated so I can rule the underworld,' said Fate.

'I need blood.'

'I know.' Fate offered her wrist. 'You only need the littlest amount, for I am a half goddess,' said Fate.

So is Ake. Orilan sunk his teeth into her wrist. A sigh of pure bliss escaped his lips. He drew in the gushing red life force.

'Enough,' said Fate.

Orilan didn't listen. He drew in the life force, savouring the icy chill of dark magic.

'Enough!' screamed Fate and dropped to her knees.

Never again. Never will I let the children of the dark use me. He let out a guttural laugh and withdrew. 'Yes, you are half human, powerful but not indestructible.'

He felt her heart slowing, then he sunk his teeth into her neck and finished her off. His broken nose healed and corrected itself into its old aristocratic shape. His seeping head injury congealed and closed leaving scabbed blood. Orilan felt the power building in his blood. His vision took on full elvish night sight. He looked at his hands and felt the power of dark magic instil itself within.

'I must kill my father; his blood is powerful too.' Orilan laughed gleefully.

A horned guard felt it's way over to investigate. The magic consumed Ori contorting his innards completely beyond repair. He laughed as *Dark Fire* burst from his hands engulfing the guard, a pile of rank ash taking its place.

Orilan teleported himself away from the crypt to Caelestis. Orilan would wait and learn to use his new powers.

CHAPTER FORTY-EIGHT

The orange sun rose against a brightly coloured sky over Relequis. Nine months had passed since Orilan had encountered Ake and she was healing well emotionally.

Lan and Ake had ridden unicorns together, held each other every night, and picnicked on moonlit nights in a field of wildflowers. Lan had been officially courting her.

Lan was nervous. He stood on a hillock lost in thought. He had tied his long hair back and made an effort to look his best. He wore a short-sleeved white shirt with a high neckline, golden thread laced up the front. Lan hated anything close to his throat but tolerated it to look his best. He shuffled his feet in the dirt, flicking up small clouds of dust onto the shining, freshly polished, black boots. He sighed and slipped his hands into the pockets of his black trousers and felt for the small velvet bag, reassured it was still there.

He saw Ake approach the hillock, she was smiling and laughing with Flo. Lan had asked Flo to invite Ake on a walk so she would be unaware of his intentions. Ake always dressed well when out with others he noticed. She wore a light blue dress that ended at her ankles. The collar and short sleeves were line with white lace. Her hair was pulled back in a simple braid, and she wore small golden slippers. Flo made an excuse of forgetting something and hurried away.

Lan drew his breath in sharply and headed down the hill.

Ake looked up at his approach, she appeared confused, and Lan laughed. He didn't know how humans proposed and had decided to do it the elven way.

'Lan, what is going on?' she asked.

'Come with me.' Lan grabbed her hand without looking at her and proceeded to walk quickly towards the forest. He stopped at the unusual entrance and stared at one of two paths. A natural archway graced one passage made up of reckless branches entwining themselves in a bid for power. The other path sported a beautiful elven-made white arch with a small silver gate. Wildflowers grew over the arch unchecked. Lan turned and stared at Ake his eyes full of concern. He began to recite the elven rite of marriage.

'You once agreed to be my lover. Would you be willing to be my mate? This is not an easy path and is often fraught with situations beyond our control. Will you join me on that path?' Lan gestured to both arches. 'These paths and the trials within will test our love and compatibility. If you agree, make your choice.'

Ake looked at him in shock. She blushed and looked down at her feet lost for words.

This will be a real test for a human woman. She has not been prepared for this rite. I hope it isn't too hard for her. Lan knew elven maidens were given some information about the rite when they came of age. No elf had dared bring a human to perform an elven marriage ritual, it was considered taboo. Elven and human mates often married under human laws. Lan intended to perform both.

Ake looked at him and smiled nervously. 'I accept your love and agree to test mine.'

Lan grinned. *How did she know the correct answer. I wonder if Flo or Dane taught her?*

Without stopping to investigate the arches further, Ake headed to the natural archway. She clambered through the branches, which snagged her dress. Some of the lace tore and branches scratched her fair skin. Lan followed without any difficulty, his natural agility gifting him easy access. Above them the canopy blocked out the sun as ancient leaves and branches wrestled for space. Lan's elven vision adjusted, and he could see quite well. Ake stumbled on the dark path.

Lan pulled her back and dragged her behind him, picking up a small branch. He used it to test the ground and disturbed the leafy entrance. A dark pit loomed before them.

Ake mumbled a few words. The area was lit briefly as she tried to conjure some light. Lan countered the spell and they were left in complete darkness.

'Magic is forbidden in this trial,' said Lan.

'I never read that,' said Ake.

Lan laughed and it echoed in the darkness. 'I wondered how you knew how to reply. No magic Ake, this is a test of how well we work together to overcome any darkness that may threaten our future marriage. A real test for mage elves who use magic for nearly everything, but not the Sidhe.'

Lan grinned at her, and Ake giggled. Lan couldn't help himself and hugged her. *She is so cute.* It took all his self-control not to kiss her. He wasn't pushing any affection on her after the events concerning Orilan. She pushed him away and her eyes glittered with mischief.

Ake took a leap of faith and barely cleared the small pit. She stumbled on landing and fell down on the path giggling. Lan cleared the distance easily and helped her up.

'Ake, you need to be more cautious,' he warned.

Ake let go of his hand and sprinted down the path. She turned and grinned at him. 'Catch me if you want me to be yours.' Ake suddenly disappeared into the darkness.

Lan swore and stopped walking. He remained still and listened intently. She was very skilled at using the shadows to conceal herself.

Dane had told him that Ake had learnt some thievery skills from Het. *Hell.* He felt in his pocket. The little bag was gone. He shook his head in annoyance. *Well, there goes that surprise.* He sighed and thought he heard gentle breathing nearby. He moved silently towards the sound and saw a slight hand movement. He grabbed her in a bear hug, trapping her arms. She gasped in surprise, and he couldn't help himself. His mouth took possession of hers and she sighed against him. He released one of his arms and pushed her up against the nearest tree one leg in between hers. He saw her blush as she felt his need for her. He realised she couldn't see him and whispered sentiments in her ear reassuring her it was him. She smiled and relaxed. He unlaced the top of her dress and his hand slipped between the bodice and her skin. She looked startled before he felt her body ignite at his touch. Her heartbeat pounded against his hand and her breath quickened. He smiled and pulled his hands back. He looked at her dishevelled clothes and her eyes sparkling with desire. *By the gods, she's beautiful and all mine.*

Lan leant down and whispered in her ear. 'I caught you. I have clearly shown that you are mine. Look how you respond to me.'

She blushed and looked away. Lan laughed and took a small step back.

'I don't know what you mean,' she said shyly.

Lan smirked at her, and his hand slipped under her dress and caressed her leg. She wore no undergarments, but he felt a lace garter. He ran his hands over it, feeling the slight bulge of something she had placed there. He retrieved the item. Lan heard her take a sharp breath and he pocketed the small bag before letting her go. He gave her a moment to fix her dress and compose herself.

'What now?' she asked.

Lan took her by the hand and cautiously guided her down the path. They came to a fork in the road. Lan listened; the darkness was void of any sound but their breathing. Ake waited patiently for him to choose. He shrugged and went to the left. They continued on for a while, content in each other's company before Lan realised they had come back to the same path.

'Let's try the other one then,' said Ake.

They went right. They walked for what seemed like hours and Lan sensed Ake's tiredness as she began to slow and pull back on his hand.

'Let's sit for a bit,' he said.

Lan saw her nod and they both sat on the path, leaning against the tree. Ake lay her head in his lap, and she soon fell asleep. *I wonder if time is different here? They are mage elves after all. What have I dragged her into?* He took off his shirt and lay it under her head as he got up. He investigated the area. He was tempted to teleport them out of there but his sense of honour towards their future marriage prevented him from doing so. He heard a strange whisper nearby and drew his knives. The voice grated on his nerves. He tried to wake Ake but she didn't respond.

'Get up Ake.'

She lay very still, her breathing getting shallower with each breath. A strange enticing being shimmered into view. An extraordinarily beautiful female elf covered in white light beckoned towards him. He put one of his knives away and hauled Ake up against him with his other hand.

'Forget her. Look at how much of a burden she is to you. Thieving from you, making you chase her and fight for her safety. You never wanted this burden, this responsibility. Relieve yourself of her. You are not good enough for her,' whispered the creature.

'She is not a burden. I am the best person to marry her, I know that now. Begone treacherous fae,' Lan muttered.

The being smiled, bowed and disappeared, but not before casting an orb of light that lit up the area. Ake opened her eyes and stared at him. He smiled and she struggled against him.

'Get away from me, get away from me,' she yelled.

Lan let her go. He looked at her, his eyes full of pain. 'Ake, it's me, what is going on?'

Ake awoke from a restful sleep to see a stranger looking down at her. He spoke to her in Lan's voice and held her in a strong embrace with one hand. She struggled against him, confused. *My biggest fear has come true. Someone is trying to impersonate Lan again to god knows what end.*

'Let me go,' she said, her voice shaking and rising to a high-pitched cry.

The man released her, his eyes full of pain. In his hand was one of Lan's knives. She turned and ran and stumbled over something nearby. She looked down and saw Lan laying on the ground. His chest rose and fell and she tried to shake him awake.

He mumbled something in his sleep. 'Ake, it's me, what is going on?'

Ake smiled and turned to the being that followed her and saw it for the beautiful enchanting fae it was.

'I am not afraid of him in any form. I will always know him,' she said, realising this was a test.

The fae smiled and bowed. 'You have both passed. May your marriage be forever blessed.' The creature disappeared.

Ake yawned and closed her eyes.

Lan was startled awake. He had only shut his eyes for a few minutes. He looked down at Ake's head in his lap. 'You are never a burden, my wife.' He brushed the hair out of her eyes and moonlight lit her face. High above, the stars twinkled merrily in the sky. Ake's eyes fluttered open, and she smiled at him. He smiled back.

'Let's go home to bed,' he said.

They stood up, finding themselves outside the forest near the archways. They looked about in surprise and started walking towards Relequis castle.

Ake grinned at him as she slipped the ring he was going to give her on the fourth finger of her left hand. It was an exquisite silver ring with a moonstone carved in the shape of a star.

'I do.' She giggled.

Lan rolled his eyes. 'I would have asked you in a more romantic manner, but you saw to it that I can't.'

Ake pouted. 'You can still try; I was just teasing.' She offered him the ring.

Lan took it and grinned at her. 'Oh, are you asking me now? I accept.' Lan tried to put the ring on his own larger fingers. 'It won't fit, sorry wedding is off.'

She gave him an annoyed look. 'Oh, ok.'

They stopped walking.

Lan turned away from her and composed himself. He looked up at the sky and his eyes twinkled like the stars above as he turned and smiled at her.

'I know, what seems like an age ago now, that I said there was harm in loving you. I meant that if I did, I'd fall uncontrollably to the point of no return. What if I'd lost you or you'd fallen for that Falcon boy. But I guess I've always known that true love has a mind of its own. Ake, I know I haven't always been there for you as we were growing up. I was a boy playing at being a man. But now let be me a man for you. My love is yours if you choose to be my wife.'

Ake was lost for words and held out her hand. He slipped the ring onto her finger. Lan was startled as she leant forward and kissed him. He fell backwards onto the ground, and she fell on top of him. He laughed and she kissed him and drew back.

'I do. I love you, Lan.' Ake stared at him, her eyes full of love. They both got up. They tried to walk past the guards quickly and head straight to their room.

'Stop,' said a commanding voice.

They turned and looked at King Serenade. They bowed their heads, trying to remain serious.

'I guess you both passed?' asked Serenade.

Lan looked up and nodded.

'You and I will have to settle some matters then now you have married my niece,' said Serenade.

'We have to have a wedding first uncle.' Ake smiled at him.

'You're welcome to plan a human ceremony. But by elven law you two are now wed. You have declared yourselves to each other and passed the trial.' Serenade glared at Lan. 'Boy, you should have gotten my permission to marry my niece and to take her through that trial. Fae can be treacherous.'

Lan shook his head. 'I may follow elven traditions for sentimental reasons, but by human law I don't need to ask permission. For Ake's sake I will honour her.' He bowed and waited for Serenade to gesture him to stop. 'King Serenade may I claim Ake as my mate?'

Ake blushed at the crude term. *Mate is so primal.*

The king dipped his head in acknowledgement. 'Tomorrow, Lan, you and I will discuss the terms of your marriage. Now go enjoy each other.'

Serenade left to discuss his news with the druid council.

Lan and Ake hurried away, embarrassed at the innuendo. They were exhausted and fell asleep in each other's arms as soon as they lay down.

—✺—

Ake's eyes opened and she watched Lan sleeping. She sighed and Lan's eyes fluttered open. He smiled lazily and closed them again. Ake laughed quietly and Lan grinned.

'Good morning.' Lan yawned, opened his eyes and blinked as sunlight streamed in through a window.

'There goes the old fallacy about elves not sleeping,' said Ake.

Lan laughed. 'I have never heard of that one before. I guess it must be our exceptional hearing, sight and our keen sense of danger that allow us to awake in time, if it threatens. That's why it must appear as if we don't sleep. Haven't you seen me sleeping before?'

'No, you always seem awake whenever I open my eyes.'

Lan kissed her tenderly and she smiled against his mouth. He drew back and grinned. 'That's because I can't take my eyes off you.'

Ake smiled. 'What do you say about us trying to forget the past?'

'Ake, are you sure?' Lan sat up suddenly.

'Help me forget,' whispered Ake.

'If you're sure.' He looked at her earnestly.

'I am.' Ake smiled at him.

Lan looked away shyly. 'I've never done this of my own accord.'

'Nor have I,' said Ake.

Lan almost cried at the pain he heard in her voice.

'I wanted the first and all the times after to be with you,' said Ake.

Lan drew Ake to him. He kissed her tenderly, painstakingly beautiful. Ake was taken aback at his tenderness, remembering their first, less than gentle kiss. Lan laughed at Ake's expression.

'Don't laugh at me, old man.' Ake pouted.

'You can't call me that now. Remember, I'm the elfling.' Lan grinned at her.

'I can call you what I like,' said Ake.

'Oh really?'

'Yep.' Ake stuck her tongue out at him.

'In that case I better do something about it.' Lan began to remove his and Ake's clothing.

Ake stopped him midway, her eyes full of uncertainty.

Lan stopped and looked down at her.

Ake was about to speak but he put a finger to her lips. 'We don't have to do this. Never feel like you have to because of my desire for you.'

Ake's eyes shone with newly created tears. Lan kissed them away. And this time Lan was stunned as Ake kissed him and took off the rest of their clothes.

Lan had his knees over either side of Ake. He was shaking. *I will have to hold back otherwise my overwhelming passion could frighten her after what Orilan did to her.*

Ake drew him down onto her and kissed him. Lan let his attraction for her still his nerves. He began to kiss her neck and laughed at her excited face. She grinned back. Ake felt his arousal and pulled away, teasing him. Ake got up and went to the bedstand and poured herself a glass of chilled rosewater. Lan feigned sleep when she came back and lay beside him.

'Okay, I'll get up then,' whispered Ake huskily.

Lan's eyes flicked open, and he pulled her to him and rolled her over onto her back. 'You don't think I'd let you get away with impudence do you my girl?' He grinned at her.

'Yep.' She smiled up at him.

Lan's eyes glittered with mischief, and he began to tickle her. Ake convulsed with silent laughter. Lan stopped suddenly, and his hands took on a new manner. Caressing her, his need for her overtook him. Ake looked at him shyly and Lan held her close.

'Are you sure?' he asked, his voice warm against her skin that was starting to burn with a rediscovered passion.

'Make me yours.'

His hands caressed her body, causing the embers of their passion to flare. His lips followed his questing hands. She parted her legs as his hips surged against hers and gasped as they became one. His mouth captured hers as he gently eased her into his rhythm as they soared to the heavens in vessels of flesh and emotion.

CHAPTER FORTY-NINE

Two weeks later, Lan stood in front of a mirror annoyed at his new outfit that the celebrant had insisted he wear. He had discussed the terms of his marriage with King Serenade the morning after he had wed Ake in the elven rite of marriage. Serenade had emancipated Ake from elven law into the care of her husband at Lan's insistence. Lan had explained he was head of the household under human law which was part of his culture.

Lan insisted he knew Ake better than anyone and would protect her with his life, never demeaning her or taking her for granted. Lan had told Serenade passionately that he wanted no more interference from druid and elves unless he asked for it. He had asked Serenade if he would promise an elf would never take Ake again without her permission.

Serenade had agreed on the conditions that Lan never used Ake's abilities for his own advancement. He had told Lan as much as he liked him, he didn't really know him. Lan had been made to swear an oath. He was never to use Ake's matrilineal link to take control of Relequis if something happened to Flo and Hau. The two men, with the help of Dane and Flo, went on to plan the human wedding ceremony for Ake.

Lan turned back to the mirror and scrutinised his outfit. *Yeah, sure it does a lot for me, but I'm sure this is what pirates would wear.* Fashion of the times that Mikaere had said. His men servants had suggested he should grow a beard. He had laughed at them and told them elves don't grow facial hair. They had blushed and told him they hadn't realised he was an elf; he'd felt pleased by that. He knew he wasn't mirror-shy, vain Ake had told him. Just like all elves.

He wore tight leather pants, which he scowled at, white long-sleeved shirt and black tunic. They had pulled his long black hair back in a ponytail and tied it with a red ribbon. His sharply pointed ears could be seen. They had made him wear a hat; he hated hats, especially this hideous one. It was a black tricorn hat, which was a hat with the edges turned up on three sides. Mikaere knocked politely and entered.

'Very good, sir, you will present very nicely,' said Mikaere.

'No, I won't, I'm not wearing these pants, or the hat. In fact, I'm not wearing any of it.' Lan began to undress.

'But, sir,' said Mikaere.

'Mikaere, please bring me a simple blue shirt and black pants, not like these tight leather breeches.'

'Very good, sir.' Mikaere sighed.

Lan grinned at his new look. Soft suede boots graced his feet, his hair was brushed until it shone and two locks at the front were plaited and beaded. He wore loose black trousers and a long blue shirt. The only jewellery he wore was a small black sapphire on a leather thong around his neck. His mother hadn't eaten meat or worn anything from an animal. He did but thanked the gods kindly every time. The sapphire made his large black eyes stand out even more. *Perfect.*

'Sir, we have ten minutes before the bride gets there,' said Mikaere.

'Okay, lead on Mikaere,' said Lan.

They left the room.

Meanwhile, Ake was getting dressed in the room she had occupied before Lan. Now they both shared it. Flo had insisted she wear white, as all brides should be allowed to wear. Her hair was braided with beads down her back, Ake wore fine white leather boots and her dress cascaded down to the floor.

Ake's sleeveless dress had a lace bodice encrusted with diamonds. The rest of the dress was in silk with pink roses appearing at various places along the hem. She wore a plain gold coronet and carried a single red rose bound with white lace. She didn't have to wear the gold mask as only a trusted few would be at the ceremony.

—~~—

Meanwhile, Drianna looked through her crystal ball and laughed. *Silly Orilan. You think I loved my daughter? She was just a burden, a useless pawn in the overall scheme of things. Yes, kill Lan, Orilan. Take Ake, do what you want with her. You, yourself, were my pawn. I'll bide my time and strike a deal with the fiends, the Shadow Masters.*

Drianna laughed gleefully. She turned the view from Caelestis and watched the wedding of her enemies.

—~~—

Lan watched Ake walk towards him down the aisle to the flare of trumpets. He swallowed hard at the sight of her. When Ake reached him, she whispered in his ear, 'By the gods you look gorgeous.'

He smiled. 'You outshine me by an elven lifetime.'

'Clasp hands.' The celebrant tied a red ribbon about their wrists. 'I am joining them in marriage with the blood that flows in their veins, and the power of their hearts. Do you both come into this marriage consenting?' They laughed to indicate their agreement.

He handed them a knife. 'Answer in kind with the blood of both your bodies and let it fall within to the chalice of Dee.'

Both Lan and Ake pricked their finger with the knife and let it fall into a plain bronze chalice filled with chilled wine.

'Now drink of each other,' said the celebrant.

Lan and Ake both sipped of the chalice.

'I pronounce you man and wife. You may kiss your wife,' said the celebrant.

'I want to say something briefly. Ake, I vow to protect you my whole life. With all my magic and skills at your disposal. I love you,' said Lan.

Lan's eyes sparkled as he drew Ake to him and kissed her gently, lingering as if he wasn't going to let her go. When he'd finished, Flo and Serenade embraced the both of them with tears of joy in their eyes.

———

Dane had managed to get leave from the druid council to attend the ceremony. Lan held out his arm and Dane shook his hand.

'Well done to you both. Be good to each other,' said Dane.

Lan released his hand and nodded. Ake hugged Dane and wandered over to talk to Flo and Serenade.

Lan glanced at his father. 'Thank you, Father. Surely the druids will leave her be now that their tool has married her. Let us decide our own path. If there are ever children I will raise them, but not to fulfil some prophecy. Do you have the document I requested you to draw up?'

Dane nodded and handed Lan a piece of vellum. Lan took a few moments to read it. Satisfied, Lan slid it into the pocket of his trousers.

'Drianna won't ever stop trying to kill her or your future son. The druids could aid you in that battle,' offered Dane.

'I know of your dark ritual. Flo told me that your druids and your king manipulated our births to fulfil that prophecy,' said Lan.

Dane looked genuinely confused. 'I know we summoned a dangerous spell to try and counter the eight-year drought. It caused widespread famine——' Dane stopped lost in thought. *Come to think of it, the words to the ritual were ancient and unknown. The candles had flared black when the circle had gathered to say them.*

Dane had felt the need to rush home and make love to his wife after the strange ritual. They had given him one night's leave on the condition he return to train a replacement as he was getting older. He had been no longer allowed to return to his family without explicit permission.

Dane had tried on numerous occasions to get leave but was denied by the head of the order. They had let him send a heartfelt message to his Regona. *As if that was enough to console me. So, they manipulated me and kept me from influencing my son and protecting my wife and daughters. There must be corruption among the ranks. I will have to get back and sift through all the trash.*

Dane was worried for his son and Ake. He smiled disarmingly at the young elf. 'I agree to the terms. Don't seek out the druids. If you ever need help from one, I ask that you seek me out directly.'

Lan nodded. 'Thank you.'

'Now, I have urgent orders I must see to.' Dane turned and strode from the room.

'Of course,' growled Lan to the retreating back.

—⁕—

Ake wandered over to Lan and took his hand. Lan's eyes met hers, his forehead wrinkled in concern. 'Dane is always in hurry to get away from me. Especially when the moments are the most important to me.' He sighed.

'Dane loves you. I genuinely feel he has your best interests at heart.' Ake reached up and caressed his cheek.

'Dane offered help from the druids then retracted the offer. That is a little strange. He told us to come directly to him.' Lan gave her a worried glance, then composed himself. 'Anyway, let's go home. I want to build on our skills in a certain area.'

Ake blushed at his directness. 'Lan there are others here.'

Lan laughed. 'No need to blush in front of amorous mage elves. They would encourage the skill building.'

Ake covered her burning face with her hands and Lan drew her into his arms.

Lan and Ake had decided to pass on a wedding feast and return to Caelestis along with their gifts from Flo, Hau and Serenade. Lan was going to teleport their gifts ahead of him and then himself and Ake within the supposed safety of Caelestis.

They knew Dane had managed to get permission from the druid council to stay at Caelestis while Lan was away for the last ten months. There had been no disturbing activity and the druid had told them it was safe to return. Lan decided he would still be wary on their return.

CHAPTER FIFTY

Orilan walked through the tomb of a thousand memories, not all of them pleasant. He wandered through the dark keep. Dust settled on the cold stone floor. Oak doors, leading to old classrooms were shut against him as if shielding happy memories from his dark purposes.

Voices of the past seemed to scream at him from the closed doors. He opened one of them and drew in the icy chill of spirits lamenting the past. Children chanted their numbers and wooden rulers rang on desktops. Laughter from children witnessing magic gone haywire. Quiet kindly words from teachers wiping away tears from children with grazes and stubbed toes. The history of over fifteen thousand years, gone in one single battle.

Orilan's hideous laugh sounded and the spirits of the evil dead echoed his and came out to play. He walked out of Caelestis and towards the river where Flo and Het had lain entwined. He would stay here plotting. *I'll give my father a happy month before he dies.* His bitter laughter echoed cruelly, but no other ears heard it.

CHAPTER FIFTY-ONE

Ake snuck up on her husband as he began to undress. Lan was standing near the underground spring in their quarters. Lan lost his balance and fell, half-dressed, into the warm water. Ake cracked up laughing. Lan gave her a satisfied grin and began to take leisurely laps.

'That was pathetic. I was intending to get in here anyway,' said Lan.

Ake pretended to be angry and pouted. Lan laughed and got out, dripping everywhere. He went and pulled the cork out of a blue-glassed bottle of brandy.

Lan winked at Ake and made a move to grab her, but she danced out of his reach. Lan shrugged and sipped his brandy and turned away from her.

Ake stomped towards him. 'Look at me Lan.'

He grinned and continued to walk away from her.

Ake stalked towards him, annoyed. 'Urgh husbands.'

As they passed the hot springs Lan smiled to himself. He turned sharply around and grabbed Ake and jumped into the water with a resounding splash. Lan laughed with glee as he sat up, holding the now empty glass.

Ake spluttered and swallowed some of the water, all the while Lan was shaking with laughter. He drew the startled lass towards him and kissed her wet lips. Ake sighed against him. He put the glass out on the stone floor and whispered that they should really take off their wet clothing. Ake's eyes mocked him.

'Wanton lad, so soon after the last time,' teased Ake.

'Not soon enough for this man.'

'Elven lad,' mocked Ake.

'Fine, an elven lad with a man's desire.'

Ake smiled languidly and swam away from him. Lan groaned and reached for her, but she swam further out of reach. He got out and poured himself another glass of brandy and went out of the cavern. Ake thought he was upset and followed him.

Lan who was quicker than Ake had reached the kitchen. He was hungry after the swim and proceeded to make a sandwich from the bags of stuff they'd brought with them.

Lan entered the kitchen; several unwashed dishes lay in a bucket of murky water. One of the cupboards was open and a bag of flour sat on the bench, half empty. Lan took up the knife he was holding as he sensed someone entering the kitchen. He sighed in relief as his saturated wife stepped through the doorway. Ake laughed at him but the sound faded on her lips. *Why is there no dust in here? This seems a little strange. Dane was supposed to stay in town only coming to check on Caelestis occasionally.*

'I noticed the mess too Lan. Maybe Dane stayed overnight and forgot to clean up,' suggested Ake.

'You are probably right.' Lan ate some of the sandwich he made. He offered some to Ake.

'I'm not hungry.'

He finished it off and picked her up, her long, wet hair falling across his shoulders.

'Now, I'm going to finish what you started.'

Ake put a hand to his face and caressed his cheek lovingly. He took her into the infirmary, which was closer. Ake laughed at his obvious and urgent intentions.

He grinned at her and pressed her into the bed, Ake's breath caught in her throat as he entered her hastily. He looked into her eyes, worried he had hurt her. Ake smiled, took his face in her hands and kissed him, slipping her tongue into his mouth. He set an urgent pace and she responded, arching her back to meet his thrusts. Ake moaned as she saw stars. Lan, face flushed with passion, looked at her proudly. His male ego was satisfied. He pushed her a little harder then collapsed beside her, spent.

For the next month they enjoyed each other, drank wine, ate heartily, and felt they'd never been happier.

CHAPTER FIFTY-TWO

Orilan thought a month was long enough. Deep within his mind he found the power he needed to bring back the mists to surround the Isle of Man'hannon. *Now Lan and his wife will stumble blindly into my clutches upon their return.*

———ᴡᴡ———

Ake and Lan looked at the mists surrounding the island of Man'hannon. They hadn't been outside for a week and had decided to go for a midnight stroll. They both thought the same thing; the mists hadn't been here for over twenty years. Lan raised his arms and said some words that sounded as chilling as the wind in a mounting storm whistling through slitted shutters.

'*Ska ripis parte.*'

The mists parted for ten seconds, and they were able to see Caelestis white against a troubled stormy night sky. Then the mist reappeared. Troubled, Lan's face grew dark and brooding. Ake shivered as coldness began to swirl around them. The wind began to howl.

Ake could see no more than three feet in front of her and Lan disappeared from sight in a swirling haze. Lan could still see her as his elvish sight procured him thirty feet of vision. He walked over to her. Ake jumped as his hand took hold of hers.

'Don't worry, I'll keep you safe,' he said.

Ake smiled up at him, eyes full of love.

'What? Here? Now?' Lan winked.

'I don't think so, we have to get home,' said Ake.

'Spoilsport.'

'Aroused elf?'

'Okay, you win.' He went to kiss her.

They both stopped as they heard hideous evil laughter alive on the air.

'I will take my inheritance now if I may … Father dear,' came a chilling whisper.

Someone pushed Ake away from Lan and Lan swore as something hit him over the head. Colours swam before his eyes and he fell into cold oblivion.

Ake looked around in complete fear and anguish from what Orilan had done to her. She was overcome with rage, at the helplessness of her position, at the gods for allowing this. *What have we mere mortals done to deserve such hate, such unwanted wrath from our divine parents? Mere mortals who strive for our whole lives trying to receive confirmation from the gods that our lives are worth something.*

A white light began to glow around the unnerved mage. Her blue eyes turned golden and golden feathered wings sprouted from her back. Her robes were torn asunder as her wings spread out nine feet in length and shaped like an eagle's. Her heritage from the gods became apparent as she took on her new form as a fire angel or Anwyn.

The white light spread out, cutting through the mist like a knife through warm butter. Ake let the rage build. Blood-red light swirled outwards from her. Orilan, attracted by the power, appeared, watching in awe at this amazingly magical and enticing creature of the gods. He covered himself in a shell of bitter black shadows. He began to stalk the goddess mage.

Ake drew in the light and suddenly it went out, leaving Ake naked in sparkling luminescence. Orilan drew in a deep breath and adrenaline pumped in his veins. He couldn't wait to have her blood circling in his body.

—∿∿—

Lan woke up, his hands rushed to his forehead. He could feel cold congealing blood and a large lump. He rose to his feet, wobbling as he did so, and opened his eyes. His vision was blurry for a few seconds as he stumbled forward, looking around. His breath caught in his throat when he recognised Ake. His Ake had finally come of age.

Lan saw a mass of darkness heading towards her.

Orilan! Lan growled and raced towards the field where the battle would soon take place.

'Ah, you are gorgeous,' said Orilan to Ake's left.

'Orilan, you come too eagerly to your death.' Her golden eyes took on a fierce determination.

'I too have the blood of a goddess swirling in my veins,' said Orilan.

'Stolen blood, ancient devil,' said Ake.

'Maybe so, but it now pulses in my body,' said Orilan.

The mage turned towards the vampyr and lifted her hands. A white fire flared from them. It was the colour of starlight. Orilan dove out of the way easily, his elven agility plainly visible. Ake frowned; Lan was slower than this.

It was true, Lan had only just arrived. Ake turned towards him and ushered him to stay where he was.

'No, Ake, I want to kill this demon who dares call me Father,' he yelled.

'You, mortal, will not succeed.' Ake grinned.

The comment had pained Lan but in this mood Ake did not care.

'Ake, don't be so sure that you can,' said Orilan.

Ake laughed, her voice now enchanting like a nightingale. 'Who do you think you are, demon? Not human, not elf, not even animal.'

'Ake, don't forget who you are,' Lan shouted.

Ake became drunk on her newfound power. 'Calm yourself little elf, I will not let this demon harm you.'

Lan, angered beyond words at this spirit girl's insults, walked down the hill and put himself between his wife and son. Lan then slid out his knives.

'You, Ake, will not take away my right. I will not budge from here. And you, Orilan, will die tonight,' said Lan proudly.

'Strong words, little mortal,' said Orilan.

Orilan lunged towards Lan, but he stepped aside easily. Orilan quickly turned and Lan, not anticipating his manoeuvrability, collided with him. *Mystic Fire* spread from his hands and Orilan screamed in pain and jumped back. Lan got his ground back and sent *Mystic Fire* arching after Orilan but he levitated out of the way. Lan, angered, sent lightning bolts firing into Orilan from behind. Orilan screamed and began to crumble.

Lan, satisfied, turned his back, but hideous laughter came from behind him. He somersaulted backwards and landed facing Orilan, not even harmed.

'*Shadow Gate* enchantment.' Orilan grabbed hold of Lan by the throat and sunk his teeth into him.

'*The offspring is often more powerful than the parent. And when this is over, I'll take her for myself,*' whispered Orilan in Lan's mind.

'*Disgusting bastard. Thinking you can just steal a woman for yourself,*' Lan replied.

Orilan grinned and broke the vampyr's kiss. This gave Lan the time he needed.

Lan punched Orilan in the face with such force it broke his nose, Orilan put both his hands to his face in annoyance. Lan sent his last *Mystic Fire* slamming into the vampyr. The dark shell of shadows protecting him faded. Orilan screamed in frustration and sent his black fire after Lan, who just managed to get away.

Lan had grown weak from blood loss, blood seeped from the head injury. Ake shimmered by his side and cast paralysis over her husband to stop him fighting. Lan felt his arm and leg muscles seize up.

'No, Ake, my love, let me finish what I helped start,' said Lan.

Ake laughed, and her answer saw Orilan go up with *Starlight* and finish in a pile of ashes. A tear rolled down Lan's cheek as the paralysis spell wore off and he slumped into unconsciousness from mere exhaustion and loss of blood.

The golden creature faded and became Ake, pale from prolonged use of high magic. She saw the pile of ashes and Lan crumpled on the ground. The look of superiority faded from her face and her grey-blue eyes showed only guilt.

In the depths of the underworld Drianna laughed, hoping this incident would turn Ake and Lan against each other.

Chapter Fifty-Three

'Don't touch me or utter any words with your vicious tongue.' Lan glared at Ake.

'Sweetheart, it wasn't that bad a thing I did,' said Ake.

'Yeah, what if someone you loved was murdered and then someone took away your right for revenge?' he asked.

They were now back in Caelestis, the morning after Orilan's death. Ake had carried him home and put him into bed in clean attire. Lan now rose and threw back the blankets and got out of bed.

'What do you mean murder?'

'His name was Orilan. Drianna stole him and made him what he wasn't. To me, she murdered Ori long ago.'

'Don't act——'

Lan interrupted her. 'Like a baby, an elfling? Don't tell me what to do, my little wife!'

Ake wondered where this would lead.

'You will listen to me,' he cried desperately.

'You don't own me.'

'Wrong. A witnessed wedding, by man's law you're mine and besides——'

'I'm a woman, I better do as my husband bids?' mocked Ake.

Lan smirked at her.

'I can leave anytime I wish.' Ake scowled at him.

'And if you did, I could have you tracked down as mutinous and punished.'

'Oh, I guess my life is in your hands master, thanks for mentioning it a little too late. I could be free and not in bonds. Oh, and I suppose I better let you beat me within an inch of my life. And did you care a thought that he was the one that attacked me?'

'Of course, I do Ake. But it's the man's job to protect his lady. And I don't hit women or children.'

'You said you could have me punished. That one is on you.'

Lan gave her a disgusted look. 'What is wrong with you? Have I ever given you reason to believe I would lay a hand on you?' Lan threw up his hands in frustration and began to pace. 'By punishment I meant you would be confined to the grounds of Caelestis for your safety.'

Ake glared at him hands on her hips. 'Besides, you are technically bound to your father until you come of age.'

Lan paused then grinned obnoxiously. 'Oh, here's a pretty piece of elvish law. I bet Dane didn't tell you this. My father never came to recognise me as his in my first year of life. So, here's the best part. I am not recognised as an elf, so I go by the laws of man. Through those laws you answer to me.'

Ake looked stunned at this and had no comeback.

'This is a ridiculous fight that is leading us nowhere.' Lan sighed and his anger dulled a bit.

'Lan, I didn't mean to upset you so.'

'You don't understand. He was my child and he hurt you. It was my responsibility to punish him.' Lan sighed. 'Maybe down the track I could have redeemed him.'

'But you wouldn't have been able to.'

'How do you know? Even if I couldn't, I should've had the chance.' Lan wiped away his tears.

Lan turned and headed away from her down the hallway and to the stairwell leading up into Caelestis.

Ake turned and sobbed into her pillow. *He must have just*

lusted after me. He only wanted me so no one else could have me, but surely not? He courted me and told me he loved me. But what he had just said to her could make any woman think otherwise. *I need to calm down. I did hurt him, and I guess he is grieving.* Ake sighed, got up and went after Lan.

CHAPTER FIFTY-FOUR

Stupid Fool. What a stupid fool I am. I should have scryed to see if Orilan was infertile due to effects of high magic. No woman he has lain with has ever conceived, yet his victims seem to gain high conception rates. Several of his lovers are pregnant to my slaves. I still have a chance. The spell over time quadruples his victim's fertility rate. In this case, Ake will be pregnant after one mating. The whore of that buck elf would be about six weeks along. I will corrupt the child, she thought hideously.

Drianna's hideous laugh echoed in the crypt and a hellhound's ears pricked up and he howled along with her. Drianna took offence to this indication that she sounded like a fellow howling hellhound. 'Shut up Bemmin. Ahh, yes, the traitor's mount. Die. He haaa.' She cackled, and the hellhound was engulfed in scarlet flames. Drianna looked into her crystal ball at the crumpled body of a young man being carried away by a druid.

CHAPTER FIFTY-FIVE

Lan stood on the balcony of Caelestis, looking out towards the sea. A faint call came from the ground below. Lan looked down and saw two hundred armoured guards and a huge caravan heading along the road to Caelestis.

One of the guards called up to him. 'Hey, you up there, we want a few words with you.'

Lan frowned and wondered what these people wanted. He shimmered out of sight and appeared in front of the man who called out in surprise.

'He must be dead,' cried the general.

Lan laughed. 'I'm not dead, I'm a mystic. What did you expect?'

'We were told that only spirits dwell within. Everyone knows that all students, servants and teachers died in the fall of Caelestis and were buried in a mass grave, the work of a spirit,' said the man eerily.

The man regained his composure and Lan looked at him closely. All two hundred guards wore a breastplate of leather armour, leather kilts, long socks and leather boots that ended like sandals at the toes. Each carried a long wooden shield and had a short sword in their scabbard. Each man wore a white cape and a bronze helmet. The man he had talked to, his helmet was gold. Lan thought he must be the general.

'What is it that you want?' asked Lan.

The general turned to face the line of caravans behind him. Five were painted red and pulled by two large, bay-coloured stock horses. The sixth, a lead caravan, was decorated in a rich purple and pulled by two black stock horses. Two bronze trumpets sounded, and Lan covered his ears at the intrusion.

'Presenting his lordship, Emperor of the Regian Empire, Cephas,' announced the general.

The legionnaires and their general turned and pumped their fists in the air and chanted. 'Emperor, Emperor.'

A balding man, with a wreath made of purple clematis flowers on his head, descended from the carriage. He was dressed in a white toga and leather sandals. A purple sash was pinned to his right shoulder and made its way around his back and to the start again. His skin was slightly tanned, his hair white and his eyes a piercing brown. Lan grinned gleefully. *They worship a balding old man. Great source of power. Sorendee is far superior.*

This time Lan would judge a book for its cover. Sure, their lord may not look like much. But this Emperor was a seasoned warrior, great speaker and the great city of Regis worshipped him. Lan had heard of Regis but had never been there. Cephas had been amazingly handsome in his younger days and had sired many daughters with countless lovers.

Ake came out through the double doors on the ground floor. She was curious and came to stand next to her husband. The emperor's eyes sparkled as he looked her up and down and Ake noticed his eyes didn't settle on her face.

'Ah, the demon man has captured a princess for his mate.' One of the legionnaires grinned at Lan.

'Lan, what's going on here?' asked Ake.

'Don't know. They haven't said yet,' said Lan.

'Do not utter a word. The emperor wishes to speak,' said the general.

'Hey, shut up you. You don't rule this island,' said Lan.

The Regians were taken aback at this.

'Sorry to inform you, we have now claimed this island. It is now part of the Regian Empire. We will now rest in our castle,' said the general.

'Hush, Mismanam. We will rest here tonight and take this man's hospitality,' said Cephas.

The men laughed meanly and whistled at Ake who scowled back and clung to her husband's side, all arguments forgotten. Cephas raised his hand, and everyone stood to attention.

'And if this man stands aside and offers us wine to drink, water for our weary bodies, fresh horses and a feast, and I the company of his woman, we will let him keep his dreary old castle. If not, it will burn,' said Cephas.

The men cheered and Lan put himself in front of his wife.

'Hang on a minute. The water, wine and food are fine, but my wife is not a part of that bargain,' said Lan.

The legionnaires held their breath and unsheathed their swords at Lan's impudence.

Cephas laughed heartily. 'Friends, let us settle down. Man, monster, whatever you are——'

'Trebrelan, Master of Caelestis. Grand Master Mystic,' said Lan arrogantly.

'Master of old stone and one girl,' jeered Mismanam.

Lan glared menacingly at him and took a step towards him.

'Shut up Mismanam, every man must be master of something. Even this hole. Why won't you let me lay with her? She's just a woman and not worth even this dump of stone.' Cephas smirked at Lan.

'What kind of husband would hand over his wife to another man? Where is the honour in that? I also happen to love my wife!' Lan scowled at Cephas.

Cephas guffawed. 'And by the looks of you she's still an untested one.'

The men laughed harder, as did Cephas who went red in the face.

Lan blushed at the insult. The men took this as if their emperor was right and they too were at loss of words for their laughter.

'You love a woman. Come on boy, women are good for two things, oh sorry, three. Lying beneath you, bearing your sons and keeping house, and you know what? I could leave you more than what you had: my child in your wife's body. I'm sorry though, I wouldn't be able to recognise it as mine,' said Cephas.

The men stopped laughing as Lan came at them from sheer anger. *Mystic Fire* burst from his hands and four of the legionnaires went up in flames. Their screams unnerved the rest of the army.

'Now, accept my offer. Hospitality minus the wife or you choose death,' said Lan.

Cephas looked at Lan in a new light. But he still wanted the girl, virgin or not, wriggling beneath him.

'I'm sorry I cannot do that. You'll have to die. Charge,' yelled Cephas.

'Ake. Get out of here.' Lan turned and spoke to her over the din.

'No, Lan, I will not leave you to them,' said Ake.

'Oh, he can't even control his wife,' the general sneered.

The army strode forth in twenty-five to a line, swords and shields at the ready. Lan set *Mystic Fire* slamming into the first line three more times, taking out fifteen men so that only seven remained in the first line. He teleported behind the last seven and with his *Call Lightning* ability took down the rest in that line.

'*Facstym mentys,*' Ake screamed in the language of the Daione Sidhe.

A buzzing began in the minds of the second line. Then an ear-splitting sound rang through their heads, and they fell to their knees as a burning fire utterly destroyed any mental capacity. There they lay on the ground babbling like babies, eyes open to the heavens, completely blank. That left fifty men and without their general they stopped and looked at their emperor for guidance.

'Fight, you fools,' he said.

They cheered and took up their swords. Lan flicked his wrists and his mystic knives slid into his hands. Within moments it began to grow cloudy and rain poured down.

'So, you think you're a god now?' Lan spat the last word at Cephas.

Cephas didn't look too fussed. Lan, in his anger, wasn't thinking straight, but Ake wondered what was in those big caravans.

Lan used the last of his magic and three men nodded off and fell on their own swords.

Ake, meanwhile, felt anger building. Wings ripped through her clothing. She began to glow and, in her place, stood her Anwyn form. *I really must do something about the naked thing.* Ake laughed to herself.

Cephas, filled with desire, looked at Ake with open lust. 'Oh, by all the gods of the empire, I must have that goddess.'

'Legionnaires, take position,' said Cephas.

Two of the huge caravan doors burst open and another two hundred men came to his aid. Lan looked forlorn and angry.

'Ake!' he screamed. 'Leave now, please do as you are told for once.'

Ake, angered by the last statement, answered by casting *Starlight*. A bright rainbow light swirled outward from her open palms engulfing the men who were awed by it. The problem with this spell was that it only killed creatures born of darkness.

The men laughed and exclaimed that she made pretty magic.

Angered, Ake began to glow with a red light. The rain stopped and the sky became dark as night. A chill wind whipped up, making every man there shiver. Everyone stopped fighting and stared at Ake, even Lan.

'Get out of the way Lan,' yelled Ake.

Lan somersaulted backwards four times and out of the range of Ake's spell casting. He looked up at the sky. His black robes flapping in the dark.

Ake's eyes became golden, and she opened her mouth. The words she spoke made everyone present feel like they'd gone to hell and back. Ake spoke to them with utter hate in a cracked and dark voice.

'*Magma manas crono.*'

The air became sweltering in a matter of minutes. Men wiped beads of sweat from their foreheads and began backing away as cracks a foot wide opened in the ground. Some men tripped and screamed as limbs bent and shattered. Smoke seeped up through the vents. The earth shuddered and a crack opened before Lan. He tripped and pain shot up through his leg as it became trapped in the vent. He almost fainted from the heat.

'*Manas hylt.*' Ake laughed hideously.

Thirty men became paralysed, magic held them in place.

'You will die in the waves of the sun,' said Ake.

The faces of the soldiers asked for mercy, but they didn't cry out, for their courage held them strong.

Lan was trapped without Ake's knowledge. Lan tried to scream for help, but a jet of steam spewed out of the vent and his call was lost in the noise and darkness.

'*Magna crono,*' said Ake.

Cephas stepped back with forty men and ran behind one of the caravans. That move saved their lives. Fire seared up from the vents engulfing the trapped soldiers. The darkness was alive with their soul wrenching screams. The fire spread quickly.

Lan tugged at his fractured leg with all the effort he could muster, eventually getting it out of the way. The chilly wind whipped up some flames nearby. Several embers struck him and burnt half his face. He screamed in agony. He dragged himself further away. The fire spell drifted away, leaving charred bodies and the scent of sulphur on the air.

Ake lay unconscious on the ground, vulnerable. Lan found a burnt stick on the ground and hoisted his burnt and useless body up. His breathing rattled in his lungs with the effort, and he moaned with the pain. The Emperor looked amazed at the buck elf's courage.

'I'll still take you on,' yelled Lan and collapsed with the effort. He tried to get to his feet again.

Cephas looked at the elf with deep respect and pity.

'Men, get a stretcher and my physician. Take the elf inside his home and tend him. Leave the woman a few moments.'

Two of the legionnaires heeded his quest and a physician followed them into Caelestis.

Chapter Fifty-Six

'Hush child. You'll be fine now,' said an older woman.

Ake opened her bleary eyes and looked up into the lady's brown ones.

'Old Ma?' asked Ake.

'No, dear, I is not your granny. You have slept like the spirits for ten days now,' said the older woman.

'Who? ... What?' Ake sat up sharply.

'Your husband is really worried about his wife,' said the older woman.

'Can I see him?' Ake smiled.

'Certainly, daughter. My son will be delighted,' said the older woman.

'You are Regona? But we mourned you,' said Ake.

'I am Kalin. You are my daughter-in-law,' said Kalin.

A chill of dread began to form in Ake's heart.

'Son, come in, your wife wants you by her side when she is ailing,' said Kalin.

Cephas entered, dressed lightly in a white silk robe and gold sandals.

'Oh, dear one, it cheers my heart to see you better.' He looked at Ake with unconcealed lust.

'Your husband loves you. I am so happy for both of you. He finally married for love and divorced his first wife. I'll leave you to reacquaint yourselves,' said Kalin.

Ake swallowed hard. Her throat became dry, and she stared at him in open contempt. 'Where's Lan, my real husband?'

'Tutt tutt. Oh, the poor thing she doesn't remember.' Cephas looked at her sadly. This was put on, unlike the feelings of lust he had for the bewitching girl. 'Oh, poor young thing. I had my physician do all they could for the boy. But after the fire got him, he went to be with god.'

'You mean you had him killed!' Ake screamed at him.

Kalin looked angry but then saddened. 'My son would never do such a thing. He is the king and founded the great city of Aldea to rule the eastern part of our great empire. He has also allowed pagans and other men to worship freely.'

'Then how?' shouted Ake, heartbroken.

'Umm, how should I put this gently? He tried to protect you and got trapped by your demonic workings and became engulfed in your hell fire. He sustained fatal wounds,' said Cephas.

'Demonic … workings … dead.' Ake wept.

'How was a young woman to know that all magic wielded by women is from the devil herself?' said Kalin.

'But I was taught differently,' said Ake.

'Well, whoever raised you taught you the wrong things,' said Cephas.

Ake's tears streamed like a river. 'I killed him.'

'The love of your life. Oh, now you must live with that knowledge. Tut tut,' said Kalin.

'Prove it to me.' Ake wiped away her tears.

'Send in Matthew the mage,' said Cephas.

Ake rose, she realised she was naked and shivered in the room's cool air. Shrieking she dove back under the covers.

A small man, no more than three foot in height, entered the room. He was dressed in rags that had once resembled robes. He was portly and his ears were round and slightly pointed. He was dirty, unshaven and his arms and hands were in chains. The halfling looked about forty and had black ringlets, tan skin and big, bright ruby eyes.

'You dare treat a mage so unjustly!' Ake yelled at Cephas.

'Those that live lengthy times and wield magic are impure and unclean.' Cephas glared at her.

'Then why did——'

Kalin interrupted Ake. 'You are young and human, we wish to steer you in the right way.'

'Just get on with the proof!' Ake stared her down.

Kalin gasped at her impudence. Cephas looked more than amused. There was a strange look in his eyes that Ake didn't recognise for lust.

'Halfling, you will get double rations tonight. Prove to this woman that her lover, Trebrelan is dead,' said Cephas.

The halfling nodded wearily and pulled out a crystal ball from underneath his robes.

'Eres moves Trebrelan,' he said.

At first Ake could see nothing, then the crystal ball showed flickers of light coming together. Ake screamed in shock at what she saw. Lan was laid out on a bed, his eyes closed. His body was covered in raw and peeling burns, Dane was standing next to him. The view shifted as if time had fluctuated. Dane stood next to a man in the midst of digging. Dane had a cloth to his nose.

'He's dead.' Ake shivered.

'Yes, my dear. And it was by you, oh how bad must you feel,' said Kalin.

Ake turned and sobbed into her pillow. Cephas sent Matthew and his mother away.

'Listen, I married you to me via a priest. So, you are not a widow and will not grow old in poverty. We will educate you in the way of Regian women and you'll want for nothing. My son, by you, will rule next. That should make you proud,' said Cephas.

Ake stopped crying and looked at the old balding man with malice written all over her face.

'I have made you an honest woman, a Regian woman,' said Cephas proudly.

'Oh, you are a horrible, evil man. I am and will always be one of the real people. The people that have the forebears of gods, a woman of the tribes.'

Cephas looked angry and disgusted. 'Do not talk about scum inside these walls.'

'I thought that you allowed men to worship as they please.'

'Sure, the common man, not pure bloods like us and especially not my wife.'

'I will not be your wife.' Ake rose to leave.

Cephas laughed at her. 'You have no choice in the matter. You are a woman, and your husband owns your body and the way you act and think.'

'You can't own my heart! I will be leaving.'

'You have no clothes, food or water. I can have you killed if you leave.'

'You won't, because then I would have won my freedom.'

Angered by this Cephas belted Ake across the face, and she fell on the bed, tears and blood from her nose mingling. Cephas came up to her and took her face in his old hands. He wiped away the blood with the sleeve of his robe.

From his robes, Cephas drew out an iron bracelet engraved with Regian incantations and slipped it on Ake's wrist. Ake recognised this as an anti-magic restraint. It could not be removed by anyone other than a priest or druid.

Ake would not be able to use any magic. She shivered, feeling helpless. Tears rolled down her face.

'Never talk back at any Regian man. They will hurt you more

than I would.' His piercing eyes bore into her wounded grey-blue ones.

He kissed her gently. Ake bit his mouth. He laughed and left the room. Kalin came in bearing a tray of two boiled eggs and bread sopped in milk. Ake refused the food and Kalin shrugged and left, leaving the tray on the bedside table. Ake sat up and stared at the tray of food. She was full of misgiving. *I wonder if the food has been drugged.* She realised she was ravenous. *The eggs are still in the shells, they would be the safest choice.* She peeled the two eggs and consumed the meagre meal hastily. Ake began to think of her dead husband and sobbed into her pillow.

Oh Lan, I said some cruel things. You didn't get your revenge on Orilan and now I have no way to redeem what I did. It seems every-one I ever love will die. I never got to say goodbye. Oh, my Lan, my love. I will never love anyone the way I did you. Oh gods, I killed him ... I killed him, she thought in utter anguish.

Nightfall, a bolt slid across metal and the doors to Ake's cham-ber opened. Cephas, naked and freshly bathed and groomed, entered. Ake jolted awake from her nightmare to see him pulling back the covers.

Ake cried out and backed away quickly and ended up on the floor. Cephas laughed and grabbed her wrist and pulled her back into the king-sized bed. He was strong and muscular for his older years. Ake screamed and aimed a kick to Cephas's chest. He sucked in his breath sharply and wrenched her to him. Ake screamed and delivered a palm strike to his face. Cephas smiled and wiped away the blood from his nose.

'Keep it up woman, it just prolongs this.' Cephas leered at her and pulled her towards him.

'No, please don't do this,' she sobbed. Ake shook with fear and desperation and tried to back away from him. 'Get away from me. Why will no one help me?'

Cephas laughed cruelly and put his face close to hers. 'I own you.'

Ake delivered a snap kick to his abdomen, Cephas grunted as he was winded. Ake used her other hand to scratch him across the face. He bellowed and belted her across the face. He went to hit her again and she used an outward block to prevent the blow. He grinned and held her arms down with one of his large hands and belted her across the face twice. Ake lay there stunned.

'Now, that's better sweet one. I must admit, you deserve what's coming to you, acting so disrespectfully to your husband. Your duty is this and whenever he wants it.'

Ake whimpered and tried to rise. He laughed at her attempt and held her down with one hand. Ake spat into his face.

'Oh, my poor little lioness, not willing to heed advice,' crooned Cephas.

He twisted her wrist sharply which cracked, and Ake cried out with pain. She lay there sobbing quietly.

'Now, who is your husband with whom you'll lie?' asked Cephas.

Ake whimpered, then composed herself. 'It was, and always will be, my husband, Lan.' Ake scowled at him defiantly.

'Silly woman. You must obey. Don't make me hurt you more,' said Cephas, and with that he was upon her. He was frightfully heavy compared to Ake's small frame. She was in too much pain and shock to fight back. Ake lay beneath him sobbing.

It was long into the night before she closed her eyes and slept the death-like sleep of the bone weary.

'Ha ha ha.' Drianna laughed.

Ahh, not one but two young to corrupt now. Two boys, brothers.

It seems her strange blood may be able to produce young from two different fathers. While it was a rare occurrence in some human pregnancies, Ake's divine blood made it more possible. *Now I will get my revenge on the two enemy families. Dee's lineage and Dane's family for trying to stop the inevitable, the dark ages,* thought the crone.

CHAPTER FIFTY-SEVEN

'Push now, you're almost there,' encouraged the midwife. Ake grunted with the pain.

The year was now 336 CE.

Ake had been in labour for seventeen hours. Cephas paced back and forth, waiting for his offspring's birth. This was his last chance at an heir. He'd had several women when Ake had become too cumbersome to lie with and, well, let's just say he couldn't seem to make any more children. Over the last eight months she had become a pliant and useful wife. She also looked good hanging off his arm. He heard her cry out again and then came a hearty scream, followed five minutes later by another weaker one.

'Oh, my gods, twins. If they are both boys that will result in problems later. Only one can be heir and they will fight for it, but boys need hardship to become strong men.' Cephas said to the guard nearby.

Ake looked at the two infants. Despite being premature, the older one was a healthy strong baby. The baby who was the first-born looked like his Regian father. Brown eyes, brown hair, noble nose, dusky skinned and clearly human. Ake looked at this child with malice. His womb brother was clearly Lan's.

He was the palest thing she had ever seen. He was a lot smaller than his brother. His ears were sharply pointed, and he had obsidian eyes that reflected the light. Ake reached out and stroked his downy head. The little boy curled his tiny fingers around her thumb. But Ake was worried about him. His cry seemed weaker than his brother's did, and he was finding it harder to breathe.

The midwife, a slave girl named Coriander, had become a friend to Ake over her time here in the city of Regis. Ake had seen the city only twice and that was while borne on a litter going to another one of those infernal dinner parties where women dressed in hideous fashions and consumed terrible food while their menfolk talked of conquering, virility and alcohol.

Regis, the once proud city, had plague, clogged water fountains and many a starving family. She had learnt they called the peasants serfs. The sewer itself flowed up onto the streets when it rained. Did the rich do anything to help the poor?

Of course not, they gave them bread, conquered countries and slaughtered men for fun. Civilised huh?

As long as a man had bread it didn't matter if his wife starved while he sat in the arena where the free bread was offered to watch a man's head be cut off. And another rich father drowned a little daughter because she was not a boy and daddy would not waste food on her. His wife would lose her love of life and he would drag her back into the house and proceed to beget his way to immortality.

The serfs may starve but peasant mothers were free to love and keep their children because most would not make it to their fifth birthday. Mothers, unbeknown to their husbands, gave themselves for an hour in the taverns on shopping days for a copper piece for bread for another week. Then, if certain herbs weren't used, her husband would become father to another man's child.

Ake held out her hands to take the elf child. Coriander looked at the child knowingly.

'Mrs, your man will be coming in here soon. You should put that little one down and hold his wee babe. He's a fine babe,' said Coriander.

She picked up the Regian child and offered up the sleeping babe to his mother.

'If you do, he might let your lover's bastard live,' said Coriander.

'Coriander, this wee babe is my dead husband's child,' said Ake.

'You were married before?' asked Coriander.

'Yeah. I'm another of the emperor's victories, I guess. What do you mean about letting a wee babe live?' asked Ake.

Coriander drew in her breath. She knew men were proud and if anyone found out that another man's son had been born of the emperor's wife, they would mock him and look down their noses at him. Coriander explained this to Ake.

'Plus, all Regian children must suffer to live. Both these babes will be taken by heavy guard and left out in the elements all night. If they survive, they are considered worthy children blessed by the gods.

'And I don't think this little one of your dead husband's will live. Then, once they survive, they will be named. A girl will take her father's name after eight days. A boy will get a name all of his own, given on his ninth day,' said Coriander.

Ake looked horrified at this information. She began thinking. Ake could pretend Lan's child had died and get it snuck out. But could she give this baby into another mother's care and never know if she would see the boy again?

'Then I will suckle that horrid man's child, there in your arms, but not before my own child. My child will be named Amities, my love,' said Ake.

Ake fed Amities and held him close, rocking and humming to him.

The little boy's breathing improved slightly, and he closed his little eyes. She placed the babe in the bed beside her. Then Ake gestured to the other little lad. Ake breast fed him with utter malice and kept him as far away from her as possible. When the little child wasn't even half-finished, Ake ripped him away from that life sustaining flow. She wanted to give her smaller son a better chance at survival than this bigger squalling child. The Regian child wept fitfully in his wooden crib laid out with wool and engraved with wolves. Ake almost felt sorry for the boy. Coriander had cleaned both the blood speckled infants and left the room for a matter of minutes.

'Ah, little one, I know you mean no harm to anyone. But you may as well learn now that life is harsh. And that anyone that will love you may leave you sooner than you want them too,' said Ake.

Coriander returned with a guard and Cephas. Ake looked at the guard disgustingly. After waking on her first night of rape she had seen the guard in the shadows. He had been there all the time in case she used her so-called demonic-given gifts. And he was there every night thereafter. Cephas looked at the Regian child in the crib with utter happiness. For this was the fruit of his loins.

'Ahh, wife, you have done quite well. But I heard another infant's cry. Is it possible I have another son? Even a daughter would amuse me after this little emperor.' Cephas beamed.

Ake's hackles rose and she was on guard. 'There is another boy child.'

'Show the little lad to me,' said Cephas.

'He is sickly,' said Ake.

'Oh, how sad of a boy of mine to be poorly, still let me see the little fellow, for you have pleased me with the sight of this boy so much that both will not go through the ordeal and have every-thing they need. On my honour. For I have had six wives who produced no male fruit and the fact that you conceived stopped the rumours that it was my fault.'

But Ake knew otherwise, her divine heritage made his weak human blood erupt with the ability to procreate. Ake took out

Amities and handed the boy to his stepfather. She couldn't conceal her joy at the look of shock on his face.

'I wish … oh by the gods, I wish I hadn't given my word before I saw this animal.'

Ake glared at Cephas. 'Too late now.'

'Don't expect me to claim this child or make it heir to anything. I will not even allow him a name. Under Regian law if a child has no name, he is no better than a slave,' said Cephas.

'I'm sure Amities won't mind.' Ake smirked at him.

'You blasphemous bitch. You, a woman named him before the man of the house even accepted the child?' Cephas scowled at her.

'Oh, but husband, you accepted him on your honour. That means he's entitled to shelter, food, clothing and a name within your household. And yours just happens to be the whole Regian Empire.'

'Oh, if you hadn't just given birth I would have you under me procuring another son. Don't expect that child of yours will be raised with my fine boy. Hey slave. Take the boy to a wet nurse in the slave pens. He may see his mother one hour a week and no more. But she will never be able to touch him again,' said Cephas.

'No, you can't do that.' Ake began to weep.

'Oh yes, I can. You will suckle my son. And you will mother him. And if you don't, that animal will suddenly have an accident.'

Ake, sensing her victory turn into defeat, gave in. At least the boy would live, and she would see him occasionally. Even if it was from a distance. Ake shed a few tears and gestured to the other lad.

'Will you name him?' asked Ake.

'No, you will. And it better be a decent one or else.' Cephas grinned.

Ake felt trapped knowing that if she named this crying thing, she would have to think of him as a person.

'No.'

'Oh yes, my dear.' The emperor laughed as his conquered bride's hope fell. 'Remember, I suffer your animal to live. Now name your only son.'

'I order. As he will order everyone. I name him Mandami.' Ake patted the child on the back as he began to cry.

'Not bad. Actually, Mandami rolls off the tongue, and it is perfect for a future emperor. For the moment there will be no accidents. Now suckle your future king,' he ordered.

When Ake began to, the emperor left.

CHAPTER FIFTY-EIGHT

Five years passed and a young child yawned with boredom as his tutor tried to teach him Regian numerals. Mandami looked out of the window to see that strange fragile boy that his mother watched daily from the balcony. He thought it was strange for an elf child to be growing up with slaves. He saw his mother weeping sometimes when the little boy came into her chambers with the other maids to dust. He decided that he must speak to him.

'You may as well finish for the day, young master, if you're not even going to try,' said the eunuch tutor.

Gaston was blond-haired with beady grey eyes, oily skin and horrid teeth. Like all scholars, he wore black robes. *Thoroughly unpleasant man, but, by the gods, he is uncannily smart,* Mandami thought as he rose along with his tutor and left the small lavishly decorated schoolroom.

Mandami wondered if Mater had finished birthing his brother or sister. He also worried if this baby would be born dead like his last two brothers Hamish and Julius. He wondered if they would live three weeks like Cephsa. Oh, even mother cried when she had died. Father had been devastated. Cephsa had been so pretty and had survived something called the ordeal. They all thought she would live. Cephsa had been a pretty little blonde with grey-blue eyes like mother and the same creamy skin. Cephsa had barely ever cried.

Mandami had never played with other children, so he hoped

this baby wouldn't die. He didn't understand why he couldn't play with that strange boy. *He couldn't be a slave*. His father said slaves never washed and that was why they were poor, and disease ridden. He wondered if that other boy bathed and maybe that was why he looked well. *Maybe it would be okay for me to play with the boy?* Mandami came to his quarters that had two guards posted at the door. He went inside for his afternoon nap that Coriander still made him take. He really thought he was too grown up for this. He lay down and closed his eyes. He told himself he wasn't sleepy and within a few moments was fast asleep.

—⁓—

Amities wondered about that boy who watched every day from that small room with that ugly little man standing at the front of it. What did he do in there all day? All he did was play and eat, and dust with his mama and sisters once a week with the Mrs.

She is pretty, he thought.

His mama, Gesha, told him to say good afternoon to her every time they went there. Then the Mrs would give mama a copper for him and her and then she would cry, and blubber thank you. He questioned why his sisters Sparra and Deela laughed at him because he was different. He thought that his Dadda might have been different and the one called Derek that lived with them and called him son, may not be his father.

He worried he would have that nightmare again tonight. The one that woke him up and made him make night water. It was the one where a man with scars on his face in tattered black robes, pointed at him and hobbled ever closer. He thought about the strange voice that uttered words in another language to him almost all the time. He had told mama and she had looked at him as if he were evil.

Mama had taken him to a priest who asked for their god to forgive his sins. Amities was made to drink sour wine and thin bread. He was then whipped by the priest four times with the end of a juniper switch, which had made him cry. Then they made him beg for forgiveness.

He had not been allowed water or food again for an entire day. He had cried all night and the crippled man in his dreams had reached out his arms and taken him away to a strange white ruin.

Someone had begun to reach out to him in his mind when he was three. The voice that spoke sounded as gentle as soft rain and as strong as diamonds. He could imagine an old man in green with grey hair, dark eyes and pointed ears. Little did he know that his blood knew its heritage and the language was elvish and came from an old Sidhe, Dane. He wondered if this really old guy was his daddy.

CHAPTER FIFTY-NINE

Ake looked over the balcony at her little son and knew how he and his womb brother were dying to meet. She had affection for Mandami. The extent of it was that Ake thought he was canny enough and that she cared if he was well, but that was about as far as it got. Ake knew Mandami adored her and that he thought Ake loved him as most mothers loved their children. Ake felt saddened by this but could feel nothing else as Cephas controlled Mandami's upbringing. Getting close to Mandami would mean being closer to Cephas.

The sound of an infant's cry came from inside the room which Ake had occupied for four years. The balcony was the closest to outside she ever saw. Sure, everything for her survival was maintained in the quarters. Ake even got books to read occasionally. Her highlight was seeing her little son, Amities once a week. When he looked at her with Lan's eyes and spoke with Lan's voice, she cried.

Mandami saw her every day for an hour. Ake even ruffled his hair occasionally and told him he was a good, kind child. He had never seen other mothers with their children, so he thought her displays of limited affection were normal. *Poor lad,* Ake thought again and sighed. Four guards below the balcony. Four outside the door. She was a prisoner in her own home, if she could call it that. Now, even the painful memories of the first eight years of her life were more comforting than this place. She had only ever felt at home in one place, the curve of Lan's arms.

Ake was now thirty-five, but her weary soul felt more like a thousand. She thought about fifty-nine-year-old Cephas and shuddered. He had more women aside from her, and he dare stick that thing in her every year as if she were another one of his mistresses. It was his duty to see that his wife was satisfied. More like it showed that he still did his imperial duty by not creating crude gossip. He had blamed her for the deaths of his children and had lost interest in her for the last two years.

Ake wondered if she would die up here. They kept knives away from her these last two years as a maid had wandered in one day and saw the blade held against her heart. Then she thought about the porcelain vase. The infant wailed again. *Another son by that god dammed evil man.*

—◊◊◊—

Amities looked up at the Mrs. He saw her go inside where a baby cried, and a few moments later a large smash sounded. Ake knew the guards would come and hid a sliver of the vase under her pillow, just in time. The guards marched in and two held her by the shoulders as a maid was called to clear the mess. Ake explained to them it had fallen when she had swept by to feed Sia.

They believed her and returned to their post. Ake looked at the newborn and did something she hadn't done since holding Amities, kissed the baby on the cheek. The child would survive because his father was sick of his dying brood. So, the baby would forego the ordeal. Ake hushed the grizzling child so the guards wouldn't suspect anything. Ake walked out onto the balcony with the sliver of porcelain and looked down at her son.

Amities watched her curiously. She waved to him, and he thought it polite to wave back. Then something strange happened, there was a blinding flash before his young eyes and the crippled man stood there, turned and pointed up at the Mrs, then at himself. That's when Amities realised this man had the same eyes as him.

Then the crippled man in tattered black robes pointed to him and whispered, 'My son. Her son. Our son.'

Ake inched the sliver through the skin on her chest and Amities screamed. 'Mama!'

Ake stopped and threw the sliver over the balcony. She looked down at Amities and let the tears fall. The guards below looked up at her in shock and then at Amities and wondered. They began to talk among themselves. Gossip spread fast. Amities sat his little bottom on the ground and pouted.

Ake saw an opportunity as the distracted guards gossiped.

———∿∿∿———

Mandami woke up at the scream and rushed into his mother's quarters. He saw his mother looking over the balcony and weeping. He went to her and slipped his little hand into her bigger one.

'Mater. Are you all right, dear Mater?' asked Mandami.

'Not with your little brother down there and me separated. And your bastard of a father forcing me to be his wife and Sia over there expecting me to care for him.'

Mandami looked frightened and released his hand from hers.

'You mean the slave boy's my brother? Don't you love Pater?' Mandami began to sob.

Ake looked at him pityingly. 'No, Mandami, I was stolen away from my husband who is the father of that boy down there named Amities. I loved my husband very much and his son too.'

'And me?' Mandami looked up at her in adoration.

'I care for you a little differently.'

'You love a slave more than a prince?' asked Mandami.

'Yes, Mandami,' said Ake.

'So, Pater is correct, my mater is just another one of his women,' said Mandami, his heart ripping in two.

'If you want to remember me that way.'

Ake walked to the edge of the balcony and suddenly a bright light flared, and an Anwyn stood in her place. Her spirit surged in her once more counteracting the bracelet for a few moments. She turned and blew Mandami a kiss. Mandami's eyes showed amazement, annoyance and then the eyes of an older child. Ake smiled sadly and waved. Mandami turned and exited the room without looking back.

Ake tested her wings, which were built for gliding long distances, and jumped. She had never tried this and lost her balance in the air. The anti-magic bracelet zapped her. Ake yelped as her body filled with searing pain, causing her Anwyn form to almost disappear. She lost her confidence and fell, landing hard but out of the way of the guards. They saw her pick up a startled Amities and run. The guards let up a cry and began to pursue them. Twenty guards came out in front of them, and Ake turned sharply to avoid them. They came to the stone walls of the palace. She looked down at her scared son, spread her wings and leapt, barely clearing the three-metre wall. Amities screamed as she did so, he was scared of heights. He wondered where the gentle Mrs went and why this fire demoness, as his mamma would say, was taking him.

'Demoness, are you taking me to the evil druid and the monster man?' He wept.

'Hush, young one,' Ake said.

They landed and the hairs on the back of her neck prickled as the serfs turned their attention to her unusual appearance. Ake shivered as a shopper dropped her parcels and shrieked, 'It's a demon's bride!'

Amities's innocent young face stared up his mother, his expression a mixture of awe and fear. 'Are you demon's bride?'

Ake's heart yearned with the need to comfort him, but there was no time for that.

Ake heard the iron gates that led to the villa scrape against the rough cobblestones. *Where can we hide?* This was their one chance, Ake ran for the throng of Regis, returning to her human form. Her gown slipped from her shoulders leaving the skin exposed where her wings had erupted and torn the delicate cloth. Remembering the skills Het had taught her all those years ago, Ake slipped past a cloth peddler and pilfered some simple grey robes without the vendor even noticing.

'Won't you get beaten by the priests for that?' asked the forever-inquisitive Amities.

Ake looked at him curiously and shrugged. 'Better my butt warm than freezing.'

Amities blushed at Ake's unladylike use of language. Ake continued among the throng and noticed a cobbler. She saw some fine hobnailed boots lined with the softest leather. These too were added to her attire. A mouse brown cloak, black leather gloves, rope, a purse of copper and a spare pair of clothing for each of them and a tinder box added itself to her collection.

'Demoness, why don't you call the fires from hell to heat your meal? Are you taking me to the demon daddy and are you both going to chew me up? I do hope god will put out the cooking fire.' Amities's mouth puckered up and he began to howl.

Amities was scared, hungry and confused. He reckoned he still wanted to live. He had never eaten apple pie, tasted cream or been to the circus. He wanted to try toffees and watch the clowns and the dancing bear. He wanted to boo at the sword-stealer clown and cheer when the knight got back his sword. He wanted to count and read with all the other poor children in the schoolhouse. But most of all he wanted a real home with parents that said he wasn't evil and didn't tease him about his looks and delicate constitution.

CHAPTER SIXTY

Unbeknown to Ake, an old lady watched her from the shadows. She had deep blue oceanic eyes and silver hair that rippled down to her feet as delicate as water and as thick as clouds. She had tawny skin that still showed the signs of magnificent beauty retiring. Like the Regians, the woman had a finely chiselled face with a proud nose. The woman was dressed in robes of a striking mauve, and she took in everything Ake said or did.

The woman stood at a smallish five feet. She slipped from the shadows, still delicate and balanced on her ageing feet. Tirian had told her of the earthbound goddess years ago. Tirian had passed on a few months later, being in her early hundreds. Clara wondered how long she had yet. Clara wanted to do so many things. She saw the pain in Ake's soul and the boy's spirit. Clara wondered if her healer's skills and air-tone enchantress voice could warm love back into that wounded aura.

Clara had watched the scene in the marketplace and followed Ake and Amities as they fled the more densely populated business area. She followed them down another alley as Ake tried to navigate her way through the city. They had entered the poorer section. Serfs lay in the street dying of plague, their bodies in various forms of decay. Children played in the street ignoring the corpses. It was now midday, and the sun was high in the sky. Rats chewed at the bodies and made nests in the discarded refuse that came with living, from fraying cloth, rotting food and the evidence of discarded bodily functions. The sweltering heat and obnoxious odours of illness and decay assaulted Ake's nostrils and she gagged. *How can anyone live this way and still worship their emperor? These poor people.*

Ake's hackles rose, and she looked around. Ake spotted the kindly looking elderly woman and wondered if she'd seen everything and would shout to the foot patrol. But the lady just smiled at her and waved. Ake thought she must be suffering from madness and must think she was somebody else. Ake shrugged and waved back. By now Amities had stopped howling and was watching curiously.

Oh, now the poor dear is coming over here. I should never have waved, oh well, there is nothing for it now. At least if the lady is mad, she will forget what she has seen quickly. Amities laid his weary head on Ake's grey-robed shoulder and fell asleep, not caring anymore. Ake then went out to meet the woman.

CHAPTER SIXTY-ONE

Dane entered the room and looked at the damaged and broken figure asleep on the bed. It had been almost six years. The man was well enough to move around, he'd even taken up Qwena, sign language. He now knew it fluently. The man before him was quite deaf and had lost the ability to speak. He had also lost all of his magic, as well as much of his sight. Dane had shed enough tears for his son. Now, it was time to heal his spirit.

Lan woke to see his father watching him from the doorway of the bare, mirrorless room. They had covered him in bandages and lotions for over two years. Halfway through the third year they had unbandaged him. They had made sure he was well fed, clean and his thirst quenched. A month later Dane had brought him a mirror and said kindly but firmly that he must face reality, unlike the servants who whispered and slunk their way around him.

He had thrown himself out of the window the night after. He had fallen two floors and banged himself up even more, but again he recovered. His father had then shifted him to the first floor and kept an elven guard outside. Lan didn't like what he had seen. He knew he would never be able to use magic again. He had begun to whistle today. At least that was a sound from his tortured throat.

Lan had to walk with the aid of a walking stick. He had one half decent leg with a slight limp and the other was completely twisted, the skin still peeling and wrinkled from the fire. His right side was also badly scarred. But oh gods, his face. He thought he would have that at least. The left side was fine apart from the scar from the horned guards, oh but the right. He put his hand up to his face. His eye was closed over and the skin around it was dry, wrinkled and many scars ran along the surface. But he knew they were not deeper than the scars that lived and brooded inside.

Lan knew that bastard Cephas had Ake and by the gods, he wondered if he treated her horribly. That made him just despair more.

He sat up and looked at his father. He knew what his father had told him yesterday was true. That being a fighter of any type is to live or die by his sword and that there was a remarkably high chance he would sustain serious injuries or never return home at all. He had said, 'Remember Het, Lan. The poor lad didn't have to fight for your palace, but he chose to and died face down in the mud with a sword in his back.'

Yeah, but he died with honour. Lan had signed back. He sighed and looked forward to the visit of Serenade, Flo and Hau. He knew these five years they had been training and securing an elven and Galli army to get Ake home. He worried that Ake was better off there with the emperor than here with a husk of a man who couldn't even tell her how much she meant to him. He wondered if Ake had any children. He questioned if Ake even knew he was alive or if she even cared.

Dane signed good morning to Lan, who acknowledged him by nodding. He wondered if his ageing father had any knowledge of Ake. He signed his question.

Dane spoke his answer. 'Several things.'

What? asked Lan.

'That she was tricked into believing you dead.'

That bastard. Anything else? signed Lan quickly.

'She has birthed six children, three are still living.'

His? asked Lan.

'Most. His two sons are living. Two other sons were born dead, and the little daughter Cephsa lived three weeks.'

That's only five, signed Lan.

'One by another man,' sighed Dane.

So, that bastard let other men use her as well. Or maybe Ake had had a lover and he or she was the offspring off that affair.

Well? And why didn't you tell me all this?

'You never asked so I thought it was too painful for you.'

The child. Did Ake get some happiness in a lover's arms?

'No.'

Oh, so did the emperor allow other men to use her?

'Oh no! He is a very proud man.'

Then, how?

'He's five years old and his name is Amities.'

Come on … Come on I want to know, signed Lan impatiently.

'He's your son Lan.'

How? signed Lan slowly.

Dane chuckled. 'I don't need to tell you how it's done Lan. I'm sure you consummated your marriage with Ake. And, well, all of Orilan's victims became extremely fertile after he bit them due to his use of high magic. With you two, phew, throw in the divine and elvish blood … well, you get the picture.'

Well, that's a cure for infertile couples then. Wow, mine. Does she love him?

'She adores him. She can't even love the others. But they were kept away from each other except once a week and no physical contact.'

Lan felt his heart contract with pain.

How do you know all this? If you have all this information, why haven't you rescued my wife and son?

'We tried. The spies who infiltrated the palace were killed

and each time security was improved. I have also been sending visions to Amities, but they just scared him. I could not contact Ake. There was some barrier preventing her using her magic. We are hoping a direct assault from our army will give us a big enough diversion so that we can again infiltrate the palace and rescue them.'

I will be going to Regis with the Galli and elf army even though I am of no use.

Dane looked pleased. Lan stood and walked. Just walked, but it felt as though he were flying.

CHAPTER SIXTY-TWO

The woman named Clara slurped her hot chocolate and placed the mug back on the table. Ake sipped hers slowly. Amities, bleary eyed, ate toffees. They were seated at an alfresco cafe near a bend in the large Regis river. The water was putrid and dangerous to drink for any human, but the serfs did so. She saw one of the gutter kids drinking it by the handful and wondered what ills would befall the youngster.

Clara had told Ake that she was the niece of the gypsies that Ake had met in her youth. She'd shouted them lunch and they had talked for hours about everything. That voice, those eyes held Ake and she felt she should talk to this woman about her hurts. Amities had fallen asleep and had only just woken. Clara said all children liked sweets and purchased them. Ake had protested but Clara waved her protestations away with a wave of her hand. The little boy was soon wide awake and had the stuff smeared over his face and hands. Clara laughed and Amities smiled back. Ake felt her soul lift and wondered if this person was more than just a little old lady with kind eyes and heart.

—⁓—

Clara had offered Ake and Amities a place to stay for a few days until the local authorities had found them. Ake and Amities had disguised themselves and they had made a run for it. Ake ducked her head out of the alleyway to see if anyone was watching. They had entered the industrial area, a collection of white stone buildings with several alleyways that led to various businesses. The air was strong with the odour of ammonia, sulphur and other industrial smells.

It was a few hours before dawn, and Ake was trying to find the safehouse Clara had arranged for them. She saw a guard walk by and pulled herself back into the dark alley.

Amities's teeth chattered in the cold and the child rubbed his hands together trying to get warm. His lips turned blue and his breath turned to mist as they waited in the cold pre-dawn air.

Ake knelt down and smiled. 'Here, let me help. I won't harm you, Amities.'

He took a step back, trembling.

'I'll show you. Look, see how I blow on my hands?' Ake held out her hands and blew on them.

Amities tried, he began to sniffle, and his eyes filled with tears.

'May I?' Ake asked, reaching out for his hands.

He put them out and closed his eyes. She cupped his hands in hers and blew on them. Amities opened his eyes and smiled. She released his hands when they were warmer.

'Now, Amities, we have to make a run to the next alley and we must be very quiet. Do you think you can manage that?' Ake gave him a reassuring pat on the head.

He nodded and they crossed the alleyway quickly and knocked on a shabby door. The door opened a crack and steam billowed out in the crisp early morning air.

'What you want? Laundry isn't open yet,' said a hoarse voice.

'Clara sent us. Bairn and mother,' said Ake.

The door opened and Ake could see women turning large vats of washing with huge paddles. Some of the water splashed over the edges of the large stone tubs. The air was humid with steam and sweat.

'Well, get in before the bloody guards get you,' said a small, wizened woman. The woman's eyes were filled with suspicion and her eyes darted around, checking no one had followed them.

They walked inside and the woman closed the door and locked it before turning to look them over.

'The work is simple. You scrub the stains out with lye soap, boil them in the vats, making sure you turn the load regularly. I won't start you on the ringers. Not yet. You get your meals and board. You will work hard if you want me to feed that boy. We aren't a charity case. Go over to that woman and she will show you what to do,' said the laundress. She pointed to a woman nearby.

Ake nodded and wandered over and the woman began to show her what to do.

—◦◦◦—

Ake was exhausted, it was nearly midnight. Amities was curled up on a pile of fresh towels. The laundress had given him some soup and he had fallen asleep quickly. The other women had returned to their homes. It had been a few weeks now and Ake had been working extra shifts to earn more than their room and board. She had a nice little pile of coins.

The child had been slowly opening up to her. She always took her meal breaks with him and tried to ask him questions about his interests and make small talk. The last few days he had been watching her work and had even tried to help her with her work-load. She had reassured him this is what mothers did when their children needed to eat. Amities had given her a big smile and began to put the towels away.

Her hands were raw and her back ached but at least her son was safe. Ake put the paddle down and sat against the wall near her.

Amities whimpered in his sleep. 'No, go away scary devil.'

He has these nightmares nearly every night, poor child. At first, Amities would back off when she woke him or tried to talk to him about the dream.

The child opened his eyes and Ake gave him a reassuring smile. Amities reached out his hand and Ake held it. 'I'm here, baby, no one can hurt you.'

Amities closed his eyes and drifted off. Ake threw a dry towel over him, and the boy smiled in his sleep. 'Thank you, Mama.'

Ake wiped away a happy tear. She smiled and lay her head back against the wall. *My baby called me Mama.* Ake closed her eyes and drifted off, content, a feeling she hadn't experienced in a long time.

CHAPTER SIXTY-THREE

General Kestrel of the army of Sorendee stood on the deck of one of the warships trying to bolster the spirits of his warriors.

'Make your empress, Elder Flower, proud. Celebrate your king, Serenade. Fight for your pagan prince, Hau.'

The army cheered, ready to come ashore. Their ship was resting at anchor in the Regis river. The ship's name was written on the ship as *Syl* but was pronounced soul.

Hau, Serenade, Dane and Lan stood looking out at Regis. They thought it already seemed defeated. The citizens were starving and diseased. People had lost their faith in their emperor and sign of rebellion had come in the form of citizens cheering them from the shore.

Flo ordered bread and small fish to be thrown to them from their own supplies. She had read that some prophet had done so, and they thought he was great. Flo thought a pet bird must think its owner is god. It's feed, water, and even the amount of light it receives are all at the behest of its owner. The serfs were like pets for their rulers, an amusement in which the ruler gained the status of god through the peasants' eyes.

Imagine if all knowledge was lost and all elders died, and children were the only ones left. They would look to the sun and the moon for answers as people have since life began. They would see law, life and love in their actions and each other's eyes. Not rolling off some man's tongue and onto a scroll for the so-called only right way to live. Thoughts like this could make a woman mad, Flo thought. So, instead, she looked at her army. *Actions. A whole four thousand actions made up of hundreds of smaller actions. Hearts beating, thoughts wandering, eyes filled with courage and purpose.* Her army consisted of three thousand tartan-kilted Galli in boots with golden torques at their throats. Some were as young as Het had been. Eight hundred elven men and women, all archers.

Then came the roc riders, the Air Sidhe. She had a mere hundred of these. The giant eagles were known as rocs, fifteen feet in height, they fought with beak and claw. Their riders were tiny elves of many hues held on by a few leathers and reigns gripped in their hands, invisible to those on the ground.

Next in line were the unicorn rider Sidhe on their dazzling white mounts whose sharp horns glinted in the morning sun. Flo had a hundred of these also. This was all she had against the armies of Regis. But her army did look fierce, all attired in the way of tribes and gods.

Flo was grateful for the ancient alliance between the elves of Relequis and the Galli. When the world was young, and the gods were new, the world was more prone to unusual seasons and great disasters. The Sidhe had tried to protect the Galli humans with their magic and wisdom until the humans became strong and founded the great Galli civilisations of Eriu and Breteyne. In exchange, the two peoples traded and made a pact to come to each other's aid if the need arose.

Chapter Sixty-Four

Lan looked at Dane and the others and then limped away. In the last six weeks he had learnt to do without his walking aid. To every other man's three strides he could take five steps. He tripped over a knothole in the planks and steadied himself on the railing.

Lan thought it would be very amusing if he put on the suit that Mikaere had suggested at his and Ake's wedding. All his nasty injuries would make him look like a strong and nasty pirate who had conquered many a country. The limp would seem authentic. He felt a tear slide down his cheek at that happy memory of his wedding.

'Ake,' he whispered. *What? By the gods I said something, maybe. I'll try it again to be sure,* he thought. 'Ake,' he drawled. *Easily done,* he thought, except his throat felt overworked. Maybe he could try to say something else. He wet his lips and felt his dry throat. He took out his ink quill and papyrus and wrote down that he wanted a drink and handed it to an elven servant, who scurried off to find refreshments to take to his room. Lan went to his lavishly decorated, mirrorless cabin and on his bedside table was a cool jug of lemon water and a glass. He poured some of the soothing brew into a glass and put the glass to his lips. He sighed as the cold thick fluid soothed his parched throat. Now he wondered if he could say the alphabet. He found out he could only pronounce the vowels, and letters k, p, s and d.

'S ... E ... See,' forced Lan and his face lit up in absolute happiness.

He knew he had better stop or he'd do too much in one day. He knew they were waiting for the emperor to come to an agreement. It could be a while, even days, before the emperor decided he was ready to deal with these so-called criminals. He was exhausted and decided to go to sleep.

CHAPTER SIXTY-FIVE

Amities felt the fear building that was the lead up to the breathing war. He tried to gulp in mouthfuls of air, but his chest was constricting quickly now. He had had this since he was two years old. It came on when he ran too hard or in colder weather. His mother noticed this and helped steady him.

They had been on the run for four weeks now. The guards had raided the laundry and the owner had helped them escape out of a back door. Ake had heard of several ships in the Regis river equipped for warcraft. She was heading there to seek employment. Ake scratched her head in nervousness. Her blonde tresses were no longer there. Instead, Ake looked like a man with short black hair and with a son who had red hair. Ake had even got Amities to call her Da.

They both wore black breeches, white tunic and red vest. Ake carried their few overused belongings in their sole backpack. She was really worried about Amities. They had run out of money and hadn't eaten for two days. The boy seemed in pain and his breath came in harsh wheezes. Ake sat him down and told him to breathe in unison with her. Amities did this and after fifteen minutes his breathing reached normality and he smiled weakly.

Ake picked Amities up and they headed up the gangplank leading onto the foremost ship. Ake noticed it was a huge war galleon with four masts.

The ship reminded her of Serenade's war galleon. She

remembered the ship was called *Syl* and was two hundred and ten feet in length and had a thirty-foot draft and was powered by one hundred oarsmen. Ake knew the ship had several floors. She noted this ship was anchored and her limp flax sails whipped in the sea air.

An elven soldier met her, and Ake found it strange to see an elf so far this way.

'Who does this ship belong to?' Ake deepened her voice.

'What's it to you, young man?' asked the elf.

'Me and my boy was wondering if we could get work?' asked Ake.

'Well, we're pretty much full,' said the elf.

'Oh, too bad. We're part of the Eriu kingdom and we need to get home,' said Ake.

'Can you cook?' asked the elf.

'No,' she said.

'Clean?' asked the elf.

'Laundry work,' said Ake.

'We don't need that. Anything else?' asked the elf.

'Heal and fight,' said Ake.

'We could always use another healer,' said the elf.

'Excellent. Do we get food, water and shelter?' asked Ake.

'Six coppers a week, food, water and you sleep on deck,' said the elf.

'But my son is poorly,' said Ake.

'That's the best I can do for you. Take it or leave it,' said the elf.

Ake looked at the boy and sighed. 'We will take it.' The elven guard led them aboard.

CHAPTER SIXTY-SIX

The army stood at the ready. The footmen first, archers behind, roc riders and mounts hovering above and the unicorn riders bringing up the rear. The general shouted encouragements to them while riding back and forth across the lines. Serenade sat astride his black war destrier. His diamond-edged sword, *Songs Edge*, sheathed. Flo and Hau stood looking down at the proud army from the deck of *Syl*. Dane was astride a female unicorn called Barmyth. The healers waited on the deck with an amazing herbal healer, Lan. Ake and Amities were not there. They had been called down to tend the dysentery patients below deck, where the rowers were.

It was dawn and the great battle was to take place on the flat plains outside the city of Regis. The Regis river wound around the great city like an enamoured serpent providing life-giving water to the Regians. The great docks were stationed further out where the tail of the great serpent-like river met the salty sea. The waves hissed like frenzied serpents as they crashed against jagged rocks.

The army of the Daione Sidhe was to face the Regian garrison of five thousand footmen and two thousand archers. They looked glorious but their proud arrogance could be their downfall. The footmen were dressed in hardened leather armour with chain mail cuirass over the top. They had red cloaks, leather kilts and full-toed boots. They were armed with iron short swords at their hips, large wooden shields and long, iron-tipped spears.

The archers wore plain leather armour over breeches and tunic; their composite bows and iron-tipped arrows were pointed at the enemy. The archers stood at the rear of the army.

Cephas sat on a huge, white war destrier. He was dressed in a purple cloak, iron chain mail over black leather armour and he wore a black leather kilt. With his double-handed iron longsword raised in the air, his army looked at him with complete adoration.

'Men. Yes, we are men. We will conquer as we have done far more vicious enemies, we are the strength of Regis. We have a duty to our proud and benevolent mother who has suckled us, sustained us for so many a century. Will we stand around and see our mother's legs thrown open as these heathens plunder her? No, we will not!' Cephas smiled.

The emperor finished his war speech; his army cheered with loud exclamations of their love for him.

The battle raged on long into the night. Many wounded lay on the deck of *Syl*. The sheer numbers of the Regians were tearing down the Daione Sidhe.

Lan was writing down lists for equipment, healing procedures and names of the dead while his band of six healers were putting the information into play. Their soldiers had taken down a few of the more organised Regians but not enough to cause an impediment.

The roc riders hadn't been harmed but they were resting at the moment while Serenade, Dane and the general discussed strategies. Another dozen Gallis were brought aboard the ship. Lan knew they would not have enough healing supplies if too many more were injured. He called for more healers and four servants rushed below deck to grab the other four healers working with the dysentery epidemic. When they were brought forth to Lan, he noticed a frail boy, a feminine-looking young man, an old woman and a small female teen elf. He sighed and wondered how decent a healer they were. *I won't get much help out of the small boy and teen girl.* He shrugged and set them to work.

—∿∿—

Cephas laughed as more elves and Gallis lay dying on the ground. Men writhed in agony as their entrails slimed onto the ground, letting off body-warmed steam into the frigid air. Heads rolled and he felt bones crush under his steed's hooves as he rode, slashing and hacking, towards the *Syl*. Blood streamed from a dozen cuts over his lean, ageing body, some of it his own, some of it from fresh dead men.

—∿∿—

Unbeknown to her father, Flo ordered a mount and drew up a sword. She rushed on some steel chain mail and leapt upon the stallion. Flo raced towards Cephas, anger and despair clouded her eyes. Cephas laughed and Hau screamed as Cephas used the hilt of his sword as a lance and knocked Flo from her mount. Serenade turned around at Hau's scream as the unicorn's diamond-like hooves came down upon Flo's fragile body. Flo felt her small legs shatter and screamed.

Serenade ordered a fresh mount and rode out to meet the emperor, for he knew they were defeated. Dane sent *Druid Fire* hurtling into a few enemies, lit torches for light with a simple thought and sent dying men peacefully into sleep. Lan heard a scream. He turned and saw a young, weaponless man rush down the gangplank without a second thought.

He admired the lad's courage but cursed his flippancy. The lad reached Flo's side and lifted the shocked, broken girl and proceeded to carry her back to the ship. He watched in anger as a white flag was lowered above the crow's nest. He saw Serenade talking to the emperor. Then Serenade turned around and galloped his mount up the gangplank. Serenade told everyone to gather the still living and draw the anchor. An hour later, *Syl* was among the other ships sailing out to sea.

⸻⁓⸻

Ake didn't know what to do. *That was Flo, my dear Flo.* She wiped a tear from her eye and continued to scrub the deck. It was dusk and the deck was caked in blood and entrails and the stench made her gag. She knew Serenade was on board and wondered why her family members were in Regis and then it dawned on her. *Could they be here for me? All that bloodshed!* She wanted to reach out to Serenade but she was overwhelmed with grief and guilt. Flo was hurt because she had tried to save Ake from Cephas. *As soon as Amities and I get home we are going to disappear and make a new life for ourselves. That way I can no longer destroy others' livelihoods.* Ake put her grief into her work, trying to distract herself.

CHAPTER SIXTY-SEVEN

Lan had signed curses faster than Dane could translate them.

Serenade had admitted defeat. To Lan, he was an absolute coward. He had surrendered, and the emperor had spared the rest of the living and told them never to set foot again in Regis upon penalty of death. Lan had demanded to know why.

Serenade had turned around and said, 'I will not risk my daughter and my kingdom on the chance that we may find one woman.'

Lan had replied, 'But we did this for her.'

Serenade had just sighed and shaken his head. 'That was when we thought Cephas still had Ake. If we had a chance in finding her, I would send more men out there without a second thought.'

Lan lay back on his lumpy bed, frustrated. His thoughts turned to the lad who had rescued Flo. No one knew his name, but Serenade was inquiring among the hundreds on his ship. He had been in his cabin since shortly after dusk. There were still about six hours before dawn, and he couldn't sleep. He got up and wandered out of his cabin, still fully dressed in his pirate gear minus the hat. He looked over the railing and watched the water caress the boat's wooden skin and listened to the gentle lap and steady rise and fall of the oars. He saw the man who had rescued Flo and his brother or son scrubbing the deck, with only the light of a single lantern to aid them. Curious he moved towards them. *I will go ask the lad's name.*

Ake looked up to see the disfigured hulk of a pirate painstakingly heading towards her and Amities. Her son began to shudder and whimper.

'Calm yourself, boy. It's just another sailor on the ship,' said Ake in her boyish voice.

Lan looked at the little lad. Even with his limited sight he noticed the dark patches under the child's eyes. The boy was diminutive in size and undernourished. *Poor child.*

'Can I help you?' asked Ake.

Lan took out some parchment, remembering he could hardly speak. It was in the cycle of the dark moon and Ake wasn't sure if she'd be able to read the mute's words. Ake sent her whimpering son off to bring a lit torch. Amities ran off. Several moments passed and the boy brought back a torch. The smoke billowed into the air as the flames greedily consumed the oiled rags.

Amities hid behind his mother. He adored his real mama who cuddled him when he had nightmares and told him she loved him and would always be there for him. Ake looked at the somewhat familiar writing.

What is your name and why did you rescue the king's daughter?

'Can you hear?' asked Ake.

Lan nodded.

'I thought the girl was beautiful. I thought I might be able to marry her, or I'd get a rich reward for me and ma boy,' she lied.

Name? Lan wrote.

'They call me Escapee.'

Strange name! scribbled Lan.

'Aye, it sure be.'

Lan noticed the Eriu accent.

Ake was trying to familiarise herself with the writing. *Where have I seen it before?*

'I recognise your writing.'

Really, have I met you before? scrawled Lan.

'Maybe. But I'm not sure where from.'

Are you from Eriu? wrote Lan.

'From thereabouts.'

At that moment, the *Syl* rolled harshly to one side as it peaked a tall wave.

'It's probably best we finish our conversation at a later date as I fear a hell of a storm is upon us,' said Ake.

Lan turned and dipped his head slightly in a respectful manner. The ship lurched again and this time it dragged all three towards the edge of *Syl*. Ake was almost flung overboard but she managed to get a grip on the railing. Lan fell atop Amities. In a desperate struggle, Lan turned so that the fall wouldn't crush the boy. He felt his back slam against the solid wood of the bulwark. Rain began to pelt down in icy torrents and the deck was saturated in seconds. A ghastly wind began to howl. Lan helped Amities stand and then eased himself up against the side of the ship. He flung out a hand to Ake. Ake placed a shivering hand in his. The ship lurched again, and Ake's hand slipped out of Lan's.

Ake now only had a one-handed grip on the outer side of the ship. Lan reached out over the ship and tried to pull her in. But they were saturated, and Ake felt her hand slipping. Amities, thinking his mother was being attacked, began pounding on his father's legs, his little fists making a futile attempt at hurting him.

'Mama! Let me mama go!' The boy wept.

Three Galli sailors came rushing over to the squalling boy. They took in the scene. It seemed as if that weird ex-mystic was trying to drown the boy that had saved his cousin. The older of the triplet sailors noticed the boy being flung overboard had feminine contours. He rushed over, pushed Lan back, who fell over, and the sailor pulled Ake back onto the ship.

The two other brothers, red flaming hair whipping and hazel eyes flashing, grabbed the boy and Lan between them. The brothers were exceptionally muscled, stocky and stood at six foot six with weather-beaten white skin. Lan tried to pull away and one of the men held him tightly. Lan scowled; the big man laughed.

Amities lashed out, trying to kick his captor. The sailor holding him held him at arm's length and commented on what a brave wee bairn he was.

Meanwhile, the eldest brother set Ake gently on her feet.

'So, lassie, my name is Hamlin, what's yours?'

'Lassie? I be a man,' drawled Ake.

The other two brothers laughed.

'Lincoln, Rafater, shut up, she been through a lot with this elfling tryin' ta drown her and such,' said Hamlin.

'Sorry, mam,' said Lincoln and Rafater. Feeling guilty, their cheeks flushed red.

Lincoln placed Amities on the deck and took the torch out of his small hands and into his large ones. He gave Amities a toothy grin and ruffled his hair. Rafater stood Lan on his feet and pushed him towards Hamish.

'Now, elfling, what have ya got to say for yeself?' asked Hamlin.

Lan stamped his good foot in annoyance and indicated to the pieces of papyrus he had been using to communicate, which were now flying away in the wind.

The rain pelted down harder. Hamlin smiled. 'Let's proceed to the galley where there is a blazing fire and our cook, Wyatt, will serve up some grub.' They all nodded eagerly and went down the nearest steps. The ship rolled to the side, a bit too eagerly for comfort.

They walked through a grimy, gloomy passageway which stretched about four metres in length one and a half metres across and seven feet, ceiling to floor and lit with a solitary torch. But at least there was a light at the end of this dark and dreary tunnel.

They entered through a grimy door into a surprisingly clean and homely galley.

A blazing fire lit the room and they all jumped as it cracked loudly. Three picnic-like benches took up the centre of the room and each had a storm lantern burning in the centre of it. They seated about six apiece. A huge bar took up the other end and had spring action half doors.

Behind this bar was a wood oven and a shelf holding wooden bowls and various cooking utensils. There were also clay mugs and several kegs of beer and spiced ales. Over the fire were two upright steel rods and a horizontal rod lay connected to the two. Attached to the horizontal bar was a hook where a huge cast iron pot hung with an iron ladle in it. The ship lurched again, and the pot swung precariously. Some utensils and wooden bowls clattered to the floor.

'Shite,' said Wyatt. He ran from behind the bar and, with the aid of the fire poker, settled the pot.

Amities looked at the cook. He was bald, tattooed, weather-beaten, bearded and rough-looking. A huge tattoo of a red dragon ran the length of his left upper arm, its serpent tongue darting forth and its tail coiled around his bicep. The man's beard was blond and his eyes a stunning emerald green. His mouth had lots of laughter lines, as did the corners of his eyes. He was heavy set, but reckoned he was big boned, and he had a big thick neck.

Amities got up and went to the bar where he began to pick up the fallen items. Hamlin winked at Amities and rose to talk to Wyatt. They began whispering and ten minutes later saw six bowls of nourishing spicy stew wafting away on the table in front of the group.

Amities ladled the stuff into his mouth hungrily and gave a watery smile to his mother. Ake laughed at his joy and sipped hers slowly.

Chapter Sixty-Eight

Captain Navita began ordering his staff to batten down the hatches, drop the sails and, those that weren't in his priority team, to get below deck. With forty years' experience the sixty-year-old Galli knew this was going to be a terrible storm. He turned his silver eyes and red-haired framed face to Dane.

'Is there anyone here who can calm a hell cat storm?' he asked.

'I have my grandson aboard. He might be able to help,' said Dane.

'Get him,' said Captain Navita.

———

Ake, Amities and Lan were now alone in the galley. Ake had explained the incident. When she was finished, Hamish had guffawed, slapped Lan on the back, whistled at Ake and ruffled Amities's hair and left with his brothers. Amities sat on the floor rolling bits of stale cheese he had found under the table into a mouse hole. Lan and Ake sat apart, staring at each other.

Lan was the first to question. 'R uoo Ake?' he asked stumbling over the letters, trying to piece them together as his speech improved.

'Yes, but you can't be Lan, and yet, I know you are.'

'They sed ta use I ded.'

'Yes.'

'They …' Lan struggled to find the words.

'Lied.' Ake shivered, finishing his sentence.

Lan stood and gestured to Ake. 'Use tired?'

Ake yawned and her head drooped wearily. Lan smiled and Amities shivered. Ake saw the pain in his eyes.

'Amities, he is a good man. Looks are deceiving.'

Amities frowned. 'Mama, I am not scared of him because of his looks. He was in my dreams.'

'Dane sent dr…' Lan looked flustered.

'Dane tried to contact Amities?'

Lan nodded.

'How come they never tried with me?'

Lan sighed. 'Did. Cud not.'

Amities took his mother's hand as Lan left the galley. They made their way to his little cabin. Lan held open the door and wobbled. Ake steadied him with her hand and Lan's hand instinctively brushed hers as she drew the hand back.

Orilan raised his arms to Sorendee and drew upon his unnatural power. His sharp canines glinted in the light of four torches. His deep blue eyes flashed sharply and his short, chestnut hair was drenched as well as the black leather breeches, leather boots and tunic and jacket he wore.

Dane looked proudly at his apprentice, whom he'd rescued from the brink of death nearly six years ago. He gave thanks to Dee every day for turning him human again after a six-week, terribly exhausting ritual. Orilan managed to bring a lull in the storm. He turned sharply and looked straight into the captain's eyes.

'Find land within two hours or we may never find it.' Orilan swivelled on his feet and strode away, back to his cabin.

Amities lay snoozing on a lumpy bed. It was two hours after they had eaten in the galley and Lan had taken his small family back to his cabin. Ake sat on a cane chair, turned away from him at an angle, watching her sleeping son. Lan sat in a corner on another chair, lost in shadow. On a table near Ake burned a solitary candle.

Ake had realised where there should be a mirror on one of the doors of the wardrobe there wasn't one. She turned to Lan and was about to ask why.

'U sor ma face,' was all he whispered.

Ake got up and placed their son under the covers. She then looked around for torch holders. There were four, one at each corner of the room. Ake took the candle and lit the torches in them. Light flared dazzlingly for a moment then steadied. Lan grabbed his hooded cloak from where it was hanging over his chair and rushed it on, throwing the hood down over his face. Ake noticed his speech had improved.

'I saw your face before.'

'That a for I no hoo u was.' Lan glared at her.

'Temper, Lan! I thought I would have more of a right, as I'm your wife. Well, I guess if you don't want me to be anymore ...' Ake sighed sadly.

'Cors u r. I hope.'

As a show of good faith, Lan slid the hood from his face, trembling as he did so and hoping that she wouldn't be disgusted at the look of him. Ake moved towards him. He held his hand up to stop her.

She looked taken aback and began to cry. 'You don't want me to touch you.'

'No! Luk at me. I'm na fit ta luk at. U on a udder hand luk ike u hadn't even got ta scratch.' Lan smirked.

With that, Ake wiped away her tears with the back of her hand. She scowled at him and left the cabin. Lan, shocked by this display of rebellion, just stared after her. He'd wanted to say lots of things to her, how he'd missed her and just wanted to hold her and listen.

She deserved better, he thought. She was a jewel, and he was just a broken and angry man that couldn't even get his tongue around the words his heart so desperately clung to.

CHAPTER SIXTY-NINE

It was pouring outside, so bad that on the flooding deck anything not tied down was sliding all over the place. The storm had started again, and Captain Navita had not sighted land. He knew the ship and her inhabitants were not going to make it. He thought suddenly of his wife and three daughters. Sasha, his doe-eyed, beautiful wife would be tucking his darling daughters into their beds. They would eagerly be awaiting their mother's tales of him while a fire blazed warmly in their room and quilts up to their noses. He sighed and called for his primary team, which consisted of six of the hardest and most experienced sailors.

Among them were Hamlin and his brothers, Wyatt the cook, Bran the only woman, Cap the kobold-killer and Zacariahn. Bran was similar to her brother, Wyatt, tall and built like a bear. Bran was forty-two and wore her hair in a pair of pigtails, her blue eyes had seen heavy combat. Cap, a tall and lanky lad of twenty-seven was the youngest of the gang. His brown hair matched his eyes and curled around his small ears. Zacarianhn was the oldest at fifty-seven and a giant of a man. His dark skin rippled with muscles and his brown eyes sparkled with a mixture of warmth and steely resolve.

'My brave men and Bran. This could very well be our last ride together and I just want to say I'm so proud of ya all. And it was bloody grand to work with ye,' the captain said.

His group cheered and grinned.

'It may not be the last time,' said Zacariahn.

'Hear hear,' said the rest.

The captain slipped back behind the helm.

Zacariahn climbed the rigging and gained the crow's nest. His night sight was incredible in the small light of a storm lantern hanging nearby. His eyes scanned the horizon for any view of land but what he saw made his heart sink. Masses of jagged rock lay in wait to tear *Syl* apart, like a predator hunting in the dark. He screamed down his warning to Bran who was lashing down objects that would make walking on the deck a danger. Bran heard her lover's cries and climbed up to meet him.

Drianna screamed with delight as her doppelgangers attacked Bran and Zacariahn. They were four feet and had thick, grey skin. They had squat, square noses and a gaping hole full of fangs where a mouth would normally be. Their two puny, white eyes were watching them coldly. They ripped the sailors apart and blood showered down onto Orilan.

Orilan looked up as blood splattered on him. He saw the doppelgangers rip Bran and Zacariahn apart. *I need to tell Dane.* The vital message of the rock sighting never made it to Navita because the doppelgangers took the form of their victims and gave the message, 'Land ho. Straight ahead.'

Twenty minutes after telling Dane what he had saw, Orilan stood watching Ake. He was about ten feet away, his breathing stilled, and blended into the night. Ake was crying. He looked towards the door she had come from, coldly. In a movement too quick for human eyes, Orilan opened the door to Lan's cabin and stepped inside. Lan, thinking Ake had come back in, looked up to apologise.

Upon seeing a man in his room, he stood quickly. Orilan gave him a fleeting glance, picked up Amities and slipped from the room. Ake turned as Lan rushed from the room. He grabbed the drenched Ake by the wrist pulled her to him and glanced around quickly.

'He got der boy,' said Lan.

Ake, looking extremely alarmed, asked who it was. At that moment, before Lan answered, Orilan appeared in front of them as if out of nowhere. He held Amities cradled in the crook of his arms tenderly, as you would a baby.

'Who are you?' asked Ake.

'Come with me now. That is if you wish to preserve your child's life,' said Orilan.

They followed him to the two lifeboats, which were covered with flax. The rain turned extremely cold and cut them all through like a knife. Orilan took the flax off one of the boats, placed Amities in the boat and hurriedly folded the flax into fours. He then lifted a heavy metal chest and stowed it away in the eight-seater rowboat. Dane came rushing out with Hau. He spoke quickly.

'Serenade won't come. He says he won't leave his ship or Elder Flower.'

'Can't they bring her?' asked Ake.

'Too weak, she'll die either way,' said Dane sadly.

'No!' Ake turned to leave.

Lan grabbed her and held her to him, strongly. She struggled against him, her eyes streaming with the rain and her angry tears. Dane ushered an extremely frightened and confused Hau into the boat.

Dane and Ori turned to the sea, raised their arms and uttered harshly, '*Larg ska.*'

The boat hoisted sharply up into the air and over the side of *Syl* and landed with a gentle slap in the water.

'Now for the woman,' said Orilan.

Lan released Ake and she tried to bolt for it. 'I have to rescue Flo.'

'*Naght*,' hissed Orilan.

Ake slumped to the ground, asleep. Lan went over to her and picked her up, his bad leg streaking with pain for doing so. He handed her to Dane, refusing to give her into Orilan's outstretched arms. Orilan looked into his father's eyes.

'You do know who I am?' asked Orilan.

Lan nodded to Dane to translate as he began to sign.

I know you are Orilan. Lan scowled.

Orilan nodded.

Lan continued. I won't be coming. Save someone whole. A child maybe.

Orilan laughed gently, almost patronisingly. 'Good, then I can be her stalwart protector.'

Lan felt his body fill with rage.

Bastard. I'm only coming so I can keep her from you, said Lan.

Dane shook his head sadly at Lan after translating. Orilan smiled; his manipulation had worked. With the same spell he'd cast on the boat, he lowered the rest of them into the vessel.

'*Moves kadaca.*' Dane cast a movement spell on their boat.

Their little boat sped away from *Syl* just as she crashed upon the jagged rocks. Screams permeated the air. A loud gurgling noise arose from the sea as the *Syl* was dragged underwater. Twenty minutes later, it was still raining but the waves were slightly calmer. And *Syl* had disappeared as if she'd never been.

CHAPTER SEVENTY

Ake sat hunched up against the side of the small craft. Her body shook with her unrestrained sobs. She turned her tear-stained faced towards Dane and his apprentice and glared at them.

'Couldn't you have combined your powers and rescued everybody?' she asked.

'No. We had used up most of our power before. My apprentice lulled the storm for a few hours, and I was trying to heal Flo so that she may come. Sadly, she was on her last few breaths when Serenade gave us the hand of Hau and ushered us out,' said Dane.

Ake went to speak but Orilan whispered sternly, 'Plus we don't have the power to thwart Drianna if she wished the *Syl* to sail to her death.'

Ake kept her tongue and turned away from them all. It was an hour after *Syl* had sunk and the spell had worn off Ake. Hau sat weeping in the corner for the loss of his ma, granddad, cousins and his people. Amities sat shivering and watching them all.

Dawn became a yellow streak on the horizon and fast approaching. The rain stopped, and the wind stilled.

Orilan swiftly reached out and grabbed Ake's wrist. Lan growled and tried unsteadily to stop him. Orilan grinned challengingly at him. Ake yelped and pulled away.

'*Dispellius.*' Orilan smiled charmingly at Ake.

Orilan was enjoying Lan's protective attempts to drag Ake onto his lap and away from him. It meant Lan was fighting for his and

Ake's future. Dane tutted and gave Orilan a disciplinary glance. Orilan shrugged. There was a click and the bracelet clattered to the floor. He released Ake's wrist and bowed his head politely, then stared Lan down. Ake sobbed, picked the accursed object up and threw it into the ocean. It bobbed briefly then sank.

Orilan turned and looked to the horizon and quietly uttered, 'Land ho.'

Everyone glanced that way. They all saw to their relief a small island with a beach and some sort of woodlands in the distance. They reached the island within the hour and the sun had risen. Orilan got out, as did Dane and Lan. Then Orilan pulled the boat up onto shore.

Lan picked up Ake to keep her away from Orilan, she protested weakly. Orilan picked up Amities. Hau clambered off the boat. Dane brought the metal chest and flax ashore. Orilan deposited Amities who went and sat next to Hau. Orilan and Dane set about opening the chest and placing its contents on the sand.

Orilan turned and spoke to Lan. 'Keep her close to you. She is full of grief and may take this advantage to run and seek solitude. We do not know what dangers lurk on this isle.'

Lan nodded his agreement and put Ake down. She stormed over to Amities and sat next to him while Lan offered the other men a hand. They told him to just keep an eye on the other three as they were only unpacking but he could help soon. Lan walked over and sat next to Hau. He put a reassuring hand on his shoulder.

'I no ya fill like ya lost all,' he said softly.

Hau turned and looked at him.

'I did,' said Hau.

'Do ya wanna tork?' asked Lan.

'Soon,' Hau said, then turned and looked out to sea.

Ake gave Amities a cuddle and placed him on her lap.

'Mama, who are these people?' asked Amities.

Ake caught Lan's eye. When she spoke, her voice was a mixture of weariness and sadness. 'The older man over by the chest is your grandfather.'

Amities looked at Dane who turned and smiled at Amities.

'I don't know who the person is next to him. The other boy is Hau, your cousin,' she said.

Hau waved sadly to Amities who waved back.

'And that man over there is Lan.' Ake stalled for a minute watching the expression on Lan's face. He was hanging on her words, waiting.

'Hello Lan,' said Amities.

'Hi,' said Lan still looking at Ake.

'Is he related to me Mama?' asked Amities.

'Yes,' said Ake.

'Is he an uncle or something?' pestered Amities.

'No,' said Ake.

Lan was waiting, hoping she'd tell the boy, even though he had been rude to her.

'He's your father,' said Ake.

Amities looked astonished. He wasn't sure whether to approach Lan or turn away. Lan looked at Ake in a pained way. Amities stood and stretched his legs and arms and stifled a yawn. Orilan gave him a sidewise glance and looked up at the sky.

The sky was a mottled grey and dark blue. Orilan felt a rain-drop hit his cheek. He looked again at Amities who was now humming a sad elven folk song. Orilan thought his mother must have taught him that, because he remembered Dane telling him his father hummed that to him when he was but a few hours old. He thought of the words.

I met my love in the dark of the night, in the woods around my home.

In the dark of the night our hearts burned.
We married when the news spread of your creation,
and lived in a small house in the woods where you were made.
The night you first cried I rode into battle.
On stretcher they brought me back, in agony from mortal wounds.
My love wept and held my hand, as I gave you my name and
died.

It began to drizzle lightly, and Orilan began to hurry and retrieve the final belongings from the box. In total, the collection consisted of a storm lantern, flint knife, two canisters of oil, three metres of leather thong and four bison skin blankets. Lan rose and limped over to Orilan who handed him the blankets.

'I sense another storm approaching,' said Orilan.

'I ust to hav that gif,' said Lan.

'I know,' said Orilan.

'Of cors u wood,' said Lan.

'Place the blankets on the ground. We will place the things in the centre and tie the blankets with the thong and carry them slung over our shoulders,' said Orilan.

He went over to the boat and grabbed the flax and strode back over to Lan. He placed it upon one of the laid-out blankets and added the lantern then wrapped it in another blanket and tied it with a metre of the thong. He added the oil and flint knife to another and wrapped it in another blanket and tied it with another metre of the thong and handed that parcel to Lan.

'Thanx fer not makin me useless cuz of the leg,' said Lan.

'It's not a matter of that. Dane's an old man. You're still young. And I'm not about to engage children and a grieved woman into men's work. Your speech is improving,' said Orilan.

Orilan felt a hardened grip on his shoulder as Lan growled in his ear. 'Ull pay fer wat u did ter her. Soon!'

Orilan grinned at Lan and talked quietly, 'Concentrate on getting strong then if you want me dead.'

Father and son glared at each other for a moment.

Orilan and Lan shrugged their packs onto their shoulders. Dane went and offered Ake a hand up as he was well brought up and always offered a lady help. Hau got the drift, rose and stood by Amities. Orilan took one last surveillance of the beach and his family, as he liked to think of them. Even though all of them didn't know who he was. He led them on, hoping they'd find some form of adequate shelter.

The ground was mushy from recent rains and consisted of mostly clay. The going was slow, and their boots sunk heavily in the mud, except for Orilan, who made it look easy walking without any encumbrance. Lan wasn't doing too badly despite his leg. He thought back to his mystic days when he could walk almost as light as Orilan was doing so now. Orilan was in front, Hau and Amities talked sadly on his left and Dane and Ake took up the rear. If his hearing were like what it used to be he'd hear their every word.

Dane took Ake's cold trembling hand in his. She gave him a weak smile.

'Grandpapa,' she said.

'I know, child. You are in so much pain. It's heartbreaking,' said Dane.

Dane stopped and held her close for a moment and they continued walking, his arm about her slender shoulders.

Lan watched the rocks either side of him slowly recede as the drizzling rain became a steady downpour. Orilan suddenly halted and quickly looked back at them. 'We must shelter now.'

He led them to a clump of boulders with wide gaps between certain ones. He chose one with a huge gap in it and handed his burden to Dane to hold. Ori then proceeded to scramble through the gap. He was gone a minute or two, then poked his head up out of the opening.

'Come, there's a very small cave down here. But at least it will be dry for the next day or two. I fear a monstrous storm approaches us from the east. We will place a boulder in front leaving a little gap and close the rest off with the flax lashed down with leather thong. Lan and I will do this while Dane and Ake gather wood and anything you can eat since you both have an advanced knowledge in foraging. And the children can take the equipment in and set it out for us nicely, there's good lads. Agreed?' asked Orilan.

Everyone was too tired to disagree. They had made little distance in the three hours they'd travelled. Orilan pushed a boulder close to the entrance of their cave, leaving only a small gap on the west for one adult to squeeze in.

Lan went in and found several jagged points above their entrance. He put the seven iron clasps attached to the flax on the points and tightened them. Then he put leather thong through the other side to tie around the base of the boulder.

Hau and Amities undid the bison blankets and laid them furry side up, three feet apart. The cave was twenty feet wide, twelve feet long and from roof to floor measured another twelve feet. The entrance sloped in diagonally leaving a four-foot slide into the cave.

Lan frowned at this, thinking that if the rain was to come in sideways they could be flooded in. He went to tell this to Orilan, but Ake and Dane arrived as it began to pour heavily.

They squeezed into the cave and Lan pulled and tied the door shut. The last of the grey light was closed off. Ori and Dane, elvish sight kicking in, led the other two into the cave. Dane, having a hint of magic left, lit the storm lantern with *Druid Fire*, which glittered a cheerful yellow.

Ake put down her meagre burden, as did Dane. Laid out on

bark were six oozing tubers, thirty-six plums, a handful of rock salt and six button mushrooms and handfuls of moss. They also had an armful of wet wood. Lan looked at the moss and smiled.

'If ad ire I'd make bread,' said Lan.

'I thought as much. I can't cook but I know it's one of your favourite pastimes,' said Ake.

Dane saw that Lan wished to say more and asked Lan if he wanted him to translate. Lan nodded.

I need two grinding stones as well as two flat rocks for baking on. I can then produce bread when the wood is dry. If we look around here, we might find what I need, said Lan.

Everyone surveyed the floor of the cave and Hau came up with the goods. He had found a small sharp stone, which was rounded at the end and three small squarish flat rocks the size of his hand.

Lan continued to sign. I'll need water caught in something as well.

Orilan spoke up. 'I suggest we eat the other food, rest and make this bread after sleep.'

The rest of the group approved.

Everyone received six tiny plums, a mushroom and an oozing tuber. The tubers tasted like eating raw turnip and everyone was only too happy to see them gone. The meagre sustenance only took a slight edge off their hunger and their gurgling stomachs protested angrily.

Ake flopped down on one of the blankets carelessly and beckoned Amities to her. Amities jumped onto her lap, and she blew on his wet belly, and he giggled and tried to bounce away. Ake tickled him, and he cried out in delight. Hau came over and sat down. Ake offered Hau a hug and he snuggled into her arms and let the tears fall.

Orilan lay down on the blanket furthest from Ake, Dane next to him and Lan took the one next to Ake and the children. Ake suggested to the boys they remove their wet outer layer and rest next to each other on one half of the blanket and she'd fold the other half over them.

The rain outside pelted down harder and the wind whistled through the gaps eerily. The lashed down flax billowed out slightly in protest. Ake, in her clear strong voice, sang an old tribal song her mother had sung to her as a small child.

Take my hand little one, and I'll take you to where the animals play.
Where if you are good and sweet, they will lead your feet to the path of dreams.
Where pans prance and fairies dance, all in a line.
In fields of green and red, children rest their weary heads.
After wishes made, and dreams are set.
Where if you listen with your heart and mind, you will experience good things of every kind.
So, take my hand, my little one and follow me to where the animals play.

Amities yawned and told Ake that that was a very happy song and within minutes had drifted off. Orilan, who'd been listening, felt a strange stirring of emotion and rolled up in his blanket and turned away. Dane gave Ake a wink and did the same. Ake turned and looked at Lan who stood and offered his sleeping place, which Ake refused. Lan was at a loss. Where would she rest?

'Wur u rest?' he asked.

'I'll crawl in with the boys. They're pretty big blankets.'

'Ake, cun we tork?'

'What's there to say Lan?'

'Bout uz.'

'I don't know that we could be together again, and things

couldn't be as they were anyway. We've both been through a lot and if we were to be a couple again it would have to be a while from now. I'm distrusting of men.'

'Do u car anee for me?'

'Maybe.'

Ake said a hasty good night and slid in with the boys and drifted off. Lan sat up for a little while full of troubled thoughts until exhaustion overcame him.

CHAPTER SEVENTY-ONE

The sky darkened, and a terrible storm reared its ugly head over the little isle upon which our heroes slept.

Orilan sat up suddenly as it felt as if evil was upon them. He looked around the cavern, all seemed well. The little lantern was the centre of light keeping shadows at bay, and he saw the steady rise and fall of sleeping bodies. All innocent to the dark, wearisome road ahead of them. He had seen visions of an inescapable darkness. They all seemed so pure and innocent compared to the dark shadow that grabbed at him any moment his guard was down. The craving for the wine of life.

Dane thought him totally cured. Impossible to resist once addicted. His disappearances, thought to be alone time, were feast times. He had to feed once a week. He was cursed with insatiable desire but blessed with amazing speed and grace. He felt he would have to feed tonight, as the storm would be a lengthy one. He should gather more food for the others while out and explore possible dangers. He slipped from his bedding to see his father turning restlessly. *Poor fellow,* he thought fondly, for a fleeting moment. But then the hunger made his body shake with need.

Orilan released the thongs of the doorway enough to exit, then fastened them the best he could from the outside. He was drenched in a matter of moments. He looked up at the black, cloud ridden, starless sky. He smelt the air and the scent of a young child close at hand reached his nostrils. The lass's heartbeat caught his ears. *So, there are other people on this island.* He moved swiftly to the place. A log cabin came into view. No light shone out through the slats of the shuttered windows. Orilan moved to the door and tested it, unbolted. He stepped inside.

Orilan stood in a one room cabin with a single fireplace and chimney. A big cast iron pot hung from a hook over the fire. Several utensils hung either side on smaller hooks. This would suit his family fine. He now swept his senses over the inhabitants, a lean young father about twenty-three was feverishly embracing his woman. They were separated from their little lass by a hide curtain. The child lay sleeping in a rocking bed, a simple box-like structure on curved wooden legs at top and bottom. He had no wish to kill the bairn. It wouldn't still his hunger anyway.

Orilan moved silently from unpolished floorboards to a soft deer rug. The man would be enough, but he wanted this place for his family. He slipped through the curtain and then closed it. He let all human emotion pass from his body and waited until the couple lay apart, resting. He killed them screaming and fighting him. He liked the resistance. Orilan licked the fresh blood from his mouth and felt a deep scratch on his face and arms. He was incredibly strong, but the lean man was tough and died fighting to the end. That had made the kill more delightful to Orilan who had gorged himself like a chieftain at a feast. His eyes gleamed an unwholesome red and he retreated outside and let the icy rain wash the blood from his face.

Lan woke suddenly as a presence slipped in through the doorway. Orilan looked his way as he tied the doorway back in place. Grey light entered for a second, as did a cold draft. His clothes dripped water steadily on the floor as he moved quickly down the slope back to his bedding and rolled up in it and turned from his father who sat watching him.

Lan had tried to sleep but it wouldn't come so he got up. His body was stiff from damp clothing and inadequate sustenance. *Orilan, I wonder where you've been at this unwholesome hour,* thought Lan. He walked over to the stack of wood and tested its dryness. It was dry enough that it would burn. He picked up the flint knife and sat upon the cold floor. With a flick of his wrist, one of his mystic knives slid into his hand. He wore them as a tribute to better days. They were made of meteorite steel, and he got a spark by banging the blades of each knife against the other. Within ten minutes he had a roaring blaze.

Lan then dragged his bedding down to the fire and sat down. He proceeded to ground the moss into moist granules to which he added a small amount of salt. Lan saw a trickle of water seeping in through a gap in the top of the flax. He cupped his hands under the steady trickle and rushed the water back over to his mixture, which he kneaded into small, thin pancake-like serves. He used the blade of the flint knife to poke some embers away from the main fire. Placing a flat rock upon them with some of the moss bread, he cooked it five minutes either side. Soon a strange smell drifted on the air like that of boiled cabbage.

Ake woke and watched Lan a moment before crawling out of her resting place. She stretched rigidly and hurried towards the warm fire. Lan, whose clothes were now dry, took off his cloak and suggested she should take off her wet things and put this on instead.

Lan, thinking she'd refuse, turned back to his cooking.

'Thank you,' said Ake.

Lan looked back at her as she hurriedly changed. He blushed and turned away. He placed another portion on his makeshift frying pans.

Ake went back and grabbed the boys' damp things and laid them along with hers on the ground to dry. She then sat on the blanket a little way from Lan. Lan turned and offered her some bread. She accepted thankfully. It was chewy and a light green in colour. It tasted like boiled celery but had a spongy texture. It was light but extremely satisfying. Ake told this to Lan who nodded politely in response.

Amities woke as the smell of cooking food reached his nostrils. His belly rumbled in response, and he rose quietly as not to wake Hau. Ake turned as her son, rubbing his eyes, slipped onto her lap. Lan offered him some breakfast, which he took shyly. As he sat there munching, his eyes never left Lan's face. Ake decided to make small talk as she was beginning to feel uneasy at the stony silence.

'Not very nice weather, is it?' she asked.

'Jus wedder.'

'Bad weather.'

'Luks lie me.'

'He does.'

The wind outside was picking up and it howled through the gap in the flaxen doorway. Lightning streaked in the sky and thunder rumbled nearby, too close for comfort. The trees outside bent over double, groaning, hoping their roots would hold. The clouds shed a torrent of tears.

Lan turned as water began to flood into the cave. Orilan and Dane sat straight up.

'Pack up,' said Dane.

He nudged Hau awake from his sleeping place and the startled teen looked quickly around and rose to his feet. Ake grabbed up the boys' clothes and wrapped them in a bison skin.

'What about dressing the child?' asked Orilan.

'He will get soaked through too quickly. Wrap the boy in separate skins and we'll carry him,' said Dane.

'Dane, can't you teleport us back to Man'hannon or Relequis?' asked Ake.

'Drianna expects that woman,' said Orilan.

'I'm sore u no oh sum plass,' said Lan.

'A slip away, when?' asked Dane.

'Last night,' said Orilan.

'Why?' asked Dane.

'To check out the potential of this isle,' said Orilan.

'What did you find my boy?' asked Dane.

'A farm.' Orilan glared at Lan for informing on him.

'So, there are other persons on this isle,' said Dane.

'Abandoned, except for a wee little lass. I locked her in after making sure she had adequate supplies available until we could get there,' said Orilan.

'Good thinking my boy.' Dane smiled at Orilan. 'I'll teleport us all there.'

The group of six were engulfed in a soft swirling blue light. The sound of delicate silver bells sounded and within seconds they stood looking at the solid wooden door of the cabin. They noticed a heavy-duty stick jammed in the door handle and tied sturdy with vine to a jutting out torch holder. Lan reached forth and used one of his knives to cut the vine. They were wet through when they entered the cabin.

An oil lantern was burning out of a little child's reach, and it gave the little cabin a homely feel. They saw a three-year-old child asleep in her cradle bed. Ake looked at the child. Her chestnut hair was mattered, and her eyes were red rimmed from crying. Ake noticed a wooden cup half full of water and a half-eaten apple and the remnants of bread.

Lan looked at the child then at the blood on the deerskin rug. He looked sharply at Orilan. Orilan gave him a scathing look and turned quickly away. Lan took the pile of wood and placed it by the hearth, while Dane slid the heavy-duty bolt on the door into place.

The child woke at the sound of people entering her once happy home. She sat up and rubbed her eyes. Ake approached her gently. The child backed away, tears starting in her eyes.

'Who you be? Where is my Ma and Da?' asked the girl.

'I'm Ake,' said Ake.

The child was biting her soft pink lips and her topaz eyes were wide with fear and curiosity. Meanwhile, Hau and Amities put on their dry clothes and boots.

Orilan ushered Dane towards a back door hidden by a black bear skin. Dane followed him into a large storage room shelved top to bottom with food, clothes, bedding, a hip bath and tools. There were four shelves in all. Dane looked astonished, then delighted.

'Well done my lad! This is exceptional scouting,' said Dane.

'It will suffice,' said Orilan.

Lan, who was curious, entered the room.

Good, he signed.

Lan was surprised when Orilan signed back.

Good you're pleased Father, said Orilan.

When did you learn to sign? asked Lan.

When grandfather chose to teach me personally, said Orilan.

Lan looked annoyed but turned to Dane with his back to Orilan as not to see his signing.

These people were probably very gentle farmers. I wonder what happened to the girl's family. There is blood on the rug, and it seems fresh, signed Lan.

'Let's ask the lass herself,' said Dane.

All three left the room.

Ake shivered as the wind threw itself against the cabin in a mad fury as if it was trying to get at them. The child jumped as thunder rumbled angrily and the rain sounded like a mass of snakes hissing.

'My Da got hurt and my Ma too, real bad,' said Carolina.

The little girl had whispered her name to Ake moments before.

'By who?' asked Ake.

'Nightmare man. He bites them then they was dead,' said Carolina.

'What did he look like?' asked Ake.

'Don't know … he gave me bread and fruit, said funny words then I sleep,' said Carolina.

Lan, upon hearing the conversation, drew in his breath.

Dane looked at him and staged a silent conversation in his head.

'Please, my dear son. Do not condemn your son for his weaknesses.'

Lan signed back. So, it was him. Father, he murdered innocent people.

'I know, but what was I to do? Ori will be my successor when the wisdom of the druids leaves on the ferry to the afterlife,' said Dane.

Great choice that was. It will give everyone the idea that people in authority can just do what they want, said Lan.

'They do,' said Dane.

You're supposed to be a druid, not just any druid but hold the status of Dun Norix, said Lan.

'Who are you to question what a druid is? Are we criminals when we eat of Dee's flesh?' asked Dane.

We hunt to survive, said Lan.

'As does Ori, my boy,' said Dane.

Does he really need to kill humans? asked Lan.

'A dreary existence on the blood of animals. Humans are his prey as animals are ours,' said Dane.

But he can survive on the blood of animals, right? said Lan.

'I suppose,' said Dane.

Then why doesn't he? He needs to be made accountable for

all he's done. Do you not care that he harmed Ake and murdered innocent people? asked Lan.

'This conversation is finished,' Dane removed himself from Lan's mind.

Lan turned and glared at Orilan. Murderer.

Orilan bared his sharp canines to Lan in a half growl, half smirk. 'One and the same.'

Animals are not on the same level as us, why not live off them? asked Lan.

'We are all of the same mother. She doesn't condemn so why do you condemn me?' asked Orilan.

Show some respect.

'Ok, then let's not argue in front of children as you want to set an example of authority … don't you?' Orilan smirked at him.

How did you know that? asked Lan.

'Druids just do,' said Orilan.

'Come, Ori, we will leave as it seems we are not welcome here,' said Dane.

Orilan and Dane vanished. *Again, my father has abandoned me for another*, thought Lan angrily.

CHAPTER SEVENTY-TWO

Ake turned at the sound of silver bells and saw Dane and his apprentice, who nodded to her, vanish.

'What was that about Lan?' asked Ake.

'Hoo nose wat druids will do nest?'

'Did you have an argument?'

Lan nodded. 'Yes.'

'Why?'

'Difrent iderz.'

Ake sighed and thought to herself for a few minutes. 'How will we leave this isle?'

'Don fink we post to.' Lan shrugged.

'Why?'

'Nuthin relly left elseware.'

'I suppose so. Don't know what we're going to do.'

'Cod try an make a life here.'

'I don't know if that's possible. We know nothing about this isle, its people or living conditions.'

The children watched the pair intently.

'Cod try.'

'What's the point? Drianna or Cephas will probably find us soon. How are two children, a teen and us two supposed to fight a goddess or Regis?' Ake began to weep.

Lan held out his arms to her. She turned from him, rose and went into the curtained off area. Ake noticed the double bed was stripped of all bedding.

Hau, Carolina and Amities complained of being cold and hungry. Lan moved the cast iron pot to one side of the hearth. In twenty minutes, he had a roaring blaze going, which soon warmed the chilly cabin and lent it a less hostile face. He then sent Hau to bring him some fish. Lan stood looking at the utensils he had available. There was a cast iron ladle, tongs, frying pan, and four wooden bowls, a wooden spoon and a large cast iron cauldron. Lan moved some warmed embers away from the blaze and fried the fish in the pan.

Within twenty minutes, the youngsters had eaten four fillets each and had settled slightly. Carolina crawled back into her cradle bed, Hau went off and sat in a corner to get some thinking space, and Amities sat down next to Lan who placed a hand on his shoulder. Amities laid his head on Lan's knee and they stayed like that for half an hour or so. Tears of happiness welled in Lan's good eye.

Lan cooked some fish for himself and Ake and placed some heated moss bread in the bowl as well. Then he sent Amities to Ake with the food.

Ake sat on the bed, knees up to her chest as Amities entered the room carrying the food and approached her. She got off the bed and took the bowl from him. 'Thank you.' She consumed the meal hungrily and placed the empty bowl on a wooden bedside table. Ake saw a mirror on it and picked it up. It had a gilded brass handle engraved with swans. Ake looked into it and sighed, remembering her beautiful long golden hair. *Ah well, you do what you must.* Ake put down the mirror then rose and parted the curtains.

Lan looked up; pity written on his face. Ake gave him a menacing look and he frowned. He wandered over to the room to see if she was ok.

'Can I have your flint knife?' asked Ake.

He gave her a sad look. 'Wat for?'

Lan kept the flint knife on his belt, it had come in handy on numerous occasions since the cave.

Hau sensed a change in the air and went and closed the curtains behind the pair.

She stared at him. 'Just give it to me Lan.'

'R u goin to harm urself?'

Ake gave him a bitter smile. *How odd for him to mention that. I nearly did.* Ake shivered at the thought of her hurting herself with the vase. She was startled out of her thoughts.

'Wan harm me?' Lan gave her a sad smile.

Ake glared at him. *How dare he think I would harm him.* 'What the hell, Lan?'

Ake took a step towards him and tried to take the knife from him and missed.

'It's more dangerous for me to fight over it,' said Ake.

'Wat do u min help mee with it?'

'With my blood.'

'Ha?' asked Lan.

'Remember my rapid healing, the one I stole from you.'

'Ahh, wen u wer in my head.'

'Yeah, that's the one.'

Lan handed her the knife and winced as Ake slit her palm. She handed Lan the knife and he did the same. Ake stepped forward and took his hand, pushing her bleeding palm against his. Blood dripped down their arms and onto the ground. Lan felt a bolt of electricity shoot through his body and his body froze in shock. His eyes rolled back in his head. Ake began to feel weak, as if all her energy was being drained.

Ake watched in awe as Lan's body and face healed. Leaving nothing but four horizontal thin white scars four centimetres long. They were a centimetre apart, on his right side, cheek to chin. Lan collapsed to his knees dragging Ake onto hers. He was breathing heavy and beads of sweat ran down his face. Ake released her hand from his and Lan closed his eyes and sat down catching his breath.

Ake sat down cross-legged and bowed her head wearily. The wind outside that had been howling through the slitted shutters dropped a little and Lan opened his repaired elven eyes and tilted his head. His restored elven hearing picked up the sound of goats bleating. But there was no feel of magical ability returning to him. He sighed dreamily and looked at Ake. He wondered if his speech had improved and tried to test it.

'Your blood is powerful. Are you ok?' asked Lan.

Ake looked at him and gave him a weak smile. 'Just tired.'

'Thank you for what you did.'

Lan appeared ecstatic as he smiled and flexed his muscles. After ten minutes Ake rose, lay down on the bed and closed her eyes. A blanket was thrown over her and her eyes fluttered open as Lan withdrew his hands. She snatched one briefly before he pulled it back gently.

'Rest well,' he whispered.

'You too.'

Ake watched him walk away and felt burning tears trickle down her cheek. *He's alive and I can't enjoy that. Cephas has destroyed us.*

The rain had stopped and the wind had died down. Ake had been asleep for hours now and Lan was wondering if she'd be okay.

Lan rose and opened one of the shuttered windows to the rear of the cabin. The clouds were drifting apart, and glimpses of blue could be seen. He saw a small red barn and a field of wheat and large patches of grass. He wondered what was in the barn and decided he'd go investigate. He asked Hau to keep check of the younger ones. He still had a slight limp but that didn't bother him, he began to hum and left the cabin.

The barn had double doors and Lan pulled one of these open and stepped inside. The stone floor was strewn with sawdust. A black billy goat, three white nanny goats and two black kids with white patches milled around him. Lan gently pushed them away and worried if there was any food for the creatures. A rooster crowed behind him, and he turned around.

Lan saw a large white rooster and four brown hens scratch at the ground nearby. Lan noticed a large barrel filled with oats and a spinning wheel and butter churn next to it. On the wall hung a couple of metres of hemp rope and a pair of shears. There was a loft with a wooden ladder. Lan climbed this and saw two bundles of hay. He grabbed a bundle, threw it to the ground and proceeded down the ladder. The goats rushed over to the food and began to chew it greedily. Lan then threw handfuls of oats over the floor for the chickens. He noticed a trough in the corner and another barrel full of water with a large wooden pail bobbing on top. The trough was empty. Lan filled it then left the barn, taking a pail of water with him, and remembered to shut the door as not to let the animals out.

CHAPTER SEVENTY-THREE

For the next few days, the group in the cabin lived off damper, fish and boiled eggs. Ake continued to stay apart from them except for meals and leaving the cabin for toilet breaks. The weather had improved greatly, and the sun was shining brightly. Lan decided to take the children to pet the goats. Carolina still didn't say much but she now came and ate with them and often played scissors, rock, paper and tic-tac toe with the boys. They drew the latter game in the dirt with a stick.

Lan decided that he'd bring back more water and oats and make porridge for lunch. He also decided that they all needed a wash. After half an hour with the goats, Lan let the goats out to graze in the grass patches. He was thankful of the fenced off wheat with these cheeky creatures about.

After lunch, Lan lugged the barrel of water inside. It took several cauldrons of boiled water to have enough for the boys to wash the toils of the road from their faces and hands. He sent the children out to play with Hau supervising. They had been told to stay clear of the woodlands. Another half an hour and he was enjoying a bath in front of the fire.

Ake heard all the commotion and poked her head through the curtains. She'd stayed in the room on her own. She had made up the bed herself and thrown one of the blankets on for warmth. Carolina had slept in her own bed, Lan and the boys in their own bison skin blankets. She saw Lan bathing and decided to have a bath after he finished. Lan saw her and blushed. Ake went and sat back on the bed. Her eyes were swollen and puffy from continuous crying and lack of sleep. Ake was mourning the loss of friends and family and working through her ordeal in Regis.

Lan finished bathing, dried himself and dressed. He then tipped the water outside and prepared a bath for Ake. She couldn't hide from him forever.

Ake, weary in body and mind, jumped as Lan drew the curtains fully apart. When he spoke, his voice was demanding and had its beautiful melodic tone again without a hint of impediment.

'Please come here now,' said Lan.

'I don't have too,' said Ake.

'I went to the effort of preparing a bath for you. I'll go outside and let you bathe,' said Lan.

'Thanks,' said Ake.

Lan smiled faintly and left.

Ake undressed and stepped into the bath. She luxuriously lathered up the soap Lan had left and washed her hair and body. Then she dried herself and put on a plain white dress she had found, it finished at her ankles. Ake dried her hair in front of the fire and put the last of the water from the barrel into the cauldron.

Ake tipped the bath water outside. She refilled the bath from the cauldron and washed everyone's dirty clothes. Then she took down the cooking implements and hung the clothes on the hooks to dry.

After an hour, Lan knocked politely on the front door, and she called for him to come in and he went inside. Ake noticed his hair was still slightly damp and it caught the light coming in through the window.

'Oh, you used all the water,' said Lan.

Ake looked panicked. 'And?'

'Hey, don't be frightened, I'm just making an observation,' said Lan.

Ake apologised quietly.

Lan looked at her sadly. *What happened to her that made her fear she would get in trouble for every little thing?*

'Don't worry, I found a river running through the woodland about ten minutes' walk from here. I wonder how they lugged the water here?' asked Lan.

'Ask Carolina,' said Ake.

'Good idea,' said Lan.

Lan swivelled on one foot and left. Ake decided she'd been inside too long and followed him.

CHAPTER SEVENTY-FOUR

Lan heaved his burden up onto his shoulders for the last trip.

He'd found another large wooden pail and now was carrying two pails tied on the ends of a five foot rod. This was his fifteenth trip, and he was exhausted. Carolina had told him this was how her daddy did it. She had asked him when he was coming home and mummy too. Lan had told her the same thing he'd told Ake when her mother had passed on. Carolina had run inside and wept.

Lan sighed. The sun was beginning to set, and he still wanted to go hunting and foraging in the woods. Ake would be a great help to him with foraging, but he wasn't willing to leave the children with the untrained Hau just yet. They didn't know what dangers could be lurking. Lan decided he would go on his own. He arrived back at the cabin and poured his contents into the barrel. He went inside quickly and told Ake where he was going. She looked taken aback.

'What, at night?' asked Ake.

'Yeah, my sight is fine now,' said Lan.

'I'm not worried about your sight,' said Ake.

'Oh, you do care.' Lan gave her a charming smile.

Ake ignored the last statement. 'Do as you wish, but I'm sure it could wait until morning.'

Lan sighed and relented. He sat down wearily. Amities came over and sat in his lap for the first time. Amities whispered in his ear, which was exceptionally loud for poor Lan.

'Mama tried to cook but she burnt it. We ate it to be nice, so you should too and smile,' said the child.

Amities gave Lan a kiss on the cheek, giggled and ran off. Lan put his hand on the spot and smiled. He watched Ake approach him with some burnt eggs and damper. He thanked her and ate it without complaint and vowed to teach her how to cook. Ake smiled at him, and he smiled back tenderly.

'We got to do something about them kids sleeping on the floor,' said Ake.

'Yeah, I know. If I had an axe I'd try and put together something,' said Lan.

'We'll sort out that problem tomorrow.'

'We've run out of fish and eggs.'

'Oh, we'll sort that out too.'

'Goodnight,' said Lan.

Lan turned and walked towards the far end of the room where his bedding was. The children were already closing their eyes. He sat down and watched them for a moment and lay down and was asleep almost straight away. Ake went to her room behind the partition and lay there thinking for a few moments before closing her eyes. She decided she would look for certain herbs in the morning to rid the dye from her and Amities's hair.

CHAPTER SEVENTY-FIVE

Lan woke to a beautiful cup of lavender tea and a plate of blackberries. He'd slept later than he usually did, due to his exertions yesterday. Ake had been up since dawn, as she often woke up shaking and scared from past nightmares. Lan praised her constantly for five minutes until Ake told him to be quiet. He pouted at her and when she went to apologise, he grinned sheepishly. Ake laughed at him shyly. It was a glorious warm day, there wasn't a cloud in the sky. Ake still looked tired, but she'd stopped crying and at least she was interacting with the rest of them.

Lan asked Carolina if her Dadda had another place where he kept things. Carolina nodded that he did. Lan asked her if she would show them. Carolina replied she would not as they were her dad's things, not theirs. He said that was true and she had every right to say no.

Ake was surprised at his kindness towards a stranger's child. Then she remembered that he was a gentle soul, despite his sometimes-rough words.

Carolina was happy with this and smiled at him and ran off to play jump rope with the boys. Amities had found the rope and was teaching the other two how to play. Lan had cut the rope into three smaller ones and one long one for joint play. Not having the tools to make adequate bedding, Lan went hunting.

Ake dragged in some sturdy wooden logs and four metres of rope leaving two metres left in the barn. The logs were seven feet long and a foot high. Ake had found them behind the barn next to a wooden chest. Ake placed the two logs six steps apart. Then every few spaces tied a cut length of rope from one log to the other.

Ake lay across her design, and it held her easily. Ake lay two of the bison skins down on her makeshift bed and cut holes in the four corners of the skins. She used the rest of the rope to tie the skins to the logs. She tested this and it again held her weight easily. *Perfect*. Ake dragged another bison skin over and put it on top and folded it back, ready for the boys.

—⁓—

Lan eyed his prey appreciatively. The doe was grazing near a thicket, and she had no young with her. He looked at his weapons. Mystic knives and a sharpened stick. He moved closer and the ground crunched under his feet and the doe bounded away. *Damn*. He had been here for hours and didn't want to return home empty-handed. *Gee, five days gone, and I am already calling it that. It has all the people I love living there. Well, almost all of them. Dane is missing.*

CHAPTER SEVENTY-SIX

Dane was filled with despair. He was attending a meeting with the druid high council to discuss Lan, Ake and their son's future. Orilan was watching everyone suspiciously.

'I say we take the earthbound goddess and her son from that buck elf and teach them ourselves,' Borrush, son of Dormalin of the Rock Fell dwarves argued. He was a burly druid, seventy years of age. The dwarf was redheaded, tawny and stout and stood at four foot two.

'I say we bring the lot of them back here and help them through this difficult period,' said a druidess called Franbaya. She was a local tribal girl with golden eyes, olive skin and dark brown hair. She was lithe and small for a human girl at four foot four.

Judan, a handsome man of thirty years, stood at six feet with blond hair, blue eyes and was heavily muscled. He agreed with Borrush.

A small, elderly, wiry man of seventy years sat undecided. He had long white hair and friendly green eyes. He was a hunchback named Tordok.

'And bring danger upon us? No, we can only risk our community and way of life for the girl and her son,' argued Borrush.

'I agree,' said Judan.

'That's selfish of you,' said Orilan.

'Dane, control your acolyte,' said Borrush.

'You have forgotten one thing,' said Orilan.

'And that being?' asked Judan.

'Your oath to go to those in need, whatever their status or path in life,' said Orilan.

'Very true,' said Tordok thoughtfully.

'As if I would leave my child alone against the wrath of Drianna,' said Dane.

'And what about her wrath against any worshipper of the true gods?' said Borrush.

'I believe Lan knows Ake better than you lot,' said Orilan.

'How would you know that, boy?' asked Judan.

'Blood is thicker than water, do you not say that to your own daughter, Borrush?' asked Franbaya calmly.

'If it were not for Lan, we would not even know that this girl is the one we seek. He found her. More than you lot ever did. So, if anything, you should get him to teach her. If you didn't know, she hates most men at the moment and then a bunch of them want to uproot her after she's finally settling down.' Orilan smiled at them smugly.

'Dane, it seems you can't even control your own acolyte and you want us to let you make a decision,' said Judan.

'Judan, thirty years, well, let's see, you're hardly old enough to be a druid and we let you speak your mind,' said Dane.

'We must vote now.' Tordok raised his hand for them to be quiet. 'Here are the options: we bring Telewanake and Amities back here and teach them, we bring them all back here after they've finally settled, or we let Trebrelan teach Amities and Telewanake where they are.'

Judan and Borrush voted for option one, Dane, Tordok and Franbaya option three.

'Seems settled.' Orilan grinned at them.

'Then you four go and sort them out,' said Borrush.

Borrush and Judan left the meeting room.

CHAPTER SEVENTY-SEVEN

Lan looked at Ake's creation and smiled. He felt an inadequate provider, not bringing back anything from his hunt. Hau and Amities climbed onto the bed gleefully. Ake told Lan not to worry about not catching anything, he could always try again tomorrow.

Ake walked over to the cauldron and ladled some soup into a bowl for him and the others. Lan was pleasantly surprised. The broth was made up of salt and onion, which Ake had dug up, and there were chunks of turnips and potato in it, she'd found in a sack in the chest behind the barn. Lan asked for seconds. After everyone had eaten, Lan and Ake tucked the children in.

'You know, I could get used to this parenting thing,' said Lan.

'I think I could get used to you being my husband again.' Ake looked at him tenderly.

Lan watched her, hoping this wasn't a dream.

'You think eventually you could love me again?'

'I could never stop loving you.' Ake smiled softly.

'Does this mean were ready to talk?'

'Yes, and we can start by you not sleeping on the floor.'

'Does this mean I'm allowed to hug you?'

'That's a good start. Let's talk.'

Lan took her into his arms and Ake began to speak of her ordeal.

'Would Hau fight for his crown? Could it be siblings would decide the fate of an empire? The struggle between good and evil would continue. Who was to know the end would lie in the choices of mortal men, women and children.' The old man sighed and stretched.

It was late and his grandson's head drooped wearily. The rest of the story could wait. The lad looked up as his grandfather stood. 'Off to bed with you lad,' said the elderly man.

The boy nodded. 'Tell me the rest tomorrow please. I need to know how their story ends.'

'Of course, my lad,' said his grandfather.

The boy turned and went to his room. The old man smiled fondly as he thought of Ake and Lan. Then he went to his own bed.

Acknowledgements

Thank you to Kim smith for helping me through the early stages of editing. Special mention to my editor Jenn Zabinskas of Red-Ink Creative. Jenn is a talented and dedicated editor who pays special attention to consistency and flow. Her comments are clear, and her suggestions are inspiring. She is witty, kind and funny and I look forward to collaborating with her again.

Deborah Daken is a talented proof-reader and editor. Her keen eyes pick up on subtle errors that are easily overlooked and she makes excellent suggestions to any changes she has recommended. She is incredibly fast and thorough. I found her to be amicable, flexible and approachable.

Thank you to all my family members and friends, especially my oldest friend and fellow writer Amy who listened to me and my wild ideas. Also, my incredible ARC readers, thank you for your support. To my dear husband who has supported my crazy pursuits, I love you, we will forever be Ake and Lan.

Meet the Author

Nadine has been an avid reader and writer since her early childhood, from publishing poems to creating her first novel at thirteen, *The Primal Heartbeat*, and publishing it in her early adulthood. *The Primal Heartbeat* has since been edited and updated.

Nadine is an avid gamer and role-player, as well as creator of fiction and fantasy novels. She also loves archery and nature.

After dealing with adversity and overcoming it, Nadine writes books that show even powerful characters are inherently flawed. That these weaknesses can often become our strengths as long as we remain true to ourselves. Nadine's writing reflects on the dark side of humanity as well as the good side and how, even though we think we are worthless, we can change our destiny, just as her memorable characters do.

Nadine's other books were written on a whim, designed for and dedicated to a special needs child who didn't relate to any of the books on the market. Seeing a representation of themself in the children's book encouraged them to improve their reading skills and develop a love of reading.

The next book of the Stars Fallen Series will be coming later this year.

ALSO BY NADINE ABRAHAMS

Ad' Astra

Ad' Astra is a collection of short stories centred around the magic store Ad' Astra. The strange goods within can either help or hinder the purchaser. In this collection of kooky short stories will you learn a lesson?

RPG Muintir Game

The inclusive RPG Muintir is set after a great catastrophe. The people must come together and battle mutagen in this shout out to home brew. The simplified six-sided dice system allows for quick and easy play. Those with diverse needs are celebrated, often having unique gifts that allow them to thrive in the world of Muintir.